THE
OTHER SIDE
Book One
Wolf Moon

Sea Elle Wolf

THE OTHER SIDE
WOLF MOON
Second Edition
Sea Elle Wolf

Table of Contents

For Mrs. Wolf

Prologue

Night of the Worm Moon

The full Worm Moon shone bright and commanding as it loomed ominously behind the clouds in the nighttime sky. The foggy Topanga Canyon neighborhood below comprised a pleasant mixture of houses and dense vegetation. A few scattered streetlamps and a staccato disbursement of front porch lights did what they could to illuminate the inky darkness that enveloped this rural neighborhood. A gray *Subaru Outback* rounded the corner, its headlights cutting through the mist as it made its way down a cul-de-sac and turned into the driveway of one of the homes. No security lights had snapped on as expected by the young couple who sat inside the now parked car.

"Huh! I guess my security lights must have gone out," the man in the driver's seat speculated while squinting up through the windshield toward his tenebrous house.

"Both of them?" the woman in the passenger seat inquired suspiciously.

"Maybe the breaker got overloaded. I'll check it tomorrow," he said, killing the car's engine and switching off the headlights. Their surroundings were now bathed in total darkness.

"Well, at least it's kinda romantic sitting here with you in the dark like this," the woman commented with mild flirtation. Then, her demeanor suddenly shifted. "Unless you've been planning to get rid of me all along? Drive me to your place, pretend the lights went out, but really you *cut* them. Do you have a large ice chest in the garage just waiting for my dismembered corpse to go inside it so you can dump me into the ocean?" she asked accusingly before cracking a smile at her morbid humor.

"Nah, I don't see the motive in it for me. For one, why would I waste a perfectly good cooler? Coolers that size are *really* expensive. Second, you're

1

pretty nice to look at, and third, you really need to cut down on your true crime consumption," he responded with a deadpan expression.

"For the last time, *I can't*!" the woman exclaimed. "Not only is it the *most* addictive genre, but it's also informative. Us women need to gain a solid understanding of all the ways in which we could be killed."

"Well, you could at least do me the courtesy of not always suspecting that it will be *me* that kills you."

"Sorry, that's not going to happen, pal. It's always the husband or boyfriend," she retorted slyly.

"Oh please, don't you think I'm more original than that?" he asked.

"You, my friend, are the most unoriginal psychopath who has ever *tried* to coax me into letting my guard down," she fired back. "But nice try, Ted Bundy."

The couple sat smiling in the car for a moment longer. They had just finished having dinner at their favorite dive bar, Churchill's, and both were full, tired, and content from a simple evening of pub food accompanied by a few rounds of beers.

"Sooo... do you wanna come in?" the man asked hopefully, to which the woman let out an exasperated sigh of mock frustration.

"Ugh, Ryan. I told you I can't tonight, babe," she said while unbuckling her seatbelt and opening the passenger door. Ryan followed suit and exited his car.

"Erika, why do you insist on torturing me?" he asked, meeting her for an affectionate hug. "Fiine! I'll admit it—I'm a complete codependent loser who is somewhat pathetic without his fiancé, but I just want to be with you. Can't you stay with me tonight?" he asked, trying to convince her.

Erika knew better—*If* she went inside, that meant Ryan wanted to have sex, which meant she would be really tired for her morning meeting. Erika was the manager of L'Ange, a chic French restaurant in town. These meetings occurred without fail every Sunday morning, at the restaurant owners' insistence, although they never attended themselves. It was just one more reason in a long list of reasons that Erika had been thinking of pursuing a new career path altogether. But what to do next? The hospitality industry was all she had ever known. Deep down, she knew there was always the option of working at her family's hotel on the East Coast; however, she had not been back there in many years—not since her mother died. Maybe she had stayed away intentionally, but also, it seemed like she could never get the timing to work out. First college, and now she and Ryan were about to start their life together in Los Angeles. Erika knew she couldn't solve all her problems at the moment, so she decided to let it go.

She guided Ryan's face close to hers and whispered sweetly, "I thought if I filled you with fried foods and IPAs, it would quell your insatiable desires."

"Well, you must feel *pretty stupid* now," he said, pulling her close while wearing a mischievous smile. "It only turned me into a powerful sex demon. A hungry, lusty wolf."

"I promise I'll get used to having a total lack of sleep after I officially move in, but for now, I have to get some sleep, so I'm prepared for that *'super necessary'* early morning crew meeting," Erika said sarcastically, then offered a sweet kiss as a consolation prize.

"I'll capture you into my lair soon enough! Bwhaha!" Ryan feigned an evil laugh, receiving the final verdict halfheartedly. After a taste of some intense affection by the light of the full Moon, the couple broke away and said goodnight.

Erika slipped into the cold driver's seat of her car and watched her fiancé as he backed away, dramatically holding his hands over his mock, broken heart. She laughed. Ryan smiled, then waved goodbye, dropping the love-sick act just shy of becoming pathetic. He turned and walked up to his unlit front porch, then after a moment, disappeared into the darkness of his house, closing the door behind him. Erika watched as various lights flipped on and then off again. Ryan was beyond fastidious about conserving energy. The front room fell into darkness, with the exception of the glow from the television. He enjoyed watching TV in the dark, just one more example of what Erika called his "vampire tendencies."

She felt a smile come to her lips as she watched this routine. Ryan was a solid, good guy. How could she have gotten so lucky? In reality, this connection took a long time to find. She had wasted a lot of time on emotionally unavailable people for far too long. Perhaps because it was a quality she saw in herself, Erika wondered. Had she subconsciously chosen partners with whom there was no hope of a future? When she met Ryan, she realized life could be different. He loved her for who she was and brought out a better version of herself. Sure, things weren't perfect between them, and physically... well... that head-over-heels feeling would come one day, she hoped, but she recognized a good thing when she saw it and was happy to have accepted his proposal.

Erika turned the key in the ignition, checked her mirrors, and backed slowly out of her fiancé's driveway. Suddenly, a quick flash of what seemed like an oversized dog raced across the rearview mirror's reflection. Erika slammed on the brakes to avoid hitting the creature. Adrenaline surged through her veins.

"What the fuck was that?!" she wondered aloud, using the sound of her own voice to calm her nerves. She checked her mirrors again—no sign of the dog or any other life form was anywhere to be seen. Erika sat back in her seat and steadied her breathing. An unexpected chill washed over her as the heavy clouds parted, and a beam of moonlight pierced through the nighttime mist.

Stepping back into the darkness, away from the illumination, a shadowy figure gazed out from within the trees. Eyes focused on the idling car in the driveway. The figure stayed hidden. Watching... stalking... waiting.

Erika reached for her phone and dialed Ryan's number. No response. She quickly texted, "I almost hit a dog as I was pulling out of your driveway. Can you make sure I didn't kill something when you get a chance?" Send. Erika resolved that it was probably best to let Ryan deal with whatever monsters were lurking in the night. With a quick look over her shoulder, she backed out of the driveway and drove off.

The dark figure watched as the car reached the corner, turned left, and drove out of sight. Slowly, the figure stepped out into the street and refocused their gaze back toward the dark house just as the front porch light snapped on.

Ryan's hand gripped the doorknob. Realizing he was only wearing a T-shirt, he grabbed a hoodie from the hall closet. Then he stepped out into the night air and crept down the driveway, scanning for an animal. There was no sign of a dog or anything else, for that matter.

"Must have gotten scared off," he muttered to himself as he continued looking around. The wind kicked up, and he pulled his hoodie tightly around his torso. Giving up, Ryan stepped back inside, flipped off the porch light, and returned the hoodie to the closet. He walked back toward the glowing light of the TV and plopped down onto the sofa, remote in hand. As he scrolled through show titles, the hairs on the back of his neck rose. *Something isn't right,* he thought. He sat up and looked around the dark room. The flashing light from the television lit up the living room in a flickering fashion, but everything appeared normal from what he could see.

Since he couldn't place what exactly felt off, Ryan dismissed it and decided to get a beer. He stood up and padded into the dark kitchen, then was surprised by a blast of cold air from an open window near the back door. He paused momentarily and wondered aloud, "Did I leave that open—?"

Suddenly, he heard a strange thumping sound coming from somewhere upstairs. Ryan quickly grabbed the baseball bat he kept near the back door. He silently cursed that his gun was upstairs, locked in a safe at the back of his closet. Creeping into the hallway, Ryan listened intently, his mind reeling, desperately trying to make sense of the scary situation.

Maybe it's just some kids or a homeless person? He thought, *or maybe it's some dude armed to the teeth who is going to shoot my ass?* Ryan had made it about halfway up the stairs before hesitating; *maybe this is a job better suited for the cops.* He reached his free hand into his pocket, searching for his absent phone, then turned to head back down the stairs. The glow from the TV flickered just as Ryan looked up, then stopped dead in his tracks. A large figure stood at the base of the stairs, staring right at him.

Ryan tore up the stairs and sprinted down the hallway toward his bedroom. The dark figure followed in hot pursuit. Ryan made it through the door, spun around, and slammed it behind him, quickly locking it. Frantically, he dropped the bat—which he had forgotten he had been holding—and pulled the dresser against the door. *Boom!* The intruder collided forcefully with the unforgiving barrier.

Wealthy with what he knew was only a small amount of time, Ryan ran to the closet to retrieve his gun. He reached a hand to the upper shelf where he normally kept the keys and blindly felt around. Nothing. He thrust a sweaty palm to the wall just outside the closet door and flipped the light on—unknowingly revealing a dark figure crawling surreptitiously through the second-story window behind him. Sensing a presence, Ryan became keenly aware of his heartbeat and the sound of another's breathing.

"P-P-please. You don't have to do this. You can take whatever you want," Ryan pleaded as he slowly turned around, and only then was the depth of his terror fully revealed.

Chapter One

The Crime Scene

Yellow crime scene tape, several police cars, CSI technicians, and worried onlookers comprised the Topanga Canyon crime scene ecosystem. The atmosphere was grim and quiet, save for the indistinct chatter between investigators and neighbors' hushed voices as the coroner's arrival confirmed their fears.

As the sun rose higher in the sky, the sound of birds chirping and a toddler's cry in the distance began to reintroduce a sense of normalcy to the scene. Suddenly, the screech of tires and a car accelerating down the cul-de-sac cut through the sullen sounds and caused everyone to turn their heads. Erika raced toward the scene after having been informed by Detective Frank Miller that something had happened to her fiancé, Ryan. Still, he wouldn't provide further details until she arrived and advised her to leave work immediately. Now, officers attempted to compassionately restrain and calm the distraught Erika, who was still dressed in the crisp white button-up blouse and pressed black pants she had worn to work that morning. She desperately tried to get past the crime scene tape to get inside the house and next to her fiancé's side. Detective Miller approached wearing a skilled poker face.

"Ms. Navarro? I'm Detective Miller. I'm the officer who contacted you."

"Where's Ryan?!" Erika demanded with panic and urgency overflowing in her voice. "What happened?! Where is he? Is he okay? Can I see him?"

"Perhaps we should step over here so we can speak more privately," Detective Miller instructed, guiding Erika away from the congregation of neighbors who all respected the needed space. Once they had a little distance, Erika quickly snapped into attention, anxiously awaiting the detective's update.

"Ryan Wilson was found by his housekeeper this morning. I'm truly sorry to be the one to inform you—" but the detective's words became inaudible at that moment when a stretcher supporting an occupied body bag came rolling out of her fiancé's home.

It seemed like all sound fell away as Erika's sight fixated into tunnel vision at the appearance of the body bag. Her entire being sank. It felt as though the floor had dropped out from underneath her, and she was hurtling toward the ground from an unknown but endless height. She felt her mouth open as her eyes squeezed shut, futilely attempting to block out the reality playing out in front of her. Erika sensed she was screaming, yet as if she were in a dream, she couldn't hear the sound of her own anguished wailing at the realization that Ryan, the man she was planning to marry... her person... was no longer on the same plane of existence as she.

The time immediately following this moment seemed to fly by in a blur. Erika vaguely remembered being taken to the police station, where she endured extensive questioning. Detectives immediately ruled her out as having any possible involvement after observing her cooperation and what they perceived was her genuine grief and anguish playing out in front of them. Investigators were all keen to find out if she had any insight into who could have committed such a heinous crime, but she couldn't think of anyone. Her fiancé had no enemies. Everyone who ever met him only had positive things to say about him.

Unfortunately, Erika had learned that Ryan had experienced a terrifying and gruesome demise. The investigators informed her that he had been viciously and brutally torn apart, almost as if attacked by a bear or mountain lion. The crime scene stumped investigators, and despite their tireless efforts, no sufficient leads surfaced, and no significant evidence emerged. It seemed that nobody had any idea what had happened to Ryan Wilson.

Following an exhaustive investigation, a thorough autopsy, and questioning everyone who had ever known Ryan, detectives were at a loss, and the county coroner's office had no other choice but to mark the cause of death as "Possible animal attack."

After shedding more tears than she had ever shed in her entire lifetime—including after the passing of her mother and grandmother—after a rushed closed casket funeral and after some futile grief counseling, Erika felt completely lost—like an astronaut who had become untethered and was now giving up, allowing herself to float out into space.

One Month Later

Erika awoke with swollen eyes again. She was exhausted. And not because she had stayed up late crying yet another night, but because she was just so tired of crying. Life felt too hard to do again today. Deciding to stay in bed, she lay there and allowed her gaze to drift over to a photograph on the nightstand. The picture was of her and Ryan holding each other on a bridge by the canals in Amsterdam. They looked happy and natural together. She studied the look of joy she had worn on her face back then. And now she lay there staring out hollowly past this picture and morbidly reminding herself—*I won't ever be happy again... Not like that... Not without him.* The dark despair of grief brought the inexhaustibly familiar sting of moisture back to her eyes once more. Squeezing them shut, the tears spilled out and streamed down her cheeks as she rolled over, away from the picture.

A tentative knock sounded from the bedroom door, soon followed by the entrance of a mousy woman wearing a Cal State Long Beach sweatshirt and holding a cup of hot tea. The person delivering the cup of small comfort was Nicole Ramirez, Erika's once college mate and now roommate. Erika sat up and wiped her tears away as Nicole sat down on the bed and handed her friend the steaming mug.

"How are you feeling today?" Nicole asked in a quiet and comforting tone. Erika shook her head and shrugged, dismissing the question. Nicole compassionately persisted, looking deeply concerned for her grieving friend. "Do you want to talk about it? I mean, I know you're already talking about it in therapy and a grief group, but I'm always here if you need someone else to talk to," Nicole sighed. "I just can't imagine losing anyone close to me at all, let alone losing a partner. Poor Ryan," she said sorrowfully.

Ryan—Erika's gaze went a thousand miles away at the mention of his name. She again began searching her memories, as she had been doing on repeat since the day he died. If she could just figure out how to put all the pieces together in the correct order, maybe she could make sense of all the turmoil and pain she was experiencing, and then, somehow, everything would be all right again. Obviously, this was not true, and solace did not come. The fact was—Erika had no memory of any of the horrible events Ryan had encountered and endured during his final moments alive. Her memory ended the moment she drove away on that fateful evening. She had gone home and got in bed, then woken up on time and conducted that stupid morning work meeting.

But there was something else. A small voice inside nagged at her. Aside from the early crew meeting, Erika knew deep down that she had left that night for another reason. She almost did not want to shine a light too brightly on this latent feeling because she dreaded what it might reveal. It was too late; the tenacity of her mind surrounding this musing felt like a dog with a bone. She could not relinquish this little nagging thought, so she futilely tried once more to reject the thought by spinning it—*maybe my intuition told me to leave that night*, she silently speculated. But Erika knew this was not entirely the case as she felt the truth come flooding into her heart, causing it to break just a little bit more. In truth, she knew she had left because she had not wanted to stay the night. And now she found herself wondering—*What would have happened if I had stayed?* She, too, most certainly would have been killed, but maybe not? Maybe her presence would have stacked the odds in the couple's favor. Together, they might have somehow escaped or fought off whatever had attacked him.

In her heart of hearts, she knew this thinking was foolish. She most likely would have been met with the same horrible fate. But maybe even that was preferable. At least she wouldn't have been left behind feeling this heart-squeezing mixture of grief, mourning, and survivor's guilt, all coupled with the innermost uncertainty surrounding her relationship altogether.

"—I mean, do you think it's a good idea right now?" Nicole asked.

Her words interrupted Erika's reproachful thoughts. Apparently, she had been talking the entire time.

"Huh? What?" Erika squinted and blinked away a headache as her awareness returned to the present moment. She had not fully heard her friend's question or anything she had been saying for the past several minutes, for that matter.

"Moving back to Nocturne?" Nicole clarified. "Of course, I support you doing *whatever* will make you happy." This sentiment did not land as Erika stared back hollowly in response. "Ah, ah... whatever will make you feel better?" Nicole quickly tried to remedy the situation and then clarified. "Whatever you *want* to do, but your support system is *here*! Your friends are *here*, in California. Are you sure *now* is the right time to uproot your entire life, leave your friends and community, and move across the country? I mean, I've known you for a long time. It would be totally different if your mom and your grandma were still there, but it sounds like you'd be moving in with a bunch of distant family members that you're *not* really even that close to. And for what? To work in some weird, haunted hotel?"

"I told you—I just want a change. At this point, I *need* it. This fresh hell feels like rock bottom. To continue living out here, in this town, where every corner of it reminds me of him... I just... I can't stay. Plus, I've always known I'd end up back at that place one day. It's been in my family for, like, a thousand years or some shit. That's hyperbole, not really a thousand, more like a hundred. The fact is I'm going to have to learn the family business sooner or later because it's going to belong to me and my cousin one day. And really, Nikki... I just need to get out of here," Erika explained resolutely.

"Let your weird cousin deal with it. Didn't you tell me he's an asshole, and he already lives out there anyway?" Nicole asked incredulously.

"Cristian isn't weird. He was just mean to me when we were little kids. I'm sure he's grown up a little bit... hopefully a lot. I mean, I haven't seen the guy since he was fourteen. Either way, I'm totally up for this. It will give me a sense of purpose. I don't want our generation to be the one that fails the great Dragos Manor or is forced to sell it to someone who doesn't understand how special it is. Really, it's the only thing I'm looking forward to at this point. And *especially* since my mom and grandma have both passed away. They both would want me to go there. I've been avoiding my family for a long time now. And let's face it, things can't get any worse at this point," Erika concluded, resolving herself once more that she was going through with this move and making this change in her life. Nicole wore a melancholy look on her face.

"I get it," she finally relented in a disheartened tone of acceptance, then asked, "So when do you leave?"

"I'm leaving in a month. I should be able to get everything sorted out in that time," Erika estimated and began plotting, which provided a nice mental break from the relentless grief.

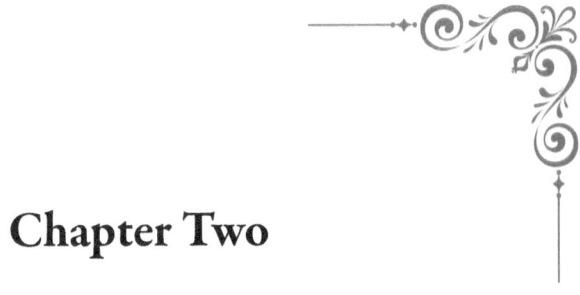

Chapter Two

Many Moons Ago

Erika Navarro was a twenty-five-year-old woman of Romanian and Spanish descent. Most of her was long—her hair, her neck, her legs. She had a pleasant oval face with emerald green eyes, offset by a cascade of ash-brown hair. Both strong and gracefully athletic, she cut a striking figure, and while many would call her a real beauty, it was her determination and resilience that most defined her.

Although Erika had lived her adult life in Los Angeles, she had spent her formative years growing up in Nocturne, a small, rural town in central Massachusetts. Her Spanish origins came from her father, who had died tragically in a car accident when she was only two years old, leaving his grief-stricken wife alone to raise the couple's only child. After suddenly finding herself a single parent, Erika's mother quickly realized she needed help raising her daughter. This inspired her to move closer to her own mother, Erika's grandmother, and a few other maternal relatives with the surname Dragos. These family members resided at Dragos Manor—a family-owned mansion that had been in the family for five generations. Back then, Erika's grandmother, Daniela Dragos, and her sister-in-law, Anastacia Dragos, were the joint owners of the family estate.

Dragos Manor was an old house with a long history. It was constructed in the late 1800s and converted into a boarding house in 1917. Then, a few years later, Dragos Manor started gaining popularity as a tourist attraction after news about reported ghost sightings began circulating. After that, the boarding house was converted into a hotel, and from that moment on, guests from all over would come to stay at the grand estate hotel and, if lucky, witness or interact with a restless spirit during the course of their visit.

In addition to Erika's grandma, Daniela, and grandaunt Anastacia—Ana for short—Erika's second cousin, Cristian Dragos, also lived in the century-old hotel mansion. Cristian was a few years younger than Erika, and throughout their adolescence, he was always much shorter, scrawnier, and more delicate, almost more feminine than she was. He was an awkward boy with pale skin, dark hair and eyes, and thick eyebrows, even as a child.

Ana was Cristian's grandmother and sole caretaker. No one ever seemed to know for certain why his parents weren't in the picture. A common explanation was that Cristian's parents simply could not handle the responsibilities of having a child, so they left, leaving Ana to care for her grandson. More and more, Ana would become angry and frustrated when anyone would raise this subject, and after a while, young Cristian ceased asking for his absent parents.

Ana insisted Cristian be homeschooled while Erika was allowed to attend the public schools in Nocturne from elementary up through high school. This contrast in socialization made it difficult for Cristian to make friends with the local children, all of whom tended to treat him as an outsider. Conversely, Erika's ability to make friendships and connections with her peers seemed effortless. This quickly became a source of contention with Cristian, and thus, a rivalry seemed to form between the two cousins.

Whenever Erika visited Dragos Manor, Cristian jealously monitored her carefree spirit from the moment she set foot in the mansion hotel. He thought she acted more like she was on holiday, just like the rest of the hotel's dusty old patronage. His life there was never so joyous and relaxed. No. His life at Dragos Manor was very humdrum and rigid, being bound under the watchful eye and stern rule of his grandmother Ana, who would keep an especially close eye on him when Erika and her mother would visit. He was never allowed to behave so casually, and Ana would instantly punish him if he started to imitate what she called Erika's "cavalier American ways."

Ana had always raised Cristian to be very proud of his Romanian heritage and would push him hard toward their culture rather than ever letting him "Americanize." While Erika could only speak and understand a little Romanian, Cristian's accent and ability to speak the language were always much stronger than hers. At Ana's behest, Cristian even made a few trips back to the old country to visit his uncle Marius, who resided in Romania.

Erika's mother and grandmother, Daniela, were usually much softer and more patient with the children. Neither ever really pressed Erika to learn the language if she was not interested in doing so. Instead, they would teach Erika about her heritage by other means. For instance, Daniela would prepare traditional Romanian comfort dishes and treats, such as sarmale and mamaliga, two classic dishes that never failed to make both children's mouths water.

This was the dynamic between the Dragos grandmothers and their grandchildren. Daniela was very loving and nurturing, while Ana was much stricter and constantly stressed rules, tradition, and respect for elders. Because of all this, Cristian seemed to resent his cousin from a very young age. Perhaps his resentment was rooted in jealousy; he couldn't fathom what it must have felt like to feel so confident, so free to be oneself, and well-liked by others. Regardless of the underlying reason, Cristian would look for subtle ways to retaliate against Erika whenever he could manage it.

Since Erika and her mother visited so regularly throughout Erika's childhood, Cristian often looked for opportunities to coax his cousin into trouble. This was easy to do because Erika was naturally curious and overly trusting. He would often pique her interest with stories of lost treasures, ghosts, and other curiosities in areas of the hotel known to be off-limits to the children.

Cristian would strike up games pretending to be searching for some curiosity in the proximity of one of the restricted areas, such as the grand ballroom, the cellar below the kitchen, the 4th-floor rooftop courtyard, or the sprawling woodlands that surrounded Dragos Manor. He would strategically shepherd his naive older cousin toward one of the forbidden entrances. Then, after a short while, he would separate from her, leaving Erika to carry out his plan. Then, she alone would be approaching the prohibited area of interest. From there, one of a few things would usually happen. If Ana caught Erika in Cristian's game, she would harshly reprimand her grandniece since she would appear to be the one with the most obvious intent of entering the off-limits space.

"Stop right there this minute!" Ana called out—first in Romanian and then again in English—on one occasion when she had caught Erika. "I told you, again and again, you are not allowed in the ballroom!" she scolded sternly with a thick accent. The young girl allowed herself to be led away in Ana's tight grasp while looking wounded for getting reprimanded. Cristian was off a short distance away, wearing a look of quiet shock upon his face at his cousin's insolence, tsking and shaking his head.

If Erika's grandmother Daniela discovered the children, she would patiently remind them which areas to stay away from in the large estate and usher them away.

"Erika, you cannot go into the cellar. It is just not safe for children without either me, Ana, or your mother accompanying you," her grandma gently reminded her once when she had caught Erika near the cellar door inside the kitchen. This happened again on a separate occasion outside the back of the house; Daniela intercepted her granddaughter at the exterior entrance to the cellar. That time, she spotted Cristian and reprimanded him as well.

"Stop leading your cousin into trouble, Cristian Dragos! Don't think I don't see you hiding over there!" Daniela scolded, silencing her nearby snickering grandnephew.

Erika's mother was not usually the one to discover the children in this game, but on the single occasion that she did, her reaction was two-sided. On the one hand, she extended understanding toward her daughter's naturally curious nature. Still, on the other, her reaction was coupled with fierce protection of her daughter's safety, which bordered on insulting Erika's intelligence.

"Believe me, Erika, I understand your desire to explore the unknown, but I need you to make smarter decisions! Promise me you will stay away from the 4th floor! Promise me now! You must do as I say whether I'm around or not. I'm not mad at you; I'm just frustrated with your incessant carelessness." Her mother's words strung. She seemed hot and cold all at once, with moments of fear cracking in her voice. "And you too, Cristian! You should know better! Can't you both have at least one working brain between the two of you," Erika's mom said, rounding on young Cristian and causing him to sulk for the rest of the day. His aunt was normally so nice to him, but he hated getting on her bad side. He had even felt sorry for Erika that day.

However, if the children were lucky, on rare occasions, their uncle Marius would discover them if he happened to be visiting from Romania. He would wait quietly for the kids to approach one of the many entrances into the woodlands, sneak into a place where he could ambush them, and then materialize from behind a tree and surprise them.

"You children should behave more like water and flow around the hard boundaries that life contains," Marius said in his ever-present sage manner when he had caught them once. The children jumped, startled by his sudden presence; a small scream escaped Cristian's lips. Erika's astonishment quickly dissolved into laughter at the recognition of her wonderful uncle. Alternatively, Cristian composed himself quickly, ashamed of having emitted such an effeminized scream in front of an adult Dragos male. Marius often noticed this turmoil in Cristian and always tried to ease his young nephew's mind.

"It's okay, Cristian. Remember, try not to deny the various versions of yourself that you will encounter on your unique path. Just like the river knows where it ought to run, carving out its way in life, the river does not question itself but merely exists."

Marius was Ana's son, Cristian's uncle, and the cousin of Erika's mother, which technically made him Erika's first cousin once removed. Still, Erika always called him "Uncle," like her cousin Cristian did. Marius adored his cousin and her daughter, although he didn't see his family often since he moved to Romania just before Erika was born. This adoration for Erika and her mother was yet another source of contention for Cristian, who desperately wanted the approval of any living Dragos male because of the family curse. As it were, the family seemed to be ill-fated with frequent deaths of its members. This motivated Cristian to frequently attempt to execute bids for his uncle's attention.

"Marius, watch how good I've gotten with my bow!" young Cristian would call up from the lawn, his heart pounding in his chest with the pressure to impress. Marius would look down from the veranda where he sat, having tea with young Erika. Cristian's moment had now arrived as he straightened up parallel to the target, nocked the arrow, raised the weapon, and drew back the bowstring. But after succumbing to the pressure of aiming too hard for too long, the arrow would fall forward to the ground before he even had a chance to fire.

"Make sure to cant your bow clockwise, so your arrow doesn't fall from your rest. Most importantly, remember to take a breath, exhale, and relax. Look for a feeling of joy in what you are trying to accomplish, and it will help relieve you of the pressure of perfection," Marius suggested to his young nephew. Cristian would turn away, face burning red hot with embarrassment. Of course, he would try again with more success the second time, only this time, Marius was not watching. Cristian looked up to see his uncle's attention focused on something young Erika had just told him.

"That was a damn fine shot there, lad!" groundskeeper Tom called out from across the lawn.

Right compliment, wrong adult, Cristian thought to himself with a hole burning in his heart.

There was one special occasion that Cristian participated in with his uncle Marius, Erika's mother, and his grandaunt Daniela that Erika was not allowed to attend. During one of Erika and her mother's routine visits, the aforementioned group would section off for the night, leaving Erika alone with Ana. Erika dreaded these nights because they were always the same—she was not allowed to play, she was not allowed to laugh or have any fun, and she wasn't allowed to see her mother or the other family members again until the next morning. Instead, she was forced to have dinner with her grandaunt, where Ana would try to force some traditional lesson down her throat, and then Erika would have to go to bed early—typically not long after the sun went down. Once in her room, Erika was warned she should never look from her window nor leave the room, no matter what sounds she heard.

Erika was told, "Even if the traveling carnival was occurring outside," she was never to look from her window. "This is a special night, and it's your duty to stay in your room and reflect." When Erika asked what she should reflect on, Ana would coarsely respond that she should reflect on the concept of "...behaving, respecting her elders, and doing what she's told."

After that, Erika would lay alone in the dark inside the large bedroom suite she shared with her mother on the 3rd floor, and she would try to *will* the next morning to come as quickly as possible. Sometimes, during those nights, Erika would have dreams of unusual parties, of wolves, or dreams of other strange creatures she had never seen before. These peculiar dreams were never commonplace to her otherwise but never failed to visit her on those particular evenings. More than anything, Erika wished she could join in with the rest of her family... whatever they were doing.

And so it was—Erika spent her childhood living between the small house just outside Nocturne—where she was most happy living alone with her mother—and Dragos Manor with the rest of her mom's side of the family and the handful of hotel guests when they would come to stay.

But as previously mentioned, the Dragos family seemed to be cursed with frequent deaths, and with such a curse, two prominent family members would come to die by the time Erika had reached the age of seventeen.

The first to pass away was Erika's grandmother, Daniela. She died of health complications when Erika was only fifteen years old. Erika's grandmother left her portion of Dragos Manor to Erika's mother, who then moved herself and her daughter into the estate full-time so they could help Ana run the hotel business.

Erika was devastated after losing her grandmother and was unhappy about moving away from the small house outside of Nocturne, which had been her sanctuary with her mother. Additionally, as soon as they had transitioned to living at Dragos Manor full-time, Erika's mom began to change noticeably. Her mother's moods grew hot and cold and increasingly became less consistent and reliable. It was almost as if some sort of switch had flipped.

Erika's mother would often disappear into the recesses of Dragos Manor late at night. When she would resurface the next day, she would seem to grow sadder and more resentful with each reemergence. She began discussing the sorrow and pain over the loss of Erika's father, something she had never really expressed previously in front of her daughter. Her mother also started making mysterious and morbid comments to Erika. Things like, "Not even death could keep me away from you," and "This Godforsaken house has been both a blessing and a curse to our family." It was as if melancholia had fallen over her mother, and she had begun losing the strength and will to escape from underneath it. Teenage Erika felt helpless and unable to help her mom and soon became affected by all these drastic changes.

Then, one day, Erika came home from school and was informed that there had been a terrible accident and her mother had been tragically killed. It wasn't until her grandaunt Ana explained the accident's circumstances that something seemed wrong. Apparently, Erika had lost her second parent to yet another car accident earlier that morning, and in fact, it had happened on the same stretch of road her father had died on when she was very young. She was at a complete loss. The news was devastating, eerie, and unfair. How could she have lost both parents so suddenly in her life? And lost both parents to car accidents on the same stretch of road, nonetheless. She was distraught and inconsolable; she had gone far beyond heartbreak.

Erika was denied when she asked if she could see her mother to say goodbye one last time. Ana told her that her mother's body had been too badly damaged in the accident, and she would be buried in a closed casket. This was just one more blow because Erika realized the last conversation with her mother had been an argument that had occurred the previous night.

The sun peeked through the gray clouds. Rain sprinkled down on the small funeral gathering, which included Erika, her grandaunt Ana, her cousin Cristian, groundskeeper Tom, and Uncle Marius, who had traveled from Romania as soon as he had received news of his cousin's untimely death. They all watched on—Marius with his arm around Erika—as her mother's body was laid to rest in the earth at the quiet Nocturne Hills Cemetery.

After losing her grandmother and now her mother—the two people she was closest to in the world—Erika saw no reason to stay. She decided to attend college in California and get as far away as possible from Nocturne and the cursed Dragos name. She wouldn't go anywhere near the East Coast for the next eight years.

It was the brutal death of her fiancé, Ryan, in Southern California that Erika would find herself out of hope, with nowhere else to go, and wanting to outrun her grief, that would converge to become the catalyst for her return to Dragos Manor.

Chapter Three

The Return

Nocturne, Massachusetts

Tires slowly rolled up the long dirt drive, crunching sparse, loose gravel and stirring up a cloud of dust as they headed toward the entrance of Dragos Manor. The tires belonged to a black *Lincoln Town Car*. As the car approached, the reflection of the grand four-story Gothic Revival estate, with its large rust-colored stones and pointed dark gray rooftops, rolled across the tinted windows.

In the backseat of the *Lincoln*, Erika sat gazing out past the loosely manicured Boxwood shrubs that framed the long driveway and took in the grounds of the large estate from her childhood. She recalled that the property sat on approximately eighty acres of land that consisted of the east and west front lawns, a variety of beautiful gardens featuring a couple of fishponds, a gazebo in the back of the house, as well as retainer's quarters, horse stables, garages, and an archery range. Most wonderfully, the entire property was surrounded by sprawling woodlands.

The black *Town Car* curved around and eased to a stop in front of the manor's entryway. The reflection of the magnificent façade remained on the tinted glass for a moment longer until the window rolled down, revealing Erika's pensive face. She took a deep breath and contemplated her new yet old home.

The car pulled away a beat later, leaving Erika alone with her luggage. The air felt crisp, but having grown up here, she had been ready for the chilly morning by remembering to dress for the weather. She wore tight black pants, a comfortable gray hoodie with a blue jean jacket over top, and white high-top Converse shoes. Her hair was long and smooth. Her green eyes glittered in the morning sunlight that peeked through the clouds. Even dressed so humbly, Erika looked beautiful as she continued to reminisce about her family's magnificent home with a mixture of pain and nostalgia. She had not been back here in a very long time, not since her mother passed away eight years ago. For the first time in a long while, she felt the comfort of being somewhere tied to her mother and grandmother.

Erika gazed up the broad front steps framed by brick pillars and an open black iron gate. The stairs led up to a set of imposing double doors constructed from solid oak panels, each featuring a large brass wolf-head door knocker. She stared at the brass wolf heads and felt long-dormant memories begin to stir in the recesses of her mind. Her thoughts were interrupted when the massive doors burst open, and like a force of nature, out stepped an elderly woman wearing a freshly starched, gray polyester dress. She was soon followed by a slow-moving elderly man wearing brown slacks, a white button-up shirt with suspenders, and a tweed flat cap atop his head. Both older people stopped just outside the open doors at the top of the steps, of which there were only three, and stared down at the familiar stranger before them. Erika instantly recognized her grandaunt Ana, who somehow looked remarkably unaged to Erika for not having seen her for the past eight years. With her stood Tom, the old groundskeeper who was actually about twenty years Ana's junior but somehow looked far more her senior.

"Good day," Ana greeted Erika in Romanian with a curt smile. Immediately, apprehension and dread crept over Erika as she walked up the steps to greet her grandaunt. She felt like she needed to watch her behavior to avoid getting scolded. Ana seized Erika by the upper arms so she could seemingly control the welcome hug, which, as Erika expected, was brief and lacked affection.

"Hi, Aunt Ana," Erika said, not surprised by her grandaunt's controlling actions. "Wow, you look wonderful! I see you've been taking great care of yourself," she remarked, truly impressed by her grandaunt's relatively youthful and healthy appearance for being—what Erika had to guess was—close to ninety years old.

"Thank you, my dear. Thank you. You know, it's like I've always said, it's good to live a clean life of temperance, free of sin and indulgences." Ana replied with a hint of pride in her thick Romanian accent. Erika then turned her attention affectionately toward old Tom, who stood waiting patiently next to Ana, wearing a big smile on his gray stubbled face.

"There she is, my little Spanish Linda," Tom gushed while giving Erika a warm hug and a scratchy kiss on her cheek.

"Hi, Tom," Erika greeted with a shy smile while hugging the familiar old man, whom she remembered giving her candy and other treats as a child. Tom always felt more like a grandpa than just a groundskeeper. When he wasn't working, he could usually be found following Ana around, trying to anticipate her every need. He was just a sweet, pleasant old guy who always seemed so impressed by everything the kids said or did, or at least pretended to be.

"You look just like your mother!" Tom continued to gush. "What happened to that little urchin of a girl I knew so many years ago?" he asked while attempting to take Erika's luggage. Erika, feeling empathy for his old age, began to resist.

"No, no, it's okay, Tom! I can carry my own bags," she started to say, but Ana intervened.

"Tom is quite capable. He shall take your luggage to your room, so you and I have a chance to visit," Ana insisted, and with reservations, Erika allowed the still-smiling old man to take her luggage from her. Her grandaunt proceeded to shepherd Erika into the great, old house.

"Come," Ana said. "Let us get you reacquainted with your new yet old home," Erika hesitated briefly, feeling a moment of déjà vu, as her grandaunt had just said the exact words that Erika had been thinking to herself when she arrived. However, she dismissed it as a coincidence and followed Ana inside.

Tom put down Erika's luggage just long enough to close the front doors behind the women as they stepped inside the foyer and into the great hall, which was now considered the lobby of the hotel. Everything was as Erika remembered. Her eyes drank in the ornate hand-carved woodworking that covered much of the house, including the grand oak staircase with its dark cyan carpets, which Tom had now started to climb with Erika's suitcases. A brief feeling of guilt returned to her once more until he reached the top of the stairs, and then Erika allowed herself to become distracted again. She gazed up at the large skylight positioned above the staircase. The high walls were ladened with intricate hand-carved gilded oak accents, elaborate murals painted in the style of 19th-century Realism, and most beautiful of all, a magnificent stained-glass window featuring the portrait of a striking dark-haired woman. Of course, Erika remembered the skylight from her childhood, yet only now felt like she fully appreciated it for the first time. A chill ran down her spine as she stared at the stained-glass portrait looming above. She knew the beautiful woman featured was a distant relative—her great-great-grandmother or grandaunt or something like that—but she decided to ask someone other than Ana about this later, as she knew her grandaunt would lecture her for not knowing.

In total, the close to thirty-five thousand square-foot mansion hotel contained thirty-three rooms. The main rooms on the 1st floor consisted of the great hall, now used as the hotel lobby; the conservatory featuring a domed glass roof; the Dragos Library full of sprawling floor-to-ceiling volumes; the grand ballroom complete with a ground floor stage and an orchestral balcony; the dining hall; the lounge containing a bar and a large retractable glass wall that would be opened during the warm summer months to the outdoor patio directly outside on the west lawn; and finally the large kitchen with a floor entrance that accessed a cavernous cellar below.

The 2nd floor contained twenty guest rooms used for hotel business, while the 3rd floor boasted seven much larger luxury suites—used personally by the Dragos family. This was where Ana and Cristian each kept their living quarters, where Erika and her mother used to share a suite so long ago, it was where her uncle Marius would reside when he would come to visit the States, and occasionally special VIP guests of the family would be invited to occupy the remaining three empty suites.

As far as Erika knew, the 4th floor only extended into a few rooms, and nobody had ever lived up there. She had once heard that Ana kept her office up there, and supposedly, there were a couple of other rooms used to store old family heirlooms or something like that. The main feature of the 4th floor, however, was the legendary rooftop courtyard. Ever since Erika was a child, she had been most curious about the rooftop courtyard but had never been allowed to go up to the 4th floor. She was always told it was too dangerous or too messy when she was younger and was told it was dilapidated and unsafe when she was a teenager.

"Follow me, child." Ana's words snapped Erika's attention back to the present moment. Her grandaunt continued, "Starting today, my task will be to acquaint you with the business aspects of Dragos Manor. We shall start on the 1st floor and then build upon knowledge, responsibilities, and duties from there. I have a great appreciation for the fact that there is a lot to learn. I remember how daunting it felt coming into our family's business at a young age, but I assure you, do not worry. We will get you familiarized with everything all in good time," Ana finished, and then, to Erika's surprise, her grandaunt walked past the concierge desk and straight toward a huge set of double doors. From Erika's childhood, she had known these particular doors led into the *forbidden* grand ballroom. Without hesitation, Ana turned both handles and glided the large, elegant doors open.

Bright, radiating sunlight came flooding into the hotel lobby. Ana moved easily and gracefully into the cavernous room, wearing an expression of obvious pride on her face as she spoke about and gestured toward various aspects of the magnificent area. Gingerly, Erika followed her grandaunt into the enormous room that was clearly constructed for the dual purpose of impressing as well as entertaining. She could only make out the murmurs of her grandaunt's speech because Erika was too awestruck to absorb or comprehend any of the facts and history that were flowing from Ana like a firehose.

The entire room was bathed in the warm glow of the sun's rays, which poured in from a set of gigantic windows on the far eastern-facing wall. Outside the windows, the late morning sunlight cascading down across a brilliant symphony of vibrant colors radiated from the flower gardens in full bloom.

"It's beautiful," Erika said in a quiet, astonished voice that ended up coming out in more of a whisper than she had intended. She cleared her throat to allow her words to come more confidently and clearly. "I'm sorry for my hesitation. We were never allowed in here as kids," Erika explained. Ana's head whipped around at the very idea.

"No, of course not! This room is a masterpiece. You children were always so destructive and so... sticky, even as teenagers," Ana added with a look of horror at the very notion of any child ever playing in such an elegant space.

"Yeah, good call," Erika admitted, still captivated by the new sights of ornate craftsmanship and art that her eyes had never beheld. Erika's eyes wandered up to the orchestral balcony. For the briefest moment, she could hear echoes of a cello concerto playing—Bach's Prelude from Cello Suite No. 1 in G Major, her favorite.

"Starting this moment, I am tasked with getting you intimately acquainted with Dragos Manor and its secrets, and by extension, all *our* family secrets as well. That way, you, Cristian, and your families will be able to carry on our family legacy after I pass," Ana said with mild, grim acceptance.

"Ana, you look so fit and healthy. You've always looked the same to me ever since I was a kid. I'm starting to suspect that you'll live forever," Erika joked in an effort to reassure her grandaunt, but Ana only stared back, unblinking at her remark.

"That fact is both a blessing and a curse of our family. Even so, we need living family members at the helm of this proverbial 'ship' so your generation can advocate for me, your grandmother, and all of our ancestors to ensure our wishes will be carried out. And of course, so that you can protect our family home, and in a broad sense, our way of life," Ana added esoterically after a brief pause, then changed the subject through the continuation of the tour by leading Erika back out of the ballroom.

"I'm very pleased you have decided to seize the destiny of your bloodline and come to join us here..." Ana continued as she closed the large doors behind them after they exited the ballroom. She then began leading her grandniece to the next part of the tour, "...even though it was by means of tragic circumstances." After she said these words, Ana chanced a glance toward Erika, who was momentarily taken aback by the reminder of her fiancé's untimely death. Ana continued, not leaving room to discuss any potential emotions, which Erika knew always made her grandaunt uncomfortable. "But we don't need to discuss that matter if it's too painful for you. As you well know, our family has had its share of untimely deaths, so I imagine this is something you, unfortunately, know how to cope with well. Taking on the responsibility of this house will be very good for you and provide very important peace of mind for our family. Once you are fully integrated into the hotel business operations, that is."

"Aunt Ana, I want you to know that Cristian and I will *never* fail you, our family, or this place," Erika tried to reassure her grandaunt, subconsciously thankful to move on from the topic of Ryan's death, but what Ana said next surprised her grandniece.

"Oh, *you* won't, but that cousin of yours might. The males in our family have always been belligerent when it comes to matters of negotiation, business, and financial affairs. That's why the females in our family have always run the household, and really, all Dragos' business matters. We are the only ones capable of managing it properly," Ana concluded matter-of-factly. Erika was stunned for a moment. Whether her shock was due to the revelation of the lack of confidence Ana had in her grandson or comprehending the weight of her family's legacy would one day be resting on her shoulders, she did not have time to discern before Ana said yet again, "Come. This way," and Ana continued to lead Erika toward other rooms on the 1st floor.

Since the subject had been broached, Erika finally thought about asking.

"So, where is Cristian?"

"Cristian has been spending much of his time entertaining some important guests we are hosting on an extended stay from Europe. Hungarians by the name of Blake and Vittoria Farkas. Siblings. They have been in the States for a couple of weeks now, staying in the empty suites on the 3rd floor as guests of honor. They all took a trip into New York City to do some sightseeing and to meet a third visitor who is joining us from Hungary named Adrian 'something or other,'" Ana said, waving a dismissive hand, "Not a *Farkas* Cristian says, but they should all be coming back here later tonight or tomorrow," she said and continued to lead her grandniece to the next leg of the tour.

Chapter Four

The Cellar

Later that afternoon, Ana led Erika through the maritime-style aluminum traffic doors into the massive rustic kitchen located in the belly of the grand mansion hotel. Mahogany-stained wood paneling covered much of the walls with old but well-made olive green and rust-colored cabinets at eye level, extending to the upper walls and sitting at ground level. A huge array of copper pots dangled from hooks hanging near an enormous ten-burner stovetop range with three large ovens beneath it. Matte-gray slate backsplash converged into cream-colored marble countertops, encircling almost the entire kitchen, providing nearly endless options for prep space. For convenience, an impressive assortment of chef's knives clung to magnet strips mounted along the walls near various countertops and cook stations. Additionally, a large island with butcher block countertops sat squarely in the middle of the open space, providing even more real estate to the already generous selection of prep and staging surface areas available. Finally, the floor was covered with honeycomb-shaped tiles of analogous shades of earthy oranges and browns.

While nothing was currently cooking at that moment, the entire kitchen seemed to be vibrating with a warm heart and soul that echoed the thousands upon thousands of meals—spanning over the past century—that had been prepared in that space. Ana regaled Erika with stories of magnificent feasts created for every sort of occasion imaginable. Giant spreads for weddings, funerals, holidays, parties, birthdays, and wakes. Dinners for celebrations, graduations, achievements, and other milestones. She explained that food cooked for the Dragos family, friends, and hotel guests alike had all been prepared in this kitchen by the long legacy of talented chefs whom the Dragos family had employed at one time or another. She pointed out that by the sheer size of the space alone, the kitchen staff would have been as many as eight employees back in the heyday of the hotel business. Still, nowadays, with minimal family members residing there and the dwindling number of hotel patronage in recent decades, Dragos Manor was able to make do with a single staff member. Chef Sabina—who was currently in town picking up some additional supplies—was their current employee and acted as the lone cook in the kitchen. She had proved to be very capable of preparing meals for the family and hotel guests when they arrived during the fall season.

Ana explained that fall was popular for the hotel as that was when the "Leaf Peepers" would frequent the long-rumored haunted New England manor. However, in recent years, despite the beautiful fall season and even despite the hotel's reputation for being haunted, the Dragos family would be lucky to fill half a dozen or so of their vacant hotel rooms. Erika's grandaunt speculated that this was due partly to the location and proximity of Nocturne being out in the "middle of nowhere." Still, Erika surmised this was also partly due to how particular Ana seemed to have become regarding whom she allowed to visit the hotel and when. It sounded as though every year, the guestlist grew more and more exclusive, and every year, the window she would allow for reservations seemed to grow shorter and shorter. To say the least, it sounded as if Ana might have something to do with the decrease in patronage.

It was now late afternoon. Ana had finished showing Erika around the massive kitchen and giving her the latest updates regarding meal service and patronage concerns. Next, she led her grandniece to a door on the floor at the back of the room. The tour for that day concluded with Ana taking Erika down into the cellar. Immediately, Erika felt apprehensive when she saw the familiar entrance in the kitchen floor that she remembered from faded memories of her childhood; particularly, memories of being scolded for attempting to go down were the ones that came flooding into her mind. Ana clocked Erika's hesitation and paused momentarily with a questioning look.

"Is everything alright?" Ana asked. We are almost done. This is the last area we will cover for the day. Then, you can rest in your room before dinner if you like."

"Sorry, I'm fine, Aunt Ana, it's just... first the ballroom and now the cellar?" Erika laughed nervously. "I spent so much time in this house as a kid and was never allowed to go into any of these places before. They were always so mysterious to me. And now I'm seeing them all on my first day back here in eight years! It's all just a little overwhelming. My whole life, I have always been curious about these areas of the house. *I've had dreams about them*. It's like, next, you'll be taking me up to the 4th-floor rooftop courtyard," she laughed offhandedly. But to this, Ana's expression grew somewhat anxious with her response.

"Erika, you must understand; I do appreciate that this must be a lot for you. Believe me, this is a lot for me too," Ana said in a tone almost resembling sympathy, but that tone quickly faded into dry matter-of-factness. "But as I told you, it is *my duty* to get you familiar with all aspects of our family's home and the hotel business. You must understand that your mother and grandmother had their reasons for making certain areas of Dragos Manor off-limits when you were young. And now *I am* the one who is tasked with 'filling you in' as they say. So, if you please, there are many things we must go through and catch up on," Ana sighed at the enormity of her task. "So I suggest we get on with it," she said in a somewhat curt fashion, then added esoterically, "Now, as we enter into the cellar—just stay close by me. We need to get it used to you going down there." This last statement hung in Erika's mind for a moment. Surely Ana had meant, "We need to get *you* used to going down there." and not the other way around. Ana must have just misspoken, but because of her grandaunt's coarse mood, Erika thought better of correcting her.

The sound of the unoiled hinges echoed throughout the pitch-black stillness of the cavernous space below. Light from the kitchen above came flooding down, slicing through the thick, stagnant air and illuminating a thin layer of dust particles floating in the atmosphere.

The path down the stairs before them looked like it yawned into a hungry open mouth that might swallow them whole the moment they set even a single foot down there. An eerie feeling followed Erika throughout the tour that day as she and Ana went from room to room on the ground floor of Dragos Manor. She had dismissed the creepy feeling, thinking surely it was caused by the lack of other people in the large, old estate hotel—it being the off-season and all. But here and now, staring down into the vacuum of darkness below, the eerie feeling felt amplified.

The steps creaked as Ana descended, followed gingerly by her grandniece. Once they both had reached the cool earthen floor at the base of the stairs, Ana guided Erika toward a massive dusty wine rack, which took up the entirety of one of the cellar walls. She began showing Erika the expansive Dragos wine collection. As she gestured a hand toward various sections of the racks, the elderly matriarch explained how the assortment was categorized.

"We have old-world reds and whites over here, new-world reds and whites over there..." Ana started explaining. Erika fought hard to pay attention and follow along. Still, she quickly found her attention drifting away from wine to the curiosity of her surroundings as her eyes began exploring the dark, musty space.

She had never been inside the cellar before this moment. The air was cool and smelled of earth and rotting wood, with a touch of something almost mushroom-like. Aside from Ana's voice, Erika could hear the small creaks and rustling sounds of unseen vermin that were probably scurrying around in the depths of the darkness, no doubt attracted to the large shelves holding jars, cans, and bins of all shapes, sizes, and colors. Jars containing every flavor of preservative, or others containing pickled vegetable varieties such as radishes, olives, cucumbers, and onions. Different types of canned goods neatly lined the shelving, and clearly labeled and tightly sealed bins held root vegetables, such as beets, parsnips, carrots, rutabagas, and turnips, sat on the earthen floor.

Erika glanced up to the far corner of the room. She saw a small sliver of daylight peeking through a crack from a second ground-level entrance and cutting through the darkness. She recalled that this entrance was located outside the northwest corner behind the house. As her eyes adjusted, she could just faintly make out the outline of a second set of stairs descending from the exterior entrance above. As her eyes traveled down the dark contours of each step, she noticed a black shape as her eyes approached the bottom. It appeared to be the silhouette of a figure crouching near the base of the staircase. Erika stared hard at the figure for a moment. *Is that a person?* she wondered as her eyes traced the large frame of a torso and shoulders, then the outline of a head on top. The black shadow leaned forward almost imperceptibly as if it were a predator crouching down, stalking its prey. The movement had been so subtle and so faint that for a brief moment, Erika questioned if her eyes were playing tricks on her.

"Ana, sorry to interrupt you, but there wouldn't be *anything* or *anyone* else down here with us, would there?" Erika asked with slight anxiety creeping into her voice as she extracted her cell phone from her pocket. Ana stopped her wine lesson, momentarily taken aback by the question.

"Why do you ask, my dear?" she questioned without reassuring that they should indeed be alone. Erika switched on her cell phone's flashlight and pointed the beam toward the dark mass at the base of the stairs. The light revealed an unremarkable medium-sized barrel with a bag of moldy onions on top of it.

"Oh no, dear. That is just a barrel of brandy. Nothing that can harm you. Now, where were we? Oh yes, this Brunello di Montalcino over here is a guest favorite! You see, they are a super Tuscan, meaning the wine draws many similarities to traditional red Bordeaux. However, instead of the traditional five red grapes of Bordeaux, this wine is one hundred percent Sangiovese." Ana went on and on with extensive knowledge of the wine collection.

Now feeling slightly silly for being startled by the darkness, Erika switched off her phone's flashlight and tried again to follow the wine lesson. But not much time had passed before her attention began to wander once more. She just couldn't seem to shake the feeling that she and Ana were not alone down there. It felt as though they were being watched. Full-body chills crawled across her skin. Then she thought she heard a faint whisper from somewhere behind her. Erika whipped her head around, trying to locate the origin of the sound. Her gaze was almost hypnotically drawn toward the far end of the cellar.

In the black recesses, she could just make out the faint outline of a narrow opening in the wall. Squinting, straining, and willing her eyesight to adjust to the darkness, she saw that it indeed looked like some kind of doorway. Inside, she saw *movement*. It appeared as though someone was standing in the door frame, staring back at her. Chills again rose on her skin as she felt more and more creeped out with each passing second. The figure then seemed to recede into the darkness as a pale bluish light slowly appeared inside, revealing that the opening was actually a hallway. Erika could see a couple of additional doorways, dusty wooden beams, lumpy earthen walls, and cobwebs. Still, all these features faded into the void of darkness beyond.

At that moment, an eerie melody filled the space around her. It sounded like the tinny crackle of music from an old gramophone. Erika turned back to gauge Ana's reaction to the bluish glow and the strange music flowing in the air; however, her grandaunt continued speaking inaudibly, presumably still engrossed in her wine lesson. Now, the music was all Erika could focus on as she slowly turned back to face the hallway. Cobwebs dangled down in long tendrils from the hallway's ceiling. They slowly began dancing around as if being blown by a mysterious breeze. Without realizing it, Erika turned and took a step toward the hallway. She had a strong, undeniable urge to cross through this alluring entrance. Feelings of optimism inexplicably began swelling up inside her chest.

Meanwhile, Ana continued on and on with pride about the Dragos' wine collection—which was ironic for a woman who boasted temperance. She hadn't noticed that her grandniece had started to wander away.

"...because as one knows, we want our guests to consume relatively young Châteauneuf-du-Pape, so we usually don't allow it to exceed one to two decades, three at the very maximum. These vintages are approaching their peak maturity soon and should be consumed within the next year... give or take."

Ana's words continued to go unnoticed by Erika as she closed the distance between herself and the hallway with its azure glow. Then something funny happened. The strange breeze inside the hallway slowly began to dissipate. The cobwebs grew very still. In fact, everything seemed to grow very still—stillness reminiscent of the eye of a storm or the stillness in that moment before a predator of the jungle strikes.

Erika's positive feelings vanished, and, slowly, a new feeling began to bubble up to the surface that she couldn't immediately pinpoint. First, she felt it in her gut. Maybe it is anticipation. Or, maybe, was it fear? As soon as Erika touched upon the possibility of fear and fright, the feeling rapidly amplified throughout her entire body at an alarming rate. *I am in danger!* she realized as her intuition finally came flooding in. An intense terror radiated throughout her entire core and threatened to overwhelm her. At the same moment, she thought she heard the echoes of people screaming from inside the hallway!

Ana turned just in time and noticed her grandniece was no longer by her side. She looked up and saw Erika very near the hallway entrance. The Dragos Matriarch called out loudly, her voice reverberating with command.

"Stop!" she yelled in Romanian, then switched to English. "That's quite enough! Stop your foolish mischief in the dark!"

Ana's abruptness startled Erika back into the present moment. She was confused by what was happening, and her automatic response of guilt and shame at being scolded came flooding back. However, as Erika replayed her grandaunt's words in her head, she vaguely realized that somehow, the reprimand did not seem like it had been directed toward her.

Shaking off the fogginess, the amalgamation of panic, dread, and anxiety began to recede as if Erika had just been awoken from a terrifying nightmare. Ana walked briskly over to her grandniece and grasped her by the shoulders as she inspected Erika's face. Other than a thin layer of sweat, she appeared to be unharmed.

"Hello?" a woman's voice called from above, causing Ana and Erika to jump. "Is anybody down there? Sorry, I'm late. I'm just getting back from my errands."

"Hi, Sabina!" Ana called back up the stairs. "We'll be right up!" Ana again turned to Erika and examined her face. Other than feeling utterly exhausted, Erika was fine. "Well... I guess that could have gone worse," Ana commented with a wry chuckle. "Come. That's enough for today. Are you hungry?" Erika shook her head to decline. She could not grasp exactly how she felt but was certain that hunger was far from any feeling she was experiencing at that moment. "You must be tired then. Come, I'll show you to your room so you can get settled." Ana led Erika out of the cellar and closed the door behind them.

The pale bluish glow returned to the hallway down in the cellar below Dragos Manor's kitchen. A mysterious breeze again picked up and began disturbing the cobweb tendrils hanging from the ceiling and walls. It was almost as if whatever lay inside was disappointed at the missed opportunity for mischief.

After a long day of travel, a tour of the 1st floor, including previously off-limit areas, and getting scared out of her mind in the cellar, Ana finally showed Erika up to her room on the 2nd floor. Erika recognized the room she used to live in during her teenage years at Dragos Manor. Her luggage sat waiting for her.

The elderly woman turned and asked, "Are you sure you don't want to stay upstairs in the suite you used to share with your mother on the 3rd? It might be more convenient to have the rest of the family nearby. We have always been saving it for you, you know."

"I know, Aunt Ana, thank you. No, this is fine for a few days while I'm getting adjusted. I'll move up there eventually, but I need some time to acclimate," Erika explained with rapidly diminishing energy.

"Very well. There is some water and fruit on that nightstand if you wake up hungry or thirsty. Sleep well, dear. We'll see you in the morning." With that, Ana turned and shut the door to the guest room.

Relieved to finally be out of her grandaunt's company, Erika examined her bedroom. She tested the softness of the bed, ran her fingers along the vanity's surface, and ended up next to her suitcase, where she began the task of unpacking. However, she did not get very far before she decided to stop and take a moment to herself.

Erika sat on the bed and gazed out from the 2nd story bedroom window. Night was about to fall, and she could hear the peaceful sounds of wildlife outside her window. All flora and fauna in the area seemed to be singing and celebrating the arrival of the brilliant full Moon that was starting to appear in the evening sky. *This full Moon would be the Flower Moon,* Erika thought to herself. Without realizing it, the sounds soothed and relaxed her, taking her mind on a peaceful and wonderful journey into solace-filled subconsciousness as she drifted into a deep sleep.

Chapter Five

The Investigation

Night of the Flower Moon

There was the modest earth below and the assured heavens above, boasting a breathtaking full Moon over the town of Nocturne. The clarity in the atmosphere that night was a rare form for this time of year and what was normally a cloudy New England sky. Dark silhouettes of tree limbs rustled eerily in a faint springtime breeze.

The horses inside the barn on the northwestern part of the Dragos property stood alert inside their stables. Someone had failed to secure the barn door properly, and now the hinged wooden door clapped back and forth on the barn frame in the evening zephyr. The horses pinned their ears back with agitation at the sound, their nostrils flaring as they sniffed a distasteful scent in the air. One of the horses nearest to the open door began squealing and roaring, either demonstrating his trepidation or signaling a warning to his stablemates of something frightening in the nighttime atmosphere.

Suddenly, the barn door swung fully open. All the horses emitted a high-pitched and piercing squeal as two large dark shadows fell across them, obscuring the fear that shone brightly in the whites of their eyes.

The next morning, Erika walked sleepily toward the top of the staircase landing, preparing to descend into a new day in her new life. She now felt hungry from not eating very much the day before, having been distracted by her arrival and absorbing as much information as she could about her old yet new home. She also still felt a little groggy after sleeping like the dead.

Just before she reached the staircase landing, the sound of a deep male voice stopped her dead in her tracks. Caught off guard, she hesitated and hung back for a minute. Then, as stealthily as she could, Erika snuck up to the edge of the staircase and peered down just over the top step so as not to be seen but enough to investigate to whom the male voice belonged. She caught a glimpse of a sharply dressed man with thick silver hair slicked back in a pompadour and a silver beard with a handlebar mustache to match. He was wearing a leather motorcycle jacket and faded black jeans. His appearance gave the impression of a 1990s UK Rockstar with a touch of biker. He definitely looked like a badass. The man was speaking with Ana in the lobby. Erika decided to hang back, hoping the pair downstairs would not notice her.

As she attempted to eavesdrop on their conversation, her interest was suddenly piqued when her grandaunt mentioned Erika by name. At that moment, the conversation paused, and the silver-haired man turned and looked straight up at the sliver of Erika's eye peeking from over the top of the landing.

"Hello, my favorite niece," Marius called up pleasantly, wearing a smooth smile beneath his silver whiskers. Ana jumped, looking momentarily taken aback, seemingly surprised by her grandniece's sudden presence. Erika stepped out fully, yet apprehensively, onto the landing, feeling like she was intruding on their conversation. Marius must have clocked her apprehension because he coaxed her further. "Now, don't make me wait. I haven't seen you in so very long. Come down and say hello to your favorite uncle," he said, turning in a welcoming manner toward her.

Erika did not need any more convincing; a warm smile spread across her face as she began to trot down the stairs toward—he was right—her favorite uncle. Once at the bottom of the stairs, she jogged the last few steps to him and jumped into his open arms, which Marius clasped around her and held her to him dearly. He was big and strong and smelled nicely of a mixture of juniper and vetiver. Erika felt so much relief that she began to softly weep. He held on for a second longer and then released her to inspect her face. Silvery tears glistened down Erika's cheeks as she beamed a smile up at him.

"Are those tears I see on my angel? Oh, sweetheart, don't cry. I'm so glad to see you." Marius spoke softly and gently lifted his big hand under her chin, wiping her tears away lovingly with his other hand.

"I'm just so happy to see you," Erika said in earnest, but then, for the sake of not offending her grandaunt, added, "All of you. I didn't realize how much I've missed everyone, and I'm so sorry I've kept myself away for so long since my mother passed." As she spoke these words, Erika couldn't help but cry a little harder.

The tears she shed were for a lifetime of loss—the loss of her father, mother, grandmother, and most acutely, for the recent horrific loss of her chosen love. She had not realized how much of a true sense of being comforted she had been lacking in her life.

Marius continued to gaze upon his niece, his face filled with loving concern and sympathy. He slowly pulled her back into a long, comforting hug. Ana averted her eyes away from the pair, uncomfortable with the display of affection and emotion.

After another moment, Marius let Erika go and said, "Mother, we're going to walk a minute in the gardens to get some fresh air." To which Ana nodded her acknowledgment, not at all looking concerned that she had not been invited—not that she would have gone anyway. Everyone knew that displays of emotion like this had always made Ana uncomfortable. Marius put a hand on Erika's shoulder and directed her out the front door into the mid-morning sunlight.

Ana stood in the open doorway but recoiled away from the sunlight, allowing the ambient shadows inside the house to cast ominously across her face. She watched her grandniece and her son as they made their way through the outdoor patio on the west lawn, then rounded the side of the house and followed a stone path leading toward the gardens in the back. Once they had disappeared around the side of the house, Ana turned and looked back at the grandfather clock in the lobby. She saw the time was 11:11 am. According to numerology, 11:11 signified a time of insight and enlightenment.

Almost as if on cue, an unseen voice with a thick Romanian accent—matching that of Ana's—began speaking to her from seemingly out of nowhere within the house.

"My poor darling. Her heart is broken so. It is such a shame what happened to that boy." Thin silvery wisps of smoke-like material began to form as the ghost of Daniela Dragos, Erika's late grandmother, materialized next to her sister-in-law Ana in the doorway. "I heard what you and Marius were discussing a moment ago," Daniela continued. "He's very upset, you know. Marius. He's convinced a werewolf is responsible. If that is the case, an incident like that can be very dangerous for our kind; to brazenly kill in the human world for other humans to discover that degree of carnage, like some wild animal attack. Maybe it was a feral? But from what the hunters have reported, there weren't any unaccounted-for ferals in the area at the time. I do hope that Marius is able to find out what happened."

"Yes, he says he's looking into it," Ana replied dryly to her deceased sister-in-law's ghost.

"And have you asked Cristian if he knows anything or has heard anything in his social circles? I know he has befriended the Farkas family pack, which is a remarkable feat considering the Dragos and Farkas families have had a contentious relationship for over a century now."

"Cristian swore it was no one from the Farkas family and has repeatedly told me that he earnestly does not know any other Lycan that it could be," Ana responded, slightly uncomfortable. Daniela must have noticed the discomfort in her sister-in-law and said nothing further on the matter but instead changed the subject.

"I want everyone in this house to give Erika adequate time to adjust to the *unique* aspects of this home, as well as our family's *lifestyle*," Daniela said firmly. To this, Ana rolled her eyes, which Daniela ignored. "I've spoken to everyone and told them to keep the parties and *wolf-play* to a minimum until the moment is right. I'm relying on *you* to have Cristian behave and make sure his friends do the same. Also, I heard about the incident with *the Mischief* in the cellar yesterday and warned them that if *they* keep up that kind of behavior, I'll send them away to somewhere far more unpleasant than a dark cellar. I see them getting wild with Erika's return to the house, and we don't need them trying to reunite with *her... the Mother*." Daniela shuttered at this latter concern. "As for me, while I miss my granddaughter and am anxious to look upon her face and speak words to her directly, I will also not reveal myself to her until she has had an adequate chance to adjust to the realities of our way of life around here."

"Oh, Daniela, you coddle her so!" Ana burst out, finally unable to contain herself any longer. "You always have! This is *Erika's* family, *her* bloodline, and *her* destiny! Neither you nor I nor any of our children, for that matter, ever had such a delicate introduction to the realities and traditions of our world. You've always been worried because Erika is Lycan recessive and cannot transform! And look at me! I am also Lycan recessive and cannot transform, and I never found our lives so disturbing or unpalatable! I have always been proud to be any part werewolf, even if I cannot transform!" Ana said with an offended tone.

"Even so, times are different, and you know very well Erika was not raised knowing anything of the reality of werewolves, let alone that she comes from a *long line* of Romanian Lycans. Her mother and I always wanted her to have a chance at a happy, *normal* life, free of traumatic experiences, such as the ones *you* and *I* endured when we were young!" Daniela's words hit Ana particularly hard, and she did not protest or argue any further with her late sister-in-law. Daniela continued, "I have no doubt Erika will come to accept all of it once she has had a chance to get used to everything because she is a strong, intelligent individual and because it *is* a part of who she is. I only ask that everyone just please give her some time. The poor thing has gone through so much already," Daniela spoke firmly, then began fanning herself with her ghostly hand as if she were becoming overheated. Ana nodded respectfully in agreement with her late sister-in-law's wishes.

"Very well, Daniela. I will make sure it is done as you ask. After all, it is my duty and responsibility as Head of Household," Ana stated stoically.

Outside, in the back of the house, sunlight reflected on the shimmering, iridescent, multi-colored scales of the Koi Carp. The sparkling jewel-like fish lazily nibbled at bugs, larvae, and anything else that could be edible, breaking the surface tension of the pond with each small O-shaped mouth gulp framed by tiny whiskers.

Marius and Erika meandered in the garden near the pond as the pair continued their conversation in private.

"Nobody could even explain what happened to him," Erika said with emotional exasperation. "The detectives said it looked like *an animal attack* of some kind, but that doesn't even make any sense! What animal could have done that?! How did it even get in his house? I still just don't understand any of it! I can't believe the investigators closed the case!"

"I'm so very sorry for your loss, Erika. Sorry you experienced that horrible nightmare." Marius offered his condolences while shaking his head in disgust and disbelief at the senseless violence.

For the past several minutes, Erika had been recounting her memories of the final moments she had spent with her fiancé immediately preceding his death, all the way through the next day when she had been called to the scene and saw Ryan wheeled away in a body bag. Marius' hardened gaze went far away as he retreated into his thoughts for a moment before returning to the present.

"I don't want to promise you anything or for you to get your hopes up just in case nothing surfaces, but I want you to know that I have a *group* on the inside who I've asked to look deeper into the case. Ryan's death was a tragic injustice, and I will do whatever I can to sniff out the responsible low-life creature and make sure they pay for their crime," Marius said with a look of angry resolve on his face.

Erika was stunned. Not only had she not seen her mother's cousin in about eight years, but the moment he was back in her life, he was already giving her all the comfort, support, and protection she had lacked. Erika now realized she was the only one responsible for the distance. Her family had always been there; they were here for her now, as if no time had passed.

"Wow... That's incredible, Uncle Marius. Thank you," Erika responded with a mixture of sadness and disbelief. "I had no idea you had any connections to law enforcement, let alone in California," she commented in astonishment.

"Well, my connections are not really in *law enforcement* per se," Marius replied mysteriously, then hesitated. Erika was momentarily perplexed by her uncle's words. Then she looked at him and took him in, taking in his appearance. She saw his gruff, tough guy exterior, and it dawned on her that she did not know what circles her uncle might be mixed up with. She quickly backpedaled.

"I'm sorry; I didn't mean to question your kindness! Please don't get me wrong," Erika exclaimed, worried her questioning may have come across as her being ungrateful or judgmental. "I do *very much* appreciate any support! I wouldn't care if the people you have on the case were the 'vigilante justice' type! Personally, I don't care how it happens—I want justice for Ryan and to find out the truth of what happened to him," she said as she stared out distantly at the thought.

Marius smiled and reassured her. "It's ok, Erika. You did not offend me. Let's just say my contacts are more akin to private investigators. Trust me, if there is anything to find out, they will sniff it out." He blinked away the somberness and smiled again at his cousin's daughter before glancing down at his wristwatch. "Oh! It's nearly noon! I need to head into town and fetch my belongings. I scheduled to have a container of my things shipped over from Romania. Now that you have moved back in again, I have made arrangements to do the same. I think it would be good if more family were around this old place," Marius said. Erika gave him a mild look of panic at the thought of him leaving, even if it was just for a couple of hours to fetch his belongings. Marius seemed to clock this as he gave her another reassuring smile. "Don't worry, my darling, I will be back later this evening. Your Aunt Ana mentioned we will have a big family dinner as a 'welcome home' for you and me. I heard that Cristian and his friends arrived back in town last night, although I haven't seen any sign of them this morning. It will be a decent-sized dinner party! I'm really looking forward to it!"

"Ok, but try to hurry back," she said with some residual anxiety.

Marius kissed Erika on her forehead, then turned and walked back toward the front of the house to see about collecting his belongings. Erika was now alone with her thoughts in the garden. A short time later, she could hear Marius fire up his motorcycle and drive off as the sound of the loud engine receded into the distance. Then, the sunny gardens behind Dragos Manor became quiet and still once more, until a new sound broke the silence.

"Argh!"

The voice had come from the stables just beyond the gardens. It sounded as though someone was struggling. Erika glanced around nervously but saw no sign of anybody else nearby, only the bright, sunny landscape. She decided to investigate the commotion and began walking toward the barn entrance.

Once there, she peeked inside and saw the interior was in shambles.

Various farm tools, riding equipment, and hay had been thrown about. One of the stable doors had been broken and had muddy prints all over it. Multiple feed bags had been knocked over, and oats were spilled all over the floor with track marks skidded through it as if there had been a struggle. The horses looked spooked and tense as the sounds of grunting and straining came from the last stall, which otherwise appeared empty.

"Hello?" Erika called out, unsure and slightly frightened about who or what might respond.

"Just a bunch of treacherous dogs..." Groundskeeper Tom said through gritted teeth as he stood up, then saw Erika standing near the barn entrance.

"Whoa, dogs did this? Can I help you clean up?" she asked, confused and alarmed. Old Tom only stared back at her anxiously and immediately advised her not to walk further into the mess.

"Ah, ah, no, it's okay, Linda. I will clean up this mess. It would be best not to get your shoes dirty in all this slop. It's nothing I'm not used to, I'm afraid," Tom assured her with a nervous smile.

"But I don't understand how dogs could get inside here and cause all this chaos?" Erika asked, bending down to pick up a broken shovel head.

"I was just cursing. There weren't really any dogs, Linda," Tom said, wearing an apologetic smile that did not linger for very long as it was replaced with a much more dismal look. It was your *cousin*... and his friends," he clarified.

Erika was stunned as she picked up another interesting piece of wreckage—a piece of equipment known as horse blinders. These blinders had a bright red bra stretched over the eye sockets.

"Cristian did this?" She asked with a mixture of horror and disgust on her face.

"Yes, he and his friends are very spoiled and selfish individuals. They have too much *Glug Glug*," Tom said, gesturing like he was drinking from an invisible bottle. "And they don't consider their actions or that someone else has to clean up after them," he explained with a look of hopelessness.

"I'm sorry you've had to deal with this sort of behavior, Tom, but it ends right now! I will speak to Cristian when I see him and set him straight. I don't know who he thinks he is, but I will not allow this kinda thing to happen with me coming on board," Erika finished, resolving to shut the behavior down immediately. She moved to leave but paused to ask again, "Are you sure I can't give you a hand?"

"No, no, really, it's fine. Get yourself some lunch or go find your aunt. I'm sure she's eager to continue visiting with you," old Tom said, then gestured to the mess on the stable floor. "I'll take care of this slop. Don't you worry about it."

Erika did not protest further but decided to find her grandaunt and discuss Cristian's unacceptable behavior. She was too old to be worried about childish games like 'tattle-tail.' Erika considered herself upfront and direct, so she aimed to address the matter head-on and nip it in the bud.

Tom exhaled a sigh of relief once Erika had finally left the stables. His gaze returned to look down at the mutilated and bloody body of the freshly killed and *legless* horse at his feet. The poor beast had just neighed its last whinny the night before.

Chapter Six

Cristian

Streaks of Shadbush, Gray Birch, Maples, and Pitch Pine flew by in blurry repetition as the 1971 black Chevy Nova tires tore down the desolate backroads at high speed. The guttural roar of the engine announced the vehicle's approach as it headed straight toward Dragos Manor. The Nova was occupied by three rough-looking characters, all wearing sunglasses and their hair blowing around in the wind.

The driver of the vehicle was Cristian Dragos. His hair was thick, dark, and tidy with a prominent widow's peak. His eyebrows looked like large caterpillars resting over the rims of his black *Ray-Ban* sunglasses, and although he was clean-shaven, his dark five-o'clock shadow was ever present just under his fair skin. Cristian took a long drag off his cigarette with his free hand, leaving his right—which wore a large gold wolf-head ring on his middle finger—grasped tightly to the steering wheel as he weaved expertly down the road with confident familiarity.

The individual in the passenger seat also had dark hair, but his was much shaggier than Cristian's as it whipped around in the wind. Blake Farkas, one of the Hungarian visitors and a guest of honor, was staying at Dragos Manor with his younger sister, Vittoria Farkas. The Dragos family was hosting the Farkas siblings after Cristian had successfully gained their friendship during a recent trip abroad to Eastern Europe. The friendship in and of itself was not an amazing feat. However, considering the Dragos and Farkas families had been engaged in a century-long feud, the olive branch extended by the younger generations from both families was quite a remarkable accomplishment. With the prolonged nature of this quarrel, the original meaning of the feud had become somewhat murky, and, as time went on, seemed to expand into more than just a Dragos vs Farkas squabble, but into a Romanian vs Hungarian werewolf disagreement.

One of the more popular rumors was that the feud's origin was based on an insult that had taken place between the two families. That once, a long time ago, a Dragos maiden was meant to marry a Farkas bachelor, but she ran away, never fulfilling the betrothal promise. The common view that stemmed from this rumor was that the Dragos family thought themselves superior to the Farkas family and then, later, that Romanian werewolves, in general, thought themselves better than Hungarian werewolves.

Other reasons would surface occasionally—the disagreement had started over money owed, a territory dispute at Romania's western border, or an insult regarding honor or besmirchment of pride. It was also said the dispute had arisen over a matter of conduct, specifically the conduct of Romanian werewolves' affinity for fraternizing with humans.

The third and final person in the back seat of the *Nova* had longer, wavy, sandy-blond hair and brown eyes and was wearing a dark brown leather bomber jacket. He looked like the type of guy who was a surfer, or he could have been one of the Dogtown skaters. This man was Curt; he was an American who had been associated with the Dragos family for nearly a decade. Curt was a human, and he also happened to be a werewolf hunter.

"So, she is there now? At Dragos Manor?" Blake asked eagerly, his thick Hungarian accent sticking around each word of his broken English. Cristian exhaled smoke from his lungs as he responded.

"Yeah, my Bunica said she just arrived yesterday morning," he replied, dialing up his Romanian accent just a little bit to better fit in with his European friend but also revealing slightly effeminized undertones in his voice.

"I cannot wait to do the meeting her finally! She looks so beautiful in the pictures you show at me," Blake said with a big, excited wolfish grin and imperfect English.

"My Bunica?" Cristian asked, momentarily confused. Blake's look of lust melted into a dubious expression.

"No cowboy, not you grandma. I met you Grandma. She not my type," Blake responded in a teasing manner. "No stupid... you cousin! Erika. Do you think she will think I am the throbbing heart, cow pie?" he asked playfully in fractured English. Cristian furrowed his eyebrows in confusion.

"Hahaha, I think you mean beefcake, dude!" Curt laughed and drawled out from the back seat. "Also, you should consider slowing your roll, amigo! Hasn't it only been like three months since she lost her dude? Didn't you say her boyfriend *just* died, Cris?" Curt asked provocatively, giving Cristian a sly look in the rearview mirror. Cristian's eyes darted up to the mirror's reflection as he shot a look of daggers into Curt's face.

"What?!" Blake exclaimed with shock. "Her boyfriend die three months ago?! How does that happen?" he asked with fragmented diction, stunned by the news. He turned to face both Cristian and Curt at once. Cristian was silently seething at Curt.

"Yeah, thanks for the info, Curt!" came Cristian's tense response, his eyes warning him not to say another word, then to Blake, "Yeah, sorry I didn't tell you sooner, Blake," Cristian said, taking on a softer tone. "I didn't want to ruin your visit with such sad news. I did say I thought you and Erika would hit it off. I think she would be interested to get to know you, ya know? Take her mind off that awful tragedy," Cristian explained apologetically.

"But you say she wants to be tied in knot. Do you think her feets are cold?" Blake asked.

"Whoa! Slow down dude!" came Curt's voice again from the back seat. "Don't overthink it. Just hang out with her; she's not going anywhere. American girls like to take their time with these sorts of things anyway."

"Yeah, thanks, Curt! But you don't even know her!" Cristian snapped, now extremely annoyed with Curt's unhelpful backseat matchmaking skills. He shot the werewolf hunter another nasty look in the rearview mirror, narrowing his eyes, as he continued. "She's pretty arrogant. Mmkay? And she's like... an *attention whore*, or something! So, she might be ready for a new boyfriend! Ya never know." While Cristian was speaking into the rearview mirror at Curt, he also intended his words to encourage Blake. Cristian flashed a toothy smile as he nodded vigorously at Blake, who only stared back at him with confusion.

"A whore? Like, prostitute?" Blake asked, furrowing his brows.

"No, no, no... sorry... let me clarify. She's not, like, an actual whore," Cristian said with a sheepish laugh. "I didn't me she charges money for— I just mean, she likes being the center of attention, so she will probably like it if you give her yours. Girls like that stuff."

"And how would you know what girls like, huh Cris?" Curt smirked up into the mirror again. Cristian mouthed—*Fuck You,* silently back at him. But Curt ignored this and continued, "Oh, you must know what women want from obeying your Bunica your entire life. Speaking of your Bunica, Cris, she's going to be really *pissed* about you guys getting into the barn last night, man," Curt taunted. "Good thing I'm a light sleeper. Old Tom called me at 3 AM this morning and told me to 'wake my ass up and come get you guys and put you somewhere you could *sleep it off.*' By the way, you're welcome for crashing at my place last night." Cristian flashed another jeering look into the rearview mirror.

"I'm about to throw your ass outta this car if you don't shut up," Cristian fumed.

"You wouldn't do that. For one, I need to get my car from your place. Second, your Bunica invited me to dinner tonight as a 'thank you' for coming to collect your rowdy assess last night," Curt said, blowing Cristian off. Blake looked more surprised than bothered by Curt's remarks.

"What is the problems? You grandma knows what we are. Is she upset about the horse?" Blake asked innocently.

"Dude, you guys *ripped that horse apart*! It doesn't have legs anymore, let alone its life!" Curt pointed out, laughing at the situation. Cristian had to admit things got a little out of control the previous night, but he knew what it was like to get caught up in the aggression that comes during transformation. At least it was an animal they attacked and killed and not a human. But deep down, he knew that Curt was right. He and Blake had gotten carried away and killed an animal on the Dragos's property. Cristian's Bunica, Ana, would be angry at his lack of self-control. This time, Cristian said nothing but fixed a surly gaze on the road ahead and continued driving.

"Again, I ask, what is problem? Everyone knows sometimes things like that can happen when Wolfy comes out," Blake pointed out in a truly bewildered way, then turned to both Curt and Cristian. "I can get you new horse legs. I can get new horse legs by three o'clock... with shoes," he offered casually while glancing at his wristwatch.

"Yeah, maybe spring for a full horse replacement, dude," Curt suggested, still smirking as he nonchalantly gazed out the window.

"It's just because *she* is there!" Cristian hissed. "Bunica and Daniela don't

48

want Erika to know about us yet. Ya know—*The werewolf thing*. It's *fucking* ridiculous. She's going to find out sooner or later!" Cristian said, feigning confidence in his remark, but he knew Curt was right. Ana and Daniela would have some choice words for him when they were alone. "Anyway, Erika will have to find out sooner or later. She will have to if she is going to marry Bla—" but before Cristian could finish his sentence, Blake interrupted.

"Oh wait, wait, wait, shut up, shut up, I love this song! Turn it up!" he requested. Cristian sighed, rolled his eyes, and reached down and twisted the volume dial on the car's stereo. Blake started nodding to the beat of the music and snapping his fingers out the window as he sang along. "..and *Am* just the devil with love to spares. Viva Las Vegas! Viva Las Vegas!"

Right on the song's chorus, the *Nova* hung a sharp right, cutting into the long driveway. The muscle car continued to accelerate while its tires fiercely kicked up dirt and gravel under the chassis as it sped toward the entrance of Dragos Manor.

Everything went silent with the engine off, and the *Nova* parked at the top of the drive until three doors *Slam, Slam, Slam* shut, breaking the silence. Blake trotted up to the front doors with the brass wolf-head doorknockers and threw open the front doors to let himself inside. Curt started to follow Blake but noticed Cristian stayed put, indicating he had something to say. Curt hung back for the inevitable lecture. Sometimes Curt thought Cristian felt like his angry wife the way he would give him cues with his body language, especially when Curt was in trouble.

"Look, I'm fine if you want to have your little *side hustle* with me to make a few extra bucks, mmkay, but don't for one *second* forget this whole deal is a lot bigger than just me or you! Nnkay? There are *contracts* in place between werewolves and werewolf hunters like you, that *you* cannot cross without royally *fucking* yourself and your career over! Got it, hunter?" Cristian was making a lot of wild gestures with his hands as he spoke; he couldn't get the words out quick enough; he was so angry at Curt.

"Hey, I'm a free agent; overall, my job exists to create balance in the world," Curt responded coolly. "Yeah, I'm making some extra cash, but also, the leverage I got over you is to protect *that girl* in there and make sure you do the same. It sucks I must blackmail you into doing that, dude! She's your cousin! Your own flesh and blood! I'd have thought *that* should be enough for you to want to protect her without being extorted into it. But clearly, you're more interested in creating your little *werewolf empire* than you are in protecting your family."

Cristian began hissing out his frustration. "Your goons were supposed to make it look like B&E gone wrong! So, it looked like any *dumbass fucking* human being in the world could have done it! But instead, your guys tear her boyfriend apart like a fucking werewolf would! Maybe they were werewolves?! I don't even fucking know! You *know* that once she finds out about us, she will *automatically* suspect one of us did it! Fuck!" Cristian spat, his hand gestures growing more frenzied as he became increasingly furious going over the details again.

"But... you can honestly tell her it wasn't any wolf that... *you*... know..." Curt smiled while tapping Cristian on the nose with each of these last words.

"Stop that!" Cristian shrieked, smacking Curt's hand away from his face.

"Just say you don't know who it was. Because... you don't," Curt responded in an overly simplified way. Cristian's unblinking, incredulous gaze continued to burn a hole into the hunter's face, so Curt switched gears. He was tired of repeatedly having this conversation. "Look, Cris, all you need to do is pay me the fuckin money you owe me and protect your cousin in there and make sure she doesn't get hurt, man. That's all! If you don't do those two things, then I tell everyone *you* hired me to put a hit on her boyfriend to free her up and lure her back to this place. And then she's *definitely* not going to join your little werewolf kingdom. I'm sure that'd piss off 'ol Farky' and send your families back into another civil war because *you* promised your cousin, *like currency*, to the Farkas family, and dude-dog in there wants his bride," Curt said, pointing to the open front doors of Dragos Manor.

Cristian realized there was nowhere else productive for this conversation to go. He clicked his tongue. "Fuck you, you little slimy hunter bitch. And don't call me Cris! It's fucking *Cristian*! Got it?" Is all Cristian could manage to retort in a high-pitched whisper as he dramatically exhaled a deep sigh, spun around on his heels, and headed into the house, stuck in his situation all over again.

"Keep your enemies closer, am I right... 'fucking Cristian'?" Curt called out mockingly after him. Then Curt laughed, shook his head, and followed him inside the house for pui de somn—Romanian siesta—before dinner.

Chapter Seven

Dinner

Later that evening, Ana, Erika, and Chef Sabina finished setting out all the traditional Romanian dishes on the large oak banquet table in the dining hall. As each dish was placed down, Erika quickly noticed a theme. Grilled minced meat rolls made from a combination of beef and lamb were set down first, followed by a dish called Honoring the Pig, which could be any part of a pig, such as in this case—ribs, tenderloin, liver, and sausage. Next was a lamb loaf dish containing a boiled egg in the center, followed by a sour meatball stew, typically made with pork. Then, to top it all off, two vegetable dishes, fried potatoes, and cabbage rolls, and for dessert, chocolate cake was included in the spread.

"Good thing I'm not vegetarian. The potatoes, cabbage rolls, and cake are almost the only vegetarian things on this table," Erika commented.

"Hmm? What was that, dear? Oh no, don't worry, the potatoes were made with small bits of meat!" Ana confirmed, missing the point. Erika counted at least four different species of animals being served that night. Still, she was also familiar with Romanian cuisine and realized there could potentially be even more animals than that.

"A lot of meat..." Erika commented after setting down the cabbage rolls.

"Yes, indeed," Ana responded, wearing a puckered smile of pride. She apparently mistook Erika's comment to mean the dinner was a prosperous bounty, instead of what Erika was actually commenting on, which was the lack of other food groups.

Erika glanced up at the wall clock. It was almost 8 PM when dinner was scheduled to start. She was a little confused about when her cousin and his friends had returned to Dragos Manor from NYC, where Ana had mentioned they had been on holiday. By the sound of the loud muscle car earlier that afternoon, she knew they had arrived earlier that day, but from the incident in the barn and Tom's remarks that morning, Erika realized that they must have also been on the property late last night. Either way, she had not seen any sign of Cristian or the others all day, and when she asked Ana, Erika was told the group was resting before dinner.

At 8 PM on the dot, a faint *ding* sounded from inside the lobby, announcing the arrival of the rest of the dinner party. Ana's head spun around excitedly as she scurried out of the dining hall to greet a crowd of male voices inside the lobby.

The *ding* sound belonged to the 1950s Otis single-passenger elevator cart located on the other side of the staircase inside the lobby. The antique lift traveled from the lobby up to the 3rd and 4th floors but bypassed the 2nd floor, which Erika always found odd. She had learned during her tour the day before that long ago, a staircase leading up to the higher floors had once been present, but sometime in the 1920s—when the dwelling had been converted to a boarding house and then to a hotel—an early model of the lift had been installed. It was later upgraded in the 1950s to a more modern Otis traction elevator model. Ana had explained to Erika that despite the description of a single-passenger elevator, the cart could actually support about 680 kilos or 1,500 pounds, approximately eight adults. However, getting that many individuals in would be a tight squeeze.

The conversation grew louder as the group approached the dining hall entryway. Then Ana and Cristian, followed by a couple of other people that Erika did not recognize, appeared in the doorway.

"Cristian! How are you, my boy? I hope you all are hungry!" Ana said to him in Romanian.

Erika was surprised to see her grandaunt doting on Cristian in a way she never had before. Cristian's expression was strained and overly stoic, but as Ana continued to swarm him, he seemed to falter out of whatever self-important demeanor he had been trying to portray. Erika saw him grow annoyed as he tried to maneuver around his grandma, and then the two fell into a rhythmic dance, attempting to get around each other. Cristian gently grabbed Ana by the shoulders and steadied her out of the swaying they had fallen into.

"I'm fine, Bunica. I'm just trying to say hi to my cousin," he said, finally untangling the old woman's hands off him. Then he looked across the room at the person he had not seen since she was seventeen, and he was only fourteen. Erika stared back at him, taking in the man her cousin had become.

Well, she thought to herself, *at least he finally doesn't look like such a scrawny, pimple-covered little weasel-prick anymore.* Still, Erika had the distinct impression that he retained an air of arrogance. He was finally taller than her, maybe standing around 5'10 or 5'11, and he possessed a somewhat intimidating demeanor that shone through his almond-brown eyes. However, Erika decided that she would not allow herself to be daunted by him. After all, they must learn to live and work together to carry on this household's legacy.

"Hello, Erika," he greeted, wearing no smile and with unblinking eyes. For a moment, his irises almost flashed to more of a yellow color than their natural brown.

"Hi," she responded in an unimpressed and subtly challenging way. The incident in the barn was still at the forefront of her mind, making her feel a little aloof toward her cousin at that moment. She was put off by his disrespect toward the home and family. Erika had changed her mind and decided not to bring up the subject with Ana that day. Instead, she thought it would be better to approach Cristian directly to resolve the issue.

Nevertheless, this was the first time she had seen her cousin in eight years, and he had guests with him, so Erika began taking long, deliberate strides across the dining hall to greet the group in the doorway. She stopped directly in front of Cristian, who stood frozen, his lip curled up in the faintest sneer. Erika gave him an annoyed look, half rolling her eyes, as she leaned forward for the mandatory hug. Cristian's hands shot up in the air as if he was about to get searched. Then he tapped her quickly twice on her back, giving her a superficial embrace. This seemed to break the tension in the room.

"Oh good! I never can tell what's going on with you, children," Ana said with ease as she headed over to the dining table and started fretting with the dishes. Cristian and Erika quickly released their awkward hug and moved away as if repulsed by the other. Cristian headed over and took his seat near the head of the table.

The two guys who were standing behind Cristian stepped further into the room. Erika noticed right away that both men were very attractive. The first of the two, a tall guy with shoulder-length sandy-blond hair, brown eyes, and a dark brown leather bomber jacket, introduced himself to Erika.

"Hey, I'm Curt. Nice to meet you," he said with a friendly, even voice. He possessed subtle yet undeniable confidence. Erika responded with her name in return and accepted his handshake. She felt a distinct visceral feeling at the touch of his hand, which was strong and rough like he worked with them. Curt flashed her an enchanting ear-to-ear smile, and she smiled back, feeling a little weirded out with herself for finding another person attractive since the demise of her late fiancé.

The two released their handshake, and then Erika watched as the muscular guy— who was taller than Cristian but not quite as tall as Curt—with shaggy dark brown hair and amber eyes stepped forward. His awkwardness was instantly apparent. He stood in front of her for a moment, not saying anything but only looking at her with a curious expression. She stood before him with arms folded; her ash-brown hair was tied up in a messy updo, black polish on her fingernails. He looked into her emerald eyes, looked at her mouth, and quickly down at the rest of her body before returning his gaze to her eyes. Erika patiently waited for him to introduce himself. Then he blurted out something in clumsy Romanian. Erika raised her eyebrows, unsure of how to respond. His attempt to speak Romanian had caught her off guard. He must have noticed this because he quickly abandoned his clunky Romanian for broken English instead.

"Hello, am Farkas, Blake. You have beautiful eye and have dropped the gorgeous. Or, I mean, you gorgeous is dead," he said, finally stumbling through an introduction and a couple of attempted compliments. However, between his nervousness, fragmented English, and faulty syntax, Blake had only managed to compliment one of Erika's eyes.

"Um, thank you, I think? But which one?" she asked, half joking. However, when Blake only stared back at her confusedly, she abandoned the sarcasm. "Sorry; Forget it. Um, I'm Erika Navarro. It's nice to meet you," she said.

Blake's body language conveyed his attraction for her, but his energy came across as shy and even slightly nervous. It was quickly getting to the point where the two had been standing there a bit too long when he suddenly extended his arms as if to hug her. Erika casually shook her head to decline the embrace, so he pivoted into a double handshake instead. She smiled, amused by the awkwardness of it all, and even decided to double down by maintaining eye contact through the long, slow handshake. Blake became visibly nervous as he was seemingly out of moves. Soon, the scene became a waggish standoff when neither broke the uncomfortable interaction.

At that moment, Marius breezed into the room. Cristian jumped up.

"Marius! I didn't know you had arrived already! Please sit here!" Cristian offered his seat, which was to the right of the head of the table.

"No, no, it's fine, Cristian. Please sit. I will dine next to my niece tonight," Marius insisted while walking up to Erika—who was still locked in the awkward handshake. He quickly kissed her on the top of her head and then sat down to Ana's left, who was now seated at the head of the table. Erika was relieved to see her uncle. "I don't mean to be rude, but I'm going to start eating," Marius announced to the room. "I'm absolutely famished!"

Everyone began reaching for dishes and filling their plates.

"Let's have dinner," Erika suggested, finally breaking the prolonged handshake with Blake as she turned, walked around the table, and sat next to Marius. Cristian, who had been monitoring Blake and Erika's interaction, sat down again. Curt was sitting in the chair across from Erika and looked annoyed when Cristian and Blake made him move over. Blake almost tipped him out of the chair, nearly dumping him on the floor.

Dinner conversation that night consisted of a lot of crosstalk. Blake and Marius discussed current events in Europe where such things were said, like— "The cabinet minister thinks trade deals with the EU are still quite possible..."

Conversations of the seasons in Nocturne included statements, such as— "...absolutely gorgeous like it is now during the spring and summertime, and while the fall gets quite chilly, it is also our busiest time with hotel guests..."

Or Ana passively making matchmaker comments to Erika about Blake. "I'm merely saying how lovely it is that our families have come together like this! Who knows, maybe one day we will all sit together like this as a real family; wouldn't that be something? Blake is a handsome devil, don't you think, Erika? Cristian, I've noticed how well you and Vittoria are getting on, which I must say is such a relief..."

Stories of the recent trip that Cristian, Blake, and his sister Vittoria had taken, which sounded like— "...we got into New York City to pick up Vittoria's friend, Adrian, who just arrived in the States. Then we started to make our way back, keeping an eye on the Moon, of course. We stopped over in Boston for a few days. Vittoria loved Boston, so she and Adrian decided to stay there for a few days longer. They should arrive in Nocturne by tomorrow..."

And even a little bit of reminiscing between the younger Dragos family members at the table, where Cristian could even be seen smirking from time to time at memories like this one— "You never liked me when we were kids, and you were my best friend! I trusted you! Even when I *knew* you were just trying to get me in trouble with Aunt Ana," Erika said while Cristian's demeanor had slowly begun to soften.

"Oh, please. You *knew* what you were doing. You were the one who became *obsessed* with trying to break the rules. You knew you were always too *charmed* to ever really get in any serious trouble," Cristian retorted, attempting to call her out.

But she only laughed in amazement. "I was not at all 'too charmed!' I *always* got in trouble for everything!" Erika paused a moment before continuing, "But she never found out what happened to that old dress of hers, did she? Do you remember?" she added with a snicker but almost immediately began to second-guess if she should bring up this particular story. Cristian's face visibly dropped, and Ana sat up straight as if suddenly realizing this story affected her. She seemingly racked her mind about which dress the children were discussing.

"Which dress? Not that beautiful flapper dress I misplaced years and years ago?" Ana asked with growing alarm in her voice. Cristian, while looking a little embarrassed, was now also smiling.

"You traitor! That was a *private* moment! Bunica, we need to give Sabina a raise! This food is delicious," Cristian snickered, trying to change the subject, but now he and Erika both had Ana's full attention, and she wanted to know what they were talking about. Cristian and Erika finally gave in and recounted a story of dressing up. Young Erika would dress young Cristian in Ana and Daniela's clothing and perform little fashion shows. One time, when Cristian was particularly decked out wearing Ana's elaborate flapper dress, high heels, long evening gloves, and furs, he had his lunch repeated on him but couldn't get the complex dress unfastened in time.

"Okay, you shut your filthy, lying whore-mouth! I forgot how this story ended!" Cristian said, laughing and burying his face into his napkin in embarrassment.

"You children are revolting!" Ana exclaimed in disgust. "And where is my dress now? I loved that dress! I'd forgotten all about it because I had thought I'd misplaced it long ago." Cristian and Erika stole a quick glance at each other, and then both burst into laughter as Erika managed to explain through gasps of air and tears of laughter.

"He buried it!" she barely managed to say between giggling breaths. "He... he had to. He laid that sucker to rest. There was shit all over it!" By this time, Erika and Cristian were busting up with laughter. Blake, Curt, and Marius were all chuckling at the story, but more so, they were amused at how vigorously Cristian and Erika were laughing. Only poor Ana did not share in on the humor; being such a serious woman, she seemed truly upset about her defiled dress.

"Disgraceful behavior. And I'm not only referring to the soiled dress but also... my grandson... wearing women's clothing. I was worried about him for a while, you know," Ana stated bitterly.

"Come now, Mother, don't be so hard on the boy. They were just children having fun." Marius said, trying to quell Ana's tension.

With this turn in the conversation, Cristian defensively regained his composure. He wiped the tears of laughter from his eyes, which now stung with the bite of his Bunica's comments. Fortunately, he did not dwell on Ana's negativity for long as he noticed the look on Blake's face. He could read that Blake's expression was a yearning to interact with Erika. Cristian caught Blake's eye and gave him a nod of encouragement. Blake saw the signal and looked over toward Erika. He took a deep breath and then made his move.

"So, how you boyfriend did he die?" Blake asked her. Any residual jovial spirit was immediately sucked out of the room with the question. Cristian waved his hands and silently mouthed the word—*No!*

"Jesus, dude," Curt muttered in disbelief while coughing into his napkin.

"Blake, with all due respect—" Marius began to run damage control on the dinner conversation, but Erika interrupted.

"No, no, it's fine," she said, then looked Blake in the eyes as she responded to his question. "He was killed. In his home. Under mysterious circumstances." She swallowed hard, eyes growing glossy, but tears did not fall.

"That is terrible," Blake remarked in a very genuine manner. He paused and thought a moment, then added, "I would want the revenge if I were you," he said, his eyebrows raised in earnest.

"Oh, believe me, I do," she agreed with a steely expression behind her eyes. The two seemed to share an understanding, while the rest of the dinner party was obviously uncomfortable with their candor.

"How you going to get them?" Blake continued as if wanting to work out the revenge plan right there and then.

"Ooookay... Well, this is romantic. Thank you, Bunica; dinner was *amazing*. I'm full, so I think I will have a nightcap and head off to bed," Cristian scoffed. "Who would like to join me?" Others began to stand and stretch, looking relieved to escape the awkward conversation. Blake glanced at Erika, who raised her eyebrows and stood up as well, then started clearing the table.

Dinner lasted approximately three hours. After everyone had their fill, including nightcaps—except Ana, of course—the party prepared to retire for the evening. Before Cristian headed up to bed, however, Erika pulled him aside.

"Hey, I just wanted to say I saw what happened in the stables last night, and I hope you're not planning to have another *wild* night like that again tonight," Erika chided. A wave of panic flooded through Cristian as his cousin went on. "I've had some pretty wild parties in my *hey*, and I know you have some guests visiting, but poor Tom spent all morning straightening up in the barn."

Cristian waited for Erika to say something more, but since no mention of any legless horses came up, he played it off.

"Oh yeah, it totally won't happen again. Hey, meet me tonight in the ballroom at 3 A.M., kay? There are some things you should know about this place. I'll show you," Cristian said mischievously, then added, "Don't worry; it's not like our childhood. I'm not trying to get you in trouble—Bunica won't even know. Besides, I'm not scared of her..." He chuckled just as Ana appeared at his side.

"Cristian," she said sternly. He screamed with surprise. The old woman had come out of nowhere. "Tom tells me you and your friends had a *party* in the barn last night, and one of the horses was..." Ana smiled a puckered smile at Cristian as he silently pleaded for leniency with his eyes. "...spooked," she finally said, not revealing the truth. "Rest assured, Cristian will not be doing anything like that again. Marius has informed me he is sending for more of his things, and he will be moving into the house for a while to relieve Cristian of the pressures of being the only Dragos male in the household until Cristian proves he can be more responsible," Ana finished.

Cristian started to defend himself, but Ana gave her grandson an icy look that told him it was best to keep quiet. She then walked away and began clearing the nightcap glasses from the table.

"Cristian, I... I didn't say anything to her," Erika started to explain.

"Ballroom. 3 A.M.!" was all Cristian could respond with through his anger and embarrassment. Then he turned and stalked off out of the dining hall.

Once in the lobby, Cristian pressed the old elevator button and thought to himself, *Fuck! Bunica is pissed. Never mind, I intend to make this princess wake up immediately. Enough of this bullshit already. Like ripping off a band-aid.* Then the familiar *ding* sounded, and Cristian stepped into the lift, the doors closing with him inside. His face twisted with anger as he rode up to his room on the 3rd floor.

Chapter Eight

The Party

The hallway outside of the 2nd-floor guestroom occupied by Erika Navarro was quiet and still until a louder-than-intended *creak* of an unoiled door hinge cut through the silence. Inside the room, Erika paused, cringing at the unwelcome sound. Then, working up the courage, she opened the door to get the remainder of the unpleasant sound over quickly. Erika slipped into the hallway in her night robe; her face winced up at the noise still echoing inside her ears. *Stupid creaky door. Hopefully, that didn't wake anyone.* It was unlikely since everyone else was on the 3rd floor. Still, she tiptoed toward the giant staircase and headed toward her 3 A.M. rendezvous with Cristian in the ballroom.

If Erika thought the 2nd floor had been dark, then the 1st-floor lobby was absolute, deepest of total darkness. She hesitated once she reached the bottom of the staircase and realized she had left her cell phone behind. That flashlight feature would have come in handy right about now. As Erika's eyes adjusted, she could hear the rhythmic ticking of the grandfather clock somewhere to her right. Cristian had said they needed to meet at 3 A.M. in the ballroom, and she was sure it was nearly that time. Taking control of her mounting anxiety, she decided to walk toward where she knew the large, hard-to-miss ballroom doors would be located.

A sudden loud sound emitted from somewhere behind her caused Erika to jump out of her skin. The grandfather clock completed its deep, resonating chime. *Okay, now it's definitely 3 A.M.,* she thought to herself while trying to steady her thundering heartbeat.

Erika hoped that Cristian was already inside the ballroom because, at this point, she just wanted to get back to her room as quickly as possible. As if answering her question, a pinpoint of light appeared in the distance of the lobby. Then, it grew into a long glowing stripe as the familiar *dinging* sound announced that the elevator cart had completed its journey. *Thank God, Cristian*, Erika thought to herself, exhaling a sigh of relief. However, when the doors parted, and the light came spilling out from within, illuminating a long strip across the lobby, it revealed... nobody was inside.

A shudder ran through Erika's entire body. Now, she really did want to turn around, yet she found herself already standing in front of the large double doors that separated her from the ballroom. She took advantage of the light illuminating her path and decided she might as well go inside.

As Erika reached for the doorknob, she suddenly heard the muffled buzz of conversation followed by laughter coming from within. She jerked her hand back. Cristian must be putting her on. *Is he having a party in the middle of the night inside the ballroom?* Now she was angry, thinking the situation she was about to walk into might be like the barn incident from the previous night. Taking control of her nerves, Erika seized the handle, turned it, and thrust the door open.

Upon entering the room, she felt the temperature drop significantly, and the smell of tobacco, cologne, peppermint, and sulfur hung heavy in the air. Indeed, the room was occupied with people, a great many more people than Erika had anticipated. Hundreds of silvery figures stood before her. She was at a complete loss. She felt embarrassed to be wearing a short night robe when everybody else appeared to be dressed in elaborate costumes. As she continued to take in the jovial crowd, little by little, she began to realize each person was less than a solid being and more of a silvery, shadowlike individual. And the costumes they were wearing appeared to be fashions that were decades out of date. The partygoers did not notice her as they continued their merriment in the brilliant moonlight cast into the ballroom through the large window on the far wall.

A group of women stood conversing near the entrance. They wore large, fancy hats featuring lacy veils, feather plumes, or flowers. A couple of women held parasols, while some were wearing muffs on their hands or animal fur stoles around their necks accompanied by enormous gaudy jewelry. A group of men not far off from them sported what looked like tuxedos with long tailcoats and top hats, and many held canes for fashion. The men smoked from old pipes—gritted between clenched teeth under their large push-broom mustaches—that stayed fixed to their mouths even as they laughed at each other's jokes.

Erika regarded an elderly woman who was engaged in conversation about temperance with a portly man wearing a monocle. Upon second look, Erika noticed the older woman had a sword stabbed through the middle of her lacy frill bosom! At the same moment, the portly gentleman pulled out a handkerchief and began dabbing his forehead, which had a large bullet hole through it! The elderly woman with the sword in her chest pulled out a large fan and began fanning herself, looking around the room as if to locate the source of heat.

Erika noticed many of the other individuals possessed fatal injuries as well, people with blades or bullet holes through their chests. Mortal wounds where their beating hearts or brains used to be. She also noticed many of these silvery figures seemed to be becoming hot, as several of them began fanning themselves and peering around the room for the heat source.

She had seen enough. Erika decided now was the moment to take her leave. She took a step backward toward the open door behind her. Suddenly, all the conversation and laughter stopped. Her movement captured the attention of the entire room. Erika froze, feeling thoroughly frightened. Slowly—as if the axis of every silvery shadowed head was bound by uniform movement—every single figure in that ballroom silently turned and looked straight at Erika.

These people are dead! They're ghosts! she realized as her mouth fell open with fear. Instinctively, she fought the urge to run. She desperately struggled to remain calm and in control as she again began to slowly back out of the room. Every silvery face was locked to her movements. All sound from the partygoers had ceased. The entire crowd remained stark still and continued to stare unblinking at Erika. Inch by inch, she walked backward out of the ballroom. Once she made it back inside the lobby, she quietly and deliberately shut the doors, turned, and took off running.

After Erika's departure, the ghostly crowd began roaring with laughter, filling the large ballroom with noise once more as the amused spirits merrily resumed their party.

Erika sprinted as fast as she could through the hotel lobby, clutching her robe around her chest, as she ran straight out the front doors into the darkness of the night. Once outside, she quickly realized she had no idea what her plan was or where she should go. Her flight response told her to keep running anyway. She ran down the drive, through the front patio, then hung a right around the corner of the house, toward the gardens in the back. As soon as she reached the garden's center, she stopped near the fishpond, in the most open area she could see.

Heart pounding with adrenaline, Erika doubled over and put her hands on her knees, gulping in the cool night air as she tried to catch her breath. Several strong emotions rushed over her all at once. She felt overwhelmed, and a desperate feeling of defeat began to sink in. Not knowing what else to do, Erika crouched down and hugged her knees. Her eyes were overbright with fear, and tears streamed unwillingly down her cheeks.

The Moon cast a brilliant blue glow that lit up the water lilies and frogbit floating atop the surface of the nearby koi pond. The soft night breeze began to cool off the thin layer of sweat on her exposed skin. A symphony of insects buzzing, crickets chirping, and bullfrogs croaking flowed throughout the nighttime spring air.

"It's all real!" she sobbed the realization aloud. All the ghost stories she heard in her youth, the legend about her family's infamous hotel—*it truly is haunted! And not just a little haunted, a lot haunted!* Erika struggled to process her situation, but her mind quickly fell into doubt. *I don't know if I can do this! I don't know if I can handle this!*

She questioned herself. She questioned her strength. With everything she had already endured this year, she didn't know if she was up to taking on this unimaginable challenge of operating a haunted mansion hotel. Despair slowly began to creep in as she realized—*I must do this. I left my whole life for this.* And just as soon as the thought came, her heart sank.

"What life?" she asked herself aloud as the familiar pangs of grief rushed back in at full force. Erika sobbed quietly. She thought about how the sun would rise soon, and then, at least, she would have some solace in the daylight. Erika wiped away her tears and sniffled as she bravely stood up and considered returning to her room; after all, she couldn't stay outside all night. In the morning, she would talk to everyone about what she had seen and then decide what she should do from there, even though it felt like a situation she would have to learn to live with.

It's Nietzsche—Amor Fati. Love your fate, right? Erika thought dismally, not noticing exactly when the nightlife had stopped its cacophony of sounds all around her.

A slight, sudden movement somewhere to her right caught Erika's attention. Her gaze traveled toward the garden gazebo. She could just barely make out a large figure standing camouflaged in the shadows. *Had it been there the entire time?* Erika held her breath. She tried to look without turning her head. Her eyes darted in the opposite direction of whatever was stalking her in the night. She saw two large wooden doors lying at the base of the northwest corner of the house. Recognizing the doorway from her childhood, Erika knew this was the entrance to the storage cellar underneath the kitchen.

She would have to make a run for it. It felt as though the large figure was anticipating her. *It's now or never.* For the second time that night, Erika broke into another outright run. She covered the distance in no time flat. Through the chaos of trying to escape, she couldn't be sure if the creature had pursued her. Erika gathered all her strength, threw open the cellar doors, and then jumped down into the darkness. She quickly spun around and swung the heavy doors shut behind her with a loud *thud*.

Total blackness sealed her inside the cellar, instantly making her regret the chosen hiding place. It was so dark that she couldn't even see her hand in front of her face. She felt her way down each wooden step, carefully but hurriedly inching her way farther and farther into the depths below. It seemed much cooler down here than it was outside. The stale air had a strong aroma of old rotten wood and the musty earthen floor. The smell brought back memories of her experience there the day before. A shiver ran down her spine as fright returned to her once more. Unfortunately, being frightened seemed to have become her "new normal" since returning to Dragos Manor less than forty-eight hours prior.

She finally reached the bottom of the steps. Her eyes open futilely wide in the darkness. Black shapes in the void of nothingness played tricks on her sight. Still, she couldn't be sure what the objects were or if they were real, with her general unfamiliarity with the space—facing outward into the abyss, where the thought that anything could reach out and grab her was too much for her to bear. So, she turned and squeezed her eyes shut, remaining close to the bottom of the staircase. She would wait a few minutes and hoped that whatever was above would lose interest and leave soon.

Stepping backward in an unknown direction, Erika immediately tripped over something bulky on the ground. Her mind flashed back to the barrel she had mistaken for a person or creature crouching near the base of the stairs. Feeling defeated, she rolled herself over and extended out a hand to locate the wooden keg. Her entire nervous system had been expecting to feel the hardness of wood, but instead, her hand grazed over something that felt soft and fleshy. It felt like organic material that deformed and yielded to her touch as her hand pressed into it. Whatever it was felt cold to the touch. Erika quickly recoiled from the unknown object on the floor.

At the same moment, whatever was stalking her outside opened the cellar doors. The illumination of the moonlight came spilling into the depths, and the object that Erika had just tripped over became visible. The thing looked like a rotting, albino earthworm-like corpse that was disfigured and left for dead in a damp cave. Before Erika had a chance to react, something even worse than she could ever have imagined happened. The body began to move! Suddenly, the terrible thing raised its head and screeched at the moonlight pouring in from the open doors above. Then it sprang up and scurried crablike into the recesses of the hallway on the far end of the cellar as though trying to escape from the bright light that shone in through the doorway above.

The sound of Erika's own scream came into her awareness. She wasn't even sure when she started. At this point, she was saturated. She couldn't take in any more horrors but could only react to each new terror as it appeared and flee from it.

No longer seeing anything at the top of the stairs, she ran back up the steps, panicked, and went outside. As soon as she took her first step back into the cool night air, Erika immediately collided with the large figure. It had been waiting for her outside. She fell back and hit the ground hard. Erika surrendered against her will. She stayed on the ground, allowing her eyes to close. Her awareness slipped away. With her last bit of energy, Erika cracked open her eyes and saw the fuzzy outline of a large silver wolf's head before losing consciousness.

Chapter Nine

Lucid

Erika's eyes slowly blinked open. She found herself lying in the middle of a clearing in a foggy, ethereal woodland environment. She could not tell what time of day it was, only that it was dark enough to make it difficult for her to discern the details of her surroundings. Suddenly, she noticed movement out of the corner of her eye. Misty visions of wolves began pacing in circles around her. She lay very still on the ground, hoping the creatures would not notice her or might think her dead. As she quietly watched the animals, Erika sensed the wolves were not stalking her but protecting her. But from what?

Just then, she saw a dark figure approaching from somewhere in the distance. As the individual drew nearer, Erika saw it was her grandaunt, Ana. Immediately, the wolves stopped circling and watched her, suspicious of the old woman coming toward them. Then, the wolves did something amazing. They formed a wall between Erika and Ana as if they were protecting Erika from her grandaunt. But after a moment, the wolves relented, permitting entrance to the Dragos Matriarch into the clearing through their furry partition. Erika put her palms on the cool earthen floor beneath her and slowly hoisted herself into a seated position.

Ana stared coldly at her grandniece for a moment before she spoke.

"There's something I've been meaning to tell you," Ana started. Erika only felt confusion at the words as she looked around the clearing again, trying as hard as she could to make out any specific details of her surroundings. She struggled, feeling tired and disoriented. "Your mother is alive!" Ana suddenly revealed. Erika blinked incomprehensively at her grandaunt's words.

"Wait... what?" Erika questioned in disbelief. "She's alive? You mean, she's been alive this whole time? Where has she been?" she pleaded with escalating anxiety in her voice, but Ana only stared back with cold, unblinking eyes. Erika wanted to chastise her grandaunt, yell at her for keeping this information from her for so long, and demand to know where her mother was. However, before she could say anything, Ana opened her mouth and spoke again.

"Kill her," the old woman ordered as she loomed over her grandniece on the ground. Erika was momentarily confused. Was her grandaunt instructing her to kill her own mother? However, it soon became clear that Ana had not spoken these orders to Erika but to the beasts nearby as one of the wolves turned his large head and fixed his yellow eyes upon her. Terror swelled up inside of Erika's chest as she watched the command set into the large animal's mind. Then his lips curled back into a vicious, pointed snarl resembling a sinister smile. The last thing Erika saw was the massive wolf lunging toward her as she jumped up to flee—

Erika awoke from the nightmare with so much force that it almost propelled her out of bed. It took her a moment to realize where she was as she looked around the guestroom on the 2nd floor of Dragos Manor.

With sweat clinging to her brow, her eyes darted around the bedroom. Uncertain of what had happened to her, she hurried out of bed but was instantly unsteady on her feet. After regaining control over her motor skills, she frantically crossed the room and opened the door leading to the hallway. Erika discreetly peered around the corner toward the staircase just in time to see the top of Ana's head as the elderly woman ascended the steps. Receding into the bedroom, Erika attempted to close the door quietly, but it didn't fully latch. The door drifted open again as she backed away. Soon, Ana appeared in the doorway and then entered the room. The two stared at one another.

"Something happened to me last night!" Erika blurted out with anguish overtaking her voice. Ana's reaction was underwhelming as she ignored the comment and gestured to the bed.

"May I sit?" her grandaunt calmly asked, but she did not wait for a response, so she went ahead and sat down at the foot of the bed. Erika remained standing, unsure of what Ana would do next. Of all the words Erika thought her grandaunt might say, she was not expecting the story that the Dragos Matriarch launched into next.

"The Dragos history in America began after many of our ancestors decided to leave Romania in search of a new life," Ana started. Unsure of where this would go, Erika relented and sat down on the bed across from her grandaunt to listen to her story. "The Hungarian Farkas family considered the Dragos family to be too... how do you say... progressive. Tension grew between our families. Nobody could seem to find any resolution. So, finally, your great-great-grandmother, Sophia Dragos, picked up stakes and moved her family away from Eastern Europe to America in the late 1800s—1884, I believe it was. I know it was a bissextile year, not long after Romania gained independence from the Ottoman Empire.

The Ungurs, that is... uh... slang for a Hungarian individual, felt the Dragos considered themselves superior. Not only had the Dragos family left Romania, and effectively Eastern Europe, but they also exited a contract between the large Romanian and Hungarian families for centuries. The contract was a treaty, but the language had become defunct with time. It was also biased toward the Hungarians as the Farkas side had originally penned it. It was the belief of many, my family included—the Lucas, that it favored Hungarian ideologies while containing shortcomings for Romanians. It was the Dragos family who took the brunt of those inequities.

After tiresome and futile negotiations, Sophia simply had enough and decided to halt them. That's when the Dragos family moved away from the territory. The Farkas family was insulted; thus, a rift formed between the two families. However, I can say firsthand that Sophia Dragos never harbored such notions of superiority. She merely put her family's best interests first and got them out from under the Farkas' control.

But of course, with distance comes misunderstanding. Eventually, it developed into almost something of a feud between the two families. Then a few other Romanian families followed suit." As Ana blathered on, Erika grew more impatient as she waited for a break in the one-sided conversation.

"Sophia and her husband, your great-great-grandfather, Florin Dragos, completed the construction of Dragos Manor in 1902. Back then, the house was usually quite full. A great many more family members were living here in those days, as well as visitors from Romania who would pass through." Ana took a moment to reminisce in the nostalgia of those early days, even though she explained that she herself did not come to live at Dragos Manor until the early 1940s. Erika seized her opportunity and jumped in.

"I'm sorry to interrupt, Aunt Ana, but this place is haunted! I saw ghosts last night! *Real* ghosts!" Erika blurted out, not caring to hear about whatever history lesson her grandaunt was trying to tell her.

"Please be patient, child. Yes, I'm getting to that," Ana said and then waited another moment as if to impress upon Erika not to interrupt again. The old woman cleared her throat and continued.

"As the years wore on, it seemed that whenever anyone from the Dragos family would visit the old country, someone on the Farkas or Dragos' side would end up deceased. As more and more family members were lost, Sophia's financial security became shaken. She had risked everything to move her family to America and sunk every last cent into building Dragos Manor. After losing her husband, Florin, Sophia was left to provide for her remaining family, so she eventually converted her grand home into a boarding house. She figured, why not turn a profit from the extra space?

Shortly thereafter, Dragos Manor became famous after guests reported seeing otherworldly spirits in the early 1920s. From that moment on, tourists from all over flocked to the boarding house, which evolved into the luxurious, haunted hotel it is today. So, you see, your assumptions are correct; our family's business model and success are directly linked to the fact that Dragos Manor is haunted!" Ana concluded with pride as she paused for a reaction.

Only, no immediate reaction came. Erika sat frozen, fear plastered on her face at the confirmation of this information. Last night wasn't just a bad dream; her experience was real. Ana sighed and rolled her eyes. She had never been one to comfort—anyone really—and the practice did not start now.

"Yes, Dragos Manor is indeed haunted. Sophia Dragos *saw to it that, with her magnificent powers.* She singlehandedly provided for our family from the very beginning. It's worth noting, my dear, that while the spirits are indeed abundant, I assure you they are mostly harmless. A simple spell ensures the ghosts themselves will never hurt you, nor anyone who comes to stay at Dragos Manor. In fact, many of the actual ghosts are deceased friends and family members! They are individuals who have died on the property," Ana added, as if this fact would make the details more palatable. Erika sat stunned for another moment before responding.

"So, we just live amongst these ghosts?" she asked, her head swimming. "And they won't hurt us?"

"That's right!" Ana said, smiling with encouragement at the progress being made. "Although, I would say it is more appropriate to say the ghosts live amongst *us*. I'm almost glad you wandered downstairs last night! Granted, I'm sure seeing all those spooks at once must have been quite a shock!" she said with an amused chuckle. "I was hoping to show you one or two of them to start, but this carries us right to the point now, then, doesn't it?" Ana was visibly pleased that this hurdle had been crossed. "Tell me, dear, why *did* you go downstairs into the ballroom late last night?" Ana asked.

"Cristian told me to," Erika responded in a deadpan tone, feeling reminded of his childhood trickery all over again.

"Well, Cristian was cruel to expose you to this truth in such a calloused way like that. Your cousin cares for you, you know. I don't know *why* he has always enjoyed teasing you like this," she said, attempting to "gran-splain" for her grandson. "Well, anyway, no harm done, though, right?" Ana asked a little nervously.

"Yeah, I think I'm alright. I just can't believe I was standing in a room full of dead people," Erika said in disbelief. Ana swallowed hard.

"Erika, you must decide if you can *stomach* all this. After all, these ghosts are going to be your responsibility one day," the Dragos Matriarch said, in an almost challenging manner.

Ana's words struck her. All her life, Erika had always wanted to prove herself to everyone, to prove that she was capable and strong enough to handle challenging situations. This need to prove herself is what prompted her to take the bait.

"Yes, I can handle it," she said, nodding her resolve. "Every family has their skeletons in the closet; ours just happen to be more literal than most. If *this* is our family secret, then I can take it." Erika felt a renewed desire to show her family and herself that she was strong enough. But then, another thought entered her mind. "Wait, why did you start that story off with the Farkas family? And why is Blake Farkas in our house right now if his ancestors are responsible for killing so many of ours?" Erika questioned incredulously. Ana was visibly taken aback.

"There are important things I need to tell you about the Farkas family, but we should save that for another time. I don't want to overwhelm you in the wake of everything you just experienced last night. Right now—"

"Wait," Erika interrupted as the rest of her memory of the previous night came flooding back to her. She had blocked out the second part of the evening, which was even more terrifying than encountering the ghost party. Erika looked at her grandaunt suspiciously. "How did I get back inside my room last night?" she asked, trying to rack her brain. Now Ana seemed worried. Erika remembered the garden, the dark figure, and the cellar. "That thing in the cellar..." Erika recollected. "And there was a white wolf?" She said as she stared at her grandaunt, realizing that those things were not just bad dreams. Erika waited for answers, but none came, as the elderly Dragos Matriarch was clearly at a loss for words. Then suddenly, a loud voice called up from downstairs.

"Hello?" the male voice called out. Both women jumped at the interruption. "Anybody home?" he inquired in a booming voice.

"Who's calling?" Ana yelled down toward the lobby. She looked startled, but Erika noticed that she also appeared a little relieved.

"It's Curt!" he yelled.

"Be right down!" Ana called back and then turned to look at Erika. "I promise, dear, I will tell you *everything* when the time is right. I don't fully know what you saw last night, but your uncle Marius said he heard you scream in the middle of the night and said he found you unconscious in the gardens. He said you looked as if you were having a terrible dream. The shock of seeing all those ghosts at once must have made you faint. He was the one who carried you back to bed. Now I will have a talk with that cousin of yours. You could have gotten hurt, and your grandmother would never have forgiven me!" Ana said with a renewed anger at Cristian written all over her face.

"Ah... Hi," Curt said as he appeared outside the bedroom door. I'm sorry; I don't mean to intrude. I'm looking for Cristian. Have you seen him? It's important that I find him," he asked, hanging back outside the door. Ana stood up as she replied.

"I believe Cristian and Blake are getting ready to go into town to retrieve Blake's sister, Vittoria, and their friend Adrian," Ana said as she propped her body in the door frame to block his view into the room.

"Groovy, I'll see if I can catch up with them then," he said in his cool tone.

"Just a sec!" Erika called out and abruptly squeezed her way into the doorway next to Ana. "I'll go with you. I want to find Cristian myself," Erika said. "I'd like to thank him for the lovely evening he showed me last night."

"Farout, I'll wait for you downstairs then... so you can get dressed," Curt said with a flirtatious smile as he glanced down at Erika in her disheveled robe. Ana noticed this and shifted to stand in front of Erika, blocking her from his view. Curt left and headed back toward the lobby. Ana turned and gave Erika a disapproving look, then exited the room, shutting the door behind her.

Once in the hallway, with neither Curt nor Erika in sight, Ana paused and exhaled a sigh of relief, thankful for Curt's interruption. She was not prepared to fully explain the Mischief in the cellar or the other entities hidden away inside the home. And she was surely not supposed to tell Erika about the Lycanthropy gene that ran in the Dragos family just yet. Daniela's ghost had made that perfectly clear yesterday morning. Erika's late grandmother wanted her to learn about all these truths in slow doses. Daniela was already going to be very angry with Ana and Cristian for the way Cristian had exposed Erika to the house spirits in such a calloused manner that he did. And what Ana said was correct—Erika could have been hurt, which would have angered more individuals than Ana's deceased sister-in-law. It would have also greatly angered the Farkas family. What if the Dragos "collateral" was hurt, or even worse, killed? If any harm came to Erika, Ana knew there would be no coming back from it... not for anyone.

Chapter Ten

The Colleague

A short time later, Curt and Erika exited Dragos Manor's front doors in search of Cristian and Blake. It was now late morning, but the sky was still cloudy and overcast.

"Let's go check the garage and see if Cristian's car is still there," Curt suggested. Erika agreed, and the pair began walking in that direction. The garage was located behind Dragos Manor on the northeast side of the property. They crossed around the east end of the estate and into the garden entrance on the side of the house, just outside the large windows of the grand ballroom.

Beautiful varieties of flowers laden the garden. Brilliant shades of reds, oranges, yellows, and purples came from Irises, Daylilies, Anemones, and Asters species. Flowering Dogwoods provided soft white and pink blossoms, and large Monarch and Swallowtail butterflies danced around the red and yellow Zinnias and Goldenrods. The bright colors jumped out, creating much visual interest in the monochromatically gray morning.

"So, how do you feel being back at this place after being gone so long?" Curt asked in his ever-present smooth manner.

"It's been... really fucking strange..." Erika had to admit, reflecting on her experience thus far. "To say the absolute fuckin least."

"I heard what happened to your boyfriend back home. I'm really sorry about that," Curt said.

"Thank you, but if it's all the same to you, I would rather not talk about that," Erika said, shutting the topic down.

"Of course! I meant no disrespect," he said apologetically, then quickly changed the subject. "So, I overheard a little bit of what Ana was telling you in your room this morning. Sounds like you had a rough night last night?"

"Yeah. I'm a little foggy on some of the details. It's almost as if I can't separate what really happened versus what was a dream. Or nightmare, I should say."

"Listen, I know you don't really know me. I could just be some asshole in the pool of assholes you have found yourself in, but for what it's worth... I would take anything anyone tells you around here with a grain of salt."

Erika looked at him incredulously. "Excuse me, but did you just call my family 'a pool of assholes?'" she asked, only slightly insulted.

"Again, I mean no disrespect. I am very close with your family. What I meant was, I think *dishonest* people are assholes, and I know your family has their share of secrets," Curt said, but Erika gave him a look to let him know that he had not repaired the damage. "Cristian *is* an asshole. I stand by that," he said firmly, then flashed her an ear-to-ear smile to break the tension. This comment and Curt's grin thawed the ice, making Erika smile as well.

"Yeah, yeah, he is."

"I know Ana means well, but I can tell you... that house holds more secrets than just a couple of ghosts. I'm sure you have gotten the sense that some sort of curse or black magic seems to be following your family. But just so you know, sometimes things aren't always as they seem, and sometimes they are exactly as they seem. In this case, it's nothing mystical. It all goes back to politics. You see—Marius living in Europe, Cristian going there, making friends with Blake and Vittoria—it's all been this 'diplomacy mission' so to speak, to try to get in good standing again with the Farkas family."

"My aunt was starting to tell me about some of that; about some sort of feud. But I sense that she hasn't told me the whole story. Do you, by chance, know what happened? I mean, it sounds like whatever it is has been stretching back for over a century now, so I understand if it's a weird thing to be asking you about." Curt seemed to mull over his response before answering.

"Yeah, I know what happened," he finally admitted, seemingly choosing his words carefully. "You see, I work in the same *industry* as your family. I know all about the great Eastern European families like the Dragoses and the Farkases. There are actually a few more Romanian families like yours in the area. There are the Lupus and the Vulpes... Cristian has friends from both those families. They came out here for the same reason the Dragoses did.

They also didn't want to *play by the rules* back home in Europe," Curt added mysteriously. "So now, over a century later, everyone is finally ready to come to the table, and funny enough, it's all because of you, actually."

"Me? Why because of *me*?" Erika asked with surprise.

"Because..." Again, Curt seemed to choose his words carefully. "You bring a fresh *perspective* to the whole ordeal. You are a Dragos female, even though your last name is Navarro, which means you are going to oversee the Dragos' legacy one day. Amongst this crowd, only the ladies are viewed as Heads of Household. The alpha female, if you will. The fact that you will be in charge one day puts you in a position of power, and all these families recognize that. Everyone is going to be trying to appeal to your good graces."

"You make my family sound like the *mafia* or something," Erika said, half joking with a nervous laugh.

"You are not too far off, actually," Curt responded with a sly smile.

"So, where do *you* fit into all of this?" she asked.

"*People,* like me, act as intermediaries between different parties, like your family, all over the world. When things start to go too far or get too out of control, my colleagues and I are here to help keep the peace and maintain balance," Curt said mysteriously while smiling. "I'm one of the *good guys*... you can trust me," he added as the pair finally reached the garage.

"So, are you, like, my family's attorney or something?" Erika asked, looking at Curt's casual—non-attorney-esque—surfer goth attire. Other than his dark-brown leather bomber jacket and long, shaggy blond hair, all his clothing was black. He wore a Siouxsie and the Banshees T-shirt, jeans, and *Converse* shoes with black laces but white soles.

"No, not an attorney," Curt chuckled as he unlatched and swung open the large garage doors to reveal the mean-looking black *Chevy Nova* sitting cold in its place. "So at least we know we didn't miss them! Good thing we started here instead of looking all over. This property is huge. I really need to catch Cristian before those guys leave."

"So, can I ask? Why do you need to see Cristian so badly?" Erika asked, not intending the question to come across as nosey, although realizing it might have.

"Cristian and I have some unfinished business we need to discuss. I'm helping him square away an arrangement between him and the Farkases,"

Curt answered without really answering. But Erika did not have the chance to pry any further as the footsteps approaching caught their attention.

"Well, well, what do we have here?" Cristian asked as he and Blake walked up to the garage, the pair looking like they were getting ready to head out for the day. Her cousin suspiciously eyed Curt standing there with Erika. Blake's black hair was messy and scattered every which way, and he and Cristian were wearing sunglasses despite the overcast day. Even so, Erika could see that her cousin's face was tense behind his *Ray-Bans*. She started to suspect that anger was just his default emotion. "What *have* you two been talking about?" Cristian asked in his pointed, effeminized way. Curt only smiled in response and ignored the question.

"We were looking for you guys, actually," Erika said, clocking the tension between Curt and her cousin. She decided to dodge his question to avoid putting Curt on the hot seat with Cristian. "We hear you two are headed into town. Can we come along?" she asked. "I know you're on your way to pick up Blake's sister and another friend, but maybe I can ride with Curt, and we can follow you guys?" she suggested. Curt's arrogant smile grew bigger at this idea.

"Sure! I would never deny a pretty lady in my ride," he replied, brazenly flirtatious.

"No! No, no... I'll ride with Curt, and you can ride with Blake," Cristian countered. "Blake, can you drive a stick shift?" Cristian asked, to which Blake stared back blankly at the question.

"A shifter car?" he asked with obvious reluctance.

"Ugh, never mind!" Cristian said in frustration. "Curt, you follow the three of us, and you can bring Adrian back with you in your car." Cristian proposed, but the suggestion came out as more of an order. Curt's eyes flashed with mild anger at the assignment. Erika decided to put an end to whatever power struggle was going on here.

"Cristian, I can drive Blake and me in your car. I know how to drive a manual transmission," she offered. "Curt said he needed to chat with you about something anyway."

"Great!" Cristian and Curt said in unison.

"Oh good," Blake added with a grateful expression.

The deep, guttural sound rose out of the *Nova's* engine as it departed the garage and headed to join the *Ford Bronco* waiting at the top of the dirt and gravel driveway in front of Dragos Manor. Curt sat in the driver's seat with Cristian in the passenger seat of the idling Bronco as they patiently waited for Erika and Blake to join them in the burly muscle car.

"Cool, so follow me, Erika, and I'll show you the way to town. I'll drive slowly, so you don't need to open that car up on these twisty roads," Curt called out to Erika, who was in the driver's seat of Cristian's beastly *Nova* with Blake riding shotgun.

"It's okay! There's no need to drive slowly or wait for me! I know how to get into town, but thank you! We'll meet you guys around the town square," she called back.

Curt shrugged and put his car in gear. As he leaned back in the driver's seat and started down the driveway, he could already feel Cristian's gaze, like a burning death ray, going straight into him. Curt sighed. The next twenty minutes into town was surely going to feel like an eternity.

In the Nova, Erika looked at the large, wolfish man sitting beside her. He was undeniably good-looking in his sunglasses, dark blue jeans, and black crewneck T-shirt.

"Put on your seatbelt," she told him, and Blake jumped into action, snapping on his lap belt. She stared at him for a moment and thought about everything her grandaunt and Curt had been telling her about the Farkas family. Right then and there, Erika decided that she should probably contribute to the diplomacy efforts and strive to be polite to their guest of honor.

She put the muscle car into gear, pressing the gas while releasing the clutch—matching the timing—which caused the engine to growl in response. She eased the car down the long driveway and onto the narrow roadway, then pulled out onto the road. After driving in silence for about five minutes, Blake took the initiative to strike up a conversation.

"You good at doing the shifting the car," he said to her over the loud, rhythmic sound of the engine.

"Thank you," she responded and smiled politely.

"You looking very beautiful today, and I cannot breathe," he said abruptly. Erika blinked, feeling jarred by the sudden shift in conversation.

"Thank you," she said again, this time in a wary tone. She was momentarily confused by his compliment, but then she pieced together that he was probably trying to say—*you take my breath away*.

"Am not flirting with you," he clarified. "I know you boyfriend just died. I will take time. I think maybe it would make you smile to know that you are beautiful." He said, then flashed her a big, toothy grin.

"Can we maybe talk about something else?" she suggested through a squinted smirk.

"Of courses," he said, pumping the breaks on his charm. He paused for a moment and then asked, "How did your boyfriend die?"

"Jesus Christ! Can we please go for five fucking minutes without someone bringing up my dead boyfriend?! You *just* asked me about that last night!" she responded in a heated tone, forgetting her recent resolve of politeness and diplomacy.

"I mean, how did he get killed? What happened to him?" Blake asked without seemly noticing her anger. Erika took a deep, steadying breath.

"I don't know. He was mauled or... mutilated. Like an animal attack," Erika confided. This caused Blake to lurch forward so quickly it startled her.

"An animal? How do you mean?" he asked seriously while removing his sunglasses. Erika tried to focus on the long and winding stretch of road in front of her, but she was having trouble as memories of Ryan began plaguing her thoughts.

"I don't know! It was..." she started but couldn't get the words out as flashbacks of crime scene photos flooded her mind. Images of blood splatter on the floor and walls, images of the claw and teeth marks on Ryan's flesh. This was juxtaposed with memories of her and Ryan lying in bed together and smiling. Flashbacks of a close-up picture of Ryan's face with claw marks across it. Memories of Ryan and Erika kissing. Flashbacks of Ryan's funeral. Memories of the sound of Ryan's voice saying, *"I love you..."*

Erika stared blankly through the windshield, far away from the present moment, when suddenly Blake lunged for her!

"Stop!" he yelled. His voice caused the haunted memories to cease and pulled Erika's awareness back into the present moment. She slammed her feet on the brakes and clutch, sending the tires into a skid, as the *Nova* narrowly missed another car in oncoming traffic! The *Nova* screeched to a halt on the shoulder on the other side of the road. Blake and Erika fell heavily back into their seats, breathing hard, as a cloud of dust from the shoulder came wafting past the windows. They turned and looked at each other.

"I am *so* sorry," Erika said in a daze. "Are you ok?" Blake nodded his head. He looked shaken but unharmed. Erika looked around and noticed the stretch of road the two were on.

"Dear God. I'm so sorry," she said as tears began spilling down her cheeks. Blake slowly reached over and gently hugged her. Erika did not protest; she hooked her arms up underneath his and sobbed into his chest. "I hate my past," she wept, the confession surprising even her. "There's so much darkness and so little to look back on and be happy about. My life feels like such a waste! It's like, there are these glimpses of happiness, but it always gets swallowed up by so much grief. I don't want to be *me* anymore. I'm sick of myself, sick of living this life. If I could wake up tomorrow and be someone else, I would do it!" she said through her sobs. Blake held her and listened.

"I don't want you to be someone else," he said. His words hung in the air momentarily, then she released him, and he let go too. She brushed the tears away from her cheeks.

"My mother died on this road," she said. Blake took in her words for a minute and then stared down at his hands.

"Am sorry," he whispered as he glanced in her direction. She nodded, quieting her familiar feelings of self-loathing, which she normally was skilled at keeping buried out of the way, under the surface, where they belong. She put a hand up to her cheek and wiped away the last of her tears. Then, she put the car in gear, pulled back onto the right lane, and continued driving toward town.

"So, I hope this ends it! You have your blood money now!" Cristian said with disdain as he stowed his cell phone back into his pocket after using a payment transfer app. "I've been having to steal it out of our family accounts for months! If Bunica finds out, she will kill me! I'll have to invent a cover story that I have a drug problem now! I hope you're happy. I have to get myself addicted to opium now! So that's it, mister! The bank is closed! Consider this bullshit-show over! It never happened! We don't ever need to discuss it ever again! And it *better never* come up from anyone on your end! It... didn't... happen!" Cristian said while clapping his hands to each of the last three words. "Let's move on! Also... *you*..." Cristian waved an exaggerated pointed finger into Curt's face, then at his genitals. "..don't need to be hanging around my cousin! Unh-uh! I don't need you sticking your nose or your *dick* anywhere it doesn't belong!" Cristian's voice kept rising higher during his rant.

"You have a lot of words," Curt simply replied, to which Cristian shrieked in disbelief. "Look, you can consider your account paid in full," Curt said. "But this doesn't mean I'm going to stop watching out for her, though. Like I said before, I'm going to make sure the girl stays protected on behalf of the 'human being' side of things," Curt challenged.

"*You* look! I know she *looks* human, but I got news for you blackmail-man, *she's not*. The '*girl*,'" Cristian made air quotes with his fingers. "As you so eloquently call her, she can create a hybrid werewolf, just like my uncle Marius, if she mates with another werewolf," Cristian reminded Curt.

"Yeah, but she also could make a human baby if she '*mates*' with a human," Curt replied, a mischievous smile spreading across his face. At first, Cristian growled but then fell into dry heaving at this thought.

"Gross! Humans creating other *unremarkable humans*... how 'totally amazing' and unheard of!" Cristian retorted with over-the-top sarcasm. "Maybe you can also feed them a poor diet, under-educate them, or, I don't know, not even provide for their most basic needs, and then really *rise above the masses*. There should be an IQ requisite for humans to procreate," Cristian said contemptuously.

"You, my friend, are a 'species-ist,'" Curt replied with obvious amusement. "Also, some of your concepts are boarding on eugenics, and that's some evil shit, bro."

"First of all, just like every other creature on this planet, my interest in humans stops at how they infringe on *my* life with their mindless overpopulation, dismissive destruction of the planet, and aggressive, entitled behaviors. Second, you don't even know how stupid you sound right now," Cristian said with an eye roll. "Do you talk shit about monkeys or carry a grudge against baboons?" he asked. "No, ya don't, because you don't even relate to your species' ancestry like that. That's how our kind feels about 'humans.' We're too far removed from your kind at this point to care. Also, 'species-ist' is not even a word."

"If that were true, then why do some Romanian werewolves *choose* to procreate with humans when Hungarian werewolves don't? Isn't that the whole source of contention for your stupid feud?" Curt taunted, causing Cristian to gasp. "Also, I didn't realize I was in the presence of such high evolutionary standards. You know, maybe *I should* consider taking cues for how to live an evolved life from a werewolf who has been living 'in the closet' for his entire life... like you," Curt jabbed, this time below the belt. Cristian shrieked again, appalled at this last remark. "How dare you!" he said.

Chapter Eleven

Nocturne

Nocturne was a small, quaint town as far as New England towns went, with just under six thousand residents. As with most small towns in this area, it had been settled in the mid-1600s, and during its early onset, it was rich with agriculture and small industry. Both the town and its residents remained largely unchanged for centuries until the mid-19th century, when viewpoints took a notable shift toward religious liberalism and social responsibilities. Many churches were erected in the area that took on strong social stances on temperance, women's rights, and the abolition of slavery.

Coincidentally, there was also a shift toward viewpoints and beliefs in the strange, mysterious, and supernatural during this religious movement. Many residents became known to be overly superstitious, adopting a macabre fascination with the ideas of various horrifying creatures wandering about the region. Stories soon began to circulate of people who wore the hides of wolves and would invade someone's property to steal livestock, goods, and even, occasionally, some innocent farmer's daughter. Stories like these had begun to spread like wildfire across county lines. Stories of shapeshifting people seemed to be allegories used to encourage people to keep aggressive or primitive impulses under control.

A particularly popular bit of local lore was a tale about a farmer's son, Ebenezer Hoffman, who needed to journey into the sprawling Nocturne woodlands to locate a lost ewe that had wandered astray from her flock. Ebenezer had asked another young man in town to accompany him through the forest. However, midway through their journey, the escort stopped, shapeshifted, and attempted to consume the young Hoffman teen. Ebenezer was able to extract a dagger from his knapsack, which he used to stab into the beast's neck. The next day, another farmer down the lane was headed out to his barn to milk one of his cows and discovered a man lying naked and dying from a stab wound to the neck. It was said that there were some black hairs, from what the townspeople could only assume was wolf fur, scattered across the man's naked body.

To the present day, the townspeople of Nocturne have maintained an overly superstitious quality and tended to be suspicious of strangers and certain families who lived in the area. Outsiders might have thought this wariness to be xenophobic in nature because a lot of the suspicion seemed to concentrate on the local Romanian families who had lived in the area since the late 1800s.

The townspeople of Nocturne had since grown accustomed to living side-by-side with their Eastern European neighbors but were always careful to keep one eye on them when they would visit town, as trouble always seemed to follow. And as far as those local legends and stories, from so long ago, of the shapeshifting peoples or people dressing in wolf skins... well, those tales had never really subsided.

"Heeeeeyyyyy!" came the loud, ear-splitting voice of what sounded like an alley cat yowling in response to a saw blade used for a violin bow. A slender hand with slender wrists and long, red, pointed fingernails waved hello to Cristian as he and Curt approached. The ruby fingernails and alley cat-saw blade on a violin voice belonged to that of Vittoria Farkas, Blake's younger sister. She came *clack-clacking* in high heels at a low-speed jog down Main Street as she jogged up to Cristian, threw her arms around his neck, and then planted her big fire-engine red lips onto his mouth.

"Heeyy, Pookie," Cristian said in a high-pitched, effeminized voice as he surfaced for air with bright red lipstick marks on his lips. He wore a placating smile as Vittoria dove back in for another obnoxious kiss on his cheek, leaving yet another set of red lip marks in the wake of her kiss. She then grabbed his ever-present five o'clock shadow chin and oscillated his face back and forth as she squealed with happiness to see him.

Vittoria flaunted a leopard-print coat and wore lots of bright red accents.

Her appearance resembled that of the late Amy Winehouse, but the similarities ended with her style, as Vittoria's voice was far from majestic.

"Pookie, you remember Curt?" Cristian asked, attempting to divert her attention away from himself.

"Hey, how's it going?" Curt politely greeted her and then extended his hand toward Vittoria. But instead of taking his proffered hand, Vittoria looked down at it with disdain as if he were offering her a cold, dead fish. Her eyes shot back up to Curt's face as her red lips retracted into a sneer, nostrils flaring like she smelled something bad in the air. She returned to kissing Cristian while whispering to him in a not-so-quiet voice.

"Baby, don't make me say hi to that hunter," she said in a baby voice with a mild Hungarian accent.

At that moment, another Hungarian visitor named Adrian stepped out of a nearby store. He was a squirrely-looking fellow with longish brown hair, big brown eyes like a Golden Retriever, and the stubble of a goatee surrounding his mouth, which sat at the bottom of his long face. He spun around in a comical, disoriented fashion until he caught a glimpse of Vittoria and Cristian and then sauntered over to the group.

"Hey, Cristian! Ma wolfman. How's your butt hanging?" Adrian asked in broken English with a hearty smile and thick Hungarian accent.

"I can confirm it's good," Vittoria drawled with a sly smile, as she grabbed at Cristian's butt, which made him squirm and giggle uncomfortably. Then Adrian noticed Curt.

"Heeey, man! Nice to—" Adrian started to say while throwing his hand up for a high five, but Curt grabbed his hand and pulled it down to a respectable handshake level, then introduced himself.

"Curt," he said tersely while forcefully shaking Adrian's hand. "Nice to meet you, too." Adrian's once-smiling mouth now hung open, as Curt's abrasive actions clearly threw him off balance.

"Sco, I mean, A... Adri—" he stammered as he tried to get his name out.

"Yeah, that's great, man," Curt said, clapping Adrian hard on the back. "Keep practicing. You'll get it one day." Cristian noticed this awkward exchange through Vittoria's swarming on him.

"Do you guys know each other?" he questioned in a high voice, but Curt immediately shook his head.

"Nope. First time," Curt said rigidly.

"N... no," Adrian gingerly confirmed as well.

"Huh! Okay, anyway..." Cristian said, dismissing the odd behavior as Curt just being his asshole-ish self.

Blake and Erika walked side-by-side down Main Street. One might say the pair even looked good together—Blake in his dark blue jeans and black T-shirt, Erika in a flowing black knee-length dress with little white flowers, and both wearing black low-top *Converse*. Light goosebumps covered Erika's arms as the sun struggled to break through the cloudy sky.

"Well, well, look at this handsome couple!" Vittoria cat-called when she spotted her brother and Erika approaching. Erika noticed the boisterous woman hanging all over her cousin, and immediately, her chills amplified.

Vittoria's smile slowly melted away and was replaced by a more ominous expression. Then, she dramatically pushed Cristian aside and started taking deliberate steps in Erika's direction. Erika stopped dead in her tracks and braced herself—for what, she didn't know.

A handful of steps brought Vittoria to stand directly in front of Erika, close enough to size her up. She then leaned in close to Erika's ear. Erika wondered what this person was about to say, but her question was soon answered as Vittoria sniffed her hair.

"I can smell your fear," she whispered dauntingly, as a viper red smile spread across her face. Erika felt extremely creeped out by the action and the comment. Suddenly, Vittoria leaned back and exclaimed, "Just kidding! One big happy family!" she shouted at an ear-splitting volume. She then seized Erika by her shoulders and guided her in for a superficial hug and kiss on each cheek, leaving red lipstick marks in her wake.

"Hi, it's nice to... err... meet you," Erika said, already suspicious of Vittoria's odd behavior. But I'm afraid you've got the wrong idea. I'm not with... We're not... a couple?" Erika stammered, gesturing toward Blake. Vittoria's smile again fell away until Blake stepped in.

"Her boyfriend just died! She needs to go into space! You got problems, Vittoria. You need to work on your social skill. You cannot just say..." Blake faltered, clearly at a loss for the English language. "And no respect..." he added. While his heart was in the right place, his valiant effort to defend Erika fell somewhat short. "And also, can everyone let there have five fucking minutes without saying her boyfriend die?"

"Okay! Caalm down, crazy!" Vittoria fired back. She was clearly more fluent in English than her brother and went on to fold in some American slang to prove it. "I was only saying that you both look *lit*. No need to get your tail in a twist, bro. Also, you're sweet to stand up for *yo bae* like that, but you need to work on your English, big brother. It's dreadful," Vittoria quipped with a laugh as she walked back over to Cristian.

Blake called out something in Hungarian after his sister, then leaned down to Erika. "Am not sure everything she says, but I just told her to be nice," he said, trying to reassure Erika.

"Don't worry about it," she replied, although she did feel touched at his attempt to stand up for her. She looked over at Cristian, who appeared uncomfortable at the attention Vittoria was paying to him. "So, where are we headed," Erika asked.

"We're headed to the Foolish Goat. It's a tavern just down the street. A couple of my boys should be there holding a table for us," Cristian responded as he gave Vittoria a superficial peck on the cheek.

As the group walked up Main Street, Erika looked up at Blake.

"Thank you for standing up for me," she said to him. Blake looked down at her and smiled warmly at her.

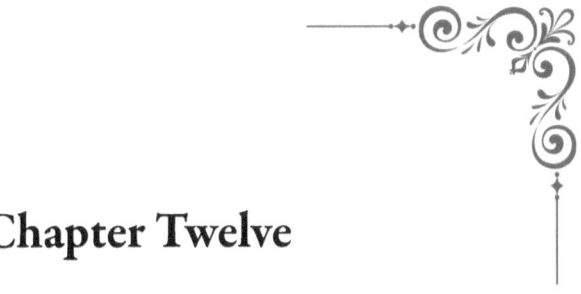

Chapter Twelve

The Foolish Goat

"He's standing right there! Plain as fuckin' day! You can see his fly is already down because the sneaky fucker has been planning this moment. And right there—when everyone's in the middle of being happy and celebrating..." Beo Aristide said, then cupped his hands to either side of his mouth and did a mock crowd roar before continuing. "Then all of a sudden... dude pulls his dick out."

"Wait, what the fuck! Really?" Beo's friend River Landis asked while laughing in disbelief. "No way. Are you serious?" River continued to laugh as he elbowed his friend Loki Lupu, sitting next to him, causing Loki to spill some beer from his overfull pint glass. Loki looked reproachfully at River as he shook his head and picked up a napkin to wipe up the spilled beer on the wooden table before him.

"Dead fuckin' serious, bruh! Just watch and see for yourself. Dude pulls his dick out, just for a second, then kinda brushes it away under his sweatshirt before zipping up his fly again. And *nobody* fuckin' notices for years!" Beo said. He was holding court inside the Foolish Goat with his brother Malcolm Aristide Junior and their friends Loki and River, all sitting at a large table in the center of the tavern.

"I knew that. You guys didn't fuckin' know that shit?" Malcolm Jr. asked in a slightly pompous manner. The group laughed and sipped whiskey and beer around a long wooden community table in the local Nocturne tavern.

"If there's a moral to be had in this story, I'd say it's for filmmakers—Don't get so caught up making your crappy B movie that you don't notice you have a dick on set," Beo said while getting the group riled up with laughter once again. "Now, if it's a blockbuster... maybe you can overlook a dick or two..."

"Ooohh, what *are* you guys talking about?" Cristian asked with a sly smile, having just caught the last bit of the conversation as he walked up to the table. Vittoria, Curt, Adrian, Blake, and Erika trailed in behind him.

"Werewolf movies!" Beo answered with a mischievous smile, which wiped the smile right off Cristian's face. Vittoria laughed as Cristian appeared to be uncomfortable. A look of wonder covered Adrian's face, as he didn't seem to be paying attention to what the group was discussing.

"Ooooooooh," Cristian managed to say, but he held the note a little too long, and his voice inadvertently came out like a tiny howl.

Moments later, the new arrivals squeezed into the open seating around the large table and mingled with the group already seated there.

"I thought I heard you talking about wieners?" Cristian asked with disappointment in his voice.

"Oh, I was," Beo confirmed with a smile. "I was talking about the rogue wiener at the end of *Teen Wolf.*"

"I don't think I ever saw that movie," Loki admitted quietly, a subtle Romanian accent coming through as he spoke. Cristian, Beo, River, and Malcolm Jr. gave their friend a skeptical look.

"What? I thought *everyone* had seen all those movies! They're pure comedy! Movies that are so bad, they're good!" Cristian said with a snort of laughter, then quickly attempted to change the subject. "Hey, so we need some more drinks for the table, yeah? Let's get those..."

"They already comin', baby boo," Beo said with a wink at Cristian, who seemed to swoon a little in response.

"I never really liked werewolf movies," Erika admitted, jumping right into the conversation. At this, the whole table looked at her like she was nuts. "I always felt they were all 'B movies' unless they appeared under a larger fantasy vehicle, like *Harry Potter* or *Twilight.* I prefer vampire movies," she stated.

"Ugh! Gross! You're kidding!" The collective response came from the whole table.

"You mean you actually like the end of *New Moon*?" Beo asked skeptically, then crudely added, "He proposes, every teenage girl in the world shits outta their vagina—*the end.*"

"Okay, maybe not *those* movies, but classics—*Interview with the Vampire,* for sure. I loved those books as a teenager," Erika defended.

"You just need to see the *right* werewolf movies. *The Wolf Man*—classic; *Brotherhood of the Wolf*—French werewolves; *Silver Bullet*—a Steven King treasure; *American Werewolf in London*—*intentional* wieners..." Beo listed off the movies on his elegantly long fingers, his skin tone a rich coffee color, and his eyes a warm almond brown with a twinkle in them. When he was finished, he held an attractive smile with big, shining teeth.

"Bae..." Cristian interjected in an amorous voice, then added, "'O'. Beo, let's talk about something else, okay?" he suggested with a puckered smile. Beo gave Cristian a mischievous—maybe also flirtatious—look in response and said nothing to protest. Erika noticed Cristian had to break his gaze away from Beo to refocus with some effort.

"So, you guys, this is my cousin, Erika," Cristian finally introduced. "Erika, these are my friends. Our little group calls ourselves the *Killers* because we're all really good-looking... Hahah! jk, jk."

"Cristian is the real killer—*Lady Killer,* that is. I don't think he's been able to keep his hands off Vittoria since she arrived," Beo teased with a hint of jealousy. A broad, pointed smile spread across Vittoria's large red lips as she again began to paw at Cristian. He, in turn, squirmed uncomfortably away from her grabby hands.

"Baabe," Cristian said, but it was somewhat unclear if he spoke to Vittoria or Beo. "Okay, where was I? Oh right, this crass asshole over here is Beo Aristide," Cristian continued the introductions as he gestured to the attractive guy who was still grinning across from him at the table. "That guy next to him is his brother, Malcolm Aristide Junior. They are Americans, but we'll forgive them for that," Cristian added in jest.

"African American Creole actually, bruh," Beo's brother Malcolm Jr. interjected. "Mom is an all-American sista. Dad is Haitian Creole from New Orléans. And they made some good-looking sons, they did," Malcolm Jr. said with a coy smile as he gestured to himself and his brother.

"You know it, bruh!" Beo chuckled in conceited agreement.

"Oh, you two are so modest!" Cristian guffawed in a friendly mocking manner but then starkly composed himself once more for dramatic effect before continuing. "This quiet, sullen character over here with resting-Eastern-European-face is Loki Lupu." Cristian gestured to his quiet friend, who had short, dark, wavy hair and a patchy beard. "Loki and his family live on the other side of our woods. His family is also from Romania, just like another family who lives out here called the Vulpes. Our friend Kessler Vulpe couldn't make it out today, but I'm sure you'll meet him soon."

"It's our woods, too," Loki said quietly with his faint Romanian accent.

"Vulpe and Lupu?" Erika racked her brain for a moment. "I think I remember hearing those names back in school," she remarked, to which Loki gave a small smile and a mildly uninterested head nod.

"Yes, I remember you. You were popular," he said flatly. Cristian resumed, finishing the last introduction.

"And last, but not least, this is River Landis. He's American but has spent time in London and Paris, so he has some culture." River looked mischievous, with wild, greasy, light brown, almost blond hair loosely slicked back on his head. He gave Erika a 'what's up' chin nod, showing off all his culture that Cristian had just mentioned.

"Hey, everyone. Nice to—" Erika started to say but was interrupted as the next round of whiskey was delivered to the table. She noticed Curt watching her. He smiled as she shrugged and picked up the glass of whiskey before her. Erika hadn't been expecting to arrive at a bar and day-drink whiskey, but the thing was... she would do it.

With shot glasses full, the group raised them and toasted to some arbitrary reason before each threw back their whiskey. Then, the group resumed disjointed conversations while another round arrived and was served to the table. After taking a second shot, Erika decided to take a breather from liquor. She stood up from the table and strolled over to the bar to order something other than whiskey.

Nobody seemed to notice as Erika wandered away, except for Curt and Blake. Both caught the other's eye as they watched her walk away. Curt glared at Blake, but neither guy made a move to follow her while the other one was watching.

"Excuse me, bartender, can I please get a beer? It's a little early for whiskey for me," Erika requested. The heavyset bartender with salt and pepper hair behind the bar turned around and nodded, acknowledging her order. While she waited, Erika glanced down the length of the bar and noticed a patron sitting at the far end who flashed her a sleazy smile and raised his glass to her. After returning a dismissive smile, Erika's focus was fortunately drawn away from the stranger as the bartender brought her the beer she had ordered. Erika glanced back toward the rest of her party and saw Cristian reach over and almost lovingly pluck an eyelash off Beo's high cheekbone. Erika clocked a comfortable energy between the two of them.

"Haven't seen you in here before," the bartender said. The comment recaptured Erika's attention, and she turned back to face him. "You with that crowd?" he inquired.

"Yeah, the guy with the thick black hair and the leopard woman hanging all over him is my cousin," Erika responded.

"Your cousin?!" the bartender asked, as he slightly recoiled from her. "Are you a Dragos then?"

"Kinda, not exactly. My last name is Navarro, but my mother's maiden name was Dragos," Erika explained as she sipped her beer. The bartender seemed stunned as he processed this information.

"So, you're Daniela's daughter's kid... er... I can't remember her name. Forgive me. What was it again?"

"Yes, Daniela was my grandmother," Erika confirmed while dismissing the second question.

"Good heavens, look at you... Daniela was a fine soul. She is missed round these parts. Be careful round that cousin of yours and those 'Killers.' I've been noticing a surge in activity round here lately that's been making my blood go cold." The bartender leaned in and whispered, "Not that I have a problem with your kind, you see. Daniela just seemed to have different rules for 'others' like your family that I don't think these new 'others' are obeying." The bartender said mysteriously. Erika stared back at him, unsure if she should be insulted somewhere in his words, so she decided not to be.

"What is *my kind*? she asked coolly while taking another sip of her beer. The bartender's mouth hung open momentarily as if he was trying to determine how to best answer Erika's question.

"Can I buy you another one of those?" the stranger from across the bar asked as he pulled up a seat beside her.

"Sure," she said without looking at him. The bartender took the opportunity to move away from the conversation and get her next drink.

"I haven't seen you here before," the man commented. "I think you're pretty."

"Look, pal, no need to melt my heart with so much charm; you'll just be wasting it on me because I can tell you right now, I'm not interested," she said as the bartender set down the fresh beer bottle before her. "On second thought, I'll pay for this myself. I'm afraid the price for it, in your mind, is more than I want to pay." The stranger beside her just snickered with delight as he dismissed what Erika had said and decided to try again with a different approach. As the man continued to whisper creepy things to her, he slowly picked up his hand and brought it to rest on the small of her back. Erika quickly jerked away from his touch.

From the table in the middle of the room, Blake's head snapped directly toward this gesture of unwanted contact. In an instant, the man who had just touched Erika's back was now suspended up against a nearby wall by his neck as Blake growled and held the man up in the air with one hand. The other bar patrons scrambled and screamed at the scene before them. The man kicked and gasped for air as he fought against Blake's vise-like grip on his neck.

"Now listen, I've told your group that you can't be rough handling my customers, or you're not going to be welcome in here anymore!" the bartender yelled over to Cristian as he reached under the bar and extracted a wooden baseball bat.

"Have you ever considered that maybe some of your customers are assholes?" Cristian innocently called back, clearly underreacting to the scene before him as if he didn't see anything wrong. "I'm sure my friend has a good reason. Um, excuse me, Blake... what did this *obviously well-bred* townie do?"

"He touch her," Blake growled as his eyes narrowed, deadlocked on the suspended man's face. Other bar patrons started to advance toward the scene, which, in turn, caused the Killers also to stand up, anticipating an escalation in the fight.

"Okay, *where* did he touch her? On her boobies?" Cristian asked mockingly while rolling his eyes.

"On her back," Blake answered with no subsiding anger.

"Oh... oookay, *on her back*," Cristian repeated. "This is gonna be fucked," he said, as he stretched and started to loosen himself up for a fight. He cracked his neck and did a few shoulder rolls.

"This guy is *the bullshit*!" Adrian growled, attempting his American 'shit-talking' skills in broken English, ready to back up to his Hungarian friend.

"Stop!" Erika shouted and walked over to Blake, who was still holding the townie in a suspended chokehold by his neck. She gently touched his arm, and Blake immediately lowered the man. Erika then turned to the bartender and the other angered patrons in the tavern. "My cousin and his friends were just trying to look out for me, but they don't need to do that. I can stand up for myself and fight my own battles," she said, then turned to the man still grasping at his neck. "Are you ok?" she asked. The man nodded unsteadily, then started to flush with anger.

"Y-y-y-you psycho bitch!" he said, immediately going down the wrong road—attacking the woman in front of him, too afraid to say anything to the large guy who assaulted him.

Erika course-corrected, "No, no, wrong way. Don't you *ever* put your hands on a woman unless she gives you permission to do so. These guys shouldn't need to be here to show you that's wrong. Don't... do... it. It is not your right to *ever* touch another person without their consent," she said firmly.

"I'm afraid your group still needs to *GO*!" the bartender said nervously. Then, something funny happened in that moment—Cristian, Vittoria, Beo, Malcolm Jr., Loki, and River all cocked their heads to the side in an exaggerated manner.

"That's fine, we'll leave," Erika replied to the bartender, still trying to diffuse the situation. "Cristian, let's *GO*," she said. Again, all the previously mentioned individuals dramatically cocked their heads to one side.

"What did they say?" Blake asked Vittoria, rejoining the crowd near the table.

"Megy," Vittoria answered in Hungarian, to which Blake also cocked his head dramatically to the side.

"Okay, I don't know what the *fuck* this is about," Erika said while gesturing to all their exaggerated head tilting, "but let's *GO*! I want to *GO*! Can we please *GO* now?!" she pleaded while Cristian and his friends continued to cock their heads this way and that with each, *GO*. "Stop it!" Erika shouted and walked toward the exit and out of the bar. Cristian and the others quickly followed her, eager to see where they were about to go.

Chapter Thirteen

Lacks

Three Months Later

The lengthy sunny days had begun to show signs of waning as the end of summer drew near. A long shadow cast across the front doors of the Foolish Goat. The shadow belonged to a mousy woman with brown hair who was wearing a CSULB college sweatshirt despite the seventy-degree Fahrenheit weather this time of year. Nicole—Erika's former roommate from California—had been able to find the town of Nocturne easily enough but wasn't having any luck finding her way to Dragos Manor. All the twisting and winding backroads through the dense woodland forest made it easy to get turned around, and she had spent the better part of an hour finding her way back onto Main Street.

After parking her rental car, Nicole approached the first open establishment she spotted in the sleepy little town of Nocturne. As she passed by the windows of the tavern, she peered inside and saw a lone bartender and a few patrons who were nursing their drinks. She went inside to see if someone there could help point her in the right direction.

The light inside the tavern was dim compared to the bright afternoon sunlight that yawned down Main Street outside. When Nicole entered the Foolish Goat, her shadow cast out into the room and danced up to the bar as she approached the people who congregated around it. The bartender glanced up at the newcomer as Nicole cleared her throat. The bartender was a large man with salt and pepper hair.

"Excuse me, but I was wondering if someone might be able to help me with some directions?" she asked politely.

"Sure thing, little lady. Would you like anything to drink?" the bartender asked.

"Actually, yeah! Can I please have some water?" Nicole requested as she took a seat at the bar. He obliged and scooped a large amount of ice into a glass and then began filling it up with water, but dumped about half of the ice out into the sink as he eyed her sweatshirt.

"Where is it you are trying to get to?" the man on the barstool next to Nicole asked as he casually reached over and placed his hand on the back of her barstool.

"Dragon Hotel... or something like that. I'm not sure I have the correct name. It doesn't seem to come up on my Maps app. Oh, thank you," she said while gratefully accepting the glass of water set down before her. The man on the barstool next to her quickly withdrew his hand, as if the back of her barstool had burnt him, and either consciously or subconsciously began rubbing his neck.

"You probably mean Dragos Manor," the bartender said.

"Yes! That's totally it!"

"You from out of town?" he asked skeptically.

"Yeah, visiting from California!" Nicole replied, taking a sip of her water.

"You gonna go stay in that haunted hotel, are ya?"

"I'm hoping to... if I can find it, that is. My friend lives there! It's her family's home, and I just wanted to pay her a surprise visit!" she exclaimed excitedly.

"Well, isn't that nice," the bartender said pleasantly. "I think I know who your friend is. That Navarro girl, right?"

"Yes! That's her! Erika Navarro!" she confirmed with excitement. The bartender and the man sitting next to Nicole exchanged wary looks.

"I'll tell ya how to get there, but I just want to give you a small word of warning, if you can please pass it along to your friend? She seems like a nice girl. And my gut tells me she might not be the same as some of the *other*... uh... members of her family," the bartender said, choosing his words very carefully. Nicole perked up, and her face took on a look of concern.

"A warning? What kind of warning? Is it about..." Nicole leaned in with a mock fearful expression, "Ghosts?"

"Ahh... er... no, not exactly. Although I have heard that house is seriously haunted, so if you're inta that sorta thing, you shouldn't be disappointed," the bartender said. The townie on the barstool next to Nicole squirmed uncomfortably as if being a party to this sort of conversation upset his belief system.

"Well yeah, everyone is afraid of ghosts in theo... theoretical ghosts, but I didn't think it was real," she said. "Just a tourist attraction. Local legend? As in made up. Right?"

"I'm not talking bout ghosts, darlin'. What I'm trying to tell you about is... Lycanthropy." Nicole looked confused at the word, so he clarified. "*Werewolves*, darlin'," he finally managed to say. Nicole sat with her mouth agape for a moment. She had been ready to retort, but not to *this* information.

"Um... excuse me?" she asked incredulously. "Werewolves?" At Nicole's disbelieving expression, the man on the barstool next to her squirmed uncomfortably again, seemingly also having trouble swallowing the notion that werewolves existed, let alone walked amongst them in their own town.

"Now, Clarence, some people reckon that mangled livestock could have been the work of some sort of wild animal or an escaped lunatic or something like that," he countered to the bartender.

"Yeah, Darren. Well, that's all hunky-dory, well and good, but what about the mangled people over the years?" Clarence asked in an ominously challenging manner. Nicole looked back and forth between each man on either side of the bar as she loudly slurped the remnants of her water.

"Well, regardless of werewolves, vampires, or unicorns, I need to get out there. So do you think one of you gents can tell me the way?"

A short time later, Nicole folded up a cocktail napkin with a makeshift map and directions scrawled on it. She put the napkin inside her pocket before exiting the tavern, then walked back out into the late afternoon sunlight.

Mere moments after Nicole had left, the doors of the Foolish Goat swung open once more, and a newcomer stepped inside. He was tall, with a silver pompadour, matching close-cropped silver beard, and handlebar mustache. The guy wore black leather biker pants, a tight white T-shirt, and a black leather motorcycle jacket with burnt orange stripes down the outer-facing sleeves.

"Uh oh. Speak of the Devil. Here comes one of them now," Darren muttered to Clarence as the townie turned his back toward the individual who had just walked through the doors. As he walked past the leering crowd at the bar, Marius Dragos removed his sunglasses and smiled at the occupant sitting in the corner booth in the back of the tavern. The booth's occupant sat inconspicuously, minding his own business and nursing a cranberry juice with a wedge of lime on the rim.

"Guess he's not thirsty," Clarence remarked, clicking his tongue on his teeth.

"Malcolm Aristide," Marius greeted the Creole werewolf in his human form. Malcolm Senior's face lit up at the sight of his longtime friend.

"Hey, ti-Marius! How's your mom 'n 'em?" Malcolm Sr. greeted Marius with an affectionate nickname derived from 'piti', meaning tiny, then immediately asked after the rest of the Dragos family, as was customary in his Louisiana Creole culture. His accent—derived from the Kouri-Vini dialect—was distinctly Southern Louisiana Haitian Creole. Marius took a seat across from him in the booth and shook his hand as he responded.

"My mom and the family are doing great; thank you for asking," he said. Marius noted that anyone who spent any length of time around Malcolm Aristide Sr. always caught his infectious smile on their own face. "And how's your family doing?" Marius asked as they both settled in comfortably across from one another.

"Mostly doing one hundred, bruh, but I tell you, those sons of mine, Beo and Junior, are always driving me crazy!" Malcolm Sr. said with mock exasperation.

"You know what, I think that is what kids are supposed to do," Marius laughed in good-humored agreement. "We have to love them, give them the room to figure things out for themselves, and do our best to steer them toward good decisions."

"Steer them away from being outright dumbasses is more like it, bruh,"

Malcolm Sr. quipped.

As far as the werewolf families in Nocturne went, the Aristide family was newer to the area. Malcolm Sr. and his wife, Shanice, moved from New Orléans to Nocturne in the late 1980s with their young son Malcolm Jr. and second son, Beo, on the way inside his mama's tummy.

With the brief catchup on family matters aside, Marius leaned in and asked, "So what have you found out?" to which Malcolm Sr. also leaned in and took on a serious yet hushed tone.

"Okay, so, I've been looking into Erika's deceased fiancé, Ryan Wilson, to see if he had ties to any suspicious individuals or activities, or if anyone had it out for him. You said it sounded like a werewolf killed him, but I wanted to be unbiased and thorough. I have spoken to everyone you can think of, bruh—werewolves, hunters, cops, gang members, junkies, pimps, prostitutes, journalists. And you wouldn't believe it, bruh. Guess where I finally heard the first whisper of something from? A little kid. No kidding... a little *sha* kid who is working as a busboy at his family's restaurant in New York City. All the way in New York City, bruh! Can you believe that?"

"How did you end up coming across this busboy?" Marius asked.

"Well, I put out the word to the 'Gather at the Goat' circuit, and you know your friend Malcolm, I'm very good at this sort of thing. Word spread through the circuit like a shockwave. It spread all the way to the West Coast and back."

"What's the 'Gather at the Goat' circuit?" Marius questioned.

"Marius, jeez, bruh. You need to get with it! You're sounding like an old werewolf!" Malcolm Sr. said in disbelief with a friendly chuckle. "'Gather at the Goat' is an expression I thought every werewolf knew about. It is for werewolves who do not know of the place they are in. They know to go to any bar, tavern, or restaurant in the area that has the word 'Goat' in the name. There happens to be some sort of establishment with 'Goat' in the name in almost every major American city. So, werewolves always know they have chances to meet other werewolves when they 'Gather at the Goat.'"

"That's good to know! I have never heard of that before," Marius exclaimed in surprise.

"Even here, bruh—the Foolish *Goat*?" Malcolm Sr. said, gesturing to the tavern they were in. "Anyway, you get the picture. So, I had asked all kinds of folks in the 'Gather at the Goat' circuit, and after a little bit, word finally came back to me that a busboy had overheard a strange conversation between a human and a werewolf at a restaurant tavern called the Buckling Goat in New York City. This kid is a werewolf. His family owns the bar, which is a well-known werewolf meeting place. He says the business has its regular patrons, but it also gets many interesting people and werewolves who pass through.

So earlier this year, this busboy noticed a traveler hanging around there for a few days or maybe even a week. He said this stranger was a human, and what caught the busboy's attention was that this human would always try to talk to werewolves who would be passing through—always the same human man, but always different werewolves."

"How did he know this guy was human?"

"By the nose, bruh... the human's scent. So, he sees this human with different werewolves, trying to talk to them, but all the werewolves did not want any part of this man. Then, one night, the busboy say he saw the human talking to a werewolf, and this werewolf would actually talk to the man. The busboy said he heard the man say something strange. He said he heard the human man say, 'Not just scare. *El Jefe* wants this guy gone. Dead.'" Malcolm Sr. paused to let Marius digest this information while he sipped his cranberry juice.

"El jefe," Marius repeated, trying the word out himself.

"But that is not everything, bruh. The busboy said he saw the same pair meet again the next night! The human and the same werewolf this time! So, the busboy was curious about what he had heard the previous night and tried to hang around close to the pair to see if he could pick up any more strange things from them. He said that the pair seemed to be making plans together and kept talking about going to someplace called 'Lacks,'" Malcolm Sr. said with a sly look.

"Lacks," Marius repeated. "What the heck is Lacks?" Malcolm Sr. smiled at the question.

"You see, I wondered the same thing myself. I had never heard of this Lacks before. Then it hit me, so I called back the busboy to ask him who was talking about going to the Lacks. Was it the human man or the werewolf? The kid said it was the werewolf who was saying 'Lacks'.

So, I'm just taking a guess, but the information I take away from this story is that I think three individuals were involved in whatever plot these *two* might have been scheming about. First, El Jefe is the boss or person behind the whole murder scheme. Second, this human who organized the werewolf to do the murder, which means this must be a human who knows about our kind. Finally, I think the third party involved is the werewolf, who might be a foreigner or traveler, someone unfamiliar with America, for two reasons. For one thing, he was in NYC, where lots of traveling werewolves and people come through. And second, I think he is foreign because I don't think he meant to say 'Lacks.' I think what he was trying to say was... LAX," Malcolm Sr. summed up, then sat back on the bench as he again sipped his cranberry juice, a coy smile playing on the corners of his mouth pursed up against the rim of the glass. Marius stared in awe at the cunning ingenuity of his friend's detective work.

"Wow... I have to say, that's very interesting. And what does your gut say about this busboy's lead?" Marius asked. "Do you think this is the trail we might be looking for?"

"In a sea of noting, bruh, this sounds like the most viable lead I've heard so far," Malcolm Sr. said soberly.

"Okay, I hear you. So, what next? Does this kid have any details about what these two looked like?" Marius asked hopefully.

"Nah, bruh, I already asked the kid this question. He said the human was always wearing a hoodie or a hat or something. The werewolf, he said, was a white male with a long face and dark hair, and that was all he could remember. I told him to call me if he ever saw either of those two again."

"Alright, my friend. Great work. I knew you were the wolf for the job. You're like a Bloodhound. You have a good nose for this sort of thing and are clearly a lot better connected than I am— 'Gather at the Goat...' I had no idea. Please keep me posted if you hear anything more. Otherwise, I'll see you and your family in two weeks at the Dragos' Sturgeon Moon gala."

"Sounds good ti-Marius. Happy to do what I can for you, bruh."

Chapter Fourteen

The Visitor

The sound of the large brass wolf-head door knocker echoed throughout the expansive stillness of the Dragos Manor lobby. A bewildered Ana marched over to answer, unsure of who it could be as she wasn't expecting anyone else that day with the six reservations that had just checked in a short time earlier. Whomever this visitor might be was in luck, however, because today Ana was in a rare, good mood. The reason for her joyful spirits was that today signified the start of the guest season for Dragos Manor. Historically, the first guests would check in starting in late August, and the momentum would continue until the year's end. Sure, Ana realized it was a rather short season, but this was the time of year when her returning customers demonstrated the most interest. Reservation inquiries simply did not happen outside of this window—at least, any inquiries that Ana approved of.

The truth was, Ana had become very stringent regarding who she would allow to stay at her family's grand home, and the guest list had been closed for years. And since the permitted guests comprised the same dedicated yet antiquated patrons who had been frequenting the hotel since the early 1970s, the number of visitors had dwindled significantly. This was due to fixed-income retirements or death from natural causes. Regardless, Ana took great pride in the long-term repeat business of her most loyal customers, who chose to vacation at Dragos Manor year after year for decades. Sure, she wasn't always prompt about adjusting hotel pricing to account for inflation, and with such long-term sustained loyalty, it was only natural that she extended a "friends and family" discount to these preferred guests.

As a result of all these factors, Dragos Manor started suffering some financial hardships in recent years. Ana had been working hard to just barely keep the home and the business afloat. Then, suddenly, this year seemed to be the first time things had drastically inverted for the family finances. Through some misfortune that the Dragos Matriarch could only chalk up to a bookkeeping error, she had somehow misplaced a great deal of money, making this guest season extra important for the Dragos family. If, by the highly probable chance, the hotel was to lose any more guests, Ana would have to consider discontinuing friends and family discounts, possibly raising prices, or even worse, reopening the guest list.

The only other way she could see around this dilemma was if the Dragos family were to, say... get a large influx of cash flow if someone in their family were to, say... marry into a wealthy family... say, someone in the Farkas family.

Nonetheless, it was an exciting time of year, and despite all these stressors and worries, Ana was on a mission. She was determined to make this the best hospitality season Dragos Manor had ever seen. She would personally see to it—hence her spirited and determined good mood.

However, her cheerful disposition faded almost immediately as Ana opened the front door to discover a strange, mousy girl standing before her. She blinked at this individual and waited expectantly to hear her business. The new arrival immediately looked intimated by the stern-looking older woman, who wore a black velvet doll dress with white frill lace on the cuffs and a gold necklace hanging well onto her chest.

"Hi," the young stranger squeaked out. "Is... ah... Erika home... here?"

"And who might you be?" Ana inquired in her less-than-warm fashion.

"Nicole?!" came the response to Ana's question, but the voice did not come from the young woman who stood before her, but from the top of the staircase behind her. It was Erika who stood in disbelief at the top of the landing. Nicole beamed a huge smile up to her friend as she brushed past Ana, and the two girls began bounding toward one another. They closed the distance and met in a long hug at the bottom of the staircase.

"Oh my God, what are you doing here?" Erika asked, excitement overflowing in her voice as she finally released Nicole from their extended hug.

"I missed you, so I decided to come see you!" Nicole responded.

"You should have told me you were coming!" Erika exclaimed.

"Yes, that would have been nice," Ana muttered, but the two younger women either did not hear her or ignored the old woman's snide comment.

"I'm so glad to see you! I'm so sorry. This is my grandaunt, Ana. Aunt Ana, this is my friend, Nicole. Um... we have plenty of room, right, Aunt Ana? We're not at full capacity. If more people make reservations, Nicole can stay in my room with me!" Erika offered, and both young women turned and looked expectantly at Ana, waiting for the formality of her acceptance and approval.

"Uhhh... yes, we have plenty of room. Plenty of linens, plenty of... ah... everything!" Ana responded, not seeing any other way out of the situation. "We are, however, ah... expecting a surge in—" Ana started to say, but then hesitated, not wanting to reveal too much, but was interrupted by Erika anyway.

"Great!" Erika said, seemingly not hearing her grandaunt's subsequent words. "Come on! I'll show you to the empty room right next to mine! Then we can go for a walk! I have so much to tell you!" Erika said, almost too excited to get the words out.

"How long will you be staying with us, my dear?" Ana asked, hoping the answer would indicate a short visit.

"I have no set time! As long as you'll have me! I've never really spent too much time on the East Coast!" Nicole's response gave Ana an idea.

"Oh, well then, you *must* see Cape Cod! Oh, and New York City. You'll be bored to death after one day in Nocturne, and I'm sure a young lady like you wants to vacation where the excitement is!" Ana suggested, grasping at straws.

"Ooh! You know what? That sounds like fun! I think I might need a vacation, too! Those places sound amazing! Maybe we can plan a—" Erika started scheming, having seized into Ana's recommendation.

Crap—Ana thought to herself in Romanian.

"No... no, no. Probably not a good idea right now, dear! We're going to be hosting a..." Ana sighed. "A gala here very soon. In two weeks, in fact. I have been meaning to discuss it with you and planned to speak with you about it today. In addition to our hotel guests, we're hosting many neighbors in the area, along with the Farkas siblings, of course, and their parents will be joining us all the way from Hungary. The guestlist has around seventy-plus RSVPs as of right now. I'm going to need you to be here for that," Ana said with defeated energy, anticipating what would come next.

"Oh! Maybe it's a birthday surprise!" Nicole speculated to Erika, thinking she had connected the obvious dots. This is not what Ana had been expecting after all.

"Ahh...Yes," she replied, having completely forgotten Erika's birthday was coming up.

"Oh!" Erika exclaimed, having the inevitable epiphany. *Here it comes,* Ana thought, a look of horror spreading across her face as she watched the train wreck unfold in slow motion. "You should stay for the party!" Erika eagerly suggested to her friend, who nodded enthusiastically in agreement.

After it was decided, the two young women trotted up to the 2nd floor to put Nicole's luggage away, then came back downstairs tangled up in conversation that seemed to have no breaths of air taken. They strolled past Ana and out the front door into the gardens to catch up.

"Shit. Shit, Shit," Ana whispered aloud. She had sincerely planned on having a conversation with her grandniece that day. A very serious, very important conversation that she had not been looking forward to all week. But at the behest of her deceased sister-in-law—and Erika's grandmother—Ana was tasked with forging the path to reveal Daniela's ghostly existence. This would invariably lead to explaining other truths, such as what *really* happened to Erika's mother and father. Uncovering that would then lead to another *small* truth about werewolf blood running through the Dragos gene pool for centuries, as well as through Erika's own veins. Oh, and finally, let's not forget that last minuscule detail that Erika was expected—by many, mind you—to marry and procreate with Blake Farkas, the Hungarian werewolf whose family detested the Dragos family!

Ana sighed out of frustration. Why was relaying all this information in a way that wouldn't make Erika run screaming into the hills, resting on her shoulders? She felt irritated with Daniela and Erika's mother for keeping these major secrets from Erika her entire life.

However, Ana had to remind herself that it did not matter what events had come before. All that mattered now was what remained to be done. That was how a *true* Head of Household would handle the ordeal. It was how Sophia Dragos herself would have handled it. Ana exhaled a slow breath to release the pressure she was feeling. She pondered the thought of her late husband's grandmother, Sophia Dragos, the founder of the Dragos Manor legacy and the strongest individual Ana had ever known. Sophia was the greatest example of the type of Head of Household and Lycan that Ana wanted to be, that is, until Sophia lost her way.

Ana shook off the dark memories of the latter years of Sophia's life as she resolved herself to a refreshed feeling of responsibility. As head of the Dragos family, it was her duty to carry out the necessary tasks for the family's greater good. Ana was also the most appropriate person to conduct this conversation with Erika, as Ana herself had a genetic makeup similar to that of her grandniece. She also happened to be a non-transforming werewolf born from a long family line of werewolves. Because of all this, Ana knew this task was her responsibility alone and that she must see to it that it was handled properly. Although now the job at hand would be *much* more difficult to execute with this annoying little *bitc... ah... friend around.*

At that moment, the Dragos Matriarch noticed a small Housefly buzzing around her wrist. She considered it only for a moment, then slapped the creature's existence from the world of the living.

Chapter Fifteen

Real Ghosts

"You were *not* kidding! This place is insane!" Nicole said while gesturing to the huge property surrounding her. "It's *creepy* for sure, but still really cool," she said, bookending her words with nervous laughter.

"You don't know the half of it," Erika responded, unsure of how to broach the subject of ghosts and hauntings. As she waited for an adequate pause in conversation or searched for the perfect segue to bring this topic up, Erika found it challenging because Nicole was bouncing around various topics and oscillating between updates.

"Erika, I have to say you *look really good*! *So* much happier than when I last saw you!" Nicole said with her classic 'foot in mouth' syndrome. "I mean! I just mean that, of course, you looked sad the last time I saw you... because you were grieving, but I'm just glad to see that you seem lighter now. You know what I mean? Maybe this place *is* just what you ordered. I mean needed! I was thinking 'what the doctor ordered' and what you—"

"Nikki, Nikki, it's ok. I'm ok. I agree with you. I do feel lighter," Erika said, calming her friend's nervous energy. Nicole looked at her dear friend with a thankful smile as she leaned in again and hugged her.

"It's so good to see you. So how about this guy you texted me about, huh?" she asked in a sly but cautious manner. "What's going on... anything to report there?"

Erika felt guilty for the smile that overcame her, especially since Nicole had known her deceased fiancé, Ryan, and knew it had only been six months since his death; surely not enough time had passed to have feelings for someone else. But she couldn't help it. The feelings were there despite any logic she tried to apply to it.

"Curt?" Erika answered, shyly providing the name she thought her friend was referring to.

"Wait, what? Curt? I thought his name was Blake?" Nicole asked with confusion. "Who's Curt?" Erika's energy shifted at the mention of Blake's name, and her smile momentarily dropped from her face. *Whoops.* Okay, now she felt like a grieving whore.

"Oh... Blake? He's... yeah, he's... interesting. Like, he's really honest, sometimes too honest, and he's genuine. I don't know. The guy totally has no filter. I'm not sure if it's a 'lost-in-translation' thing or a cultural thing, but he's inappropriate most of the time," Erika said, subconsciously shaking her head. "It's obvious my family wants to set me up with him because he comes from a big Eastern European family like ours, but I also think they are trying to squash some shit between our families or something. I don't know. It's not my shit. It makes me not want anything to do with him."

"I see. It's just the way you've been texting about Blake. I thought there was something there. It reminded me of how you used to tell me about Ry—" Nicole caught herself and backpedaled. "So, who's Curt?" she asked, changing the subject.

"Curt is... uh... just a friend. That I've made out here. He's another one of Cristian's friends, or he works with my family... something like that," Erika simply said, but again, a subtle smile betrayed her lips.

"Ahhh. Mmkay. I see," Nicole commented with a teasing, all-knowing smile; her tongue rested on the back of her molars. Well, I'm looking forward to meeting any and *all* of these gentlemen," she said, and then asked, "How about your cousin?"

"Oh my God! Cristian is totally *gay*!" Erika whispered, and both women laughed at the tension breaker. "I'm only laughing because it makes *so* much sense! I'm actually really sad for him because I know the only reason he's still 'closeted' is because of my traditional-ass Aunt Ana! You saw her!"

"Ahhh. Ya, she is scary as *fuck*. Definitely gives off Lady Tremaine vibes," Nicole agreed.

"As you may or may not know, gay people are still not really tolerated in much of Eastern Europe. Like, there are still massive anti-gay purges in Chechnya in recent history. It's fucking evil! Which now makes me feel bad for Cristian all over again. I do love him even though he's a total bitch to me and always has been."

"Yeah, yikes." Nicole winced at the Chechnyan fact. "That is super tough. I couldn't even imagine. Okay, I'll be a little nicer to him than I was planning on being."

"Yeah. So, he's pretending to date Blake's younger sister, Vittoria. The thing is, I can't tell if she is *aware* that she's his 'beard' or not. I don't know. But just watch out for her, okay? She's very lacquered and loud, as they say."

Erika continued downloading updates about her life and the people around Dragos Manor to Nicole. After the conversation had been flowing for a bit, she felt brave and seized her opportunity.

"So, funny story, *true story*. Um, this place is *super* haunted," Erika blurted out.

"Oh my God, I totally felt that the moment I got here! It feels like this one friend's house where I used to spend the night when I was eight. *I swore* I woke up one night and saw, like, a floating, *bloody head*. I'm pretty sure it was her grandma or something," Nicole finished dramatically, pausing for effect. "Also, the people in town told me this place is full of ghosts. Oh, and werewolves, for that matter! So, I was already expecting some news like this!" Nicole joked, half rolling her eyes.

"Um, yeah. I'm just giving you a heads up because there's a strong possibility you might see some..." Erika searched for the right words to convey the magnitude of the otherworldliness the spirits of Dragos Manor had brought to her consciousness and concept of reality. She landed on "...*pretty fucked up shit* during your stay here." A subtle look of terror fell over Nicole's face like a dark rain cloud, replacing her previously jovial expression. Erika realized she had scared her friend and clarified. "I'm sorry. I'm not trying to scare you. I don't know anything about werewolves, but I'm just trying to prepare you. I mean, I'm talking about *real ghosts*! I've seen them! I actually can't stop seeing them now, in fact. I mean, they really don't give a shit where they pop up. The good news is they don't seem to be out and about during the daytime. You might catch something funny out of the corner of your eye, like a small silver ripple, or kinda like when you stare at a light, and it leaves an impression burned into your retinas. It's funny; I've seen them here since I was a kid! I used to call them *spooky slivers*. But they sure do come in the evening. Recently, they have been rehearsing their 'haunting acts' for the tourist season. The first guests finally checked in today, so I expect we'll see some sort of haunting activity tonight. But again, please don't be scared of them. It's all just an act. They are harmless and typically very casual in front of our family. Sometimes a little too casual, actually," Erika said, then recounted a few recent encounters with the house spirits.

One encounter happened the other night when Erika was getting ready for bed. After brushing her teeth, she used the restroom before turning in for the night. Just as Erika sat on the toilet and was getting ready to relieve herself, she glanced up and noticed a female ghost sitting directly across from her in the bathroom. The female ghost appeared to be in her early to mid-twenties when she passed away from a very apparent bullet wound to the head. She stared at Erika with unblinking eyes. Uncomfortable with the sudden presence of this ghost during a moment of privacy, Erika hesitated, unable to relieve herself. The young female ghost wore a judgmental look on her transparent face, with one eyebrow sharply raised.

"Um... do you mind?" Erika asked.

"Yeah, I do! You disgust me," the ghost replied with repugnance.

Another ghostly encounter happened late one night just last week. Erika had gone downstairs to get some drinks for her room. She passed by two spirits she remembered seeing when she had inadvertently crashed their ghost party shortly after arriving at Dragos Manor. One of the ghosts was the portly man with the bullet hole in his head, and the other was the woman with the sword stabbed through her bosom whom he had been conversing with at the party. The two spirits seemed to be married, or at least had been married once long ago when they were alive, and they seemed to be engaged in an argument midway up the staircase.

"Really, Roger! The Dragos are good enough to host us, and all they ask in return is that we contribute to entertaining the hotel guests on occasion," the female ghost said.

"I'm fine with the arrangement, Estelle darling, despite the fact Sophia Dragos killed the pair of us, thus cursing us into this state of eternal damnation forever and ever on her estate, very nice property, mind you. Do you remember when we wanted to purchase this plot of land? But then the

Dragos family came and scooped it out from under us. All I'm saying is I would like a turn with clanging the chains about for once," the portly male ghost called Roger complained to his late wife. In turn, Estelle clutched the ghostly chains she was holding a little more preciously to her chest, making sure to move around the sword that was stabbed through her bosom.

"Darling, don't be passive-aggressive with that story just because Sophia's great-great-granddaughter stands there before you. It's not polite. You know very well the Dragos family spared us from suffering the great Influenza we had both contracted in the early part of 1920, which you and I were doomed to perish from. Also, we could *not afford this land* anyway on a Bookbinder's income. Now here..." At that, Estelle pulled the sword out from her chest and offered it to her ghostly husband, Roger. "Why don't you do something with my sword?" she suggested in feeble consolation.

"Keep moving, girl!" the ghost named Roger complained and pulled a translucent handkerchief out of his breast pocket, which he used to dab his ghostly sweat from his face. "You give off terrible heat. I only want to rehearse for a minute or two tonight, Estelle. I'm not looking forward to when we must do this in the coming week. The living always makes me so *damn* hot!"

"Dear!" Estella reprimanded her husband for his shocking language. Then Erika continued down the stairs, leaving the phantom couple to their negotiations about who would get to rattle the chains and who would do something with the sword.

"You're not kidding me, are you? It's like real ghosts?" Nicole asked in disbelief. "Where did they come from?"

"I'm told that most of them are deceased relatives or people my family once knew. I'm not sure how they all came to be concentrated here at my family's home, but the good news is they are all pretty mundane. You don't need to be scared of them."

"Sure! I totally believe you. It's just, maybe I could sleep in your room with you? Like I can totally sleep on the floor or something," Nicole suggested, still looking a little uneasy.

"It's just so crazy to think about!" Erika said, ignoring Nicole's request.

"Like, to actually try and wrap my head around." Erika had a look of wild excitement in her eyes as she pondered aloud to her friend. "Being a ghost that walks in the dimension of the living. What does that mean spiritually? That they do not want to *go on*? Or maybe they can't go on for some reason, like Roger said— 'Cursed in eternal damnation'?" Erika's face twisted up with wonder. "Like, what if something were to happen to me? What if I was to meet an untimely death that left my spirit feeling like it had been wronged out of this lifetime, and I was unable to advance on to whatever cycle of energy that our souls are meant to evolve into?" Erika's wild excitement and speech slowly faded away as she drifted into the velvet fuzziness of contemplation before arriving at the root of her questioning with almost childlike innocence and wonder. Then she vocalized her question aloud, "Would I haunt?"

Chapter Sixteen

The Meeting

As Erika and Nicole continued their stroll through the back gardens in the receding afternoon sunlight, signs of the evening began to creep into the summer sky from the east. On the other side of the property, a makeshift meeting of misfits gathered inside the garage of Dragos Manor, far off from any potential eavesdropping of hotel guests or spirits.

In attendance at this meeting were a group of the young werewolves of Nocturne who called themselves *the Killers*—Cristian, Beo, and his brother Malcolm Jr., River, and Loki, as well as the group's leader, Kessler David Vulpe. Marius and Ana Dragos were also invited, although neither were group members.

"Why is this whole ordeal taking so long?" Kessler Vulpe demanded. Loki Lupu nodded in tense agreement to Kessler's line of questioning. "Our families, in particular," Kessler said, gesturing to himself and Loki, "are very keen to know when this union is going to be finalized. We understand that István and Irene Farkas are coming here to Nocturne, and we all know they are expecting to arrive to the news that their son Blake is going to marry the Dragos female! We are all eager to put this one-hundred-plus-year-long feud behind us! The only reason Cristian was able to gain the Farkas family's trust in the first place was because he convinced them that Erika was available for their son and that she could give him offspring with unique gifts, such as the ones Marius possesses! I don't think they would have allowed their son and daughter to have traveled all the way out to the U.S. otherwise!"

Ana stood strong and stoic but visibly uncomfortable with the chosen meeting place—inside the garage next to Cristian's parked *Nova*. "You can tell your families that we are working on it," she responded in a rigid, authoritative tone. "After all, you cannot force the girl to fall in love with

Blake Farkas."

"Oh, OH, oh. What's love got to do... got to do with it?" sang Beo with his comedic timing. Cristian smiled, bit his lip, and turned his face away, unable to tolerate how cute Beo was sometimes.

"Now, just calm down, everyone. All you young pups are so tense. You need to learn to relax a bit more," came Marius's even voice. I know your families are all very anxious to resolve the bad blood; believe me, the Dragos are more eager than anyone."

"That's easy for you to say, Marius! You have been able to *live* in the old country for decades now! No one will harm you with your unusual abilities, Dragos or not!" Kessler called out. "Our families all migrated here to America over a century ago, seeking freedom to live how they wanted to, but nobody realized that meant not being able to return to our homeland again for fear of retaliation! *Make* her marry the Farkas wolf already!" Loki murmured audible support for his leader's words.

"My point is," Marius continued, ignoring the comment. "Times are different. Erika *will* be the head of the Dragos' estate and family once my mother moves on to join the spirits of the rest of our family. No disrespect, Mamă; I wish you many healthy years to come," Marius said affectionately to Ana. "If Erika is to ever be with Blake Farkas in a romantic capacity, it will be her decision alone. She needs to *choose* him, and the only way for that to happen is for us to be patient, release our attempt to control something that we cannot, and let come what may. The good news is they do seem to have an undeniable connection. You've all seen them interact. I think they understand each other, and that is a good thing. That will make a very strong foundation for our households to build on top of, but only if *they* choose it. Not us."

"We don't care *how* it happens, so long as it happens. The Sturgeon Moon party is in two weeks. The Farkas family will be here for that. All our families will be here. This bullshit feud needs to end," Kessler said in a menacing tone.

"Speaking for the American werewolves, we don't have any vested interest in traveling to Romania or Hungary or wherever," Malcolm Jr. said, jumping into the conversation. "But my father says we do have an interest as a species in encouraging those wolves with intra-species conflict to resolve it. The Dragos and Farkas feud has gone on for way too long. Territoriality is one thing, but a feud that has lasted this long is almost embarrassing for all of us."

"Your father is a wise werewolf, Malcolm Jr., and I agree with him about seeking a resolution, but there has to be another way."

"Cristian assured us this would be resolved very soon," Loki quietly added.

"*Cristian* should *not* be making promises for others. For one thing, striving to control another is *not* something anyone should desire to possess. To make a finer point, *none* of these decisions are his." Marius countered, turning a stern gaze in his nephew's direction. Cristian sat casually tipped back in a wooden chair beside an old, rickety table near a cluttered workbench. "Nevertheless, we hear your concerns and understand that everyone will be here for the party in two weeks. We appreciate everybody's eagerness for a resolution, but you should all be prepared that *no such announcement of any union between Erika and Blake will be made.*" The Killers started shifting around restlessly and murmuring words of protest to Marius' statement until Cristian raised his voice loudly over the commotion.

"Let's not get ahead of ourselves, everyone!" he called out. Everyone in the garage turned and looked in his direction. "We keep getting overwhelmed by the big picture, thinking we need to solve all our problems at once. We need to break it down. Compartmentalize. Take it day by day. Erika's here. She's single. She knows about the family business—well, the ghost part anyway. Just getting all of *that* to happen was hard enough." Cristian scoffed. This last statement seemed to catch his uncle's attention, as Marius opened his mouth as if to say something, but Cristian ignored him and continued. "Now, the next step is simple; we need to tell her about her roots and what *she is*," Cristian said. "As always, my beloved Bunica, Uncle Marius, I respect you both, and it's your decision how to handle this task. Please feel free to proceed however you wish, but know... *I will* see to it that she gets a reality check if you don't," Cristian stated simply with subtle threatening undertones. Suddenly, he tipped his chair forward so quickly the front legs hit the ground with a loud *clap* on the floor. Everyone jumped. "Like ripping off a Band-Aid," he said with a mischievous smile.

The Killers seemed taken in by Cristian's confidence and promise to drive the romance story plot forward between Blake and Erika. Kessler looked

117

proud and relieved to have a Dragos insider like Cristian to help ensure things moved along as expected. Cristian suspected that if the decision were left up to Daniela's ghost and Marius, they would allow a rare recessive werewolf, like Erika, to marry some human. Then, they would miss the opportunity to create remarkable Lycan offspring—like Cristian's father and Uncle Marius.

Marius stared at his nephew's face and saw that Cristian was serious about breaking the news to Erika if neither he nor his mother got the job done, and got it done soon. He also sensed something else about his nephew. Something that wasn't sitting quite right with him. Cristian's comment, *'Just getting all of that to happen was hard enough'* Marius made a mental note that he would speak to Cristian about this remark once the meeting had concluded.

"My grandson is right," Ana said. "We need to tell Erika about the Lycanthropy gene. It is my fault that she does not yet know of her werewolf family lineage. My late sister-in-law thought it would be best to break the news slowly so as not to frighten the girl, but I fear too much time has passed. The onus is on me and me alone. The time is nigh, and the older generation of Farkas will be arriving in town soon. I have not been forceful enough and have allowed various distractions to prolong the inevitable. I will get her alone as soon as possible, and I will tell her," Ana stated resolutely.

"Alright then. I see no need to belabor the point," Kessler said, his demeanor lightened. I believe it is happy hour. Who wants to go grab a drink with me?" With that, the crowd began to vacate the garage individually to avoid drawing attention. Marius was one of the last to leave. He briefly glanced back at his nephew as he strode toward the exit, heaved the heavy door open, and walked out. Cristian and Beo were now alone in the garage.

"You seem pretty confident that this is all going to end well," Beo said, walking over to Cristian, who finally rose out of his chair.

"Yes, well, fake it till you make it, right?" he snickered, giving Beo warm bedroom eyes.

"Such a 'Cristian' thing to say," Beo said, wearing a look of love with undertones of worry on his face. Still, Beo's concern regarding his lover's involvement in werewolf politics did not stop him from moving closer to Cristian. The pair nonchalantly interwove their fingers together as Beo voiced his fears aloud. "I'm worried about you. Worried you are making promises on something you can't deliver to Kessler and the other families."

"You underestimate me," Cristian said and planted his mouth, surrounded by his five o'clock shadow on Beo's luscious, soft lips. Cristian knew his boyfriend was worried that he might somehow get hurt if things did not go as he had promised with Blake and Erika's union, but this did not worry Cristian. He only felt there was one path forward; it was success or nothing.

The garage door opened again, and the kissing pair sprung away from each other so quickly they looked like two snakes striking in opposite directions in the recesses of the garage. Marius stood quietly in the doorway, clearly noticing he had interrupted something. Beo lurched forward and walked right past Marius and out through the garage door without saying a word. Cristian's face wore a look of pain, knowing his uncle had most likely seen something, but he was unsure how much. His heart pounded, burning with shame and hatred for himself inside of his chest. Marius walked in and stood next to his nephew.

"I apologize. I did not mean to burst in on you. I only wanted to speak with you and was waiting for everyone else to leave." Cristian's eyes stung with tears that he wiped, sniffed, and tried to blink away, which only further irritated his eyes. He couldn't find the words that would fit past the lump in his throat. Marius continued, "You know, there is great importance in a reptile who sheds his old skin, for the old skin no longer serves him, so he releases it. The snake is not sad to lose his former self, nor is he surprised by the new life he encounters once he has shed the old one. This is how he grew and became who he was always meant to be."

"Thank you, Uncle. What is it you wish to speak to me about?" Cristian asked, thinking he understood what Marius was trying to say but also desperately wanting to change the subject as quickly as possible.

Marius raised his hand and brought it to rest upon his nephew's shoulder, "I want you to know that I love you no matter what," Marius assured while looking Cristian in the eyes. Cristian was thankful when Marius moved on. "The reason I want to speak to you is because of something you said during the meeting just now with the ah... *Killers*. By the way, I wish you all would pick a better name, but I remember being young once, I suppose. Decision-making wasn't a strong suit.

My question to you is—When you were talking about Erika arriving at Dragos Manor, her being single, and your methods for revealing the house's ghosts to her, you also said, 'Getting all of that to happen was hard enough.' What did you mean by that? I know you were responsible for one of those things; you showed her the ghosts, but I must ask—was there any deeper meaning behind that remark?

Craaap, Cristian thought to himself but said aloud to his uncle, "Oh, yeah, I just meant that... I mean, none of us knew if she would ever decide to come back! I mean, it was pretty clear she didn't want anything to do with us or this place for a long time. Like seven years, eight years, something like that."

"But Erika might never have come back at all had she married—had her fiancé not died, that is," Marius reminded his nephew. The theatrics of the pained look that overcame Cristian's face as he sucked air in through his teeth and winced, some might have said, was over the top.

"Yeah, I know it's just... just... Terri... horri... just... ahhhh... really not... not... good," Cristian stammered as he barely managed to get the words out. "Believe me, Uncle, nobody more than I wishes those were not the circumstances that led Erika back, but she's here now, and I suppose you are right; we all need to wait and see what happens," he said with an ever so subtle gulp. Marius studied his nephew's face for a moment longer but said nothing further.

Chapter Seventeen

The Talk

Dusk lay its gentle cloak of soft, eye-pleasing oranges and yellows upon the western horizon far beyond Dragos Manor as Erika and Nicole finished their stroll in the back gardens. The pair headed toward the outdoor patio attached to the hotel lounge, where happy hour would be hosted during the guest season, so long as the weather was agreeable, such as that night. The two friends followed a dirt path framed by various flowers, small slate stones, and decorative solar lights that stood about ankle-high. The path led them around the west end of the house toward the front patio.

Most of the year, the Dragos family would simply jump behind the bar and fix their own drinks for themselves, but now that guest season was upon them, they had brought a young bartender named Sam onto their staff. This was his third season working for Dragos Manor. By this point in the evening, the young bartender was busy at work, pouring different liquids into jiggers, muddling various herbs, or grating an assortment of spices, mixing all needed components into a shaker with the precision of an alchemist. He then rhythmically shook and poured beautifully colored drinks into glassware of all shapes and sizes. He added the final touch by putting the perfect garnish on each glass before loading them all onto a tray and personally delivering them to tables on the outdoor patio.

During this time of year, when the weather was still nice enough, the most direct route from the interior lounge to the outdoor patio was through the large retractable glass wall—that operated similarly to a dock door—located on the southwest end of Dragos Manor. The patio floor was made of charcoal gray slate stone tiles that elegantly transitioned into deep mahogany wooden beams inside the hotel's interior lounge.

Despite the cooler temperatures of the late August evening, the patio provided a pleasant ambiance with heat lamps blazing, making the space quite comfortable and toasty. Soft cello and violin music played over speakers mounted on either side of the retracted wall. Solar curtain lights were draped down the parameter fence that encircled the entirety of the patio, bathing the area in a pale, warm glow.

A group of elderly guests sat merrily around small tables, sipping their cocktails, taking in the scenery of the expansive front lawns surrounded by dense forest and mountains in the distance. It was magic hour, and this time of day was particularly breathtaking with the remnants of the receding sunlight to the west and the first whispers of stars overhead. A few other guests had chosen to sit in chairs near one of the fireplaces inside the lounge and gaze out through the retracted glass wall to enjoy the cool summer evening from the comfort of an indoor setting.

"Oh my God! It's so beautiful out here! I can definitely see why you wanted to come back," Nicole said in awe as she and Erika emerged from around the side of the house and beheld the peaceful scene before them.

"The killer thing about this place is that it happens to have a fantastic bar," Erika said, then held out her elbow to Nicole. "Shall we retire to happy hour then?" Fortunately, Nicole was on the same page.

"Why yes, indubalet... indubitably. That sounds lovely," she answered with a mock air of sophistication as she took Erika's proffered arm. The two women headed toward the nearby gate leading inside the garden patio.

As it turned out, the Hungarian visitors, Blake, Vittoria, and Adrian, all had the same idea about happy hour. The siblings and their strange friend sat conversing at one of the patio tables with drinks in front of them. Blake and Erika locked eyes from a distance as she approached with Nicole beside her. He nodded his chin toward her with a subtle smile, making his entire face and eyes light up and soften at once.

"Whoa! Check out that tall glass of sex juice," Nicole whispered loudly to Erika, not even attempting to hold back her drool.

"Which one?" Erika asked.

"The one who's looking right at you!"

"Oh. You think he's attractive?" Erika asked, almost a little surprised.

"Ahh, duh!"

"That would be Blake, and that's his sister Vittoria, and that other guy there is their friend Adrian," Erika explained without pointing. Of course, she logically knew Blake was very attractive, but for whatever reason, she tended to overlook his sex appeal, which Nicole was visibly responding to. Maybe it was because Erika was familiar with his personality that made her feel so unenthusiastic toward him. Feeling guilty, she reminded herself yet again that she should ease up on her outlook toward Blake. After all, he had been nothing but sweet to her, even if he chronically suffered from foot-in-mouth syndrome.

"Uumm, that girl does not look very friendly," Nicole commented apprehensively.

"Yeah, be careful around her. I get the sense she doesn't like me very much, even though she pretends to," Erika replied in a low voice.

Blake stood up as the women approached, while Vittoria and Adrian remained seated. Vittoria looked as dismissive and unimpressed as ever, and Adrian looked as bewildered as ever.

"Good evening, Erika. You look nice," Blake said with a smile as soon as she was in earshot.

Nice... Not a bad start, Erika thought to herself.

"You are so beautiful. Am glad to see you have more fat on you by now," Blake said, holding his hands up in a substantiated way.

"Oh my God," Nicole said in disbelief. "Did he just say that?"

"Steady big brother," Vittoria drawled disinterestedly. Adrian turned to Vittoria and laughed at Blake's ignorance in conversing with the fairer sex.

"Ladies' man," Adrian said with a snort.

"What did I say? I mean, she looks nice! When I first met her, someone died, not going to say who, but she were very skinny. Probably because she was sad. I don ever want her to be sad. So, I am trying to say that I think she looks much happier and healthier by this time," Blake finished his well-meaning but poorly-delivered compliment with a broad smile.

"Ookay," Nicole said to Erika. "I see what you mean about that foot-in-mouth thing."

"Is this you friend?" Blake asked, gesturing to Nicole, who offered her hand. Blake took it and introduced himself with his surname first—as is customary in Hungary.

"Good day. Am Farkas, Blake. Nice to meet you," he said.

"Blake, Vittoria, Adrian, this is my friend, Nicole, from out west. She surprised me today with a visit," Erika explained.

"Yeah! A surprise visit to see the birthday girl! Whooo!" Nicole added and then playfully nudged Erika.

"What?" Blake turned to Erika with an expression of shock. "Is your birthday?"

"No," Erika cleared her throat. "In two weeks." Then she braced herself for his response and realized she often did this when conversing with him.

"Am so happy am here, and I get to party you. Party? Party?!" Blake's face twisted up into a question as the word confused him. "Is that the right word?" he asked.

"Celebrate," Vittoria offered while sipping her drink.

"Celebrate! Yes. That is what I want to do. I want to celebrate you," came Blake's surprisingly sweet response. Then he followed it up with a victorious fist pump as he exclaimed, "Party!" in his thick Hungarian accent.

"Did someone say party?"

The group turned to see Kessler approaching, followed by the Killers—minus Cristian and Beo. Ana trailed behind them. Immediately, Erika noticed her grandaunt wore a strained expression on her face as Ana set her sights directly on her.

Uh oh, that's a look that says she needs to speak to me about something important, Erika mused.

"Erika, my dear, would you kindly come with me? I need to speak to you about something important," Ana said almost verbatim to Erika's thoughts.

I got it right. Erika smiled and excused herself from the group and followed her grandaunt as they headed toward the inside lounge.

As Ana and Erika walked away, Erika heard Kessler striking up a conversation with the Hungarian visitors about the party that would be happening there in a couple of weeks. Erika wished she could have stayed and been a part of that discussion, but she sighed quietly to herself as she followed her grandaunt through the retracted glass wall into the lounge.

Ana scanned the room for a place where the two could speak privately. She settled on a service closet near the bar.

"This way, Erika. Kindly follow me if you would, dear. I need to speak to you immediately about something very serious. Something we've been meaning to tell you," Ana sighed, "for nearly all your life." Ana led Erika into the service closet, shutting the door behind them. Once inside, she spun around and faced her grandniece. Erika looked so much like her late mother. Ana began to feel light-headed with the gravity of the situation weighing down upon her. Erika stood amid cleaning supplies, extra light bulbs, propane tanks, and a ladder and stared blankly at her grandaunt, visibly bracing herself for what sounded like a very intense conversation.

"It's okay. I can take it. Whatever you have to tell me, you should just say it," Erika encouraged with matter-of-factness. Ana closed her eyes and nodded firmly. She took a deep breath and was about to speak when she was interrupted by a knock at the closet door. Ana exhaled in exasperation as she immediately lost track of her words.

"Give us a few minutes, please!" she called out forcefully, but the door to the service closet opened anyway. It was Sam, the Dragos bartender.

"Forgive the intrusion, Mrs. Dragos, but the young men are... ahh... fighting on the patio. It's disrupting the other guests."

"Oh, for *fuc*—God's sake!" Ana said, almost swearing, then she and Erika hurried out of the service closet to see what was happening.

Night had fallen. It was quite dark outside on the patio with the New Moon in the sky that night. A table and a few chairs had been knocked over. Blake and Kessler were wrestling on the ground, both deadlocked in the other's grip.

Loki, River, Malcolm Jr., Vittoria, Adrian, and Nicole all watched the fight with varying degrees of interest as it unfolded before them. A group of elderly, silver-haired hotel guests were also spectators to the commotion, albeit from a safe distance at a nearby patio table. Most wore expressions of shock and horror on their faces, apart from one elderly woman called Mrs. Johnson, who had a feisty personality. She was one of Dragos Manor's longest-running patrons. She and her family had been coming there every fall since the 1970s. By this time, the long-widowed Mrs. Johnson wore an amused and mischievous smile as she eyed the two strong young men wrestling on the ground.

"What happened?!" Erika asked with alarm as she and Ana hurried up to the scene.

"Yes, what happened," Ana demanded with visible anger.

"Tear his shirt off!" Mrs. Johnson yelled with a raspy cackle. Vittoria smiled at the old woman with amusement before explaining to Ana how the fight had started.

"The dumb, Marlon Brando-looking one mentioned he was planning to bring some attractive *human females* with him to the party in two weeks... apparently, that is his *kink*," Vittoria recounted, giving her take on the matter.

"Human females? Kink? What?" Nicole questioned aloud to the group. Everybody ignored her, and Vittoria went on.

"My brother did not like that because, as we all know, this subject is a major source of contention amongst our kind... shall we say, romantically fraternizing with people is not done where we come from. Then my brother said, 'blah, blah, blah... people knowing about you is just asking for silver.' Then the dumb-looking one said a bunch of unintelligible words and called us 'show dogs,' and then I think he even called my brother *a Frenchie* or *a Poodle*, something like that, but I can't be sure; it was all quite hilarious," Vittoria explained with amusement. "Then Blake said 'yada, yada, yada... I would rather be a show dog than be a people lover, people fucker? I can't fully remember, then my brother said..." Vittoria cleared her throat and did her best impression of Blake's deep voice. "'I don like you people fucker face; I don like you people fucker behavior; And I don like *you*, People Fucker!' To which the *People Fucker* said, 'Dude, you can go fuck your...'"

The last words that came from Vittoria's lips made everyone, including Mrs. Johnson, gasp as they pertained to the fornication and inbreeding that has the potential to occur in purebreds and show dogs.

"Then after that, Blake simply excused himself to me and little mouse-face over there," Vittoria said, pointing to Nicole, whose eyes lit up overbright as she frowned at the comment. "And now the two are tangled up just as you see them in this very fucking moment."

"Rip his *people fucker* head off, Blake!" Adrian encouraged, poised to jump into the fight. "We will fuck you up, *People Fucker*!" he growled to Kessler.

"I dare you to try," Loki said in a low, dangerous snarl. Tensions were mounting.

"Can someone please tell me what this is all about in plain English?" Erika asked, completely perplexed. "What does 'People Fucker' mean?"

"Kessler!" Ana sharply reprimanded while ignoring Erika's question. "You are interfering with the Dragos family business and making an ass of yourself in front of our honored guests! You know I will not tolerate this!" she said firmly. Blake and Kessler were eye to eye. Kessler said nothing to Ana's chastising of him but continued to glare at Blake through gritted teeth. It was Blake who responded.

"Am sorry, Ana," he said, taking the higher road as he finally released Kessler. Adrian lurched forward in anticipation but eased back when he saw the fight was relenting. Blake and Kessler stood up and brushed themselves off.

"This ends right now!" Ana ordered sternly to the pair, then rounded hard on Kessler. "What do you think you are doing?! Be sure I will speak to your grandmother and mother about this." Ana was so angry she forgot all about the important conversation she had been trying to have with her grandniece.

"Never a dull moment around Dragos Manor!" Mrs. Johnson cackled. "Too bad their shirts didn't get torn off!"

Chapter Eighteen

Losing It

Night of the Sturgeon Moon

Black linens stretched across long buffet tables with steaming chafing dishes full of delicious foods. The string quartet softly played a musical composition, Haydn's String Quartet in F Minor, up in the orchestral balcony. The grand ballroom was abuzz with wait staff and caterers, all of whom were busy making sure arrangements were set just right for the end of the summer gala at Dragos Manor, which was moments away from commencing.

Groundskeeper Tom, who sported an old suit with only minor moth nibbles, was wrestling to draw the large, heavy drapes shut on the massive window on the grand ballroom's east-facing wall. Outside, the rain had been falling steadily for most of that day. Nighttime loomed hungrily on the horizon, poised to swoop down and swallow up the final morsels of daylight. This would make room for the magnificent full Sturgeon Moon that would be the centerpiece for that evening's festivities.

Ana spun around anxiously as she searched through the crowd for her grandniece. The elderly Dragos Matriarch wore a magnificent black sequin dress with sheer sleeves and a cape that flowed off her back and connected onto her sleeves like giant bat wings. The dress featured soft white feather accents from mid-waist down to the floor and sparsely placed on the sheer cape.

"I cannot believe you have not told her yet, Ana!" came the disembodied voice of Daniela Dragos's ghost. A small sliver of silver mist briefly rippled through the air near Ana's face before disappearing again as the ghost chastised her sister-in-law.

"Believe me, I have attempted a few times now, Daniela!" Ana fired back.

"We keep getting interrupted. There have been so many distractions between guest season starting and planning this event. You know that hosting all our Lycan neighbors is always a large undertaking," she explained defensively. "Not to mention, hosting the Farkas family here tonight!"

"I can appreciate how busy you are, dear sister, but the time is nigh, and it simply must be done. Frankly, I don't care how you accomplish it at this late stage."

"Daniela, please. We wouldn't even be in this mess had you allowed us to tell her immediately upon her arrival. Not to mention, oh, I don't know... told her *at any point during her life!*" Ana said with mounting frustration, which she quickly got under control. "But I did as you asked. I have always done what you asked. And now, please, all I ask in return is that you cut me some slack. I am the one who must face her. Not you!"

"That's because I don't have a face, Ana!"

"Oh, please. You are just a little pale, that's all!"

After a moment, Ana finally spotted Erika walking down the staircase with that little annoying friend at her side. Both younger women wore black cocktail dresses, and Nicole wore a white fedora atop her head. *Why did that little pest have to choose now to visit?* Ana wondered in exasperation. It didn't matter. Ana Dragos would not allow any more hiccups or roadblocks to deter her efforts to speak with her grandniece this time.

"There she is. I'm going to speak with her now. I implore you, please don't follow us. I need you to give me some space to do this," Ana requested of her invisible sister-in-law.

"Very well. I won't follow you. But hurry and do it now," Daniela's disembodied voice demanded.

The living Dragos Matriarch began making her way toward Erika as she cursed herself inwardly for allowing the entire past week—and the entire summer, for that matter—to slip by without the important conversation taking place. Ana had been so preoccupied with planning the annual Sturgeon Moon Gala that family, friends, neighbors, and hotel guests all looked forward to attending every August. This year in particular, the gala was even more significant because—as Ana had mentioned—the Farkas family, Blake, Vittoria, and their parents, would be among those in attendance.

The time is nigh. Ana heard Daniela's voice replaying in her head as she weaved her way through the increasing crowd toward Erika. She only paused occasionally to give a quick smile or "hello" to new arrivals, but Ana was a Lycan on a mission. She quickly made excuses to everyone she encountered, citing the need to attend to a pressing matter.

Erika and Nicole followed an elderly woman wearing too much sweet-smelling perfume into the grand ballroom. As Erika turned to whisper something to her friend, she noticed her grandaunt approaching, cutting through the crowd like a shark. Ana wore a look of determination on her wizened face. *Oh no, what now?* Erika wondered. The week leading up to the party had been so chaotic and flown by so quickly with all the preparations that had to be made, and every day seemed packed with things to do, tasks to complete, and arrangements to be made.

Glancing around the ballroom, Erika spotted Curt, who looked very handsome. He wore a tan suit, a black dress shirt, and no tie. He was waiting for a drink from a pop-up bar set up for the party in the grand ballroom.

"See that tall blond guy standing by the bar? That's Curt."

"Yowzah. *That's* Curt? I see what you're saying! Ooh la la, I didn't realize there were so many hot guys in Nocturne. Maybe I should consider moving out here!" Nicole said with a click of her teeth.

"Hey, I need to speak to my aunt for a moment. Why don't you introduce yourself to him, and I'll catch up with you both when I'm done," Erika suggested.

"You don't need to ask me twice! No sweat! Hopefully, you won't have to work all night and can actually enjoy your own party, birthday girl," Nicole said, flashing her friend a quick smile before turning, setting her sights on Curt, and making her way toward him in a predacious manner. She looked like a lioness stalking an Antelope or Ibex near a watering hole.

"There you are," Ana said almost breathlessly. "I need to—"

"You need to speak with me. I know. Should we go somewhere?" Erika suggested with mild exasperation, beating her grandaunt to the point.

"Yes, thank you, dear," Ana responded with a look of relief. "Let's go somewhere where we won't be interrupted," she suggested, then led Erika out of the grand ballroom and toward the conservatory next door, which was sure to be empty.

The conservatory was quite chilly, slightly damp, and laden with a wide array of plants, but most importantly, it was completely free of distractions. The vegetation scattered throughout the space benefited from UV exposure during the daytime from the high domed glass ceiling and many large windows in the room. Because of this, however, the conservatory had very poor insulation, leaving it to be either the hottest or coldest room in Dragos Manor, depending on the time of day or season.

Ana eased the doors shut behind them, then turned with some apprehension toward Erika, who was already beginning to softly shiver as she waited for whatever conversation Ana had so desperately wanted to have with her.

Muffled sound filtered in through the wall from the ballroom next door, but other than that, the room was almost completely quiet. Ana gestured to a musty, old, antique chaise lounge, and they both walked over and sat on the cold, stiff fabric.

"Erika, you'll have to forgive me in advance for the brevity of this conversation we are about to have. Even though other family members played a part in keeping certain details—" Ana paused, took a breath, and then restarted. "Regardless of anything you may have been told—" She faltered again. "After all, it is my responsibility and my responsibility alone that this conversation has not occurred yet." Ana stopped again and clicked her tongue against her teeth in apparent frustration. "I'm sorry, dear. I'm just getting so tongue-tied. I believe you would agree that we both would prefer to get back to tonight's event, so I will just come right out and say what I have to say. That alright with you, dear?"

"Yes, Aunt Ana. I agree that would be for the best," Erika said, trying to subdue the dread she could feel creeping onto her face. Then Ana finally came out with it.

"Erika, our family, *your family*, is a Lycanthrope family. There I said it!" Ana blurted out all too abruptly. They both stared at one another for a moment; then Ana giggled quietly, and Erika wasn't sure why. She wasn't even fully clear on what the confession meant. "Oh, my goodness," Ana chortled. "You don't know what a relief it is just to get those words out. Pheew," she said, sounding almost drunken with relief. For a moment, Erika did, in fact, question if her longtime sober grandaunt was indeed intoxicated, but knew it was highly improbable for a woman of probably seventy-plus years of never touching *the drink* to start now. Ana composed herself and continued. "I'm sure you'll have questions, but I've been trying to tell you about this information for so, so long," she said, seemingly giddy with relief. Erika, however, only sat wearing a look of confusion on her face. Ana's pleased expression waned into a more serious one as she offered, "Werewolves, dear."

"Werewolves?" Erika repeated, wanting to make sure she had heard Ana correctly. *Ooohh boy,* she thought to herself. Of course, she did not want to treat the elderly woman in any sort of condescending way. After all, her grandaunt had remained in peak physical condition for so long that it was only a matter of time before something began to slip, and it now seemed apparent that it was her mental health was deteriorating.

"That's right," Ana said encouragingly. "I'm sure you must have a thousand questions, but first, let me explain the basics. Your grandmother, your mother, Cristian, and Marius are all *transmogrify dominant* or 'changing' werewolves. You and I are 'unchanging,' or *transmogrify recessive* werewolves, which are very rare, but we are still werewolves, nonetheless. It's called *transmogrify recessive* werewolfism when one is born from a long lineage of Lycanthropy, but we do not have the ability to transform. Some think that *transmogrify recessive* werewolfism occurs as a result of werewolves procreating with humans, as both my birth father and your father were. *Humans.* But I do believe it can also happen sometimes with *transmogrify dominant* werewolf couples as well.

Furthermore, Blake and his sister are also *transmogrify dominant* werewolves; in fact, many of the guests attending the party tonight are *transmogrify dominant* werewolves. Oh dear, we are short on time, and there is so much to explain. You must understand, Erika, I have been a proponent of telling you all this information... well, for most of your life, in fact! But your grandma Daniela, oh, she's here too, by the way! Her spirit is, at least. And she can't wait to visit with you." Ana was all over the place, rapid-firing revelations. "Your grandma did not want any of us to tell you because it was your mother's wish. You must understand she thought she was protecting you. Personally, I always thought keeping something like this from you would only do more harm than good. I was just talking to Daniela about it the other day. Anyway, it's done now, and there you have it," Ana concluded, but then apparently remembered another matter.

"Oh, one more thing. I should also warn you about a little announcement I must make tonight. You see, I need to say something to the crowd tonight, and I don't want it to catch you off guard. Really, I did not mean for the *whole* summer to go by. I just don't know how it happened, but we need to win over the Farkas family tonight. The hotel is in... well, we're in trouble, Erika. Financial trouble. The Farkas family is very well off, and I... well, all of us were hoping that..." Ana seemed to be backing herself into a difficult subject. "We just need your help to save our family home." The Dragos Matriarch had tears in her eyes now. This surprised Erika, and she leaned in to comfort her grandaunt, but Ana raised a hand and blocked the affectionate gesture, shaking her head. "No, we don't need to get emotional right now. After all, we do have a room full of guests next door. I'm only hoping that any questions you have are ones you can ask quickly?"

"Dear aunt. I understand everything you have told me," Erika replied with pity and compassion for her elderly grandaunt. Erika noted that she would need to get Marius and Cristian involved, get them alone to speak with them, and tell them about all this. They would have to make decisions together as a family, as well as get Ana some medical help to gauge how far gone she may already be. This was probably the onset of Dementia or Alzheimer's, definitely an issue with her cognitive faculties. "I guess I do have one question; why didn't you tell me the hotel was in financial trouble? I mean, I've been wondering how we could stay afloat with such a short season and with so few guests."

"Oh, my dear, you know these things just happen. Times change, interests change. The hotel isn't as popular as it once was," Ana explained. "It's our hope that an influx of funding, maybe from the Farkas family, could help right the ship, so to speak. So please understand that I may need to say something tonight that is a tiny embellishment of the truth," Ana said as she held her fingers up an inch apart.

"I think I understand what you've been trying to tell me about Blake and his family now, Aunt Ana. I want you to know I'm *happy* to help however I can." Ana looked so overwhelmed with gratitude toward her grandniece.

"So, no questions about the werewolf aspect of this conversation then? Does that mean... oh gracious. Does that mean you knew about us then, did you? Did Cristian tell you?" Ana asked with mild bewilderment.

"No, Aunt Ana, he didn't tell me. I've known all along," Erika said with a twinkle in her eye.

"Well, there you have it! All this worry for nothing! I can't believe you've known! Wait until your grandmother hears about this!" Ana laughed, putting a hand atop her head as she chuckled about how silly this ordeal had been. "We can discuss this matter further after the party if you like. There is so much we need to catch up on! Oh, and your grandma will also want to speak with you about everything!" Ana stood up, and Erika followed suit.

Erika realized she felt closer to her grandaunt somehow, even though the bond she felt at that moment was forged under the pretense of a delusion. She briefly wondered if playing along with the story would cause Ana any harm. Hopefully, humoring her aging grandaunt was ok for tonight, but Erika recognized it might not be a good thing to entertain long-term. A medical professional should be able to advise appropriately once the family engaged someone. Still, the whole ordeal seemed almost bittersweet. While she hated the thought of her family member's decline, Erika had to admit she was very impressed by Ana's creativity. Her grandaunt had always been such a serious woman that Erika was surprised that a mental decline could yield such a wonderful imagination. And while Ana being adamant that Daniela was still alive wasn't too farfetched, especially living in a house *full* of spirits, thinking their entire family were werewolves was very far-out indeed.

Just as Erika and Ana were about to exit the conservatory, a small sliver of silver mist rippled momentarily through the air before disappearing again.

"Oh! A spooky sliver!" Erika exclaimed.

"A spooky what?" Ana questioned, then glared at the spot they had just seen the apparition.

"That's what I call the ghost slivers that sometimes appear in the air. It's nothing," Erika replied offhandedly. But Ana's face looked unamused as she responded.

"I see. Erika, why don't you head back to the party? I just realized there is something I need to deal with here, dear."

"Okay, are you sure? Is there anything I can help you with?"

"No, no, not at all, dear. It's just an annoying little task. You go on ahead and have a good time. I will see you later."

"Okay, sounds good, Aunt Ana," Erika said, then opened the door and exited the conservatory, heading off to find Nicole and Curt.

Ana leaned forward and slowly closed the door behind Erika.

"You can come out now, Daniela," Ana said dryly out into the room.

"Annoying?" Daniela questioned as she appeared.

"It is annoying! I asked you to give us some space! The task was stressful enough without having you judging and critiquing me on the invisible sidelines!"

"On the contrary, dear sister, I thought it all went rather well! Much better than I had expected, in fact. I wonder how Erika found out about us. The sweet child didn't seem shocked at all, did she?"

"She did not. I agree; I'm quite pleased with how well that went. I only wish I could occasionally have a private conversation around here without someone listening in. Now, if you'll excuse me, Daniela, we have a party to host."

Chapter Nineteen

Fang Hang

The grand ballroom was buzzing with conversations from the increasing number of partygoers, and more were still arriving every minute. A faint chill ran down Erika's spine as she recalled the night she had seen a party very similar to this one, except all the attendees at that party were dead. She shook off the chill as she noticed Cristian and Vittoria standing at a nearby table, holding some plates of food. Vittoria reached over and attempted to wipe something from his chin, but he turned away; his body language not seeming to convey any sort of intimacy toward her. Erika walked over to say hello to the pair.

"Well, well, look at what we have here," Vittoria drawled, looking Erika up and down. "Don't you look nice? Just sweet enough but with a tinge of heartbreaker around the edges."

"Thanks. You look nice too, Vittoria," Erika said flatly, ignoring her snarky remark. Vittoria wore a form-fitted red dress. Her hand, featuring red nail polish, rested on her hip as she reached into her mouth with the other hand, then extracted an elastic strand of pink bubblegum and began spinning it around her index finger.

"Good evening, all you gorgeous folk!" Beo said smoothly as he approached the group, looking quite fine in his black suave, plain-weave two-piece Hackett suit, with brown leather dress shoes and no socks. Cristian lit up at the sight of Beo but suddenly changed as he quickly put his arms around Vittoria. Cristian began kissing her vigorously on the cheeks while Vittoria giggled with delight. Erika found this transition to be quite jarring and turned to see what caused this abrupt change in her cousin's demeanor. As she had suspected, it was because Ana was approaching.

"Is everyone having a good time?" her grandaunt asked, beaming with pride at how the evening was shaping up thus far. Beo started to respond, but Vittoria cut him off. Erika noted that this was done almost competitively.

"Anastacia, you are such a gracious hostess. We're having a fabulous time. You have been so wonderful to lodge my brother and me in your fine home," Vittoria said with sweet venom dripping from her teeth, which flashed through her bright red smile.

"Well, you and your family are the guests of honor, so our family feels gratitude over your presence here tonight and always. Again, I do apologize for that little incident with Kessler a couple of weeks ago. You know how these young pups can be! I spoke with his grandmother, and he will be skipping the party tonight, so you need not worry about any more trouble from him! Hopefully, Blake was not too inconvenienced?"

"Not at all," Vittoria said, still smiling.

"Also, I must say, you two look very smart together!" Ana said, reaching out and smoothing down Cristian's suit. Vittoria also took this cue as an opportunity to fix Cristian's hair, then kissed him on his cheek, leaving a bright red lipstick mark behind. The two women laughed and began to increase their grooming of Cristian, who quickly grew irritated with the attention. He winced and gave an accommodating yet phony laugh as he squirmed uncomfortably out of their grips.

"That's so... sweet..." Cristian's voice was high-pitched as it trailed off, and then he glanced around nervously for a way out. "But have to... Beo! Um, would mind uh... I just have to go... away," he said, grabbing Beo by his jacket sleeve. The two headed off toward the restrooms.

"I don't like that creature," Ana muttered darkly under her breath as she watched them walk away. This comment caught Erika sharply off guard. *Creature?! Oh my God, did she just say that?* Erika thought to herself as she stared at her grandaunt in disbelief. *Oh no! Is Ana totally racist? Did she just call him a 'creature' because he's black?*

Outwardly, Erika wore an uncomfortable look of horror on her face. She did not want to make a big scene at the party just in case she had misunderstood Ana's words and intent, but Erika was also not one to give a racist "pass" to the older generation. She decided to keep an eye out for the disgraceful behavior and resolved to speak with her grandaunt if she noticed any unsavory comments again.

As if remembering Vittoria was still there, Ana stirred out of her dismal mood and allowed a smile to return to her face once more as she retreated into a more positive sentiment.

"I'm just *so* happy you are so fond of my grandson! I think you two look so good together! So natural!" Ana said, raising her happy, clenched fists. "And tell me, dear, what time will your parents be arriving this evening?"

"They should be along any moment, "Vittoria said. They landed earlier today and are driving in from Boston. Unfortunately, they will only be visiting for tonight and then will continue to tour the United States since this is their first time visiting."

"Oh dear! Really? What a shame! Maybe they will reconsider after tonight's party? I have a feeling they will be quite pleased with the outcome of this evening's affair," Ana said with a mischievous smile, then glanced nervously at Erika.

"Possibly," Vittoria somewhat agreed. "Of course, I will bring them over to introduce you, Ana, as soon as they arrive."

"You are a real treasure, Vittoria. A gem!" Ana said, touching Vittoria's cheek with palpable adoration as the female Farkas flashed another sweet yet viper-like smile. Then the Dragos Matriarch turned and walked away to go play hostess and socialize with other guests.

Erika found herself in a position she never had before—she was alone with Vittoria. This was the moment she had been waiting for. She had been wondering if Vittoria knew about Cristian's sexuality. Cristian being gay seemed very apparent to Erika, but if Vittoria really had feelings for him, maybe she was too blinded by love to see the truth. Erika decided to do a little digging.

"So, you and my cousin seem to be very close?" Erika started.

"Hmm," came Vittoria's response in mock amused agreement.

"How long have you two been... seeing each other?"

"Since I arrived." Vittoria's eyes rolled away in disinterest with her brief response.

"And do you like it out here? Do you like the people?" Erika pressed on.

"*People*?!" Vittoria laughed, but Erika was not quite sure why. She was getting nowhere with this line of small talk, and Vittoria was clearly stonewalling the questions, so Erika thought she should just go for it.

"Cristian and Beo seem to be *very close*. You can tell they definitely have something special in their... friendship. Anyone can see they're very bonded. My cousin can be a dick, but I'm glad he has someone like that in his life." *Your move*, Erika thought. Vittoria slowly turned and raised one dark, drawn-on eyebrow at Erika. Vittoria wore a cynical look on her face, and then, as if finally answering Erika's underlying question, she responded.

"Fang Hang," Vittoria said dryly.

"Fang Hang?" Erika questioned.

"Yes. I am your cousin's Fang Hang. It's code for the 'traditional title,' so to speak." Erika looked confused, so Vittoria rolled her eyes and offered further explanation. "There is a well-known term for individuals like me who get on well with individuals like your cousin and help mask who they truly are. 'Fang Hang' just adds the letter 'N' to both words in the term and is a clever way to make the term apply to our kind. Fang Hang."

"Oh, I see. So, you *are* aware? Good, that's good," Erika said, then asked for clarification, "What do you mean by *our kind*?" But Vittoria only ignored this last question and instead fired back her own underlying concerns about Erika.

"Yes, I know about Cristian, but who I don't know about is *you*!" Vittoria hissed, bringing her biting venom back around full circle. "I see you playing the innocent '*Good guy*' character—the real hero in this story. Or maybe worse—you think you're on some pathetic hero's journey. But I have news for you—everyone can't always be the good guy. It doesn't matter who you are. I don't think you have a clue what you're doing here. I think you ended up here by *pure* circumstance, and you are *not* some powerful, soon-to-be Head of Household. But I do think you *are* going to break my brother's heart no matter what your fucking bullshit intentions are."

"Hi," Blake said as he and Adrian walked up. Vittoria recoiled from her strike as Erika stood dumbfounded, mouth agape in shock from the professional hit. Blake wore both a charming smile and a nice black Prada suit. Conversely, Adrian was wearing a look of wonder as he gazed around the party wearing an awkwardly fitting suit, possibly a rental.

Erika glanced up at Blake for the briefest of moments, wearing a completely stunned expression, before turning and wordlessly departing from the group. As Blake watched her leave, his smile faded. Then, he snapped his head back to his sister.

"What did you say?" he demanded. But Vittoria only looked up at her older brother with innocent eyes as she sipped her cocktail through a straw, a coy smile playing on the corners of her viper-esque red lips.

Erika was distraught as she wandered over toward Curt and Nicole, who were conversing near the pop-up bar. Nicole threw her head back and let out a particularly loud laugh at something Curt had just said—so hard, in fact, that a snort escaped in the middle of it. She quickly clapped a hand over her mouth in embarrassment, trying to conceal what had already happened. Nicole must have noticed the destroyed look on Erika's face because she immediately snapped into serious mode.

"Oh my God! Are you okay?" she asked as she grabbed Erika's arms and inspected her friend's troubled face.

"Yeah, I'm fine. Blake's sister is just a real fuckin bitch," she responded, still trying to recover from what had just happened. "I'm okay though; just fuck her." Then Erika thought about it again and immediately felt bad for saying that. "I mean, I guess not 'fuck her' entirely. She *is* doing something really great for my cousin, but that bitch is fake as hell otherwise."

At that moment, the string quartet finished playing their set, and a DJ—who had discretely set up next to the classical musicians on the orchestral balcony—took over the musical entertainment for the remainder of the evening. The DJ, an attractive African American girl with a mohawk and wearing a black one-piece Bauhaus swimsuit, started playing more modern music. With the change in vibe, the whole room started to liven up and dance.

"Would you ladies care to dance with me?" Curt asked. The invitation dislodged any residual negative feelings Erika had felt as Curt took her and Nicole by their hands. The three began dancing and having a great time spinning around the dancefloor.

As the evening wore on, the crowd was having a good time. The boisterous energy was palpable in the ballroom, and the evening was on a steady incline, ostensibly headed toward being a huge success. Curt, Erika, and Nicole danced the night away. At the same time, a seething Cristian sat at a nearby table with a doting Beo, a mercurial Vittoria, the bewildered Adrian, and a melancholy Blake.

"God, I hate that guy," Cristian fumed as he kept his glare fixated on Curt dancing with his cousin and her friend.

"It's hard *not* to hate that guy," Beo agreed. "But the truth is, I can't stand most werewolf hunters. They all seem to have; I believe the clinical term is—narcissisticus-*arrogantous-dickous-superiority-complex.*

It's like, just because you 'maintain balance' or whatever," Beo said, making air quotes, "..doesn't mean you're qualified to be in that role. *Nor* does it mean you are not just some power-hungry sociopath that lacks empathy and happens to have a tiny dick. As a result, you feel the need to prove your self-worthiness by throwing your weight around while rubbing it in society's face that you 'maintain law and order' by murdering... let's just say it everyone...other versions of God's creatures. But I also *happen* to think Curt, in particular, is a stone-cold puckered asshole," Beo finished, taking a breath after his long tirade.

"Yeah, fuck that guy. I don't like him either," Adrian said, chiming into the conversation out of nowhere.

Cristian sat stewing over Curt's reckless flirting with Erika and her friend. His mind then flashed back to the line of questioning Marius had been asking him about a couple of weeks back in the garage, and he grew even angrier.

His thoughts began to run wild—What if Curt's people hadn't been as careful as he'd sold them to be? What if Marius already knew about Cristian's involvement in the murder of Erika's loser fiancé in California? Marius could just be biding time, waiting for the right moment to reveal the truth. Cristian couldn't just sit back and let that arrogant fuck, Curt, get away with it; with any of it! Cristian knew he needed to act and get out in front of this thing! After all, he was the only one trying to ensure that things went the way that everyone fucking expected them to with Erika and Blake!

I'm the only one with this family's best interest at heart! Cristian thought. *I would be* way *better suited for Head of Household. Not only would I improve things around this place, but I would fiercely guard Dragos Manor until I took my last breath! Bunica always said I reminded her of great-great-Bunica, Sophia Dragos, who built this home and made it what it is.* Cristian took pride in this comparison and realized he needed to take immediate action.

"Blake, get up. Come with me," Cristian said, suddenly standing with renewed focus. Blake reluctantly stood up and followed Cristian, who had already begun snaking his way through the crowd toward the trio on the dancefloor.

Curt had just reached out to place his hand on Erika's waist, but Cristian walked through the middle of their dance, intercepting his hand and substituting it with an awkward Blake in the hunter's place. Cristian leaned in close to Erika.

"Um, yeah, I need to talk to Curt," he shouted over the loud music. Can you please show our guest a good time? Dance with Blake," Cristian ordered more strongly than suggested. Then he gave her a small push toward Blake, who stood awkwardly nearby. Cristian turned his icy stare toward Curt and silently directed him to follow as he headed toward a relatively empty corner of the ballroom.

At that moment, a slow song came on over the P.A. The song was "Shrike" by Irish artist Hozier. Blake stood in front of Erika. He held out his hand, silently inviting her to dance. She looked down at it momentarily like it scared her, but recognized she was feeling this way and immediately rejected the fear. She did not want to allow anything or anyone to have this sort of effect on her, so she decided to simply remove its power as she defiantly reached out and took his hand. The pair began to slow dance to the music.

Nicole's gaze lingered longingly on Curt as he receded into the crowd with Cristian. "Bummer," she said aloud, then turned back to Erika, who was now slow dancing with Blake. Erika's eyes floated up to Blake's as the melody of the music flowed sweetly through the air. A small, knowing smile crept across Nicole's lips as she did a solo slow boogie backward, retreating toward the sidelines. Now Blake and Erika were alone.

"I did not know he was bringing me to dance with you," Blake admitted sheepishly. "I hope is ok with you."

"Yeah, sure, Blake. I'm glad to dance with you," Erika answered diplomatically. A smile rested peacefully on his face as he held her gaze, but then was broken by a small chuckle of joy that escaped his lips.

"Sorry. I laugh because I feel happy. I find out that wishes come true. A moment ago, I was sitting over there and wishing I could have the chance to dance with you. And now here I am. I get to," he said, still smiling.

Erika stared back at him with a poker-faced expression. She had purposefully been avoiding the subject of Blake's unspoken feelings, which she had almost undeniably been feeling simmering just underneath the surface all summer long. And now, deep down, Erika realized the prospect of these feelings frightened her. They were the reason why she had been so standoffish toward him. Flirting with Curt, the way she had been, was one thing. That was harmless. There was no risk involved. She didn't have anything on the line. There had never been this palpable feeling in the air with Curt like there was when she was around Blake. But everyone's continuous steering her toward dating him or commenting on their non-existent relationship made it difficult. Even that bullshit comment Vittoria made just moments ago—that Erika might somehow hurt him; might somehow break his heart. Comments like those made Erika feel defiant and not want anything to do with Blake romantically. So, she had simply decided not to lead him on in any way. In doing so, Erika had decided to avoid getting to know Blake at all. This way, she could circumvent any confusion altogether. The most annoying part of all this, though, was whenever she did happen to interact with Blake, just as they were now, she only ended up liking him more.

Blake moved his hand from her waist and slowly ran it higher on her back. His touch felt like a loving caress. It disarmed her just enough that she subconsciously let her guard down.

"If you want to dance with me, you should just come over and ask me yourself," she challenged.

"I saw you dancing with somebody else. That is who you choose for you dance partner. I would not get in the way. I have more honor than that," Blake explained.

"Ya know, just because I am dancing with someone doesn't mean I only have to dance with him. I can dance with you, too."

Blake thought a moment before responding. "For you... there would never be a line. Just you. Always first."

Erika was caught off guard by the simple complexity of his words as the music began to pick up into a faster tempo once more.

Meanwhile, across the ballroom, in a far corner, stood Cristian and Curt.

"So, this is quite the party your grandma is throwing tonight, *'Fucking Cristian'.* These *female* Heads of Household really know how to run things," Curt jabbed through his small talk, knowing this was a sore subject for Cristian.

"First of all, I could throw this party. In fact, I could throw a *way* better party. And second, who knows, maybe things *will* change someday, and I might be running things around here. And my first act would be to disband the Wolf/Hunter Treaty and finally put an arrogant *fuck* like *you* in your place. That could happen ya know, especially if my cousin falls for some basic-bitch human like yourself and leaves the position wide fuckin open! I mean... what the fuck do you think you are doing?"

"Just dancing, buckaroo. Don't get it twisted... your panties, that is."

"I am this fucking close," Cristian held up his index finger and thumb an inch apart in Curt's face. "I don't fucking trust you. I think your guys were sloppy in LA. I think Marius knows something is up. I think you are going to royally fuck me, and I'm going to be left standing here, holding my motherfucking dick!"

"Funny, I thought getting fucked by me would be something you'd enjoy. Then I could be fucking both Dragos cousins," Curt taunted as he did subtle thrusting motions with his hips. He clearly no longer gave two shits about maintaining any sort of civil relationship with Cristian. "Look, Cris, don't you get it yet? *You* don't hold any of the fuckin cards here, I do! I didn't *just decide to blackmail* you as an afterthought. I decided to do it *the moment* you asked me to take care of your little problem in LA. That's why I agreed to do the job in the first place! I own you now. And I am the one controlling this situation. You showed me what a dickhead, piece of shit you were when you asked me to do something so awful that would most definitely traumatize your own flesh and blood, and now it's done. You can't touch me. So, stand the fuck aside."

Cristian was absolutely livid. In the deep recesses of his abdomen, he felt the moonlight just outside the heavy drapes pulling at the familiar vicious entity that had been dormant within him for most of the month—dormant, that is, until the full Moon rose high in the sky, just as it was that very evening.

Cristian could not speak; he was so angry. He turned on his heel and stormed off, away from Curt, his irises completely without color, just black hollow holes. The sound seemed to fade all around him as he took deliberate steps in what felt like slow motion, exiting the ballroom and crossing the lobby toward the old elevator. He needed some air.

Chapter Twenty

The Rooftop Courtyard

Erika's eyes followed Cristian as he exited the ballroom. Slowly, she stopped dancing. Blake didn't seem to notice any of it, not even that she was no longer dancing, as he continued awkwardly singing along to the song that was playing.

"So raise you glasses you are wrong, in all the right days, all the other dogs!" he sang the lyrics incorrectly. "We will never be, never be—"

Erika found his enthusiasm endearing because she could tell he was genuinely having a good time. However, simultaneously, she had been clocking the escalating tension between Curt and Cristian in the corner of the ballroom. She thought Cristian looked the most visibly upset she had ever seen him, and she was worried he might do something drastic.

"Hey, hey... Blake," Erika said, putting her hand softly on his arm. Blake stopped dancing and was immediately attentive to her. "I'm sorry, I need to go check on Cristian. I think he's really upset. Maybe you can dance with Nicole for a bit, huh?" she suggested, waving Nicole over from the sidelines. A very willing Nicole stepped up to the plate. However, the smile and good time faded from Blake's face.

"Oh... no, is ok. Thank you. I only want to dance with Erika," Blake said with deflating matter-of-factness.

"He's so charming. I think he likes you," Nicole yelled sarcastically through the sound of the crowd toward Erika. "I'll see if I can go find Curt. See if he wants to dance some more. He's a thirst trap anyway," Nicole said with a sly smile on her face. Erika nodded, then made her way out of the ballroom to go after Cristian.

In the corner of the ballroom, Curt lingered back for a moment longer after Cristian had departed. He had seen Erika stop dancing with the Farkas werewolf and then go after her cousin. He now watched as her friend weaved through the crowd, undoubtedly looking for his companionship on the dancefloor once more. Curt knew he had pushed Cristian really far this time, but he simply no longer cared. Things had been this way all summer with Cristian's endless angry asides, and Curt was tired of it.

As Nicole drew nearer, he strategically side-stepped behind the crowd and positioned himself out of her line of sight while simultaneously retreating in the opposite direction. While he didn't mind humoring the friend, it was Erika he had his sights on. She was the clear conquest. Curt sensed that if he continued to play his cards right, he would easily have a shot with her.

Once inside the lobby, Erika glanced around for any sign of Cristian and noticed the elevator's needle was in motion. She walked toward the old lift that she had not ridden in since she was a teenager and saw that the indicator had come to a halt, parking itself on the 4th floor. She sighed and pressed the call button. After a moment, the needle responded as the lift slowly descended to retrieve her.

Curt maintained a good distance away from Nicole, who seemed to finally give up on the search for him as she returned to the bar to order another drink. A sigh of relief passed through Curt's parted lips as he relaxed and stopped moving through the crowd like a Pied Kingfisher positioning itself in front of the sun to mask itself from unwanted view. As he glanced around the room, trying to decide the best place to wait for Erika's return, something else caught his eye—or, actually, *someone*—that strange, distasteful little fellow who was a friend of the Farkas siblings.

So, Adrian, is it? Just my fucking luck, Curt thought as he tensed his jaw and stared hard at Adrian. As if sensing someone was staring at him, Adrian turned his head and looked directly at Curt. The two stared at one another through the crowd, and then, after a minute, Adrian stood, maintaining eye contact with the hunter. For the briefest moment, Curt was afraid the little fool was about to approach him there, in front of everyone, but Adrian, while quirky, was not dumb. He turned and walked toward the restroom. Taking the cue, Curt followed.

On the elevator ride up, Erika became acutely aware that she had never seen the 4th floor. After all, she had been forbidden to go up there her entire life, and the habit—or more apropos, *rule*—seemed to have carried over into her return. All circumstances considered, she did not think Ana would complain or protest about this visit. Erika would eventually have to see the 4th floor anyway if she intended to take over Dragos Manor one day, right? More importantly, she was checking in on the welfare of her cousin. Remembering Cristian and how upset she had seen him downstairs, Erika began feeling concerned for her cousin again. But she had to remind herself this was Cristian we were talking about here, and he always seemed angry. In the same vein, she also understood how nuanced his life was and felt sorry for his troubles. She cared about him and, of course, didn't want him to be unhappy.

The lift cart had now almost arrived at its designated destination. From what Erika knew of the 4th floor, Ana's office was up there, and there were rumored to be some rooms that stored old family heirlooms and whatnot. And, of course, there was the legendary outdoor rooftop courtyard. Beyond that, Erika was unsure what else to expect. When the elevator finally *dinged* to announce its arrival, she was surprised that the doors behind her opened. She had never noticed that the elevator was double-sided before.

A hallway with three doorways stretched out before her. Being aware of the size of the house, Erika realized there must be rooms upon rooms of unaccounted-for space up here. On the floor, discarded clothing was strewn all over, leading down the length of the hallway toward the door at the far end. The clothes appeared to be Cristian's formalwear, forsaken and cast to the ground. While Erika wasn't sure what this could mean, hopefully, she was not intruding on anything private. Regardless, her gut told her to proceed with the welfare check and confirm her cousin was okay, even if it meant walking into an awkward or embarrassing situation.

As she stepped out of the lift, Erika peered at the doorway to her left. It contained what one would expect to see—a door. To her right, however, there was no door whatsoever. Instead, whatever this entrance was had been sealed off with aged brick and mortar.

First, Erika tested the door handle to her left. As she almost certainly suspected, the doorknob would not yield—locked. This must be Ana's office. Next, she turned her eyes almost magnetically to the bricked-off doorway on her right. She sensed that whatever lay on the other side was immensely alluring, as she felt powerfully drawn to it, compelled to find out what it was. *Maybe I will get the opportunity to find out one day*, she thought. Her senses screamed at her that it was something she *must do*. Erika realized that she had hypnotically lifted her hand to the wall as she lightly grazed her fingertips down the rough surface of the old bricks. *Pity...* she thought.

Erika had to forcibly break her gaze away from the bricks as she raised her eyes to the third and final doorway at the far end of the hallway. The discarded men's dress clothing led up to this door, which was just slightly ajar.

A moment later, Erika pushed open the door at the end of the hallway and beheld a magnificent sight. The bright, starry night shone breathtakingly above and reflected down onto what looked like a smooth glass floor at her feet, which stretched out awe-inspiringly in front of her. She had never seen anything so beautiful.

As her eyes adjusted to her surroundings, little by little, more details came into focus by the light of the full Moon. The courtyard was in a state of disrepair—broken Greek-style pillars and crumbling concrete pedestal railing stretched out along the edges of the high courtyard atop Dragos Manor. Garden boxes most likely once held manicured ornamental plants were now overgrown with wild thistles and weeds. Piles of discarded debris were stacked against the sides of stonewalls bearing the gray shingled pointed rooftops that poked up like battlements and framed the far corners of the courtyard.

Erika cautiously lifted a black high heel and stepped onto the glass floor. Surprisingly, the floor yielded to her step and immediately sent an icy sensation shooting up her leg as the mirrored floor began emitting ripples from the origin of where her foot now rested. She realized what she thought was a glass floor was actually a giant puddle of water from that day's rainfall, which had since stopped. The evening air was calm and crisp. The bright, starlit night was silent and still. Erika drew in a deep inhale of the cool, fresh, rain-scented night air into her lungs. She felt as though she might cry from the sheer beauty of the peaceful place she was standing in.

Back downstairs in the ballroom, Ana scanned the room for any sign of her grandniece or grandson. She was already feeling the pressure from the expectations swimming around the atmosphere that night as numerous whispering faces glanced in her direction. She knew exactly what those whispered comments were pertaining to—Would there or would *there not* be a big announcement that evening? She would have to say something. At the very least, she would have to extend a sort of olive branch, especially after István and Irene Farkas had just made a tremendous effort to come all the way out from Hungary. They had done so expecting to hear news of their son's engagement to Erika Navarro, the rare non-transforming werewolf and the biggest olive branch that the Dragos family could possibly offer. With that, the Farkas family would gain the possibility of having hybrid grandchildren similar to Ana's offspring.

Betrothals were common in werewolf culture, at least in traditional werewolf culture. Unions were arranged and chosen based on desired traits in offspring rather than romantic feelings. Survival of the fittest. It was simply nature. Most importantly, it was tradition. It was the younger generation that had been moving away from this practice and moving toward selecting partners based on "romance" and "feelings" for another creature. Ana scoffed at the very notion. Deep down, she knew she would have to make this announcement. There was simply no way around it—too much was at stake. Even if Marius and Erika would both be shocked and angered by this announcement, anything less would be seen as an insult and a waste of the Farkas family's time.

At that moment, Marius came rushing up to his mother. "I just heard from Blake that Cristian got upset over something, and Erika has gone off looking for him!" he said urgently. "Have you seen either of them, Mother?"

"No, I haven't, and I don't appreciate Cristian indulging in his dramatics on such an important evening," she said crossly, taking the news quite personally.

"Mother. If Cristian is angry, there is a chance he could have gone outside. You know... to blow off some steam. If Erika follows him out there..."

"Oh no, it's ok, Marius. I haven't had a chance to tell you yet, but I spoke with Erika! She already knew about our family! We're good on that front. Now, please go and find them both and tell them both to shape up and get their butts in this ballroom. If Cristian has already changed, then just tell him to wait outside. The others will be out there to join him shortly."

"Okay, I'll find them. And mother... do not... I repeat, *do not* make that announcement. You are Head of Household, but I strongly advise you to rethink the idea. It won't end well. It will almost certainly have the opposite effect you want it to," Marius said and then gave his mother one more look of warning before hurrying off again to go find Erika and Cristian.

"Son of a bitch," Ana hissed through a long exhale. Her son's words had rattled her and made her second-guess everything.

Inside the restroom, Curt walked in and saw Adrian standing and urinating at one of the stalls. Crouching to a knee, Curt inspected the base of the two stalls in the room and saw they were unoccupied. Standing back up, he slowly walked over to the urinal next to Adrian, unzipped his fly, and began to pee. Curt knew anyone could walk in at any moment, so he decided to make this quick.

"Hi, Scott. Or I guess it's Adrian now," he started.

"Of course, am not going to tell you my real name," Adrian fired back.

"No duh, *Scott fucking Howard*! You may as well have said Jacob fucking Black or Remi fucking Lupin!" Curt shouted.

"Remus," Adrian corrected.

"I don't give a fuck! Of all the places you could have been visiting, I found you in New York Goddamn City for Christ's sake!" Curt said, shaking his head, angry with disbelief. "Just remember, I paid you a *fuck-ton* of money for your discretion."

"And what is *fuck-ton* in Kilos?" Adrian asked sarcastically. Curt raised his fist as if he would punch Adrian in the nose. Adrian flinched, but then Curt just lightly tapped him on the cheek.

"Eww, gross! Wash your hands. You disgusting me," Adrian said with repulsion.

"Shut up and pay attention. I paid you. A deal's a deal. That means you *don't* know me. That business where you almost said 'hi' to me on the street! What were you thinking? If I find out you have said anything to anyone, particularly to Cristian, I will make you regret the day you ever met me. Please tell me you haven't told anyone. Tell me you haven't told Cristian."

"You have nothings to worry about," Adrian said in broken English, staring forward with a hard look on his face. Then he zipped up his fly, turned, and walked out of the bathroom, leaving Curt behind as he seethed silently to himself a moment longer. This was the first and only time he would have this conversation with Adrian. If another conversation needed to occur, it would only be to discuss which way Adrian preferred to die. Curt zipped up his fly, flushed the urinal, and stood there composing himself a moment longer.

Upon exiting the bathroom, he ran straight into Erika's friend, Nicole; apparently, she had been heading toward the restroom herself.

"Oh! There you are!" she said with excitement. I'm gonna use the ladies' room really quick, then do you wanna get our swerve on?" she asked, doing a little boogie move. Curt exhaled, deflated at the question, and almost pulled a muscle in his face, trying to keep himself from rolling his eyes.

A strange sound detached Erika from the good feeling she was experiencing. It sounded like the rhythmic padding and frantic splashing of an animal galloping through shallow water. Erika spun around and saw a very large black wolf—much larger than she would have thought a wolf to be—running straight toward her from across the courtyard. Without hesitation, she turned and ran back through the door into the safety of the hallway. Once inside, she slammed the door shut with as much speed and strength as she could muster. At the same moment, the large black wolf struck the other side of the door with so much force it almost knocked Erika off her feet. But she stood strong, bracing with all her might against the closed door! She reached down and quickly deadbolted the lock to prevent the creature from getting inside.

The sound of hastened footsteps from somewhere behind her caused Erika to jump. She was easily startled after the encounter she had just had with the ferocious animal mere seconds before. She turned to see Marius running toward her, his face wearing a look of deep concern.

"Erika, are you alright?! I've been looking for you everywhere—" he started, but she frantically interrupted.

"The... there's a wolf out there! It almost got me! It may have gotten Cristian! I followed him up here!" she explained, her voice shaking so hard she almost couldn't get the words out quickly enough. Marius stood frozen for a moment. This caused Erika to grow anxious as she waited for him to comprehend this information and have some sort of appropriate reaction. However, his face only shifted to an expression that conveyed that he was neither surprised nor alarmed.

"No, Erika," he sighed. "That *is* your cousin. Here, let me speak with him." With that, Marius boldly stepped up to the door. He unfastened, opened his dark suit jacket, and quickly unbuttoned his dress shirt to expose a thin white undershirt. For the briefest moment, Erika thought she saw something move on her uncle's chest underneath his T-shirt. She thought her eyes were playing tricks on her. Marius reached his hand out and placed it on the door handle. "Stand back," he advised, then forcefully pulled open the door.

A large bulge appeared from the center of Marius' chest, stretching his undershirt tight to the breaking point. From the center of the bulge, the contours of a long snout came protruding out as two large, furry ears poked out through the top of his collar. His T-shirt was now very taut, filled with both Marius' human form and what appeared to be the shape of a large canine head occupying the area just under the thinly stretched fabric. At that moment, the snout opened its mouth, revealing the outline of numerous sharp fangs, which instantly tore through the thin undershirt. Suddenly, the large head of a silver wolf extended out from Marius' chest. He held his coat open as the silver wolf's head glanced around with a snarl on its lips.

The black werewolf—which was apparently Cristian—spied the silver wolf head extending from his uncle's chest. In a fit of uncontrolled emotion, wolf Cristian lunged right for the other creature's head and grabbed the silver wolf on either side of his jowls with his large black paws. Then, the two werewolves began engaging in a vicious, snarling dogfight, maneuvering rapidly, jaws snapping at one another.

For a single, terrifying moment, Erika stood wide-eyed and stared in horror at the scene before her. Finally, her fight or flight response kicked in, and she turned and ran away, leaving the horrible sight and sounds behind her.

Chapter Twenty-One

The Announcement

Erika burst out of the elevator onto the 1st floor. She ran through the hotel lobby and then back into the grand ballroom. The music had stopped, and everyone was listening to Ana as she addressed the crowd from the stage. Most people had smiles on their faces and seemed to be having a great time, blissfully unaware of the horrors that played out on the rooftop above. Erika stared in disbelief at her grandaunt on stage. *Ana wasn't crazy! It wasn't a delusion!* Erika realized in a panic. She had to find Nicole and get her friend the hell out of there!

"...the joining together of our two great families," The Dragos Matriarch said and raised her hands out toward the Farkas family, who stood in the middle of the ballroom. Blake, Vittoria—and what Erika could only assume were the Farkas parents—appeared to be quite pleased in the spotlight. The crowd applauded enthusiastically. Erika thought Blake looked as though he was going to throw up. She did not have time for whatever was going on right now. She frantically searched the crowd for Nicole as her grandaunt's speech continued.

"Again, I would like to extend my most sincere and humble apologies for my family's absence during this joyous announcement, but I can assure you all that they are just as excited as I am. And now that everyone has had their fill of food and drink, I must request that the waitstaff kindly exit the ballroom and get set up on the lounge patio for the party's conclusion. The weather has been cooperative, and it appears the sky has cleared up significantly. There should not be any more rainfall this evening!" Ana said in a delighted spirit.

The waitstaff obliged and began to take their leave as if expecting this cue. They placed half-full platters of food and half-empty trays of drinks onto nearby tables and then filed out through the ballroom doorway one by one.

"Is it me, or do they look a little... scared?" Nicole asked. Curt also seemed anxious as his eyes darted nervously around the room.

"Thank you all for being so gracious as to hold back transformations as a gesture of respect toward this evening's affair, our home, and the Dragos family. We know it gets more uncomfortable to do so as the night progresses, but please feel free now to 'loosen your ties,' so to speak," Ana said with a clever smile. The crowd emitted muffled excitement and laughter in response as some began to undress, taking off coats or jackets and unbuttoning dress shirts. "As always, all we ask is that no damage be brought to the property and, of course, please do not harm any of our animals nor the humans we have invited here tonight. We will offer to perform memory work on those who need it. Also, a reminder to please take it easy on the catering staff this year. Their group has served us for many years, so while they should be used to it by now, please spare us the trouble of finding a new catering company," she finished pleasantly. This time, an exaggerated murmur of disappointment mixed with mischievous laughter rolled through the crowd.

"Um... harm? Did she say harm?" Nicole asked nervously, but Curt's attention seemed fixated on Groundskeeper Tom. The elderly man hobbled through the crowd, walked up the stairs onto the stage, past Ana, giving her the briefest look of adoration, and over to the large window where he began fiddling with the curtain ropes.

"Ahh... what is happening?" Nicole asked as the crowd grew silent. Curt looked down at her solemnly. His eyes seemed hollow, much blacker than Nicole had noticed before. The words that came out from his lips were very dry and thin.

"Just stay close by."

Tom heaved a mighty pull on the ropes, and the heavy drapes quickly dropped to the floor to reveal the massive window they had been concealing. As the light from the full Moon came flooding into the room, two things happened—first, the crowd instantly more than tripled in size as the moonlight revealed hundreds of silvery figures occupying every open space between the living partygoers in the grand ballroom that night. The second thing that occurred was happening to many of the living partygoers. Fur, teeth, claws, and tails burst out of tuxedos and dresses.

Vittoria, Adrian, and Blake all transformed; werewolf Vittoria looked particularly vicious. The Farkas parents, István and Irene Farkas, both morphed into werewolves. The entire Aristide, Landis, and Lupu families all transformed. Kessler's parents, Elena and Andrei Vulpe, both transitioned into Lycans.

Erika's eyes were stricken with panic at the horror she found herself in as she stood in the middle of a room full of ghosts and werewolves! The beasts moved in a pack-like formation as they thundered like ferocious hellhounds around the ballroom before making a beeline for the exit.

The catering staff stood outside, listening and waiting. New bottles of wine and Hors D'oeuvres of bloody steaks and other cuts of meat were spread out on fresh tables on the outdoor lounge patio.

One waiter leaned toward another and whispered, "I can hear them coming. I hate this part. I think I liked it better when they used to make a little effort to try at least and erase our memories."

"I don't think it ever really helped any," another waiter responded. "All the memories just played out in my nightmares. I think they stopped doing it because it was too much work. The effort of erasing our memories was just the *honeymoon phase.*"

"This gig alone is paying for my kid's braces," a third waiter commented. "So, just suck it up, guys."

Just as he finished saying these words, the front doors of the house burst open, and a pack of werewolves, all shapes and sizes, came bounding out of the estate like the hounds of Hades. They ran fiercely all over the front grounds, a few veering off toward the patio directly toward the catering crew.

"Remember, team, they're not allowed to hurt us," came the unsteady voice of the staffing manager. But as the snarling wolves bounded closer and large teeth could be seen flashing in the brilliant full moonlight, fear got the better of them. All twenty-six of the full waitstaff started screaming as they broke out running, trying to escape from the gnashing teeth and snapping jaws that pursued them. The commotion caught the attention of more werewolves, who joined in pursuit.

As he ran from a large, spiky-furred brown wolf, the staffing manager wondered why he continued to accept this job year after year. Yes, the money was *outstanding*, but was it worth all this? He turned to see large jaws snapping at his behind. To his knowledge, no one had ever been killed... *yet*. But getting caught was not great either. As he continued running, the staffing manager pondered the idea of going back to school to pursue a career change.

With the room now largely cleared out, save for a few ghosts and about a dozen or so of the silver-haired guests, Erika saw Ana walking toward her, her wizened face conveying a look of satisfaction.

"Great party as always, Ana!" feisty Mrs. Johnson called out as she raised her glass to the Dragos Matriarch.

"I'm glad you are enjoying yourself, Grace!" Ana shouted back with a smile as she approached Erika. She turned to face her grandniece and exhaled a pleased sigh as she triumphantly looked around the party's aftermath. "Ahhh... this evening went well, wouldn't you say?" But Erika only stood with a perplexed and frightened expression on her face as she stared back at the old woman or creature or whatever the hell she was. Erika had known her grandaunt all her life but was only now seeing her for the first time. Ana noticed the look on Erika's face and mistook it for shock toward the announcement she had made, which Ana was unaware that her grandniece had not actually heard.

"Oh dear. Yes, I'm sure my speech probably came as quite a shock to you. You see, we—" But Ana did not have time to say anything further as Erika turned on her heel and ran out of the ballroom into the lobby.

Where is Nicole?! Erika frantically wondered. Fear took over at the thought that something bad may have happened to her friend. From the corner of her eye, Erika saw a nondescript feminine figure slipping into the unlit dining hall across the lobby. Was that Nicole? She went after her.

The lights were off inside the dining hall. The room appeared to be empty. Erika noticed one of the traffic doors leading into the kitchen was swinging ever so slightly on its hinges before it came to a rest. Someone had just gone through it. Erika ran across the empty room, pushed open the door, and entered the dark kitchen. There was no sign of Nicole or anyone for that matter anywhere. Whoever it was must be moving quickly because Erika herself had been running as fast as she could after them.

A soft *thud* came from behind the cellar door on the floor. *How did she get down there so quickly?* Erika wondered, but she did not ponder this for long. Instead, she lurched forward, ripped the cellar door open, and plunged into the depths of the darkness below. In the stillness of the kitchen, everything was quiet, that is, until the cellar door swung shut, apparently closing by its own accord.

The sound of the door slamming overhead caused Erika to jump. The benefit of what little light she had been receiving from the dim kitchen above had now been snuffed out. The cellar was bathed in complete and total darkness. She couldn't even see the next step down the staircase before her.

She began carefully feeling her way down the stairs when suddenly, the entire cellar became illuminated with an ambient blue light. The eerie azure glow seemed to be all around her without a visible source. Even though Erika had no idea where the light was coming from, she did not care because she could now see the path in front of her. She quickly finished descending the stairs and stepped onto the earthen floor. The memory of the creature she had stumbled over came rushing back into her mind, causing her to hesitate as she momentarily lost her nerve.

Erika was about to turn around when suddenly she heard the faint sound of crackly music playing from an old-timey gramophone. Then, she heard the muffled sound of a woman's laughter. It sounded like Nicole's laugh, coming from somewhere inside the hallway at the far end of the cellar. A slight breeze moved through the thick, stagnant air and seemed to coax Erika toward the hallway.

"Nicole?" Erika called out apprehensively. She gingerly took a step toward the yawning mouth of the pitch-black hallway. The giggling had stopped and was replaced with the sounds of heavy breathing and soft moaning. Erika again hesitated, questioning if she should continue. Her mind was spinning with images of werewolf parts coming out of her uncle's chest, with thoughts of her gay werewolf cousin and dozens upon dozens of werewolves running loose outside.

On top of that, her mind was now being bombarded with thoughts of Curt and Nicole possibly having sex just around the corner. The hallway ended abruptly, or so she thought, but Erika realized that it curved around to her right. She felt her way around the corner and soon found herself inside a small, dimly lit room.

Inside the strange and musty room, she saw the tall frame of Curt leaning over a woman lying on her back on top of a table. The woman was moaning softly. Erika could only assume it was Nicole. He was bent over her, his busy hands moving all over her body, while his face was very close to hers. Soft, breathy moaning sounds of pleasure came from Nicole's parted lips. Erika didn't know why, but she felt triggered by the scene unfolding before her.

"What the hell, Nicole?" she asked with disappointment, surprised by her own jealousy. At the sound of her voice, Curt abruptly stopped moving. Then he slowly stood upright but kept his back facing toward Erika. When he finally did turnaround, Erika saw that he was wearing a surgical mask with inky blotches flecked onto it. In his latex glove-covered hands, he held surgeon's tools that glistened with a viscous dark liquid that Erika could only assume was blood. His eyes possessed a demonic quality about them as they peeked out over the bloody mask.

Nicole's eyes fluttered open as if waking from a blissful dream of distant pleasure. She blinked and looked over, with unfocused eyes, at Erika. A hoarse laugh escaped her throat, and then she looked down and noticed the bloody, gaping cavity in her exposed abdomen. As her eyes became more focused, they grew overbright with fear at realizing what was being done to her. Her breathing became more rapid and erratic now. She tried to scream, but only a raspy whisper escaped through her lips.

Curt took a menacing step toward Erika. She stood frozen with fear, unsure of what to do. She fought the urge to run, determined to stay and try to help her friend. Suddenly, Curt's arm shot up rigidly into the air like a marionette on a string. His hand held the scalpel poised, ready to stab down. Immediately, he broke into a disjointed sideways run toward Erika. She flinched and screamed at his jarring, unnatural movements. Curt was almost upon her. He violently stabbed the scalpel downward, but just then, the gigantic figure of a werewolf appeared out of nowhere. The large creature jumped in front of Erika, blocking her from the stabbing blade. The werewolf stood up strong, bracing himself for a second attack, but as he got into a fighting stance, neither Curt nor the mortally wounded Nicole was in the room any longer.

Erika sat up on the earthen floor, not even realizing when she had fallen.

"Are you okay?" the creature asked—to Erika's surprise— in Blake's voice.

She must have been knocked to the ground when wolf Blake jumped in front of her to shield her from the surgeon's blade. He quickly reached his paw around to feel for the damage the scalpel had inflicted, but there was no visible wound, nor any blade stuck anywhere in his massive canine body.

Black patches began to appear across Erika's field of vision, like missing pieces from a puzzle. She was losing consciousness. Wolf Blake rushed to her side. She saw his mouth moving but could not hear any of the words he spoke as she fought to remain awake. She blinked, desperately trying to retain what she could see of the world around her. Then she sensed she was no longer on the floor but being carried in large, furry arms.

Glancing over the werewolf's shoulder, with her last glimmer of sight, Erika saw a faint, blurry vision of a lone figure standing inside the cellar. The dark, feminine silhouette stood daunting and unmoving inside the hallway, her features rapidly diminishing into ambiguity as the blue light faded. Erika tried to blink for sight, but none came. She knew her eyes were open, but she could only sense the echoes of the cellar that they were now leaving behind as wolf Blake carried her up the stairs toward the safety of the kitchen. The cellar door closed behind them. Dark stillness returned to the underground space once more, obscuring everything below, including the mysterious woman, into total darkness.

Meanwhile, back upstairs, Curt and Nicole descended the staircase from the 2nd-floor level back down into the hotel lobby. Nicole no longer looked frightened, nor did she possess any mortal wounds. In fact, there appeared no indication of anything Erika and werewolf Blake had witnessed inside the cellar just moments ago. Likewise, Curt also seemed like his normal self, with no demonic air about him whatsoever. The two seemed quite calm and at ease as Nicole shivered and swung a jacket around her shoulders.

"Thanks for coming with me, Curt. I just needed to grab a jacket but was too scared to go upstairs by myself... ya know, with *ghosts* and *werewolves* running about," Nicole laughed, having been let in on the secret. "I can't believe this night! I wonder where Erika went. Maybe her scary aunt had something else for her to do... ya know, besides *promise herself to Blake Farkas in marriage*! That was really weird! Why would her aunt say that? Erika has not mentioned anything to me about being engaged to a werewolf! I wonder what that was all about." Curt stared with a grave expression at everything Nicole was saying, a displeased look on his face. It seemed as though he, too, had also found Ana's announcement troubling.

Chapter Twenty-Two

Recurring

Althea's eyes slowly blinked open. She found herself lying in the middle of a clearing in a foggy, ethereal woodland environment. She could not tell what time of day it was, only that it was dark enough to make it difficult to discern the details of her surroundings. Suddenly, she noticed movement out of the corner of her eye. Misty visions of wolves began pacing in circles around her. She lay very still on the ground, hoping the creatures would not notice her or might think her dead. As she quietly watched the animals, Althea sensed the wolves were not stalking her but protecting her. But from what?

It suddenly dawned on her that she had seen this all before. Althea knew it wasn't her that the wolves were interested in at all. She turned and looked beside her, and there, lying next to her was a beautiful dark-haired woman who was fast asleep. Althea had seen this woman before. In fact, she had seen this entire sequence of events play out before. She gazed down at the woman's face and beheld her beauty. *Erika.* Althea somehow already knew this person's name, but she couldn't be certain how.

Just then, she noticed a dark figure approaching from the distance. As the individual drew nearer, she saw it was a man, but Althea also sensed he was not a man at all. He had a distinct *animal-like* quality about him. He was very good-looking, with dark hair and thick eyebrows, and he had a five o'clock shadow even though he looked freshly shaven.

The wolves stopped circling and suspiciously watched as the man approached. Then, the wolves did something amazing. They formed a wall between the women on the ground and the dark-featured individual, almost as if they were guarding Erika and Althea, protecting them from this mysterious creature who resembled a man. After a moment, the wolves relented to this stranger, permitting him to enter the clearing through their furry partition. She slowly lifted herself off the earthen floor into a seated position as Erika remained asleep beside her.

"There's something I've been meaning to tell you," the creature-man said, but Althea got the distinct sense he was not speaking to her but to the unconscious woman beside her. "Your mother is alive! She's waiting for you. You must go find her," he suddenly revealed. Althea blinked, trying to comprehend his words. Before she could respond, someone else spoke.

"What?" It was Erika. Althea didn't realize she had awoken. "My mother has been alive this whole time? Where has she been?" Erika pleaded with the creature-man, but he only stared back cold and unblinking at her.

Althea could feel Erika's hurt and frustration. This made her want to defend her, to fight for her. Althea wanted to yell at the strange creature disguised as a man for upsetting Erika, but before she could say anything, he opened his mouth and spoke once more.

"Kill them," he ordered while staring right at Erika. Then something unexpected happened; his gaze shifted to look directly at Althea as well. One wolf turned his large head and fixed his yellow eyes on Erika and Althea. His lips curled back to reveal a pointed smile. The last thing Althea saw was the wolf lunging toward her and Erika as they jumped up to fight back!

North Hollywood, CA

Althea awoke with so much force she almost flew out of bed. It took her a moment to realize where she was as she looked around her surroundings. Exhaling a long sigh of relief, she relaxed into her soft bed and felt solace in the comforting familiarity of her bedroom.

It was a room that was full of interesting artifacts. Various-sized jars of tinctures, herbs, and powders sat on mounted shelves. An impressive assortment of crystals and stones, a collection of various tarot card decks, along with some candles, incense, and bundles of sage, sat atop the surface of an altar in the northwest corner of the room. Many houseplants were scattered on tables, countertops, and bookshelves, which contained shelves upon shelves of books by well-known clairvoyants, Wiccans, and astrologists—her favorite being the works of the late great Raven Grimassi on the subject of Italian witchcraft. Althea's cat Gingersnaps had been asleep at the foot of her bed, and now the orange tabby cat lifted its head and began softly purring, her eyes still half-closed from sleepiness.

Althea was a woman in her late twenties who stood around five feet, eight inches tall. She had dark hair—although she tended to change her hair color and style often—and large brown eyes. She was a magnificent beauty with pale skin and a kind heart. She lived in an apartment above the metaphysical shop she had owned and operated for the past few years in North Hollywood called Stellar Remnants.

Residual feelings lingered from the strange dream Althea had just awoken from, but she wasn't quick to shake them off. She had learned long ago that such dreams were important, particularly given her unusual *gifts*. Althea had this particular dream once before. As she had done the first time, she sat, switched on the bedside lamp, and grabbed the journal she kept on her nightstand for this very reason. She wanted to capture as many details as possible while the dream was still fresh in her mind.

Thumbing back to May of that year, Althea located the earlier entry she had recorded from this—now recurring—dream about this mysterious woman named *Erika* and the wolves. For the time being, she ignored what she had previously written in her earlier entry and instead set to work writing out as many details she could remember from the recent dream:

Environment—Woodlands, nighttime, fog

Erika—Asleep, confused, afraid, frustrated, lost? Althea took a moment and marked a star next to Erika's name.

Creature-Man—Intimidating, homicidal, homosexual? Revealed Erika's mother was alive, then ordered wolves to attack to kill.

Question—Is Erika's mother alive? I haven't seen proof of life in dream(s).

My feelings—Protective, friendship, love?

Althea paused and adjusted her mind to be more fluid and less focused to allow the rest of the content from her dream to flow through herself more easily. Then, finally, the deeper understanding came to her as it always had. She resumed writing once more:

Love. There is no question about it. It will be important for me to help Erika become aware of her inner light despite so many who will try to dull her shine.

At times, Erika herself will even attempt to snuff out her own precious light. She has been struggling. She can't seem to find her power and is about to journey through the underworld. There's a very good chance she won't make it. She will need me; she needs my help.

Althea finished writing as the vague message being fed to her by her inner voice began to dwindle. She called this voice her *Obvious Voice*, the one connected to the *true source* that fundamentally knew right from wrong and good from evil. Some might have called this voice a conscience, but it was more than that. It was more like extremely sharp intuition that had the ability to be prophetic, so long as Althea listened properly. The voice came from the whispers of generations of women before her, some of them ancestors and others complete strangers, but all with a common deep sight connected to *the source*. While particularly strong in Althea, this voice was accessible to anyone who could quiet their minds and surrender their will.

After capturing her notes from the most recent dream, Althea glanced back at the May entry and noticed that the notes she had scribbled down were almost identical, except for two key points. First, the May dream featured an elderly woman instead of the creature-man. Althea had forgotten that discrepancy, as the two figures who had accosted Erika had a similar nature. Maybe they were related. The second difference was that in the first dream, Erika fled, whereas in the second dream, she jumped up to fight beside Althea.

Based on the sequences of events and differences in both dreams, Althea felt certain her path was destined to cross with Erika's. While she knew it was only a matter of time before she would encounter this person, Althea also understood how *roads* worked and that there was nothing she could do to make it happen before it was time for their paths to cross. So, she relinquished control, the way she had been taught when beings like herself were connected to time, space, consciousness, and the universe. Instead, she focused on what she invariably knew she should—the things in her control.

Althea sat back and began planning to fortify and strengthen herself to ensure her own needs were met. If she had a future with this person, they would face hardship together, and she would need to come from a place of strength to help guide this powerful woman, Erika, to find her inner strength.

Nocturne

Erika woke up with so much force she almost fell onto the floor. It took her a moment to realize where she was as she looked around the room she had just awoken in. Eventually, she recognized it as her grandaunt Ana's room on the 3rd floor of Dragos Manor. She had only been in here a few times when she was younger. With sweat clinging to her brow, her eyes darted around the expansive, sterile bedroom suite. The room was so tidy it resembled a museum full of antique Edwardian furniture.

Unsure about what to do, Erika rose from the chaise lounge she had been sleeping on but was instantly unsteady. After regaining control of her motor skills, she frantically crossed the spacious room and opened the door leading to the hallway. Erika discreetly peered down the corridor just in time to see Ana rounding the corner at the far end and heading toward her. Receding into the bedroom, Erika attempted to close the door quietly, but it didn't fully latch. The door drifted open again as she backed away. Soon, Ana appeared in the doorway and then entered the room. The two stared at one another. It was Erika who spoke first.

"I want to get as far away from this place as possible," she said, fighting back tears. Ana crossed the room, took a seat on the chaise lounge, and gestured for her grandniece to sit down at the other end. Erika did not budge.

"Very well," Ana said. "I understand you must be very upset."

"That is a *fucking* understatement," Erika growled. Ana paused and studied her grandniece for a moment.

"Erika, I'm going to speak plainly. I feel that is what you will appreciate most at this moment. You are a werewolf, even though you do not change. Your family are all werewolves."

"Was it one of you?" Erika interrupted.

"Sorry, dear?"

"Was it someone in this family?" she demanded, but Ana was seemingly not following her line of questioning, so she clarified. "A werewolf killed Ryan, isn't that right?" Erika's demeanor grew dark as she fought to control her emotions. "To get me to come back to this Godforsaken hell hole. Don't

167

lie to me! I saw one that night. Was it one of you who did it?"

"Uh... er... no, dear... It was no one from this family, nor any werewolf that we know. You see, we've been—" Ana stammered.

"Where's Nicole? I want to find her, and we're getting the hell out of this place."

"I assure you Nicole is safe. I know you had a scare last night down in the cellar. Blake told us all about it. He brought you out of there, you know. The Mischief—"

"What is that *thing* down in the cellar?"

"I'm trying to tell you, dear. The spirits that reside in the basement, while brash and mischievous, are harmless. They are called the Mischief. These non-human phantoms don't have a tremendous amount of respect for the living, which is why we force them to reside in the cellar. The Mischief's spirits will penetrate your mind to project hallucinations in an effort to frighten you, but they are only a fabrication. They are not real. Your friend is fine, but unfortunately, she does have to leave today."

At that moment, a car horn sounded from far below outside. Erika's mouth fell open as she turned and ran to look out from Ana's bedroom window. She saw Nicole hanging out from the back passenger window of a taxi, waving her arm vigorously to say goodbye to Erika up on the 3rd floor.

"Farewell! It was so good to visit with you, dear! Unfortunately, I must be going home to California now, as my studies will be resuming in the Fall. Until next time, dear friend!" Nicole called up in an out-of-character speech pattern. Then she recoiled into the taxi's cabin as the vehicle drove away.

"Wait!" Erika called after her, then turned to her grandaunt, who looked sheepishly guilty while desperately attempting to appear innocent. "What did you do to her?' Erika asked in an icy tone.

"Hmm? Oh... well, we... I had to, errmm...." Ana cleared her throat, apparently very uncomfortable. "...perform a small memory charm. Just a tiny one," she said, holding up her fingers an inch apart. "We must do that for human visitors who live outside of Nocturne. The towns... ah... people here know... some are familiar with... For instance, the catering company—"

"What about the guests?"

"Hmm? Oh, well, yes, they know about us as well. Most of them have been coming here for decades, you understand."

"Never mind. It's probably better this way. At least Nicole won't carry the trauma that I am experiencing right now."

"May I just ask," Ana jumped in. "Are you upset about my little announcement last night? Or are you angry because of your run-in with the Mischief?"

"What? What announcement? I'm upset about all of it! My family are all fucking werewolves! How am I supposed to react to that?"

"Oh dear. I thought we settled this last night?" Ana asked with confusion. "I thought you said you already knew!"

"I thought you lost your Goddamn mind! I thought you were just turning into a doddering old bag! I didn't think you were fucking serious! Now I'm going to ask you..." Erika's blood reached a boiling point, and her voice caught inside of her throat. She cleared it and continued, "...to ask you again." She paused, closed her eyes, and swallowed hard. When she continued, her voice was only slightly more measured than before, but she was still a powder keg, nonetheless. "*Who* killed him? My fiancé, Ryan. Which one of you did it?"

"Erika, I assure you, and I say this with the utmost sincerity, *no one* in your family, and no werewolf our family associates with killed your poor fiancé. I swear upon it. Our kind has a way of telling if the blood of murder is on a werewolf's paws... we can smell it."

Erika stared hard at her grandaunt, digesting everything and weighing all her options, but unfortunately, she was only operating with less than half of any dwindling common sense. She was mentally and physically exhausted. *Dear God. I could use a drink,* she thought to herself, but she knew there would be nothing to drink in Ana's room.

"Erika, I need to speak to you about a very serious matter regarding Blake Farkas," Ana said, visibly trying to tread lightly.

"Yeah? What about him? He saved me last night," Erika said, realizing her statement was true. The small gratitude she felt toward Blake was quickly overshadowed by her anger and frustration toward her family. *The pack of lying werewolves.* How could they keep this secret from her for her entire life?! Her own mother had been a werewolf! Erika wanted to go down that line of questioning, but before she could say anything, Ana caught her attention with the next thing she said.

"Erika, our family is in a lot of trouble," she said as her expression grew hollow.

"What kind of trouble?" Erika asked with diminishing energy. Ana's eyes shone with what Erika thought could only be tears, but none fell onto the elderly matriarch's cheeks.

"Oh, dear, please forgive me. I'm so very tired. Every kind of trouble! I'm worried for Cristian." Ana seemed to be trailing off and getting distracted, but she caught herself and stayed the course. "We're in political trouble with the European wolf families; I don't think our pack out here in America can sustain much longer. They are going to wipe us out.

We're in financial trouble. The bank wants to take our house because of years and years of unpaid back taxes owed on the property. I feel like our whole world is a mere house of cards about to topple over at any moment. We simply cannot bear all this burden at once. I feel like I have failed our family. This has only happened since I have been in charge. That is why I had to make that announcement of your engagement. I hope you can forgive me, but we have no choice. The union will solve so many converging problems." Now Ana wept.

"My what?" Erika asked flatly.

"Your marriage. To Blake Farkas. To end the century-long war and to save our family home." Ana pulled out a handkerchief, softly blew her nose, and dabbed small tears from her cheeks. Erika looked at her grandaunt for a moment, then turned and stared off one thousand yards away in disbelief that this was the life she found herself living and the family—her family—that she would one day be responsible for.

Ana surreptitiously peeked an eye out from behind her handkerchief and glanced at her grandniece. Erika turned around and caught a glimpse of Ana as she quickly covered her eyes with her handkerchief once more and continued to weep. Erika mustered up the most compassionate tone she could summon for the words she would say next.

"Yeah, I'm not doing that."

Chapter Twenty-Three

The Hand Mirror

Erika felt extremely frustrated as she exited Ana's suite and entered the 3rd-floor corridor. She pulled the door shut behind her, then paused momentarily to compose herself, her mind reeling from everything she had experienced. Ana had basically just told Erika that *she* alone could resolve all her family's political and financial turmoil. More than that, Erika was *expected* to resolve all of it!

Ana had said, *"I don't think our pack out here in America can sustain much longer."* Running through a mental checklist of all the people who had been lost in their family, Erika began to put the pieces together. She wondered if the Farkas family killed her parents. Maybe even killed Cristian's parents. Maybe even... Ryan! Which made the idea of Erika marrying Blake Farkas that much more absurd! Not only marry a fucking werewolf but marry into the family that may have murdered so much of hers! Yet, something in Erika's gut told her things were still not adding up. However, she did have the stamina to go back into Ana's room and ask more questions now.

She was exhausted. For the time being, Erika pushed everyone else's problems aside and focused on her own. She needed to figure out what her next move would be and where she should go after she left this Godforsaken place. Again, the realization hit her that she didn't know where else to go. She would just be starting over anywhere she went. Maybe she should look up her relatives on her dad's side. Or maybe she should just go back to LA. But the thought of doing that made her feel defeated. She simply did not want to live there anymore. Instead, despair sank in as Erika gave up on trying to solve her problems at that moment.

Her eyes traced the intricate patterns on the ornate Persian rug beneath her feet. Little by little, the familiar details came more sharply into focus. Erika roused from her dismal thoughts and took in her surroundings. A latent feeling had been stirring inside her chest, and now she realized what that feeling was about. She was on the 3rd floor. Erika had not set foot up here since returning to Dragos Manor.

She glanced down the hallway toward the door leading into the bedroom suite that she had once shared with her mother some eight years ago—longer than that, even, she realized. She had shared that suite with her mom when she was just a child. Once Erika and her mother moved into Dragos Manor during Erika's teenage years, she chose to reside on the 2nd floor to have her own space and privacy.

For a long moment, Erika gazed at the room with a mixture of curiosity and longing but couldn't decide if she should go inside. A soft *click* of the door mechanism sounded from down the corridor as if answering the question for her. Then the door mysteriously drifted open and sat ajar eerily beguiling. Erika was frozen.

"Hello?" she called out. Only silence responded. Glancing around, she confirmed that no one else was around—save for Ana, who she knew was still inside her bedroom suite. Finally, curiosity got the better of her. Erika took deliberate steps toward the open doorway.

The door to the large suite slowly inched open, and Erika peered inside. The cavernous room was pitch black and felt like the darkest dark of forgotten corners from her youth. She stepped into the stale, abandoned suite. As her eyes adjusted, not only did the room's features come more sharply into focus, but so did her feelings about not seeing it for so long. Her heart panged as she lamented the loss of her late mother.

As she ventured deeper into the dark space, she almost immediately noticed the dim outlines of large pale objects around her. Surrounding her, in fact. She extracted her cell phone from her pocket and switched on the flashlight. A beam of light came to life on the tiny phone, illuminating a small circumference of her surroundings. The large pale objects were, in fact, furniture covered with dusty, dull sheets, giving each the appearance of large off-white and yellowing ghosts. She pointed the flashlight beam up to a mounted wall clock—it was stopped at 6:59. Erika recalled that the sheets on the furniture and the stopped clock were practices once done by the bereaved after someone had died. She did not know why this superstitious practice was done, but she made a mental note to look it up later.

As she took another step deeper into the void, then suddenly, Erika caught sight of movement out of the corner of her eye! She jumped. Her blood ran cold as she stifled a *yelp*! Erika swung her flashlight around, but the beam bounced back toward her. She steadied her breathing as she realized she was looking at her own reflection in a standing floor mirror in the corner of the room; the reflective surface was partially uncovered.

Shaking off the fright, Erika walked over and pulled back the dusty sheet to reveal the large antique mirror in its entirety. She recognized this mirror from her childhood. Next, Erika walked over to—what she knew was—an antique vanity in the corner of the room. Again, she pulled back the sheet covering, revealing a familiar oval-shaped mirror atop the cherry wood vanity. She paused, running her fingertips along the surface, disturbing a thick layer of dust, and leaving a trail in her wake. Taking a seat on the bench, Erika set the phone down next to her, so the beam of light cast upwards toward the ceiling, giving herself general visibility of her surroundings.

Little by little, memories from Erika's childhood came trickling in.

She remembered playing dress-up with her mother when she was just a little girl. Erika was around ten years old at this time. Young Erika laughed and wiggled as her mom gently reached out and steadied her daughter's chin, then dabbed some lipstick onto her daughter's small lips. Erika remembered reveling in this attention. She remembered the smell of her mother's perfume delicately dabbed on her wrists. As a finishing touch, her mother wrapped a costume feather boa around the lavishly dressed little girl, again making young Erika squeal with delight. Her mother's loving smile burned in those moments of long-ago memories.

In the present moment, adult Erika sat at the dusty, forgotten vanity inside the dusty, and forgotten suite, and yet, a small smile rested on the corners of her mouth. *That had been a time when I was truly happy*, she thought. The bittersweet feeling stayed with her as she turned her attention to the items on the vanity's surface. She remembered everything from her childhood in those happy days so long ago. There was an organizing tray, a hairbrush and receiver, a perfume atomizer, and a manicure set.

Erika sighed as she looked into the vanity mirror and took in her own hardened reflection staring back at her. This was not the face of the once happy little girl from those pleasant memories. No; this was the face of the jaded and cynical woman she had become. Then, something caught her attention. Her gaze shifted within the mirror's reflection. Behind her, standing in the dark recesses of the bedroom, stood the dark silhouette *of a woman*. Erika gasped and jumped, accidentally knocking her phone—and only source of light—to the floor! She whirled around to see who was behind her, but her ill-adjusted eyes only stared futilely into the black void of the enormous suite. She frantically retrieved her cell phone from the floor and directed the flashlight beam toward the far corner of the room. But the suite appeared to be empty. Erika spun back toward the vanity mirror and confirmed that the dark figure was nowhere in sight.

She thought her eyes must be playing tricks on her. Erika reminded herself that she should not reasonably discount the possibility that some spirit might be in the room with her. After all, Dragos Manor *was* an *established* haunted house. She tried to reason with herself, to tell herself not to be afraid, despite her heart pounding defiantly inside her chest. She was still working on regarding the spirits of the house as commonplace. Resolving herself once more, she took a few deep breaths to steady her nerves. As she continued inspecting the contents on the vanity, she periodically glanced into the mirror's reflection to confirm she was indeed alone.

Refocusing her attention, she opened the top drawer. Inside, she found a small pewter powder box with a matching makeup brush, a few pearl-encrusted combs, and some elaborate antique hair pins that she remembered seeing her mother wear occasionally when she was younger. Lastly, there was a familiar pewter hand mirror that she had forgotten even existed. The hand mirror was placed facedown, and, like everything else in the room, it had a distinct aged and forgotten quality to it. Her mother had always told her that this hand mirror was a valuable Dragos family heirloom passed down from her great-grandmother.

Erika took one more precautionary glance into the vanity mirror to ensure she was alone before reaching for the hand mirror. She delicately traced her fingers along the intricate paisley design on the pewter antique before grasping the handle, lifting it from its resting place, and turning it toward her face. She saw herself staring back at her. Again, she glanced behind her, first in the hand mirror and then again in the vanity mirror, confirming she was alone. However, she noticed something odd when her gaze returned to her reflection in the hand mirror. The reflection staring back at her, while it was indeed Erika's face, appeared to be different somehow. Her face bore dark circles under her eyes. She almost looked tired. Or maybe sick. As she continued to inspect her face with mild alarm in the hand mirror's reflection, she thought—*Wow, I look like shit.* She ran her fingers along the side of her eyes and cheekbone, then traced the deep crow's feet that she had never noticed before. It was as if something of her familiar appearance was missing. As if the shine of her spirit had been dulled. Or the light behind her eyes had been snuffed out. Frankly, this image of herself startled her.

Again, her gaze shifted to the room behind her, and again, the dark feminine figure stood behind her, but it was much closer than before. Chills rose on the surface of her skin as she fought to remain in control of herself. She did not jump but instead held the figure in her sight in the hand mirror's reflection. This time, she did not dare turn around for fear of losing it again. Then, after mustering up what courage she could, Erika finally addressed it.

"Mother?" she asked; the word came out in a whisper from Erika's lips. The entity did not respond. It stood there, looming ominously in the shadows... silent... seemingly staring right at her. Erika's breath grew louder as anticipation mounted. Then, a faint *knocking* sounded from the doorway. Erika jumped and gasped, startled by the sound.

Chapter Twenty-Four

The Truth

"Knock, knock... May I come in?" Marius asked, inching the door open a little wider. Erika quickly glanced back to where she had seen the figure standing, then swung around wildly to check the hand mirror, then the vanity mirror's reflections. Just as she had suspected, the figure was gone. "I hope I'm not interrupting anything," Marius said apologetically as he approached. "I can come back if you need a little time to yourself, but I was hoping to speak with you after what happened last night." His demeanor was somewhat sheepish.

"Don't be sorry," Erika responded in an icy tone as she put the hand mirror back in the drawer. "After all, you all were just doing as you were told. I was just completely not—" Erika faltered with her response as she was emotionally running out of steam. She fought for composure. "Expecting my family to be—" Then, with a sudden surge of rage, she finally found the words. "Fucking werewolves! I mean, Goddamnit! This is it! I've had enough! I want answers, and I want them right Goddamn now! No more piecemealing family fucking truths, secrets, and other bullshit to me!" she yelled, then pleaded, voice cracking. "Please, I just want the truth. Be honest with me."

"Okay, Erika," Marius said. "You are right. I will be honest with you, right here and now, but I have brought someone to help explain. You deserve the truth," Marius assured her, then paused as if waiting for the individual to arrive. Erika wondered who the hell they were waiting for, then after a minute of no one showing up, Marius spoke outwardly into the air, "Aunt Daniela? Can you please join us? We're waiting!" he called out into the large room. Erika slowly nodded her comprehension as silvery wisps of shadow-like mist materialized beside her. Soon, the familiar shape of her grandma came into form.

"Hello, dear," Daniela's spirit softly greeted. Erika stared back hollowly at her grandmother's ghost.

"Grandma. Hi," she dryly greeted.

"My, how I've missed you," Daniela said with apparent emotion.

"Was that... was that you in the room with me a moment ago?" Erika asked with bewilderment, gesturing to the far corner of the room where she had previously seen the feminine silhouette.

"Pardon me, dear?" Daniela asked, seemingly confused by her granddaughter's line of questioning. Erika sensed that Daniela was treading carefully to avoid further upsetting her.

"That figure behind me... in the mirror. Was that you watching me?" Erika asked again.

"No, dear. I do not detect any other spirits in this room, nor on this floor for that matter. We actually don't permit resident ghosts onto the 3rd floor, except for me, of course. We want the *living* family members to have some privacy, after all. Mind what you say on the 1st and 2nd floors, though. It's almost guaranteed some unseen soul is lurking about and listening," Daniela explained in a lighthearted manner, apparently hoping this news might bring Erika some solace and ease. However, Erika did not feel solace or any sense of ease. "Erika, I know what you must be feeling about all this, but I—" Daniela started, but Erika interrupted her.

"Was it my mother? Is she here?" Erika asked, still very distracted by the mysterious phantom she had seen. Marius and Daniela exchanged nervous glances.

"Unfortunately, no, dear. Your mother never found her way back here," Daniela explained uneasily.

"Please stop calling me, dear," Erika responded with frustration. "Someone or *something* was in this room with me right before you arrived. I saw her!"

"Alright, Erika," Daniela said soberly. "I believe you. But before we discuss what or whom you may have seen, your uncle and I need to speak with you. We want to provide context surrounding the missing pieces of your life, so I must ask for your patience while we do that. Is that alright with you?"

Erika surrendered, nodded her head, and braced herself for what she could already sense was going to be very emotionally charged information.

"Thank you. Now, the most important thing you need to understand is that you come from a long line of lycanthropy. That is, werewolves, dear... I mean, Erika." Erika wore a deadpan expression on her face as Daniela continued. "You, yourself, have the Lycanthrope gene inside you, but as you know, *you do not metamorphosize* like you saw your cousin and uncle both do, but that does not make you any less a werewolf than they are. And Erika, you must understand that you *are* a werewolf. It's in your blood. Your mother could transform, I could transform. In fact, *most* werewolves transform. It's what we do. And not because we were '*bit*' as the legend goes, although one can create another werewolf by doing that. However, our kind does not like to create new wolves recklessly. So, in our family's case, Lycanthropy is in our ancestral DNA." Daniela paused and asked, "Does this make sense?"

"Not at all," Erika wryly responded.

"You must understand, the family—" Daniela sighed. "*We* did not tell you about this at *your mother's* request. Because you cannot transform, your mother wanted you to have the chance at a 'normal' life, so to speak. We all pleaded with her to make you aware of it so you could make an informed decision. But you were *her* daughter, and she thought her way was right. Then, after she passed away, you left, so we thought... maybe it was best just to let you lead a normal life as your mother had requested. Please don't misunderstand me. I love and respect my daughter, no matter what happened to her in the end, but I always knew this day would come, and I have been dreading facing the betrayal you must surely be feeling at this moment," Daniela confessed.

Erika listened, trying to piece together all this new information with what she had already learned about werewolves, ghosts, family feuds... *Oh! Family feuds!*

"Wait, the feud!" Erika exclaimed. "So, is that how my father died? Was he a werewolf that was killed in the Farkas feud? Is that how my mother died? Did someone in the Farkas family kill her?" Erika asked with a sudden surge of anger rising in her belly. She felt ready to lash out if the answer was any form of a "yes," knowing that the Dragos were *hosting* those Farkas monsters inside their home.

Again, Daniela and Marius exchanged worried looks. Erika clocked this exchange and dialed back her anger. "I'm sorry. I'm sorry," Erika said, giving them space to respond. "Please just tell me the *whole* truth," she pleaded, holding back the anger bubbling under the surface.

"Your father was a *human*. Your instincts are correct; he did not die in a car accident, but he was only ever involved in one battle, and that was a battle with alcoholism, which he tragically lost when you were very young. He had the affliction of the drink, and unfortunately, it just had too strong a hold on him," Daniela explained with a pained expression.

An inappropriate laugh escaped Erika's lips. The laugh was triggered by the banality of the news of her father's cause of death. She had never really known her dad since he died when she was a toddler, and the only story she had ever been told was of a fictitious car accident. Her laugh was because out of all the extraordinary information she had learned about her family in the past twenty-four hours, to hear her dad had actually died of such a mundane human affliction as Cirrhosis was almost comical to her at that point.

"Ah, okay," Erika said, not feeling the need to push this particular subject any further. "And my mother?" To this question, Daniela sighed and visibly braced herself.

"Erika, your mother was a very powerful and respected werewolf. She would have been Head of Household after Ana passed on. Again, your instincts are correct; there was no car accident. However, she, too, was not killed by any involvement in wolf 'politics' but by her own accord. Erika, she committed suicide, dear," Daniela said with a look of personal pain. Erika was stunned. Slowly, her heart sank through the floor as she grasped for meaning in her grandma's words.

"That doesn't make any sense," Erika responded incredulously. "She would never..."

"Sweetheart, I know this news must be very difficult for you, but what your grandmother said is the truth," Marius chimed in, backing up the ghost of his late aunt. Now tears fell openly down Erika's cheeks.

"No! No! That's not possible! That's not true! Mom? Mommy!" she jumped up and desperately called out for her mother as she searched wildly around the dark room. "Mom!" Erika called out, crying into the darkness. Marius went after her. He caught her in his arms and attempted to calm her, but she fought hard against him. Even so, Marius held on until she surrendered to his embrace.

"Shhhh, my sweet darling, shhh... Erika, she is not here. Not like she used to be anyway," Marius said, attempting to comfort his late cousin's daughter.

"Erika, there's more to tell you, but we can take a break if you would like to," Daniela offered while floating over to where Marius was holding her granddaughter. Erika sobbed into Marius' chest for another moment, then leaned back and abruptly wiped her tears away with the back of her hand.

"No. I don't need a break. Let's do it. I want to get it all out now." Erika tried to gain control over the emotional roller-coaster she had been riding since returning to this Godforsaken place.

"The last and most important piece of this story is about you. Again, we have not been truthful with you for *far too long*, but that ends now. If you have all the information, you can make your own decisions from there," Daniela said, then took a deep breath. "Erika, we have reason to believe you carry a very unique werewolf gene. The reason we suspect this is actually quite simple. As I mentioned, you *are* a werewolf born from a long line of werewolves. However, your parents were a union of a powerful werewolf mother and a human father. Of course, there have been others born from similar couples before in history, but as far as our kind is aware, most, if not all, offspring were still able to transform.

You, however, demonstrate *no* werewolf traits; that is, you do not transform. In the werewolf community, it is speculated your genetic makeup is ideal to mate with a *full* werewolf, for then there is a very strong possibility your offspring could end up being *hybrid werewolves*. Your uncle Marius, here, is an example of a hybrid werewolf. He has the werewolf traits but has complete control over all his unique gifts. He can change whenever he likes, regardless of the time of day, full Moon or not. As you saw, he does not need to change fully but can call out pieces of the wolf gift from different parts of his body. There are very few werewolves like him in Lycanthrope record history.

Marius is the offspring of your grandaunt Ana, who is another non-transitioning werewolf like yourself. You see, Ana was also born of a union between a werewolf mother and a human father. And yet, because of this, she was shunned in the werewolf community in Eastern Europe when she was a young child and was sent to live with the Dragos family, who had established a life here in America. Your great-great-grandmother, Sophia Dragos, took in the exiled child and vowed to fold her back into the werewolf bloodline by betrothing her to one of her werewolf grandsons, Elek Dragos. I was married to Elek's brother Robertino 'Bob' Dragos."

"Grandpa Bob was a werewolf, too?" Erika asked in disbelief. She only vaguely remembered her late grandfather but had heard stories about him nearly all her life.

"Yes, dear," Daniela confirmed. "So, this brings us to the reason Blake Farkas and the Farkas family would be willing to lay down a century-old feud if you would consider taking him as your life partner. You are a very desirable mate for any werewolf bachelor. Not to mention you are next in line for Head of Household here at Dragos Manor," Daniela stated. "There you have it. Now you know," she faltered, "e... everything," she stammered.

Erika looked back and forth from her uncle to her grandmother's ghost as she took in the gravity of what Daniela had just explained. She thought long and hard as she considered her careful reply.

"Yeah, I'm not doing that." Erika's words came out clear and cold, then she turned on her heel and walked toward the exit. "Thanks, Grandma! Thanks, Marius!" she called back dismissively. "I understand that me finding about this shit show now isn't *entirely* your fault, but either one of you could have told me, I don't know... at any fuckin point in my life, so you both aren't off the hook. Also, I'm not buying this '*my mother committed suicide*' bullshit so be prepared to circle back on that one later on. It's been real for now, but I've had enough."

"Aunt Daniela, will you please just tell her," Marius said with mounting frustration as he gestured his hand toward Erika. "You see what happens when this family keeps secrets. I wouldn't blame Erika if she got on a plane and never returned."

"No, I won't tell her because I don't want her going there too, Marius!" Daniela shouted angrily. "I won't! Not that..." she said in a lower voice following her surge of anger.

"Well, you two sort it out because I've got news for you both—I'm not going fucking anywhere, except downstairs to the bar, then with my newfound bottle of liquid '*no fucks given*' I'm going up to my room to have some fucking down time, alone with my whiskey!" Erika said. She was about to exit the suite but remembered something. Then, she doubled back and walked across the room to the vanity. Erika ripped open the top drawer, grabbed the pewter hand mirror, and slammed the drawer shut again before storming out.

Downstairs, Cristian, Blake, and Adrian all sat with a group of elderly, silver-haired hotel guests inside the lounge. The group was enjoying afternoon cocktails and exchanging antidotes. A pair of senior women were in the middle of being enamored with Blake's devilish good looks and seductive Hungarian accent when suddenly Erika stormed into the room, moving like a determined force of nature toward the bar.

"Oh my. Looks like the poor dear might be upset," one of the silver-haired women commented.

"Yes..." Blake and Cristian agreed aloud in contemplative unison. They all watched as Erika walked right up behind the bar and threw open the countertop door with a loud *bang*—startling everyone, including Sam, the bartender—then began tracing her finger along the whiskey labels on the shelves.

"Umm... boss? Lady? Miss Erika? Um... would you like me to get something for you?" Sam feebly inquired.

"Nope, Sam!" Erika yelled in dismissive reply. "I got it!" Then, she finally found what she was looking for. She selected a bottle of ten-year-old Pappy Van Winkle. With her newly acquired liquor bottle, Erika turned, exited from behind the bar, and started toward the exit.

"Hi, Erika," Blake called out to her.

"Fuck off!" she called back without turning around and walked straight out of the room. Blake and Cristian's jaws hit the floor as they watched her leave. Adrian buried his face in his hands, snorting with laughter. Then, not knowing what else to do—except knowing for damn sure that neither of them was going to go after her—Blake and Cristian slowly turned back to their happy hour company. Cristian sheepishly snickered to the group. The wily elderly Mrs. Johnson sat beside Blake and elbowed him in the arm, winking a wrinkled, cheeky smile up at him.

"I think that young lady likes you," Mrs. Johnson said with a twinkle behind her aged eyes.

Chapter Twenty-Five

The Man from the Bank

Several Weeks Later

The tires of a pearl white *Nissan Altima* crunched up the long dirt and gravel drive. Reflections of gray storm clouds sitting just beyond the gigantic house rolled across the reflective surface of the car as it inched to a stop in front of Dragos Manor. The small stuffy man in the driver's seat squinted up through the rain-flecked windshield as the wipers cleared the droplets. He glanced down at the cabin clock—almost noon. It seemed he had some trouble finding his way to Dragos Manor on this gray, stormy day. None of the twisting roads were clearly marked, and he very quickly got lost. As a result, he had spent the better part of his morning—longer than he had intended—winding down the wet, unnamed country roads. Now his bladder ached, reminding him of this fact. While he was not typically keen on asking residents to use their toilet facilities, especially with the type of business he conducted, he didn't see that he had any choice in the matter today. Nature was calling.

The man turned off the car's engine, then glanced down at the stack of paperwork on the passenger seat. Everything appeared in order, clearly marked with color-coded sticky tabs. However, he already knew this. In fact, he had somewhat obsessively confirmed more than a few times that morning.

Seizing the stack carefully in one hand, the man tucked the papers protectively under his raincoat and exited the vehicle. He shut the driver-side door, taking extra precautions to shield the important paperwork from the falling rain. The man walked up the broad steps and then carefully extracted the paperwork from under his coat as soon as he was under the awning at the front door. As he looked up, he immediately felt apprehension about knocking on this particular set of doors. He contemplated the large brass wolf-head door knockers that stared back at him, and then a chill ran down his spine.

The sound of rainfall beaded down on the large stained-glass window portrait over the staircase in the lobby of Dragos Manor. Ana took long, crisp strides toward the bar to speak to the wait staff—of which there was only Sam—about a supply order when she heard the front door knocker. She cocked her head to the side, wondering who might be calling. When she opened the front doors, she observed a meek, stuffy little man wearing a wrinkled suit and mildly wet raincoat standing before her.

"Yes? May I help you?" she asked suspiciously.

"Indeed, you may, ma'am. My name is William Sullivan, and I'm a representative from the New England Independent Mortgage Corporation. I'm here today to follow up on some documents that are pending your response. May I ask, are you the homeowner here? Mrs. Dragos, I presume?"

"Erg... yes, but I don't understand. The last person I spoke to said we were granted a grace period to respond. Oh dear, what was that person's name..."

"While that is indeed the case, Mrs. Dragos, it is common practice for mortgage companies such as NEIMC to begin the foreclosure process at least three to six months from the first missed loan payment. If in the event you—"

"Foreclosure?! What?! No, no, there must be some mistake. You see, we own this house, but I had to take out a Home Equity loan to—"

At that moment, a loud crashing sound came from the dining hall, followed by the loud bellowing echoes of male laughter. Ana lurched toward the dining hall to investigate the cause of all the commotion, leaving Mr. Sullivan alone in the open doorway.

Still grasping his important stack of documents awaiting completion and signature, Mr. Sullivan stepped inside and closed the front door behind him.

Ana rushed through the dining hall doorway to see Cristian and the Killers—Beo, Loki, River, Vittoria, Adrian, and Kessler—all rolling with laughter. Malcolm Jr. stood looking helpless amongst a huge pile of shattered dishes and cutlery scattered across the floor. A particularly rowdy laugh flowed out of Kessler. Cristian saw his Bunica, and the smile quickly dropped from his face as he snapped to attention.

"Hey, hey, shut up! It's not funny, you guys! Malcolm? Jeez! Look at you. You're a... fucking mess. Pull yourself together!" Cristian said with a snicker as he tried to suppress a smile.

"Well, maybe if you assholes would have helped me, or I don't know, had any fucking waitstaff in this place besides a single cook, Sam, and Old Tom, I wouldn't have dropped these dishes!"

"Cristian!" Ana sternly interrupted. "What do you think you are doing?" Her face was angry and expectant as Cristian opened his mouth to respond.

"Whatever I fucking want to!" came the loud echo of Erika yelling from the top of the staircase. Ana blinked and spun around in bewilderment. She turned her head back into the lobby to see Erika descending the staircase. Blake trailed behind with pleading body language. Her grandniece was visibly intoxicated, still gripping the bottle of Chateau Margaux in her hand.

"Uh oh. Here comes '*the pride and joy*' of Dragos Manor now, out for one of her rare belligerent appearances," Cristian said sarcastically, commenting on how Erika had largely been keeping herself isolated since the Sturgeon Moon party and had not been in a good mental state since.

"I don't even know you, dude, bro, dog, babe!" Erika yelled at Blake.

"Erika please, can you put your voice more quiet? I just want—" he urgently pleaded. She abruptly rounded on him halfway down the stairs.

"I know what you want! You want to do some 'ole fashion, outdated betrothal bullshit that a guy like me just doesn't want a girl like you for me to be your boyfriend let alone your wife!" Erika responded belligerently, as if trying to show Blake the absurdity in all of it.

Back in the dining hall, Cristian and the Killers all winced at the painful exchange. Vittoria turned to everyone and said, "I'd just like to say that while his English *is* getting better, he hasn't got a chance of understanding that one."

Mr. Sullivan from the bank stood helplessly in the lobby, his instincts screaming for him to leave as he saw some sort of family dispute unfolding.

However, the stack of papers in his hands and his bladder reminded him that he needed to stay.

"Erika! Cristian! Both of you, come with me this minute! I need to speak with you at once!" Ana yelled loudly, oscillating her head in and out of the dining hall doorway to address Cristian, sitting at the banquet table, and Erika, who was now almost at the bottom of the staircase. Erika came around the corner into the dining hall and squinted at the mess of broken dishes scattered all over the floor.

"Keep these wild animals away from me! Haven't you ever heard of a leash? Heh heh..." Erika said, doing a drunken Jon Lovitz impression. Nobody else seemed to get the humor of her poorly executed impression, so Erika explained, "*A League of Their Own*? Anybody? Oh, never mind. It wasn't some terrible werewoof movie so y'all probal never seen..." she slurred, then hiccupped as her voice trailed off.

"Oh, I love that movie!" Adrian offered enthusiastically but then dialed back his fervor once he saw nobody else was joining in. Blake came sulking into the dining hall, looking miserable. He took a seat next to his sister at the long dining table and then let out a long, audible sigh of frustration. Vittoria raised a hand with long, red, shiny nails and patted her older brother on his slumped shoulders. Cristian sighed and rolled his eyes as he dramatically stood up from the bench, and then he and Erika followed Ana into the kitchen for one of her infamous lectures.

Mr. Sullivan from the mortgage company took this opportunity of everyone being distracted and craned his neck around in search of a bathroom. He didn't want to start opening random doors, so he searched for someone—anyone other than *that family*—to ask. There was no way he would walk into that dining hall, as it sounded like sheer chaos was occurring inside. He saw what looked like a bar or lounge area and started toward it. Once inside, Mr. Sullivan discovered a young bartender polishing glassware.

"Excuse me, young man. Can you please direct me to the nearest restroom?" However, the young bartender did not indicate he had heard Mr. Sullivan's request as he continued his cleaning duties. Mr. Sullivan drew nearer and noticed the young man was wearing headphones as he worked. His bladder was screaming now, and he was about to tap the young man on the shoulder when he noticed the brass letters over a door to the left of the bar marked "Lavatory."

Mr. Sullivan left the oblivious bartender to his duties and took urgent strides toward the bathroom. As he extended out a hand, about to enter the bathroom, he was suddenly aware of the sound of a woman sobbing quietly within. He hesitated, retracting his hand, thinking the facilities might already be in use. As the sobbing continued, curiosity got the better of him, and he pushed the door open.

Like everything else in Dragos Manor, the lavatory was laden with Edwardian décor. The bathroom parlor was dimly lit by wall sconces and contained a vanity, antique cupboard, chaise lounge, elegant standing floor mirror, and other decorative ornaments. The sobbing was louder now that he was inside the room. He turned toward two stalls at the far end of the room where the crying sound came from. He didn't want to be rude, so first, he tried clearing his throat. When the crying did not cease, he called out.

"Hello? Are you alright, miss?" The sobbing abruptly stopped at the sound of his voice. Mr. Sullivan was immediately worried he'd overstepped. "My apologies; I did not mean to startle you. I just heard you weeping and thought—" He did not know how to complete his sentiment, so instead, he decided to switch gears. "Do you need me to get any assistance?" Still, no response came, nor any further sounds of tears.

Mr. Sullivan took a tentative step toward the stalls. The silence and stillness seemed eerie after having just clearly heard someone weeping. He reached the stalls in just a few steps, then slowly raised his hand and brought it to rest on the door of the first stall. Ever so slightly, he gave it a small push. The door yielded, slowly drifting back to reveal it was empty. Mr. Sullivan shifted his gaze to the second—now clearly occupied—stall but decided it was probably best he just use the facilities and take his leave as quickly as possible.

He closed the door behind him and quietly lifted the seat. The sound of his streaming pee being released into the toilet water was loud, so he began softly whistling in an effort to mask the unpleasant sound. His eyes glanced toward the partition that separated him from the adjoining stall. He finished as fast as he could, flushed the toilet, and then stepped back out into the lavatory parlor.

As he washed his hands, the sound of the woman crying resumed once more. This time, it was much softer and more subdued than before. Mr. Sullivan shut the water off and turned to face the second stall once more. He cocked his head to one side; his heart truly ached for this person's sadness. In fact, he had always had a soft spot for women's tears, and not in any sort of creepy way. Mr. Sullivan had a genuine, honest urge to comfort this stranger, but he knew this was not how society operated, although he thought maybe it should be. The world might be a better, more compassionate place if people comforted and consoled strangers.

Before he realized it, Mr. Sullivan stood in front of the second stall as the weeping softly continued. Again, he raised his hand and brought it to rest on the door of the stall. He didn't even mean to push, but the door yielded to the weight of his hand and began to drift open. Mortification overcame him as he realized he was actively intruding into someone else's private space! The crying immediately stopped. Mr. Sullivan began to frantically muster up the words for an apology, only to find... the second stall was also empty.

During this time, when Mr. Sullivan was having his unusual experience inside the lounge lavatory, Ana excused Sabina—the Dragos Manor chef—from the kitchen and then fiercely rounded on Cristian and Erika.

"So, *this* is what the future of Dragos Manor has to look forward to?! How can I confidently pass on knowing our family's home is going to be left in the care of you two dismissive, careless individuals?" Cristian stood with arms folded defiantly, and Erika was propped up against the kitchen countertop, her mouth completely purple with red wine stains. Ana *tsked* and exhaled in exasperated disgust before continuing. "This is not working! I need to speak to Marius at once. Maybe he'll reconsider my request for him to step in, even though it's not customary for males to run the household. I would rather *break* tradition and have more confidence with him stepping in than—"

"Well, if you're open to allowing a male to be Head of Household, why don't you let me do it, Bunica? I love and cherish this home and family more than anything. I could do just as good as any female Dragos HOH has," Cristian offered pridefully, seeing his chance at the opportunity and jumping on it.

"Excuse me? Dragos what?" Ana asked incredulously.

"HOH—Head of Household, grandma," he clarified.

"Yeesss, you should let him do it, Aunt Ana! Aww, I think you would make such a pretty queen," Erika slurred, staring at Cristian with adoration as she tried to pet his face. He jerked his head away from her touch with aggravation.

"Erika! You need to pull yourself together," Ana said firmly. "Now I understand you are upset about... well about everything, but this is *still* your home, and we are *still* your family. Now I need to know you are not just going to abandon your duties and responsibilities just because of the way you are... *feeling*." Ana choked on the word with visible repugnance. "As we stand here now, we have a caller in the lobby. He is a collector. Well, more than that. He is trying to begin the process of foreclosure on our home."

"Wait...what?" Erika asked more soberly now.

"He can't do that!" Cristian's voice grew high-pitched with alarm.

"Wait a second; isn't this house... like a thousand years paid off? Were there even mortgage loans given out in the 16th century?" Erika slurred sarcastically.

"19th century," Ana corrected, clearly unamused. "And yes, this house, of course, never had a traditional mortgage, so to speak. The primary ongoing costs have always been operation, property taxes, and upkeep. So, a few years ago—" Ana's voice had been escalating with the whole explanation, so she stopped, took a deep breath, and composed herself once more before continuing. "A few years ago, the profit-to-cost margin inverted. I did not want to compromise the integrity of the high level of quality that our guests have come to expect here at Dragos Manor. Otherwise, I thought we would never be able to recover if our reputation was to suffer. I took out a rather large home equity loan against the house, thinking if I could just somehow increase the flow of..." Ana stopped, apparently flustered once more. "Anyway, things have not turned around the way I had hoped, the way we *needed* them to. On top of that, it seems as though I may have misplaced or mishandled some money." Her tone was distraught as she explained. Cristian sank back a little at this remark—knowing what money his Bunica was referring to.

"Now the man from the bank is here. Right now! In our lobby! And I just don't know what to do," Ana said, almost laughing inappropriately at the situation. Erika and Cristian stood there confounded. They looked at Ana. They glanced at each other. Cristian wore a mortified, dumbstruck sneer on his face. Erika held her hand on her head as if she had a headache, either from the heavy news or from drinking all morning.

"Can you two please, if nothing else, pull yourselves together long enough for me to try to negotiate with his distasteful visitor? I might be able to buy us some more time. Cristian, can you please get your friends the hell out of here?"

"Ugh, we were trying to have brunch! And please call us the Killers. We are an organization, not some schoolyard gang of—"

"I will not! It's an immature and idiotic thing to call yourselves!" Ana fired back dismissively. "It is also a very good example of *why* I would never let you be head of this family. You need to grow up!" she said harshly, then turned to Erika. "Erika, I've tried to give you the freedom to process and feel everything you are feeling," she said, again making a face as if the word tasted badly. "But now I'm afraid I've run out of patience, and we have all run out of time! We've all had to make sacrifices and do things we don't want to, but that's just the way life is. It's tough, and it's unfair. Your family needs you. We need you to suck it up, put on your 'Head of Household' pants, and you can start by just being *open* to the idea of marrying Blake Farkas." Ana slapped her hand down on the countertop with exasperation.

Cristian heard Ana speak these words to his cousin. His heart panged that his Bunica would never put so much stock and faith into his capable hands. He could envision turning this place around, making it a place that visitors from all over the world would want to come to. But he knew this would not happen without some sort of miracle. Cristian dug deep, searched his heart, and channeled his inner Head of Household, as he thought to himself, *for the greater good...*

"Bunica is right, Erika. We need you to do this. I'm begging you. Please consider marrying Blake," he said, tearing his heart asunder with his innermost desires to become Head of Household, battling with the sacrifice needed for the family's best interest. Erika wiped her face, smearing her makeup further. Her lips were bright purple.

"I need to do some thinking," she said in a less-than-clear voice as she slowly shuffled out of the kitchen.

"God and our ancestors, please help us!" Ana said. "Cristian, if you would kindly clean up and get your friends the hell out of my house, I would really fucking appreciate it," Ana said, then turned and departed from the kitchen as well, leaving Cristian standing alone, feeling sorry for himself.

Chapter Twenty-Six

Outside the Closet

"Heey," came Beo Aristide's soft voice as he poked his head into the kitchen through one of the traffic doors. As he had expected, Cristian stood alone and brooding inside.

"Hi," came Cristian's quiet response. Beo walked in, the aluminum door swinging shut behind him. He approached Cristian, exuding tenderness and compassion.

"Junior says he's sorry about the dishes. My brother can be a real clumsy asshole sometimes. I'm sorry, too, boo. I should do a better job to help keep those guys under control. I made them all take off. Thought that might be best with how upset your Bunica is. Vittoria is the only one left out there. We can help you clean up if ya like, my pretty bae," Beo gently offered. Cristian's lip quivered.

"She's not even open to it," Cristian said with frustration.

"Who's not open to what, honey?"

"My Bunica," Cristian answered, tears now openly falling, "She's not open to passing the house over to me after she's gone. Because *I'm not a girl*! She doesn't think it's proper or just doesn't think I can do it. But I have so many good ideas! No one has ever even asked me for my opinion."

"What are your ideas, my love?" Beo asked. Cristian blinked his tears away.

"Like I would totally have, like ya know... a club night thing. With Go-Go dancers and... and... like Leather Nights," he sobbed. "I know it's not what she's used to, but it would totally make money!"

"Oh babe, come here," Beo coaxed as he lovingly reached out for his lover; however, Cristian jerked away from the affectionate gesture.

"No, what are you doing?! I can't. My Bunica could come back at any moment," Cristian whispered with his usual paranoia over the prospect of any display of affection toward Beo within the Dragos Manner walls.

"Oh, don't worry, honey. I saw Ana heading toward the lobby. Plus, I accidentally overheard that news about the Dragos' financial troubles..."

"Accidentally?"

"Okay, I had my ear to the door. Anyway, me thinks she's gonna have her hands full with that man from the bank for a bit."

"It's not just my Bunica I'm worried about! There is literally a house full of spirits with big flappy ghost lips," Cristian fretted.

"Well, I defy any ghost in this kitchen right now to get in the way of true love!" Beo said doggedly. "Also, I heard that ghosts *love the gays*! Yeah, little-known fact—ghosts are not Homopho-BOO-c... haha! Get it? Like 'Boo!'" Beo chuckled at his own pun. Cristian only stared back at him with an unamused expression. "Look at me like that all you want to. At least I made you stop crying for a minute," Beo pointed out.

"Look, I'm really upset here!" Cristian exclaimed.

"Okay, okay. I know. You right. I'm sorry, *Boo*," Beo said, then bit his lip to stop himself from laughing once again at the genius that seemed to flow from him effortlessly.

Ana walked back into the lobby expecting to see Mr. Sullivan waiting for her, but to her surprise, he wasn't there. A small sigh of relief escaped her lips. *Maybe the little creep gave up and left. Or maybe the commotion frightened him off.* At the possibility of the latter thought, Ana felt a small amount of gratitude toward Cristian and Erika for their reckless behavior that day, especially if it meant not having to deal with that unpleasant character.

With a tight smile on her face, Ana started to double back toward the dining hall to ensure everything would be cleaned up to her satisfaction. Just before she was about to slip back into blissful taskmaster mode again, however, Mr. Sullivan appeared once more in the lobby. His face was white as a ghost as he hurried out of the lounge.

"Mrs. Dragos. If you please," he firmly called out before Ana could disappear into the dining hall. *Drat*, Ana thought to herself as she froze. Mr.

Sullivan walked with a sturdy gait as he approached her.

"Mr. Sullivan, there you are!" she said, feigning a pleasant demeanor. "I do extend my most sincere apologies for that frightful display of uncivilized behavior from my grandson and grandniece! I can assure you it shan't happen again."

"Indeed, Mrs. Dragos. Now if you would be so kind as to—"

"Oh dear! How careless of me!" Ana interrupted again, "Where are my manners? I haven't even offered you something to drink!"

"No, thank you! Now, Mrs. Dragos, if you please!"

"Nonsense, I will be right back," Ana said, raising a hand into the air and heading back toward the kitchen. *That's it; I will have to perform a memory charm on this little pest*, Ana thought. *A drink ought to do the trick.*

Back in the kitchen, Beo took Cristian into his arms and quietly shushed away his tears. This time, Cristian surrendered to the comfort of his lover's embrace as he continued to weep.

"I don't understand," Cristian sobbed helplessly. "'*It's tradition. It's not custom. It's not proper. It's not normal*,'" he said, imitating his grandmother's voice through his tears. While some of his pain had to do with his role in the household, deep down, Cristian knew that another part had more to do with his struggle around his own sexuality and his grandmother's acceptance—or lack thereof. "It's like, change the damn tradition then," he said futilely. Beo slid his hand under his partner's five o'clock shadow chin, tilting his mouth toward his lips, and gave Cristian the sweetest kiss.

The sudden appearance of Ana in the dining hall caused Vittoria to jump. She had been sitting at the table, waiting for Cristian and Beo to reemerge, but was hanging back to give them privacy in the kitchen, which was the very place the Dragos Matriarch was now briskly heading toward.

"Ana!" Vittoria called out in a loud voice. Ana stopped, momentarily taken aback.

"Goodness, I didn't see you there, dear!" she said. "You startled me."

"Forgive me, Ana. But I'm glad I caught you. May I speak with you for a moment?" Vittoria asked, trying to think on her feet, knowing she needed to signal Cristian somehow. "It's about Cristian!" Vittoria called out loudly.

"Very well," Ana said with a strange expression on her face as she studied Vittoria. Suddenly, the elderly matriarch darted toward the aluminum traffic doors that led into the kitchen as she responded. "But I'm afraid it will need to be later. Right now, I have a pressing matter to—" Ana pushed open the double doors and immediately saw Beo and Cristian kissing. The two jumped away from each other almost as if they were spring-loaded. It was too late. Ana had seen everything.

"I knew it," she said darkly, inhaling sharply through her nostrils.

"Oh fuck!" Cristian wailed.

"Oh fuck," Beo echoed grimly.

Ana spun sharply on her heel and left the kitchen.

"Bunica! Wait! I'm sorry! This isn't what it looks like! *He* kissed me!" Cristian yelled as he went after his grandma. Beo's face fell into sharp dismay as Cristian ran out of the room.

Back inside the lobby, Mr. Sullivan stood waiting. He glanced down anxiously at his wristwatch, then back toward the lounge where he had used the bathroom just moments ago. A deep chill ran down his spine. Just then, Mrs. Dragos reappeared once more and marched with tremendous force toward an old elevator in the back of the lobby. Mr. Sullivan was about to call out after her but was interrupted by the loud begging and pleading coming from a younger man who was pursuing her.

"Grandma, please! You have to believe me! I'm not like that! I was just about to punch that asshole in the face! It's so disgusting! Bunica, ppp-please!" he pleaded through desperate, angry tears. Ana stepped into the open lift and rounded harshly on her grandson.

"Stop it! I have always known! Today was hardly necessary, but I'm glad I know for certain now." The elderly woman seemed livid as the elevator doors closed. Her grandson was left behind weeping loudly in the wake of her departure.

At that moment, Mr. Sullivan felt a tug on his coat sleeve that startled him and almost made him jump out of his skin. He looked down to see an elderly silver-haired woman had quietly sidled up next to him. She gazed up into his eyes and gave him a cheeky smile.

"You know why I love this place?" the elderly woman asked. "I love it because *anything* is possible here." With that comment, she pinched Mr. Sullivan's butt, causing him to jump once more.

"Madam! Please contain yourself!" Mr. Sullivan exclaimed with surprise. That was all he could take. As he turned to leave, Mr. Sullivan shrieked when he almost collided with the tall, blonde stranger wearing a dark brown leather bomber jacket. Apparently, this newcomer had just let himself in through the front door.

Chapter Twenty-Seven

Self-Destructive

It was late afternoon atop the 4ᵗʰ-story rooftop courtyard. The rain had stopped falling, and the gray clouds parted just enough to let the sunshine through. Despite the warmth of the sun's rays, a tenacious chill lingered in the air.

Erika had washed the wine stains from her mouth and was now reclined in an old deck chair. The emerging sun dually warmed her face and dried her tears, and the crispness of the air sobered her as she sat silently with her thoughts. *What a mess. How did I end up here, at this place in my life? Should I just give up and marry Blake Farkas? He is sweet to me. I can tell he cares about me. Plus, holy shit, I guess I am supposedly some kind of werewolf. Maybe this is where I belong. Maybe this is my fate. And I'm just fighting it. I have the power to save my family home... Blah, blah, blah, blah...*

Erika's mind was spinning. She was sick of thinking. She was sick of herself, sick of all of it. Erika grew more and more numb with each passing moment. Her mind and soul were descending into a dark place. She was feeling sorry for herself. Her body ached with cravings to drink more. Not just to prolong the hangover that was rapidly descending upon her, but also so she could just shut it all off, to not feel the things she was feeling. As she lay weeping softly, a white dove landed on the courtyard railing. She blinked her tears away as she watched the beautiful bird and pondered the concept of life.

A muffled *ding* sounded from down the hallway, indicating someone had again arrived on the floor. After a moment, the door leading out onto the courtyard opened, and out stepped Curt. His appearance startled the dove, causing it to fly away. Erika was irritated by this exchange of living creatures in her space.

"Well, look what the werewolves dragged in," he drawled, making a feeble attempt at lightheartedness. Curt walked over to where Erika sat and looked at her with a cheesy grin. However, he must have noticed she was upset as the smile fell from his face. She addressed him without looking up.

"How did you know I was up here?" she asked.

"I... ah... got here a little while ago. I let myself in, and I saw you get onto the elevator. I was going to follow you, but then Ana came out and got into the elevator shortly after you had. By the way, I get the distinct impression she knows about Cristian now. There was a big scene downstairs."

"Knows what about Cristian?"

"Um... that he's gay," Curt said, as he pursed his lips together and winced. This news snapped Erika out of her apathetic mood.

"What? Oh no! Poor Cristian!" she said, knowing this turn of events was going to be bad for her cousin. "Was Ana really angry? What happened?"

"I'm not sure. I think I just caught the tail end of it. But Ana and Cristian are in their separate corners now, which is probably good, all things considered. And yes, to answer your question, she seemed angry... very angry."

Erika sat back, stunned by this news. At the very least, she was glad to hear Ana and Cristian were taking space. A small feeling of guilt crept over her as she decided not to check on the situation and add more problems to her already full plate. She needed to take care of herself first, for once.

Erika sat up and looked at Curt. It dawned on her that she had not seen him in several weeks, not since the party. Frankly, she hadn't even noticed because she had not been coping well since discovering the truth about herself and her family. In fact, Erika had been spending most days drinking alone in her bedroom.

"So, where have you been? I haven't seen you since the party," she asked in an offhanded yet suspicious way.

"I've been working," he responded cryptically. "But I've been thinking about you..."

"Do you think you can do me a favor and cut the crap?" she scathingly asked. "I haven't seen you since the party where I *thought* I saw you either hooking up with or torturing my best friend. And you've just mysteriously and conveniently been away 'working' this whole time?"

"Yeah, I heard about that. I always knew there was something down in that cellar, but I didn't know what exactly. But just so we are clear, that thing you saw was definitely, one hundred percent, not me or Nicole. We were upstairs all night."

"Upstairs? Like... in her room? Did you guys hook up that night?" Erika asked, wondering if the Mischief might somehow have been projecting aspects of reality.

"No! Not at all! I meant upstairs, as in—on the main floor. It's not Nicole who I'm interested in," he said, then hesitated as if he was considering saying more, but Erika did not give him the opportunity to elaborate.

"So, what is this secret thing you *do* for a living, and how does it relate to my family?"

"Funny thing about that; I'm a werewolf hunter, actually," he said very candidly, then paused for the invariable questions that would follow. Erika squinted into the distance and slowly nodded.

"Right. Of course! Of course, you are. But say, did you know you are in a house full of werewolves?" she asked with a wry laugh. "Did you know *I* am a werewolf?"

"You are not a werewolf. You do not change. You are a person," he said, rejecting this notion as he took a seat next to her on her damp deck chair. "But regardless of what you are, the hunters don't hunt werewolves from the large established families. We have contracts in place with them. We typically only terminate the werewolves who are accidentally created from wolf bites. Unauthorized Lycans or 'Ferals' as we call them. They're pretty much viewed as the *bastards* of the werewolf world. They are not 'domesticated' like the genetic Lycans are, so they tend to run amuck and go around biting and propagating more like them. There was a flare-up after your family's party back in August. It happens. We can't tell who is responsible for the first bite, but the large werewolf families are always very apologetic and cooperative after it happens."

"That's fucking terrible," Erika responded with a mortified expression on her face. "And my kind doesn't get upset that you are killing other werewolves?"

"Not at all! They don't want them around just as much as anyone! Those rogue werewolves are not good for your family's kind. They bring too much 'bad press,' so to speak." Also, families like yours are surprisingly protective over *who* can *be* a werewolf." While Curt's response seemed to satisfy Erika somewhat, it didn't entirely.

"Has anyone ever tried rehabilitating these rogue Lycans, or whatever you call them? The bitten werewolves?" she asked. "Help them adapt to werewolf culture? I mean, they only turn into werewolves around the full Moon, right? So that means there must be an opportunity to reason with them after they are human again?"

"You are a very kind and compassionate person with a big heart, but if you met one of these *bitten* rogue wolves, you would understand. No amount of reasoning with them in their human state will negate the wild animal that comes out of their untamed, feral blood once they turn. We'd be talking years upon years of rehabilitation that might never yield the desired results." Erika considered Curt's explanation and decided not to press the matter further. He took a moment before repeating the latter part of his original statement.

"So, I told you I've been thinking about you... a lot," he repeated. Erika's eyes wandered up to meet his. Curt held her gaze coolly and steadily. While she knew romance was likely on his mind, it was the furthest thing from hers. Erika could almost see his ideas of lust flash across his eyelids like a theater marquee. However, in addition to feeling awful and hungover, she was also still a little bit drunk, but more importantly... she was feeling self-destructive.

Erika licked her lips and brought her hand to her mouth as she paused, contemplating what she could feel she was about to do next. Curt did not move but continued to stare into her eyes. He was there. He was a human man. Erika didn't know what to do with anything else in her life right now, but she knew what to do when a guy was looking at her the way he was at that moment, and she knew it was easy. The easiest thing in the world, in fact. She moved her hand away from her mouth, leaned her body forward, and kissed him hard on the mouth.

As the passion gained momentum, gradually, bits of their clothing began to get peeled away. First, Curt took off his leather bomber jacket and dropped it heavy on the floor as Erika unzipped his fly, then shifted her focus to partially undressing her lower half. She knew he had probably been hoping for a kiss maybe, but he did not hesitate, nor did he question his luck as the fiery sequence of events rapidly unfolded. Both stood partially naked now outside in the sunny yet crisp and chilly afternoon air. With him inside of her from behind, Curt continued to kiss her face and neck, but Erika was glad once they got moving so she could have a chance to get warmed up.

Chapter Twenty-Eight

Fear, Shame, and Grave Mistakes

Back inside the dining hall, Cristian sat pink-faced and puffy-eyed, his tears finally slowing and drying on his cheeks. Vittoria comforted him while Blake and Adrian sat with them at the table. Neither Blake nor Adrian knew exactly what had transpired since they had left the room with the rest of the Killers after Ana had taken Cristian and Erika into the kitchen to scold them.

Blake managed to catch Vittoria's eye. "What happen?" he quietly asked with concern.

Vittoria explained something in Hungarian, then Blake seemed to understand the gravity of the situation.

"Oh, I see," Blake said. "Is okay, my friend. Is no problem," he said to Cristian.

"You idiot, of course it's no problem!" Vittoria hissed at her brother and then put her arms protectively around Cristian's head, messing up his hair.

"Wait a minute. But I thought you two were..." Adrian hesitated, seemingly choosing his words carefully. "...doing the fucking?" He was apparently putting together that Vittoria and Cristian's relationship could also be falling apart at this very moment. Cristian sat up, out of Vittoria's arms, with messy hair, and looked at her while he sniffed back more tears.

"Vittoria is the best friend... that I've ever had," he said with a small sob. Vittoria listened as she petted his face affectionately.

From the first moment they met, Cristian and Vittoria had formed an immediate bond. Yes, maybe it was true that Vittoria had initially thought Cristian was attractive when she had first laid eyes on him; after all, he was very beautiful, but she instantly saw who he was and offered to play the part of his doting girlfriend to appease his grandmother. Cristian was blown away by the ease with which he and Vittoria got on. He was also very pleased at how delighted their fake relationship had seemed to make his beloved Bunica. No one had ever seen him, seen his truths, seen his core so quickly and made the decision to love him unconditionally for exactly who he was the way Vittoria had.

Cristian hugged her now and buried his face into her long black hair that rested on her shoulders. In return, she again tenderly wrapped her arms around him. Then, after a moment, he resurfaced.

"You guys, I feel bad for how I treated Beo. I didn't have a choice! He and Malcolm Jr. don't understand how traditional Eastern Euro families work, and how deeply frowned upon it is to be gay..." Cristian trailed off defensively.

"Don't worry about Beo for now, my love," Vittoria comforted. "It was good he left to help defuse the situation."

"It's all of these *perceived traditions*; they're stupid, outdated ways of thinking." Cristian once again daydreamed about the possibility of him claiming the Head of Household title after his grandma passed on. Dragos Manor had been his cherished home for his entire life! But this role was reserved for Lycan females—reserved for Erika.

Remembering Erika, Cristian flushed with anger once more. He glanced over at Blake and noticed that he, too, was looking as if he carried a heavy heart. "Blake, I'm so sorry. What was going on with you and Erika earlier? What were all those unpleasantries we heard being exchanged down the stairs?" Cristian asked. Blake only shook his head at the question.

"She is very upset at me. She won't even gives me a chance to explain how I feel," he responded with a crestfallen demeanor.

"Speaking of Erika. Where is she now?" Cristian asked.

The thin, curved sliver of the waxing crescent Hunter's Moon broke through the evening clouds as if to say it was indeed a lucky night for hunters. Erika and Curt redressed themselves after an inspired marathon session of sex, which, while it alleviated some of Erika's pent-up and angsty feelings, still left her with the familiar hole in her heart, as well as a full-blown hangover. She marveled at how quickly the regret came rolling in.

"Ya know, I've had feelings for you since the first moment I saw you," Curt admitted with a subtle giddy tone as he pulled his leather bomber jacket back over his shoulders. "Or maybe you didn't know. I know I'm not always the easiest person to read."

"I think I could tell," she said dismissively, not feeling eager to discuss the subject. "But I have also not been in the headspace for romance," she admitted. The familiar negative thoughts from everything that had transpired over the past several months returned like a lightning bolt and rolled thunder across her mind and heart. Curt seemed to notice this sudden change in her.

"Look, I know this past year has been crazy for you, to say the least. I can't imagine how you must be feeling. But for what it's worth, I'm here for you. I really care about you. And frankly, I don't usually care about anyone. Feeling this way is kind of a *big deal* for me because sometimes I have a difficult time feeling *anything* for another person at all. Maybe it's my work. Maybe it's the state of the world right now. Either way, I'm glad to be having these feelings, especially since they are for you. We don't have to continue this if you don't want to or if you are not ready to, but I really hope we do." Curt pursed his lips and swallowed hard. He stared at her, searching for some sign of his fate.

Erika was quickly beginning to feel overwhelmed at the very notion of this conversation taking place. When she decided to sleep with him, all she had been trying to do was attempt to seize control over at least one aspect of her life. She had just wanted to decide on at least one thing for herself, but unfortunately, the decision had been made while she was drunk and feeling emotional. Now, as reality was setting in, she realized the layer of complexity this interaction would certainly add to her current circumstances.

"Curt, listen, I..." she started, but she didn't need to say anything further. He saw the rejection written all over her face.

"It's okay. I understand. How bout we just keep this to ourselves for the time being?" he offered, and Erika relaxed.

"Yes, thank you. I think that would be best. Please don't tell Cristian. He has enough on his plate. I should go find him, actually." Curt nodded his acquiescence and wrapped one arm around her shoulders, then gave her a quick kiss on the forehead.

Erika and Curt walked down the long hallway toward the elevator. As they passed the brick wall, Erika's eyes wandered up to it, as they tended to do every time she passed it. Then she glanced toward Ana's office and noticed the door was cracked open. Her blood ran cold at the thought that her grandaunt might be inside.

"You go on ahead," she said in a hushed voice to Curt, nodding to show him Ana's open office door. "Did anyone see you come up here?"

"I don't think so. I snuck up after things seemed to calm down a little downstairs. I was hoping to talk to you in private," he whispered back, then flashed her a flirtatious smile.

"Okay, good," she whispered, no longer in the mood for flirtation. "See if you can sneak your ass outta here. I'm going to hang back."

"Sounds good." He looked as though he wanted to kiss her goodbye but seemingly thought better of it. "Is it ok if I hug you?" he asked hopefully.

"No!" she replied in a quiet but forceful tone, just wanting to get rid of him.

"Fine. I'll see you soon, I hope," he whispered. She feigned a smile but said nothing in return. He grinned at her as he pressed the call button for the lift.

Once the elevator doors closed and Erika was finally standing alone in the hallway, she took a deep breath, pushed the office door open, and peered inside. Fortunately, nobody was inside. Ana must have forgotten to lock the door after her last visit. Taking the opportunity to explore the previously inaccessible space, Erika started to snoop around. She didn't know exactly what she was looking for, but stumbled upon something that piqued her interest—a toolbox sat in the corner as if waiting for her to notice it. She crouched down, and after interminable fishing, she found some items suitable for her needs—a hammer and chisel.

Downstairs on the 1st floor, Cristian and Vittoria sat alone and in the dark at the long banquet table in the dining hall. Night had fallen. Blake and Adrian had left. Blake was still feeling melancholic over Erika, so he had decided to take some time to himself. Adrian had made his way to the bar to meet up with the silver hairs for happy hour. As an extra special treat, Chef Sabina set up a polenta bar in the lounge to warm everyone's stomachs, given the weather being so chilly outside that day. The dining hall was quiet that evening since everyone was assembled in the lounge. Vittoria continued petting Cristian's head, trying to comfort him.

Suddenly, the crystal chandelier snapped on overhead, flooding the room with light. Marius was about to enter the dining hall but lingered in the doorway, his attention captured by something behind him in the lobby. Cristian hurriedly wiped his eyes when he spotted his uncle approaching, but he was relieved to see that Marius was distracted.

"Is that you, Curt? Where are you coming from this evening?" Marius asked innocently. "Were you meeting with my mother upstairs?"

Cristian's ears perked up at the mention of Curt's name, as well as questions regarding where he was coming from. He furrowed his thick eyebrows and cocked his head to one side in curiosity. Cristian knew his Bunica had no open business with the hunters. He quickly stood and briskly walked over to join Marius in the dining hall doorway. Sure enough, there was Curt, seemingly having just stepped out of the elevator cart behind him. Curt wore an uncomfortable look on his face.

"Oh, yeah... no. I was... uh... looking for..." Curt stammered. "Erika," he finally said. "Yeah, I had accidentally ended up with her friend's... watch. It uh... fell off at the party, and I had it in my pocket for... I was holding it for her, and I must have forgotten. Anyway, I gave it back now," Curt said, fumbling through the explanation. Cristian's mouth was agape in suspicious disbelief. His broad eyebrows furrowed to a converging point as he glanced from Curt to the elevator doors and then back again. Vittoria's head soon appeared next to Cristian's in the doorway.

"Okay, well I trust you found Erika and returned her friend's watch then?" Marius asked.

"Yup, we're good," Curt said, then began crossing the lobby toward the front doors.

Vittoria stepped out from behind Cristian and Marius and began to pursue

Curt ominously, sniffing the air in his wake. Marius and Cristian watched her in bewilderment, unsure of what she was doing.

Sensing the vicious female werewolf in human form following behind him, Curt stopped and turned to face her dead-on. Still, she kept approaching; a menacing stare fixed on her beautiful face as she held him in her sights. Reinforcing his stance, Curt made his frame solid and spoke deeply, as one would to deter an advancing wild animal.

"Stop right there! Don't come any closer!" he commanded, but still, Vittoria did not stop.

"Curt! There's no need to come out of the gates and use that tone like you're the police!" Cristian barked, appalled at Curt's behavior toward the Dragos' guest. "Just fucking ask her." Then to Vittoria, "Hey Vittoria, angel?" Cristian called after her. "What are you doing, babe?"

Vittoria finally stopped just feet from Curt, who anxiously stood his ground. A threatening glare was fixated on the she-wolf's face. She took one last subtle sniff of the air between them and then glanced downward toward his crotch. A mischievous grin slowly spread across her large, red lips as her face shone with baleful amusement.

"Oh, nothing," Vittoria called back in a whimsical voice. "I was just disappointed to see him going so soon, especially after he had just *come*," she said, then turned around and walked back toward Marius and Cristian, both of whom watched her with eyebrows raised.

"Umm... exqueeze me?" Cristian whispered to Vittoria as she walked past him.

"Oh, nothing, darling. He just reeks of fear, shame, and grave mistakes," she drawled.

Curt turned, red-faced with anger, and burst out through the front doors, almost slamming them shut behind him.

"You kids should know better than to provoke the hunters," Marius chastised mildly.

"Whatever, that hunter is an asshole!" Cristian fired back. Marius ignored this comment, and instead, he studied his nephew's face for a moment. Cristian's eyes darted around nervously with confusion. "What?" he asked defensively.

"Cristian, are you okay?" Marius asked. "I'm noticing a dullness to your normal shine."

My God, how does he do that? Cristian wondered as he realized his face must still be carrying a residual wound on it. He would have to do something about that later, maybe a mud mask or some Botox or something. For now, he did not want to relive the whole ordeal that had happened earlier that day all over again with his uncle. Cristian knew Marius had always been a very connected and in-tune Lycan. He always seemed to be able to pick up on more things in the moment than were seemingly present. He looked down at Vittoria, who stood silently staring back at him, ready to follow his lead.

"Yeah, I'm fine. Bunica and I had a little disagreement, is all," Cristian said and forced a fake smile as he downplayed the situation that had transpired. Marius was quiet for a moment as if he was contemplating Cristian's very soul. Then he finally spoke.

"We are constantly traversing down various roads in life, Cristian. Sometimes, these roads will bring us to the great heights of the tallest mountain top. Other times, these same roads can also lead us through deep valleys of the darkest shadows. When you encounter another atop a peak, it feels like God and the universe remembered to shine the sweetest ray of light directly on you. Conversely, when you encounter individuals while journeying through a valley, it can feel like heart-squeezing sorrow. Unfortunately, sometimes we part ways with someone we once knew, cared for, or even loved and leave them behind in the valley forever. This is such a shame because we forget that moments, no matter how grim, are fleeting. It's important to remember to forge on and carry the strength in our hearts that we felt atop the peak. Otherwise, we run the risk of missing out on the majesty of a dawning sunrise," Marius said.

Cristian and Vittoria both stared blankly at him. Cristian shook his head with incomprehension.

"Marius, with all due respect, what the fuck are you talking about?" he scoffed. Marius again studied his nephew with a pensive expression on his face.

"Trust me, nephew. It will all be fine. It will either be fine, or it won't be fine, but that is also fine," he said, then took Cristian lovingly into his arms. Marius held his nephew while Vittoria stood on the outskirts. After a short while, she leaned in and awkwardly joined the hug, putting her arms around both Marius and Cristian.

Chapter Twenty-Nine

The Mother

An old phonograph revolved hypnotically, sending the crackling and staticky yet rich-sounding melody of Feuermann's *Sonata in A Minor* into Ana's dimly lit bedroom suite. Ana stared hollowly into the middle of the room as she lay despondent in her bed. The faintest *tapping* sound came rapping on her chamber door, followed by its opening just wide enough to permit entrance to the devoted estate groundskeeper who carried with him a tray of hot tea. Old Tom balanced the precariously full tray holding a hot teapot, cup, and saucer, as well as some biscuits that he knew Ana liked, although he was aware she would most likely not eat them until no one was looking.

The specter of Daniela Dragos sat in an antique armchair at Ana's bedside, rolling her ghostly eyes at her disheartened sister-in-law. Groundskeeper Tom finally managed to make it to Ana's bedside, as he carefully set the tray down on her nightstand, then got to work pouring a cup of the steaming steeped liquid, fixing it just the way he knew she liked it. His old grip trembled with arthritis, causing the China to *clink* together as he worked.

"Oh, come now, Ana, be reasonable," Daniela's ghost said, trying to break the somber mood that was thick in the gigantic room. "You know times are not as they used to be! This sort of thing happens and is more common now, in fact. Also really, to some degree everyone has always... known."

"I don't wish to speak about it," Ana responded firmly.

"You are still Head of Household, and you have the power to change things! Change outlooks and perspectives! Every day is a new opportunity for us to be different to challenge the status quo, and the changes can start as soon as now! Just accept the boy for who he is. Or who *they* are. I don't know if they have a pronoun preference?" Daniela pondered, surprisingly aware of the times, not just for being an old Lycan but for being an old, *dead* Lycan. But Daniela's consideration for gender identity and pronouns was lost on Ana.

"I am not concerned about multiple people, so I don't know what *they* you are referring to. I am only concerned about my grandson!"

"Ladies, if I may. Maybe Ms. Ana simply needs some time to process and come to terms with the news of our dear Cristian. After all, we all thought we would see him be married one day," Tom glanced down at Ana as if they shared the mutual pride in this thought, "that he'd have little ones padding about."

"He can still have all those things; it just might not be with a... female Lycan," Daniela said, to which Ana clicked her tongue and exhaled a forced, exasperated sigh.

"You know this sort of thing was still a *crime* even just a few decades ago in Romania," Ana correctly pointed out. "You could serve jail time. Cristian knows better."

"Ana, this is not something that individuals should *know* to do or not do, nor is it a way they *choose* to be! Your grandson has been gay his whole life! Everybody saw it! You simply refused to face that fact!" Daniela was exhausting her patience with her sister-in-law.

"I simply give up. As far as I'm concerned, Erika just got a promotion today. She can take over immediately. I'm done trying to do right by this family. All I am met with is grief and lack of cooperation. Let come what may to this household. I am a very tired, very old Lycan."

"Ana, you cannot just wash your hands of the situation! You remember what Sophia Dragos told us when we married her grandsons?" To this reminder, Ana's gaze went far away.

"*There will always be choices to be made, but always choose our family first,*" Ana recited from memory of her late grandmother-in-law.

Back then, Ana thought she had a grasp on the realities of the burden she would one day come to bear as Head of Household. She was so young then, so naive. And so very wrong indeed. Everything was far more complicated than she could have ever imagined. It was the world that had changed, not her.

"I know it's hard to see, Daniela, but that *is* what I'm doing. I am just getting in the way. I'm an obsolete old Lycan. I've already fulfilled my legacy by creating my remarkable offspring who are inarguably the most magnificent Lycans of all time. After a lifetime of trying to uphold what I thought to be proper and just, I cannot simply change my mind and heart. Let the children deal with it now—all of it. I am very tired," she repeated with exhaustion. Daniela saw it was futile to argue with her stubborn sister-in-law any further at that moment. Tom stood protectively over Ana but offered nothing further. Ana turned to him and requested, "Tom, please go locate Erika and bring her up here to see me. It's important that I let her know the final pieces of the story now."

"Ana, please, I beg you, don't do this. We can't have her digging around in the echoes of the past. It will be her demise... just as it was for her mother. You know how profoundly it affects female Dragos. It is strong enough on the pair of us, and we are both married into the family! Not even blood! Please, I implore you to reconsider until Erika is more fortified of mind and spirit."

"Daniela, dear, sweet sister-in-law, I am through. Finished."

At that moment, the door to Ana's room creaked open, and Erika stepped through the doorway. Tom, Ana, and Daniela all looked at her with stunned expressions for a moment; then Tom turned to Ana with an open-mouth smile as he pointed to Erika, confirming he had indeed located her.

"Yes, thank you, Tom," Ana said with unamused praise. The Dragos Head of Household adjusted herself to sit higher up in bed. As Erika approached, she noticed her grandma's ghostly face wearing a look of deep concern as she sat by Ana's bedside.

"Please, come sit down, Erika," Daniela coaxed.

"Nope, I'm all set; I'll stand, thank you," Erika declined defiantly and remained standing where she was, not five feet from the bed.

"Very well, have it your way," Ana said dryly, "Congratulations, Erika Navarro, Dragos Manor is yours. I am retiring effective immediately. You are now Head of Household." She paused for dramatic effect. The room went silent now, save for the music that was still softly crackling in the corner.

"I'm sorry, can we turn *that* off?" Erika asked, gesturing to the melancholy phonograph situation that was happening near them. Tom obliged and scurried over to pull up the needle, making a slight scratching sound as the music stopped. "This is because of what happened with Cristian earlier today, isn't it?" Erika asked, aware she was taking an emotional shot at her grandaunt.

"This is *because* I can no longer bear the burden of trying to keep this property, business, and family afloat any longer. I am a very old Lycan, perhaps too old and defunct for this world. I think what is best is for you to take over and do what you will with the place. Do as you see fit."

"And what if I turn down the job?" Erika challenged.

"Then I guess it would fall to Marius and Cristian, and any offspring..." Ana stopped as if the words she was starting to utter had struck a very deep, very painful nerve. "It would fall to whoever wanted it before the bank takes it away," Ana finished dismissively.

Erika thought for a moment. She felt more of a sense of ease now that she was holding all the cards for once, but wisely, she decided not to play her entire hand at once. Instead, she sat back and waited to see how the events would unfold. As of right now, Erika could take over as Head of Household if she wanted to. Fine—she might be able to turn things around with the business, but Erika was not stupid. Doing so would require a huge influx of revenue. She would need to figure out some things first but thought there must be some way to achieve this other than marrying Blake Farkas for his money. That was just not an option in her mind. And there was no chance of ever having any true feelings for him with everything that had happened. Erika pushed the income problem aside for a moment and refocused on the core subject of taking over as Head of Household.

"What is the *most* important thing I would need to know if I am to make an informed decision about taking over?" Erika asked. "I'm sure there will be many details that will need to be handed off, but what is the *most* important thing I need to take away from this room today, that will contribute to either the success or demise of my being Head of Household?" she asked, making frank eye contact with her grandaunt. Ana's eyes were steely and deadlocked with her grandniece. Daniela brushed a translucent hand stressfully over her ghostly face, then began to fan herself with her other hand, appearing to become overheated. Tom bit his top lip and glanced down nervously at Ana.

"Well, there are a few spells you will need to learn to maintain the house spirits. They are quite simple, actually. Other than that... you will need to know about the Mother," Ana answered finally.

Chapter Thirty

The Admission

Two Weeks Later

Cristian walked up to the set of double doors leading into the Dragos library, quietly muttering a rehearsal.

"Heeyy, how's it..." He stopped, cleared his throat, and made an adjustment. "Heeey, just checking in— Heey just wanted to see how it's going. If you ever want to run anything by me..." *That'll work,* he thought. Cristian paused, composed himself then knocked on one of the doors. He opened it and poked his head inside without waiting for an invitation to enter.

A roaring fire burned bright in the large fireplace inside the Dragos library. The flames illuminated the many volumes on the bookshelves directly surrounding the stone hearth. The glow tapered off into the ambient room lighting as the bookshelves stretched further away toward the ceiling, floor, and far walls. It was an impressive collection, indeed.

Erika sat in a chair pulled up to a modest-sized table, which she had repurposed into an office desk, positioned a couple of yards from the fireplace. Boxes upon boxes of documents—that Erika herself had carried down one by one from Ana's office—were stacked up behind her. She was busy at work cross-referencing various piles of papers, pausing occasionally to input a particular detail into a new laptop that she had purchased just for Dragos Manor record keeping.

So far, reconciling Dragos Manor, LLC's financial state of affairs had taken Erika just about two weeks, and she was still working to get it sorted. She had spent many hours sussing out relevant information from old, faded hardcopy documents, most of which had not seen the light of day since their creation. She was now busy at work, organizing all the pertinent data into a complex digital master spreadsheet that she had put together.

"Heey, I just wanted to check in and see how it's going. See if you have anything you want to run by me?" Cristian offered with an accommodating smile as he approached her desk. Erika glanced up, but her hands continued typing.

"Hey, Cristian. Yeah, for sure. I'm not trying to bypass you from this process. I fully intend for both of us to run this house as a joint effort. I just thought it might be quicker if I dug in and organized all this stuff and get the relevant information into a place where we can start to have meaningful conversations around it. I'm getting close to having a snapshot of analytics we can discuss. Then we should even be able to start talking about strategy for increasing revenue forecasting going into the next fiscal year," Erika rattled off. Cristian stared back at her wide-eyed with bewilderment, as much of what she had just said went over his head.

"Uh-huh. So, I was thinking... we should talk about maybe having like... a dance night?" he suggested. "Ya, I have a lot of ideas for how we can make this snore-fest into a much more badass..." he began to suggest, then pivoted in an effort to match Erika's tone. "Um, for how we can increase the modernization of the..." he waved his hand, gesturing wildly around the room as he searched for the word he was looking for, "...business."

Again, Erika looked up but continued typing as she tried to multitask by giving Cristian half her attention. This delayed her response to his comments.

"Yeah! Definitely! That sounds really great. I want to hear all your ideas," she replied seemingly in earnest, but then her demeanor changed. "It's so weird," she remarked. "I see what Ana was talking about. It seems like some money has gone missing. I'm sure it's just gone into one of these thousands of expenses, but I can't seem to find it anywhere!" she said, trying to troubleshoot aloud. Again, Cristian slinked back as he recalled the money he had to steal from the hotel business to pay off Curt's extortion for the murder of Erika's fiancé. He shied away from this topic and avoided commenting on his cousin's speculation altogether. Instead, he changed the subject.

"So, like... how do you know how to do all this stuff anyway? Is it something you can like... teach me?" Cristian asked but instantly regretted doing so, as it all sounded boring to him. While he wanted to be capable of running the business, he was hoping that creating some kind of cheat sheet would suffice. "I thought you worked in restaurants?"

"Um... yeah, I did. I used to manage restaurants and went to school for art, but I guess I've always just had a mind for this sort of thing. I can usually figure out most things that I don't know how to do with a little research and some intense YouTube-ing," Erika said and smiled.

"Okay! That sounds like something I could get on board with," Cristian replied hopefully. "I know you are officially the Head of Household now, but I want you to know that I want to stay involved in the decision-making around here. I'm not trying to step on your toes, and you clearly have all of this part..." Cristian gestured to the masses of paperwork. "..taken care of, but I was thinking maybe we could like... run it together? Like a team!"

"Yeah, for sure!" Erika agreed in a seemingly genuine way. "But listen, I'm trying to get to a good stopping point with this stuff before Curt gets here. I have a meeting scheduled with him in a little bit," she said, glancing down at her watch. At this, the smile dropped from Cristian's face and was replaced with a dark cloud. *Fuck this guy!* he thought, fighting hard to stifle his burning rage. He only slightly managed to do this, however.

"Oh! *You have a meeting with Curt*! She has a meeting with Curt!" Cristian muttered erratically. "Don't think I haven't noticed how much time you've been spending with him!" his tone was tense. Erika was not stupid. She had to know this conversation would happen. She and Curt were being so obvious about it. As she looked up at Cristian, Erika finally stopped what she was doing. He stared back down at her, angry and expectant.

"As Head of Household, I have a responsibility to interface with all colleagues who are involved with this family from a business standpoint. I've been trying to repair some tension that obviously exists between our family and the hunters. I'm trying to open up lines of communication and be transparent about our cooperation with these longstanding deals. It's important that I develop this relationship in my new role. Anytime there is a change in ownership, it's good to reach out to ensure consistency, if not promise improvement."

"What about his evening visits?" Cristian asked suspiciously.

"I was just getting to that. Outside of what I have just described to you, Curt and I have a friendship. It's nice to talk to another human who is around my age."

"But he's older than you, and also, you're *not* human!" Cristian reminded her.

"That may be true, but all my life, I thought I was. I think, all things considered, I have done a pretty remarkable job adapting to all of this, but at the end of the day, I still feel like a human. It would be different if I could transform, but I can't, so really, I don't feel any special way at all. I just know that *if* I have a baby one day, there is a possibility it could come out as a werewolf... even if I were to have a baby with another human," she said evenly. At this last comment, Cristian's face flashed with anger.

"So, you *are* fucking him!" Cristian accused. "What about Blake?"

"My love life is really no one's business but my own. I have a meeting with Blake later this afternoon. I'm not sure what everyone's plan was, but I'm not going to marry him for his money. I plan to approach him to see if we can talk reasonably about bringing any bad blood between our two families to an end and see if I can convince him to become a silent investor in Dragos Manor, LLC, until the time we can get the business in good standing. I think it would be a mutually beneficial endeavor."

At that moment, Curt tapped on the open door and walked into the room, holding a brown paper bag. Cristian glared at him as Erika nodded hello.

"Apologies, is this a good time?" Curt asked respectfully to Erika.

"It's a perfect time; come on in," she invited. "Cristian, let's find some time to discuss your ideas very soon. I'm genuinely excited to collaborate with you on the future of this business." Cristian, not knowing what else to do, kept his mouth shut and squinted a fake smile at Erika's comment. He turned and walked past Curt, shooting him a look with daggers in his eyes. Curt smiled politely and surprisingly refrained from saying any instigating comments.

"Cristian, can you please close the door behind you on your way out?" Erika asked. Cristian sneered his compliance, then turned and bowed deeply and dramatically as he walked toward the door. Neither Curt nor Erika seemed to notice. Curt approached Erika and handed her the bag. Cristian continued to peer suspiciously back inside at the pair for as long as he could, even as the door was closing behind him. Erika extracted a wrapped sandwich from the bag. Cristian scoffed, gave up, and allowed the door to close fully.

Outside the library, Cristian was fuming. He wasn't dense. It was obvious that something was going on between Curt and Erika and it was *completely* fucking up his plans for her to marry Blake. Even if Erika could talk Blake into some bullshit investment opportunity, Cristian knew how werewolves operated. They were an *old-school* crowd. There were more wolves in the Farkas family to appease and convince than just Blake. The Farkas family wanted their *Marius wolf,* and the only possibility of that happening was for Erika to have offspring with a full werewolf—Blake. Erika had been right about her assumption of having a child with a human; while her offspring might still come out as a werewolf, Cristian knew there was almost certainly *no way* it would come out as a hybrid werewolf, like his uncle.

As the thought crossed his mind of Erika and *Curt* having children together, Cristian threw up a little bit inside of his mouth. *That's it! I'm done playing around with this fucker.* Then, the realization struck him like a bolt of lightning—*I need to get rid of him. Curt needs to die.* With this revelation, Cristian started taking deliberate steps to find Vittoria so the pair could plan how to accomplish it.

A short time later, Cristian found Vittoria and Adrian sitting outside on the lounge patio, bundled up under an umbrella and propane heat lamp. A light drizzle sprinkled down all around them as the two were enjoying a new prohibition-era whiskey cocktail that Sam, the young bartender, was trying out called *The Angel Face Cocktail.* The drink was rumored to have been named after a mobster called Abe "Angel Face" Kaminsky, supposedly known for robbing speakeasies in the 1920s, or so Sam had told them. Cristian sat down at the table next to Vittoria.

"Hey, where's Blake?" Cristian asked in a hushed tone, to which Vittoria clicked her tongue and rolled her eyes.

"My idiot brother is getting ready for his meeting with Erika this afternoon," Vittoria drawled. "The bonehead is very excited that she will finally speak with him."

"That's good. He shouldn't be involved in this conversation anyway. Listen guys... Curt. *Hunter dick.* He's outta here. I'm done with him. He's gone *way* too far this time. I strongly suspect he is now fucking my cousin!"

Cristian rattled off in disgust.

"Of course, they're fucking. I thought you already knew?" Vittoria asked, eyebrows raised.

"Wow," came the shocked response from Adrian. "That is seriously fucked up."

"Tell me about it!" Cristian agreed. "So, the three of us need to figure out how we *remove* him from the equation... permanently," Cristian whispered. Vittoria shrugged her unfazed agreement while a worried expression crossed Adrian's face. Both Vittoria and Cristian noticed.

"What is it?" Cristian asked.

"You guys..." Adrian sighed. "I need to confess to you something," he said, with a look of dread falling across his face. "Am sorry I did not say anything sooner, but he threatened to me if I did. But since he is going to die now anyway, I should probably tell you.

Vittoria, you know how I know lots of kinds of creatures and peoples? When I first got to America, I heard through one of my people that an American hunter was looking to hire a werewolf in New York City to do *a job* in Los Angeles. What am trying to say is, I already knew that hunter Curt because he hired me to kill someone, or I thought that is what he hired me for." As Adrian struggled to get his story out—and not just because he struggled with English—he seemed worried that at any moment Cristian and Vittoria would become angry with him for keeping this information from them.

When Adrian finished, Cristian's jaw hit the floor. He already knew the *job* that Adrian was describing. Vittoria stared at Adrian with an impassive look on her face.

"Am sorry I keep this from you both," Adrian said with deflating spirit.

"Wow, that is *so* crazy!" Cristian replied mechanically, feigning ignorance about Adrian's confession and wondering how much he knew. "So, tell me... was it just Curt who hired you? I mean, was anyone else with him or involved?" Cristian fished. Adrian swallowed hard as he stared back at Cristian.

"He say there was a boss. *El Jefe.* But I never... he was never there with us. It was only Curt and me," Adrian stammered. "The worst part is when I got here to Dragos Manor, I saw Curt was in this town and met all of you."

Adrian sighed. "I figured out that it was Erika's boyfriend who got killed."

"Vittoria!" Cristian interrupted in a high-pitched voice, causing her to jump. "Can I speak to you in private for a moment?" Cristian asked with alarm in his voice. Adrian looked down at the ground, apparently worried he was in deep shit. He stood up to leave.

"Am so sorry, Cristian. Please don't tell Erika. She is going to be so angry," Adrian said, with a look pained look on his face. Cristian could feel the blood draining from his face as he said nothing in response. Adrian nodded sullenly at his doomed fate, then turned and walked away toward the bar. As soon as he was out of earshot, Cristian spun around to Vittoria.

"*It was meee!*" he hissed in an urgent whisper. "I hired Curt to get one of his low-life associates to kill Erika's boyfriend so I could lure her out here and make her available for your brother! This whole thing is so fucked! We definitely have to kill Curt, and now I need *you* to find out if Adrian knows anything about my involvement. Because if he *does*, then I need your fucking *word* that you will force him to take that secret to his fucking grave, otherwise..." Cristian paused, shaking his head, his face stark white. "I'm sorry... I'm sorry; I know he's your friend, but this situation just got so much fucking worse. I can't believe it was..." Cristian threw a silent tantrum, punching the air. "*..fucking Adrian,* who Curt hired! *Jesus,* I just can't fucking believe that. I mean, what are the odds, right!" he finished in a panicked whisper, barely having taken a single breath during his entire tirade. Vittoria simply stared back at him with loving amusement on her face.

"Do not worry, my darling. I will find out what he knows, and I promise you, I will do whatever is necessary to protect you. I will keep you safe. You were very thoughtful to do all that work for my dear, sweet brother."

"Uh ma God, thank you! Thank you," Cristian said, kissing Vittoria on her face with mild relief. Then, he resumed his scheming once more. "Okay, this bullshit with Curt cannot go any further. This *needs* to happen tonight! I'm going to wait for that hunter *dick-squeeze* to come out of the library and see if I can get him alone. I'll do my best to keep him around until nightfall. There's a big *fuck-all* full Moon in the sky tonight, and if I can get him up to the rooftop, I need you and Adrian to meet me up there. This fucker is about to have himself an ac-ci-dent." Cristian said, enunciating each syllable. "Okay, this part is very important; his death *has to* happen outside of the house! He cannot even be touching it when he dies. Otherwise, his ass will just be haunting the house as a ghost for eternity, and I *definitely* can't have that. We have to push him off the roof onto the lawn. Try to make it look like an accident. It's roughly a seventy-foot fall, that should do the trick," Cristian finished. Vittoria nodded her vicious agreement. She had previously told Cristian that she had no problem with killing humans and had never experienced any negative recourse from it.

"I will speak with Adrian and find out what he knows. I will convince him to help us kill Curt, and then, if need be, we will see what needs to be done about him," she reassured.

"Oh my God, I could kiss you," Cristian said and exhaled a sigh of relief.

"You know, I would let you, darling," Vittoria replied, then flashed a smile with her viper red lips.

Chapter Thirty-One

Jesus Freak

Back inside the library, Curt and Erika chatted casually near the fireplace. The pair had finished a late lunch, and Erika was now getting ready to meet Blake to discuss her business proposal with him. Seeing his window of opportunity dwindling like the nearby fire, Curt decided to apply a little playful pressure. As Erika turned her back to him and started organizing a few papers on the desktop, Curt walked up behind her and put his hands on her waist, causing her to jump.

"I told you, not here! It's too risky. The walls have eyes and ears," Erika said, pushing his hands off her.

"I can't take it! It's so hard waiting for the few and far-between moments we get to be together," he pleaded in an almost pathetic tone. "Maybe we should just make it known? Come on, you're Head of Household. Everyone has to do what you say, right? They would have to accept us."

"There's nothing to 'make known,' and there is no *us*," Erika said as she gestured back and forth between them. "This is not a serious thing. It's only been like two weeks. We're just messing around to pass the time, and don't make me regret that I'm even doing that much." She turned back to finish what she was doing on the tabletop, then scattered the embers in the fire enough for it to diminish fully. Curt thought this symbolic action was appropriate for his unrequited advances.

"Don't I get a say in this? Or do you expect me just to shut up and continue allowing you to use me like a tool? Make me feel cheap?" he asked jokingly but also slightly sulking.

"The latter," came Erika's response as she tapped him on the nose. "If you cooperate, maybe I'll meet up with you tonight. We could have a drink and bang it out."

"Great, more car sex," he remarked halfheartedly, then Erika gave him a look to let him know she could even take that much away, so he changed his tune. "But I shall take it gratefully!" he said.

The pair exited the library. Erika waved goodbye as she trotted upstairs to fetch a jacket. Curt started to walk through the lobby toward the front doors with a smile on his lips when, out of nowhere, Cristian came walking up like an unstoppable force and ambushed him.

"Ballroom. Right now. I'm not joking," Cristian ordered in broken commands. Curt released an audible exasperated sigh through his teeth, rolled his eyes, and followed Cristian, who stomped ahead into the ballroom. Cristian closed the doors, concealing them both inside.

At the same moment, Erika appeared again at the top of the staircase, zipping up her Patagonia puff jacket. She trotted down the stairs and through the lobby, but she didn't have any inclination that the impromptu meeting was taking place behind the closed doors of the ballroom. As she walked past the lounge, she glanced in and briefly noticed Vittoria and Adrian sitting alone in the far corner, huddled together in what looked like a private conversation. Erika did not pay this any mind. She stepped out into the reassuring New England drizzle. Once outside, she took a deep breath and thought about how much she liked the rain and appreciated that it kept things green and made her heart peaceful.

The lounge was a very cozy place at this time of year. The room possessed so much warmth in all aspects of the word. There were two fireplaces with roaring fires on the southwest and east walls of the room and a variety of couches, sofas, booths, cocktail tables, and chairs for guests to choose from. Kerosene sconces adorned the walls and emitted a soft, warm glow for lighting ambiance. During the cooler months of the year, as it was now, the glass wall remained closed to keep all the comfy warmth trapped inside.

After seeing Erika pass by and look in their direction, Adrian and Vittoria moved over to a booth with a high seat backing so anyone passing by would not see them engaged in their sensitive conversation. Once settled, Vittoria resumed her inquiry.

"And so, as far as you know, the hunter hired you, and you don't know who the other party involved was? The boss... *El Jefe*?" she hissed out her line of questioning in a hushed tone.

"That's all I know, I swear!" Adrian responded for the third time, his voice urgent and flustered. Indeed, he seemed to be standing steadfast by his answers. He claimed not to know who the other player in this game was. However, Vittoria realized that Adrian might still be trying to protect himself if they were unsuccessful in their plan to kill Curt.

"Darling Adrian, I'm only going to ask you this one more time, and I promise you, of the beings to fear in this situation, you should fear me above that hunter... who *will* die; this I assure you. You should fear me not because I would ever bring harm to you but because betraying my trust will remove me from your corner. You will have to face any consequences alone should the truth come out. Now, for the last time, do you know who *the boss* was?" Her gaze was steely as she held Adrian's eyesight. And it was effective. He cracked. Adrian sighed out a long exhale.

"Cristian... Am pretty sure that *El Jefe* is Cristian. At least, that's what the hunter says to me in New York. He only mentioned it once or two times. I do not think he meant to say the name, and I think he forgot he said it to me. Curt never knew I would actually meet him. I suspect it was Cristian who was the boss of this job."

A look of shame instantly crept across Adrian's face at the previous lies he had told Vittoria, followed by a look of worry over what might come next after his admission. Vittoria, on the other hand, did not react. Instead, she sat back in her chair and momentarily contemplated Adrian. He was her friend. She was fond of him and had never considered harming him or allowing anyone else to. And while Vittoria held a tremendous amount of love for Cristian, surely if she were to inform him of Adrian's awareness of his involvement in the matter, Cristian could become very dangerous for her friend. Possibly, Cristian may be convinced in the short-term, but if paranoia got the better of him, he would probably never feel at ease regarding Adrian.

So now Vittoria clearly saw her task at hand. She would have to instruct Adrian to become even more fortified with this information than he had been with her, especially with Cristian. However, before she would lead Adrian down this road to conceal the truth, curiosity got the better of her, and another question sprang to mind. She rolled her gaze back toward her friend sitting across the table. His face was anxious, as he had been waiting for her to say something.

"So... how did you do it then?" she asked, piqued by morbid curiosity. Adrian blinked, trying to catch up with the shift in her line of questioning.

"Oh... I didn't kill him," Adrian clarified, having previously omitted this detail.

The elevator *dinged* in the Dragos Manor lobby, announcing the passenger's arrival from the floors above. Out stepped Marius Dragos wearing black leather motorcycle pants and a black long-sleeved Hawkwind T-shirt. He strolled casually yet with a sturdy gait toward the hotel lounge. As he passed one of the elderly silver-haired guests, he nodded hello. Mrs. Johnson responded by sneering her lip in an attempted seductive snarl while simultaneously swiping the air with a cat claw motion in his direction. Marius humored her as he jumped back, very spry with his footwork, then playfully allowed a sly grin to appear on his lips.

"Good afternoon, Mrs. Johnson," he greeted the aggressively coquettish old woman as he continued toward the bar. Once inside the lounge, Marius glanced around the room and passively noticed various guests were scattered about. Some guests sipped drinks, while others quietly read books, and others were engaged in conversations in hushed tones. Marius started toward a closet in the back of the lounge to retrieve his riding gear—a helmet and jacket—when a piece of a conversation caught his attention.

"...and then we landed at Lacks."

Lacks. The word danced around in his head for a moment, and then a strange feeling told him to turn around to see who had spoken the word. In a nearby booth sat Vittoria Farkas and her friend, Adrian. The two appeared to be engaged in a private conversation.

"Hello, Marius," Vittoria said, her iconic smile appearing on her face.

"Vittoria, Adrian. Good afternoon," Marius said, nodding his head toward them in greeting.

"And what are you up to on this crisp autumn afternoon?" she asked.

"I'm headed into town to meet Malcolm Sr. at the Foolish Goat and am just grabbing my helmet for the ride," Marius explained in banal fashion.

"Very nice. Make sure you take a warm jacket, too. It's chilly out there. I think we might be expecting some more rain later," Vittoria forecasted.

"I will do that. Thank you, Vittoria," Marius said with a smile. As he continued toward the closet, Marius was struck by the feeling that he had just lost his train of thought. He was supposed to do something, or there had been something else he had meant to do in this area, but he couldn't think of what it was. Saying hello to Vittoria and Adrian must have knocked the thought out of his head. It would come to him later. He shook it off, grabbed his helmet and a thick motorcycle jacket, and then shut the closet door.

On his way out, Marius waved goodbye to Vittoria and Adrian, who gave him a smile and a head nod, respectively. As soon as he was out of earshot, Vittoria rolled her eyes back over toward Adrian.

"Do you think he heard anything?"

"I do not think so. I did not say anything about the kill. I was talking about getting to the airport. Lacks."

"Oh, right. I was going to ask what you mean by that, but we should probably continue this conversation another time. Marius popping up was a good reminder that you never know who could be listening," Vittoria drawled. As she said these words, a silver smoke-like mist rippled through the air near the pair before disappearing again. Vittoria stared wide-eyed at the anomaly. "What was that? That was strange," she said.

"Oh! Spooky sliver!" Adrian commented. "I think it means there is a ghost right there."

The large front doors with the brass wolf-head doorknockers swung open, and Marius stepped out, decked out in leather from head to toe. The protective riding gear made Marius look like a badass as he reached up and secured his black carbon helmet on his head—his best helmet for riding through rainfall. Turning the key, his *Zero Engineering T5 Blackie* roared to life. Marius walked the bike backward, steering the handles around. Once in position, his left hand worked the clutch, and his left foot worked the gear shift as the throttle took over, and he rode off toward town to rendezvous with Malcolm Sr. at the Foolish Goat.

Again, Marius joined Malcolm Aristide Sr. in the back corner booth at the tavern in downtown Nocturne.

"Ti-Marius, thank you for meeting with me on such short notice," Malcolm Sr. said in greeting, shaking his friend's hand as they took a seat.

"Of course, Malcolm, my dear friend! Thank you for meeting me here. As you know, it's almost impossible to speak privately at Dragos Manor."

"You read my mind, bruh!" Malcolm Sr. said, nodding his head. "I know there is barely a private corner at your house. The walls have ears with all those ghosts lurking about."

"So, what is it? Did you find something else out?"

"So, get this, bruh... I heard back from that busboy again! The one who works at his family's werewolf speakeasy in New York City. He said he had been thinking about something. Another detail he forgot to tell me about those two suspicious characters when they had been coming around there. But then the kid said every time he went to contact me, he couldn't find my phone number!"

"So, what was the extra detail?" Marius asked.

"Okay, bruh, but first, I want to say that this detail could mean anything. I'm not accusing anyone of anything. The kid said that after we spoke the first time, he said he forgot to mention that he thinks the man, not the werewolf, but the human man... he thinks that the man was some kinda Jesus freak." Malcolm Sr. paused and then took a deep breath before continuing.

"Why does he think that?" Marius asked.

"The kid thinks the man might have been a Jesus freak because the kid heard the man say the word 'Christian' a few times," Malcolm Sr. again paused to let Marius digest, but he did not expect Marius' sudden reaction.

"Oh my God!" Marius exclaimed loudly, which caused the sleepy patrons across the bar to jump in alarm. They all turned and shot annoyed glances in Marius and Malcolm's direction. The pair ignored this and continued their conversation, Marius lowering his voice this time. "Oh my God, Malcolm! On my way here to meet you... I heard that Hungarian wolf, Adrian... I heard him say the word Lacks! I *knew* I had heard that word somewhere before! It made me pause for a moment because I couldn't quite place why it sounded familiar! Anyway, holy shit!" Marius said in quiet exclamation, his mind reeling at what this all could mean. Malcolm Sr. looked back at Marius with an expression of shock on his face.

"Marius, my friend, this could be really serious. I think we should take a step back," he advised wisely.

"I appreciate your concern, Malcolm, but don't worry. I don't plan to accost Cristian or Adrian about this. I will simply start by asking my nephew some questions to see if he knows anything about this information you have uncovered. And let me be clear: I am prepared to get a truthful answer," Marius stated in a manner that, while not threatening, seemed more dangerous than threatening.

Chapter Thirty-Two

The Other Side

It was a cool, smoggy day in North Hollywood. Althea peacefully organized a new stock shipment inside her metaphysical shop called Stellar Remnants. She casually laid out different types of polished stones, manifestation candles, amulets, crystals, varieties of sage, palo santo, and other items onto display tables and shelves. So far, the morning had been calm and uneventful for the most part. The shop had opened at 11 AM, as it normally did, and foot traffic had been slow since it was a weekday; only one or two customers had come in, and it was already getting late into the afternoon.

The front doorbell sounded, indicating someone had just entered. Althea lifted her head to greet the new arrival but did not see anyone in the shop. *Must have been a tremor, or passing truck, or maybe even some lost spirit who had jostled the bell*, she thought, dismissing the incident. But then something else happened. A woman chatting on her cellphone walked past the shop window. While she had never seen this person before, something about the woman made the hairs on Althea's arm stand at alert. The woman was the mousy type. She was chatting away on her cell phone as she casually glanced inside the shop window and inadvertently made eye contact with Althea. A shock wave shot through Althea's entire core when their eyes connected. It would have been a 10.0 on her intuition Richter scale. Then, as if traveling through the window of this stranger's eyes, Althea saw an image of the girl from her dreams pop into her mind. *Erika,* Althea realized. And then it was over just as quickly as it had all happened. The moment had passed, and the woman talking on her cell phone was gone. Standing up a little unsteadily, Althea tried to move quickly to go after the woman.

Once outside, Althea looked down the sidewalk in the direction the woman had been heading. There was no sign of her. She jogged a little way and peered around the corner, down the adjoining street. Again, there was no sign of the woman anywhere. With some difficulty, she decided to let the incident go. If the woman had left, the opportunity had also decided to leave, so Althea consciously decided not to overexert her will too strongly into this matter. She would continue to wait patiently. The time would come. The entrance onto that road would come. Althea peered up into the sky and whispered a quick prayer that she hoped this stranger Erika was doing alright... wherever she might be.

Back in Nocturne, the light drizzle was progressively turning into proper rain drops with each passing moment. A bank of gray clouds approached dauntingly from the east, accentuating the nightfall on the horizon. Blake and Erika walked side-by-side through the vibrant green gardens, with multi-colored fall leaves covering the ground all around them. The fall air was fresh and damp.

"So, what do you think of my idea?" she asked, after having just laid out her business proposal to bring the Farkas family on as silent investors to Dragos Manor, LLC. The premise of Erika's pitch was a twofold approach—For one, she tried to sell the opportunity as 'good for their species' if one prestigious Lycan family helped to elevate another. Second, this opportunity would allow Blake to join Erika and become part of the next generation of Lycans who were freethinkers. They had the power to make changes and resolve outdated conflicts that had existed between the two families for far too long. Conflict that no longer served any function, nor had any relevance to either of them. Erika had peppered in words and phrases such as 'diplomacy' and 'gesture of goodwill.' All of this while assuring Blake it would be a profitable endeavor for the Farkas family, so long as they could agree on the terms of investment, as well as an appropriate timeframe for demonstrable results.

Blake had been listening intently to Erika's thorough and well-thought-out business plan, never once interrupting, but only occasionally asking a question or two during an appropriate pause in conversation. As a result, it seemed the proposal had been effective.

"I think it is a very good plan. You impress me, Erika," Blake somberly complimented. "But it is not me you need to ask for this. It is my mother. You could also ask Vittoria. She would be the next Head of House in my family."

Erika was touched by Blake's positive reaction to her ideas. She had suspected it would have to be the Farkas females who she would ultimately need to convince but had decided to approach the situation in small doses. She thought it better to approach Blake first and get him on board, and then there might be a higher chance of success with his mother and sister.

At that moment, Erika regarded Blake in a more objective light. He was so kind and gentle. He had always been so sweet to her, even despite his tendency to be overtly blunt at times... or most of the time. And yet, she still felt the familiar barrier she kept so fortified between them. Now, wanting to establish a potential business relationship with the Farkas family and also get past years and years of defunct bad blood, Erika dug deep and challenged herself to tear down the wall that she so painstakingly kept up. After all, Blake was really not a bad guy. She resolved herself to make a concerted effort to sort out any lingering issues between them.

"I would like to address a couple of things with you. If that's okay?" she said, and then, after Blake nodded his consent, Erika continued. "The first thing I want to ask about is the feud between our families. Is there any way you would be willing to come together with me to help me figure out how we can put an end to it? To help figure out how to bring our families together and find a lasting solution and resolution that will be upheld back in Europe?" Erika asked in earnest. Blake only smiled at this. "What is it?" she asked.

"Nobody back at my home knows what this *feud* means," Blake chuckled.

"What do you mean?" Erika asked in surprise.

"There is maybe some reason that we think we know about. We think maybe it is because in Europe, werewolves stay hidden away from humans. Also, Romanian werewolves started *mating* with humans. This is a law... how you say no good? Illegal! Hungarian werewolves do not do this," he said. "But there is nothings wrong with a werewolf who is half-human," he added, knowing Erika herself was half-human. "In fact, it seems we were wrong. Look at you, uncle. There is no wolf like him, and he came from a werewolf who is half-human."

"What about all the killings? I heard the Farkas family is responsible for several Romanian werewolf deaths."

"Maybe one hundred years ago, this may have happen, but I don't know any Farkas that has killed a Dragos in recent time," Blake said resolutely.

"Are you serious? I don't believe it!" Erika said incredulously, pulling her jacket up around her wet face as she and Blake finally retreated under the cover of the garden gazebo. The two stood looking out into the rainfall as Erika contemplated aloud, "I guess just like most misunderstandings and conflicts in society, they are surrounding perceived differences and false truths," she mused. "So why was everyone pushing so hard for us to get married then?" she asked. To this question, Blake lowered his face, obviously trying to conceal his wound.

"Erika, I heard about you for a very long time. My parents want me to meet you because you would be a suitable partner. You Head of House and could maybe give them special grandpup, like Marius. At first, I like all those things too, but then I meet you." Blake lifted his gaze from the floor and looked directly into her eyes. "And I don't think I will ever find another like you in this world. You are amazing, special creature."

Erika looked at the surprising clarity in his eyes as he spoke. The rain hammered down on the rooftop of the wooden gazebo. The chilly October air smelled pleasantly earthy as the two of them stood there together. Erika felt a warmth and closeness to him that she had to admit she had always felt. Then, the totality of her circumstance, coupled with all the revelations she had learned since returning sank in, and panic swelled inside her chest. She took a deep breath, trying to thwart the onset of a panic attack.

"I'm in way over my head," her voice broke. Blake appeared surprised at the change in her demeanor.

"What's wrong?" he asked with growing concern. "Are you sick?"

"I'm trying to take up the reins like a boss, ya know?" she started with a quivering voice, "but I'm so scared. I'm so scared, and I feel so lost. I've never done *anything* like this before! Never run a haunted mansion hotel. I have never been a werewolf. I never knew werewolves and ghosts even existed, let alone see them up close or be related to them! And I'm doing it all alone!" Tears welled up in her eyes at the feeling of helplessness that was flooding in and clashing against her futile struggle to have control. "And on top of it all, I found out there is *something* in that house." Her voice now struck a chord of pain as she pointed toward Dragos Manor. "It's upstairs, shut up behind a brick wall. And I constantly feel it *bursting* to come out!"

"What is the thing, Erika?" Blake asked with care and concern. Again, her voice caught in her throat as she attempted to respond.

"*The Mother,*" Erika finally managed to say. "Ana says it's some sort of fragmented soul. I'm not very clear on exactly what it is, but it feels like a drug. The desire to let it out is stronger than I can bear. But supposedly, no one can let it out. If it gets out, there is a very strong chance that it will kill me, maybe even kill others. But my mother is up there! She got lost in her own pain, trying to fortify it away." Erika now put her face in her hands and wept in despair. Blake got closer and gently wrapped his arms around her. She did not protest as she allowed herself to yield to the solace of his strong embrace as she cried helplessly like a child into his large chest. Blake spoke softly, attempting to comfort her.

"I understand you are not expecting any kind of this life. I understand it must make you feel like a great shock. But this side of the world you see now... this *is* your world. It is everybody's world. This side has always been here in plain sight, only most human peoples do not see it. They cannot see it. It is, as you call it, a shift in perspective. You tilt a little bit what you see to the side, and then you see clear through to the other side—the whole world has always been here. The other side might seem strange, unusual, sure, but also on the other side has magic and possibility. Remember the chicken on the road story? Is the side the chicken he wants to be on," Blake explained.

Erika looked up into his face. As usual, he wore a sweet, soft look in his eyes as he smiled down at her. She understood most of what he was trying to communicate to her. He was telling her most people are closed off to their surroundings and that it takes a shift in perspective to see the magnificent, the extraordinary, and all the possibilities that life has to offer. It was all so comforting and wise, and most of his message had yet to get lost in translation. The only part where he had somewhat lost her was the 'chicken on the road story' part.

"What chicken on the road story, Blake?" she asked, stepping out of his arms but still feeling comforted by his presence.

"Why did the chicken cross the road?" he asked with a smile.

"To get to *The Other Side*," she responded with a smile. Blake smiled back, seemingly pleased that they shared the answer, as they both stood side by side and stared out into the rainy evening from under the gazebo's covering.

"No, you're wrong! Your story doesn't hold water! Let's face it: our lineage was probably not caused by evolution. The first werewolves were most likely the result of something more divine, like from aliens, or something..." Cristian was on a figurative soapbox going down a road and had no idea where it would end.

"Ooohh my God, I don't care!" came Curt's annoyed response. Cristian now paused his tirade and raised his hand to his mouth. He chewed his nails idly as he glanced nervously toward the large, drawn curtains. *Curse Tom for being so diligent about closing the curtains on days the full Moon was due,* Cristian thought to himself. *If only I could get a sense of what time it was.* As he explored his abdomen, down inside the pit of his solar plexus, Cristian couldn't yet feel his wolf stirring inside of him.

"Look Cristian, I don't know what the fuck you're *crappin' on* about right now, but I'm gonna take off, dude," Curt said while slapping both hands down onto his thighs as he stood up. He clearly had enough after sitting in the same spot for so long listening to Cristian go on and on. First, they discussed the feral werewolves that sprang up in the wake of the Sturgeon Moon party, then recent complaints the townspeople had been having regarding the werewolf activity, then lastly, Cristian's speculations of the origins of werewolves. He knew he had to capture the hunter's attention long enough to keep him there until the full Moon came out that night. Cristian decided to finally dive into the real conversation topic he knew Curt wouldn't be able to resist.

"So... I hear you hired *Adrian* to do one of your non-werewolf kills this year. That's interesting!" Cristian said ominously with a smug expression on his face. Curt stopped dead in his tracks just as he was about to exit the ballroom. He didn't turn around. Cristian knew he got him. "Yeah, he told us, Adrian, that is. He told us you hired him to do a hit on Erika's boyfriend in California," Cristian taunted. Curt remained unnervingly still for a moment longer, then finally turned around. His expression was like stone. Then Cristian went for it. "*You* need to stop seeing her. This won't end well for you."

"Sorry, pal. I can't do that. Sure, I hired Adrian, but you hired me."

"Erika needs to choose Blake. I won't let you get in the way of that."

"Again, that's never gonna happen, compadre."

"You think you can just stonewall me into getting what you want, but you can't!" Cristian was angry. "The truth is—you have a problem; I have a problem. Let's talk about your problem first—*you* hired Adrian to kill Erika's boyfriend. You did that! Do you think Erika is going to want anything to do with you after she finds out? Sure, you can *try* to incriminate me. I'll flat-out deny it. Adrian will go along with whatever Vittoria tells him to. So, that will be everyone saying one narrative and only *you* saying the other. If you don't stop seeing Erika, I will tell her," Cristian threatened. To this, Curt clicked his tongue as he stared off into the corner of the room with arms folded. He was visibly angry at the nerve Cristian had.

"And your problem?" Curt finally asked.

"My problem is simple. You. Everything else is largely in place and has the potential to go forward, so long as there are no roadblocks. And all I see in front of me is one greedy, arrogant fuckin roadblock. Just step aside, and both our problems will be solved. Erika will never know you had anything to do with killing her boyfriend. You have your money. Take it and get the fuck out of Nocturne. Have the Wolf Hunter's Association send another hunter to the area since you guys are so insistent that this region needs one. But it's not you. Not anymore. Do you understand me?" Cristian said. Curt unfolded his arms and took a few casual strides forward until he was right up in Cristian's face, looming over him menacingly. Cristian stood his ground, taking in how much taller Curt was than himself, as he stood dangerously close.

"And suppose I just take the whole ship down with me? I tell her you hired the kill—she believes me or doesn't—and then suppose there's an accident and... she gets hurt, or worse, maybe gets killed?" Curt threatened in a quiet, daunting tone. Cristian's face twisted up as he furrowed his brows.

"Dear God! You really *are* a psychopath, aren't you?" he said incredulously.

"That's rich coming from a 'Killer,'" Curt said mockingly. His eyes flashed, revealing the void of black emptiness that lay behind them. "You have no idea what I'm capable of," he said darkly.

"Well, I suspect someone is going to be telling her something very soon. It'll be interesting to see who finds her first," Cristian challenged. With that, Curt did not waste one second longer talking to Cristian. He turned on his heel and walked straight out through the ballroom doors.

Once in the lobby, Curt craned his neck around and searched, trying to decide where to go to look for Erika first. At that moment, Vittoria emerged from the lounge across the lobby. She also appeared to be searching for someone.

"Oh," she said, in almost a theatrical tone. "Have you seen Cristian? Erika and my brother are looking for him. They just went upstairs to the 4th floor to retrieve something from the office and asked Cristian to meet them up there." Curt glared down at the she-werewolf in human form and brushed past her without saying a word. He headed straight toward the elevator at the far end of the lobby. Once the doors parted, Curt stepped into the cart and turned back around. Vittoria was nowhere to be seen.

On the ride up, Curt's thoughts ran wild. He would have to try with every fiber of his being to convince Erika to leave with him that night, and he knew this would not be easy. Curt knew she did not think that their relationship was anything significant, let alone enough to warrant her blind faith in him. He would need to be convincing. *This is just fucking perfect,* he thought. And that bit about killing her, of course, Curt had been lying. He had meant what he had told Erika—she was the first thing that had made him feel *anything* in a very long time. He would not let that go without a fight. But he knew the timing could not be any worse with the full Moon due to arrive in the sky that night.

Back in the lobby, Cristian, Vittoria, and Adrian stepped up to the elevator and watched the needle as it approached the 4th floor.

"Nicely done, Vittoria," Cristian said, referring to the lie she told to steer Curt upstairs.

"Don't mention it," she drawled. The needle stopped, signifying Curt had arrived on the 4th floor.

"Get him," Cristian said. The eyes of all three werewolves, still in their human form, began to turn black with the prospect of what was to come. Then, all three soon-to-be werewolves split up, each taking separate paths in pursuit of their prey. Cristian and Adrian ran out the front door, undressing as they went, while Vittoria pressed the elevator's button, calling the cart back downstairs.

Chapter Thirty-Three

The Altercation

Night of the Blood Moon

Lightning strikes lit up the night sky, and the sound of distant thunder came rolling in a few moments behind it. The rain splashed down hard on the 4th-story rooftop courtyard. Large pea-sized droplets pelted down into the pooling water that collected upon the courtyard's stone floor, making the appearance of thousands of small fish amid a vigorous feeding frenzy. The surface of the massive pool jounced and jostled this way and that.

Heavy boot falls slapped down hard, causing the puddle to slosh and thrash with each running step as Curt raced into the center of the courtyard. Having not located Erika inside Ana's office, as Vittoria had stated, he now frantically searched for her outside on the rooftop courtyard. However, he already knew the she-wolf had most likely tricked him. His instincts now blared an alarm that he was in danger.

With no hesitation, Curt ripped open his brown leather bomber jacket and grabbed two large, silver, fixed-blade Bowie knives that he always kept holstered in the jacket's lining. In one swift motion, he loaded both knives point-side downward into a chambered snake-strike grip in each of his hands, then positioned himself into a tiger crouch, ready for a fight. With rigorous focus, he kept his eyes fixated on the door leading back into the hallway to the elevator.

A long moment of silence passed, save for the large beads of rain that relentlessly plunged like a liquid swarm into the rooftop lake all around him. From behind the closed door, Curt heard a faint, high-pitched dinging sound announcing the arrival of the elevator cart. More silence. More waiting. The raindrops echoed deafeningly in the night, dulling his senses as the anticipation mounted. A minute went by and then another.

A damp bar towel swirled in circular motions, leaving streaks of disinfectant and water in its wake. The young bartender whistled as he worked to keep the drink service area clean.

The sound of the large front doors opened then shut again, and soon Marius stood in the lounge entryway, scanning the room. Normally, around this time, Cristian, the Farkas siblings, and their friend Adrian would be finishing up their pre-transformation cocktails before heading out into the night. And since the autumnal equinox had brought much darker night skies, tonight, in particular, was the perfect backdrop for the bright blood Moon that was due in the sky any minute.

"Sam. Have you seen Cristian and his friends?" Marius asked with some urgency in his voice.

Curt grew impatient and began to rise out of the fighting stance he had been holding for some time now. Slowly, he began to walk toward the door. He did not dare take his eyes off it. As he got closer, the door drifted open ever so slightly to reveal a faint sliver of light from the hallway on the other side. Again, he stopped.

From somewhere behind him, he heard the faint padding of paws splashing through the rainfall. His reaction time was just a fraction off. He turned and was mauled by Cristian in his werewolf state, but Curt was able to roll and maneuver out of the Lycan's grasp. A second werewolf, wolf Vittoria, now burst through the door. Then a third werewolf, wolf Adrian, breached the east wall and joined in the fight.

All three werewolves relentlessly attacked the hunter who worked hard, fighting Beatrix Kiddo style, to fend off each new enemy that came at him in rapid succession. Curt's silver knives slashed through the wet night as all the werewolves agilely dodged them. They knew those knives meant certain death for any of them since all hunters were equipped with knives made of sterling silver.

Back under the dry protection of the gazebo, Erika awoke feeling quite cozy and warm. She and Blake had spent the past hour laughing, joking, and bonding over great conversation. Then something unexpected happened. The two eventually snuggled up together and quietly watched the rainfall for a while. The sound of the rain must have lulled Erika to sleep, as the sound of distant thunder now woke her. She felt comfortable and safe, feeling Blake's secure warmth next to her. As she stirred, she stretched, looked up at him, and saw she was cuddling with a large werewolf. He was sleeping and breathing softly next to her.

At first, Erika felt startled and somewhat afraid, still very much not used to the creatures, but as she steadied herself, her fear diminished. She took in the black werewolf peacefully dozing next to her. Erika smiled to herself as she allowed her heart to warm at the sight of this large, beautiful creature who she knew cared about her so much.

She yawned, laid her head back against him, and gazed idly out into the cold, rainy night. The silhouette of Dragos Manor stood erect against the dark and stormy sky. Suddenly, a flash of lightning lit up the entire landscape before her. Erika noticed four figures—one human and three werewolves—engaged in what looked like a vicious fight atop the large mansion estate. She jumped up, waking wolf Blake in the process.

"Blake!" she yelled out in a panicked voice. "Something's happening up there! Look! On the rooftop courtyard!"

Wolf Blake fixed his sharp vision in the direction Erika indicated and saw the fight in progress. His keen werewolf eyesight did not need the illumination of a lightning strike.

"Find Marius!" he instructed but did not wait for her response. In a flash, wolf Blake took off, bounding through the rain toward Dragos Manor. As he ran, bits of tattered clothing fell away from his canine body. Erika fought to keep her wits about her despite her growing panic. She, too, sprang out of the gazebo and ran through the rain-soaked gardens toward the house to find Marius, just as Blake had instructed.

A soaking-wet Erika burst through the front doors of Dragos Manor, startling some elderly silver-haired guests with her drenched and frantic appearance. Ignoring and moving past them, Erika ran into the lounge. The bartender was stocking new liquor bottles behind the bar when she appeared.

"Sam! Have you seen Marius?!" she asked with urgency. Sam opened his mouth to respond but didn't need to, as Marius again appeared in the doorway.

"Erika, there you are! Are you okay?" Marius started to ask, but she cut him off.

"They're fighting! On the roof! You've got to come quick! Curt—" But Erika was winded and couldn't get the words out. At this, Marius turned and ran out of the lounge, into the lobby, and toward the elevator. Erika hurried after him.

Marius and Erika arrived on the rooftop courtyard a short while later to find a skilled fight underway. Curt swept a kick underneath wolf Cristian's leg in a lightning-fast movement, sending the werewolf flying off his feet with a wave of rainwater in his wake. Then, Curt turned—just in time—and narrowly missed an attack from wolf Vittoria. The she-wolf recoiled when Curt lashed out his fist, which gripped a silver Bowie knife.

"Son of a bitch," Marius growled through gritted teeth, as he stared in horror at the mess that was unfolding before him.

Wolf Adrian and Curt seized one another, and a great struggle ensued. Wolf Blake finally appeared on the rooftop and immediately began trying to fend off his werewolf sister and wolf Cristian in an effort to protect the American hunter. Curt successfully broke free from the scuffle with wolf Adrian and, in the process, managed to slash him across his shoulder with his Bowie knife. Wolf Adrian clutched his paw to the smoking, bloody wound with an angry snarl on his wolf lips.

"We have to stop them!" Erika yelled at Marius, worried about Curt's safety. Then she rushed forward and attempted to intervene in the fight. Wolf Cristian was about to lunge for another attack on Curt, but Erika suddenly grabbed him by his shoulders. Wolf Cristian rounded ferociously and focused his large, snarling werewolf face just inches away from his cousin's face. *Oh fuck*, she thought, as she instantly regretted her decision.

Meanwhile, Marius took bold strides forward while simultaneously transforming with each step. His limbs were the first of his body parts to change. Pale fur-covered hands, forearms, calves, and feet came shooting out of his clothing, ripping his jacket cuffs and pant legs. Then, his thick silver hair atop his head began to spread onto his face and merge with his beard. A long, furry snout with pointed teeth stretched and emerged out from the contours of the face he had once possessed. Finally, a large, thick silver tail came bursting out of the seat of wolf Marius' pants. The gigantic silver werewolf stood on hindlegs for a moment as he released a commanding howl up at the blood Moon. Then, he bent down from a bipedal stance onto all fours. Wolf Marius shook like a dog, sending the remainder of his tattered clothing and rainwater flying every which way, leaving a large, silver werewolf standing before them.

Erika's instincts screamed at her to be afraid of this large, black werewolf that was snarling and growling in front of her, but as she looked into wolf Cristian's eyes, all she saw was that little *asshole* of a cousin she had grown up with. He had always maintained some sort of distance from her, and Erika had no idea why. She had only ever been kind and supportive to him, and all he had ever done in return was be a self-centered, mean-spirited, arrogant little jerk of a family member. Channeling all her frustration that she felt toward her cousin, Erika wound up a tight fist and punched him square in his nose. Snout bloodied; wolf Cristian grabbed his face and let out a very feminine scream. He was surprised that she had punched him in the face.

Erika realized she may have made a huge mistake by punching a werewolf in the nose. She began to retreat toward an old junk pile that was stacked up against a far wall in the courtyard. Wolf Cristian pursued her and tackled her hard as the two cousins crash-landed into the pile of old crates, discarded bottles and cans, and soggy boxes. Erika struggled against her werewolf cousin in the rain-soaked debris. Their struggling knocked over a crate, dislodging an old tennis ball and sending it rolling toward them. Erika got an idea. She wrestled one arm free and grabbed the tennis ball, then turned and whistled to wolf Cristian. Surprisingly, it worked. Wolf Cristian stopped fighting with her to see what she had whistled about. Erika gripped the tennis ball tightly in her hand. Her werewolf cousin froze with pinpoint focus as he watched the ball. The two cousins lay tangled up amongst the debris and stared at one another. The tension between them was palpable in this strange standoff.

"Go get it, boy!" Erika said as she threw the ball as hard as she could—considering she was mostly pinned on the ground. Wolf Cristian's face conveyed how desperately he wanted to deny what would inevitably happen next, but he could not. His willpower betrayed him.

"Son of a bitch..." he whispered in a quiet, defeated tone through gritted fangs. He released Erika, picked himself up off the ground, and went to fetch the ball.

Wolf Marius, wolf Blake, and Curt skillfully fought side-by-side, trying to subdue the relentless attacks from wolf Vittoria and wolf Adrian. Erika ran back to where the group was fighting and stared in horror at the violence playing out in front of her. Just then, wolf Cristian appeared at Erika's side, standing on his hind legs. He wore a pleased expression on his face as he presented the retrieved tennis ball in his hand. Erika knew if she did not continue to distract him, he would resume the attack on Curt with the others once more. Feeling bad about what she was about to do next, Erika put a hand on wolf Cristian's shoulder as if to say, "Good boy," but instead, she pivoted around and kneed him in the balls. Her werewolf cousin yelped, then doubled over in pain, as he grabbed his testicles hidden beneath the thick fur between his legs. He dropped onto his knees and dropped the tennis ball, which splashed into the puddle of water next to him.

While Curt was fighting off an attack from wolf Vittoria, wolf Adrian lunged straight for the hunter's throat. A blurry flash of silver cut through the dark, rain-soaked night as quick as a striking snake and made contact with its target—wolf Adrian's temple. After that, wolf Marius and wolf Blake were able to subdue the Farkas she-werewolf as they drove her back from the brutal scene. Curt withdrew the blade, and wolf Adrian immediately collapsed heavily onto the ground. His werewolf body began to change back into the form of a naked human. The rainfall finally began to relent all around them as the group all stared down at Adrian, who lay dead on the 4th-floor rooftop courtyard.

Chapter Thirty-Four

The Real Killer

Curt stepped over Adrian's dead body, which lay in a cocktail of blood and rainwater. The rain had stopped falling, and the clouds began to clear as he walked brazenly—albeit spent of energy—toward Erika. She ran up to him and threw her arms around his tall shoulders, hugging him tightly, obviously thankful that he was unharmed. Wolf Blake turned away from them and lowered his head. Wolf Vittoria growled with rage and disgust. Marius and Blake, still in their werewolf forms, now stood as a barrier between the hugging pair and wolf Vittoria and wolf Cristian—who was still on the ground after getting kneed in the groin by his cousin.

Wolf Marius was about to ask what the fight was about, but now, seeing Curt and Erika hugging the way they were and the reaction from the Farkas siblings, he did not need to ask. Instead, Marius knew he needed to run dual course damage control—both with the attack on the hunter and the disappointment the Farkas family was experiencing with an unfulfilled betrothal promise. *What a mess*, wolf Marius thought to himself.

"Please forgive our family, Blake and Vittoria," wolf Marius started, first addressing the werewolf Farkas siblings. "I know this story has not turned out the way you may have wanted it to, but that shouldn't negate all we have come to know of one another. Our family has been privileged to host you in our home, lives, and hearts. I'm very sorry this happened to your friend. He was a... unique fellow. But as you both know, there are laws against werewolves attacking hunters, so I must urge you both to set aside your personal feelings on this tragedy and see reason. Please do not pursue any punitive recourse. That would only make this already terrible situation much worse." Then, wolf Marius looked over at wolf Blake. "Blake, I know you must be disappointed, but listen to me, pup, the best and most lasting form of love happens when individuals choose each other. You want equity. Two strong pillars to equally hold up the foundation of your household," Wolf Marius said with compassion. "Do you understand what I'm trying to tell you, my friend?" To this, wolf Blake sullenly nodded his large wolf head.

Next, Marius looked down at his werewolf nephew, who sat defeated in the puddle where we had dropped to his knees in pain. "Cristian," Wolf Marius sighed. "We are your family—Erika, me, your grandmother. It would be best if you were protecting our family *first* above all costs. I understand you meant well and were only trying to help repair the damage between our two families, but I fear you've only created more damage here tonight with expectations getting shattered. My only hope is that Blake, Vittoria, and their family will be able to forgive us."

Wolf Marius then shifted his focus to the hunter. "Curt, I know there is a chance you may be angry at the events that have taken place here tonight and may be considering retaliation, but you had to understand your actions to pursue Erika were going to create problems with all the expectations flying around. I'm not saying you two did anything wrong, but I hope you can view tonight's situation through a lens of compassion and understanding. *I beg you* to please allow this to end here and now, with no further consequence to any wolf here tonight, other than the life that has already been tragically lost."

Curt's expression was steely as he held an immaculate poker face. He said nothing to wolf Marius and instead turned to Erika. He placed his wet, bloodied hand on her cheek, then leaned down to kiss her. Wolf Blake again turned his face away at this display of affection. But Erika sharply pulled away from the kiss. Curt stopped and searched her face. Wolf Vittoria looked down at her dead friend, who lay bleeding and naked in a puddle.

"So, she loves you even though you killed her boyfriend, Hunter?" Wolf Vittoria called out to Curt. A look of shock slowly fell over Erika's face as she digested the she-wolf's words. Now it was Erika's turn to search Curt's face for anything to indicate the validity or falsity of wolf Vittoria's statement. If nothing else, everyone was at least waiting for Curt to deny the accusation. But he didn't.

"We should go somewhere to talk out. This has all gone *way* too far," Curt said, changing the subject. His smooth demeanor returned once more. Still, he did not address wolf Vittoria's accusation.

247

"No," Erika said adamantly. "What is she talking about? Is... is that true, Curt?"

"Of course, it's not true!" he replied defensively. "That dog over there would say anything at this point because, guess what, they lost!" While Curt attempted to yell out the words with conviction, Marius noticed that he faltered a bit.

"Ah... alas, it is true, though. That hunter killed your fiancé. Adrian told me so himself. You see, this hunter hired Adrian, not knowing he was our friend and going to show up here with us. Adrian was worried about you finding out, but he's dead anyway, and *that* guy killed him; the same guy who killed your boyfriend—right there!" Wolf Vittoria pointed her paw and claw square at Curt. "Adrian said he thought he had been hired to kill the human himself, but that the plans had changed once they got there that night."

The Night of Ryan's Murder...

Adrian, in his werewolf state, crouched behind the bushes near Ryan's driveway. He had been positioned in the same spot for a while now, and by this time, his back began to ache. Finally, he heard what he had been waiting for—the sound of the car starting up in the driveway. The two people had taken their sweet time getting home and then saying goodbye to one another.

Taking a deep breath, wolf Adrian jumped up and ran past the back of the car as the tired screeched to a halt, then he took cover once more behind some nearby hedges. He waited for several minutes before he heard the car start to drive off again. Chancing a glance over the hedge, wolf Adrian saw the figure of the strange human who had hired him back at that bar in New York City. The man stood in the middle of the road, watching the car as it drove down the street before disappearing around the corner. Wolf Adrian stood up and joined the man standing on the moonlit road.

"I made sure she see me, but not for too long... just like you tell me to," werewolf Adrian confirmed.

"Good work, *Scott*," the man complimented in a low whisper—clearly thinking Adrian's name was Scott.

At that moment, the front porch light of the house the pair were standing in front of switched on. Curt's face became illuminated.

"It's *Go* time," Curt said, looking up toward the bright porchlight. Wolf Adrian—AKA Scott—briefly cocked his head to one side upon hearing the word "Go", then suddenly Curt took off like a flash as he stealthily ran toward the back of the house. The sound of the front door opening finally got wolf Adrian moving, too. The werewolf quickly bounded off in the direction Curt ran, just as Ryan stepped outside and began scanning his driveway.

Once wolf Adrian made it to the backyard, Curt instructed him on what he was to do next.

"Okay, Scott, pry open that kitchen window, climb inside, and hide somewhere on the ground floor. I'm going to scale this wall and climb onto the roof. I'll get inside through that window up there on the 2nd story, then we'll both close in on and kill this fuckin loser," Curt said coldly. "Remember, we just need this dude outta the picture. Got it?" Wolf Adrian nodded enthusiastically in agreement. Curt began scaling the back wall of Ryan's house.

For his part, wolf Adrian began prying open the kitchen window with pleasant wolfy thoughts swimming around in his head. *Oooh, I like this! So much fun getting pays for killing stupid crybaby human!* With a little force from his werewolf strength, the window finally yielded. Once inside the house, wolf Adrian began tiptoeing through the dark kitchen toward the living room, where the only light came from the glow of the television.

The sound of the front door opening startled wolf Adrian, so he hurriedly jumped inside the kitchen pantry. In his haste, he failed to clear his tail out of the doorway in time, and it got smashed inside the pantry door. He bit his paw, struggling hard to stifle a scream.

Up on the rooftop, Curt wrestled to pry open the bedroom window. Unfortunately, it seemed the window had an extra security latch that he had not anticipated.

"Fuck!" he swore aloud through clenched teeth, as he strained against the window with no success. Curt scanned his surroundings to see what he could use to pry or smash the window open, but nothing apparent was in sight. For a moment, he considered using one of his Bowie knives that he had holstered in his jacket, but he quickly dismissed this thought, as his knives were brand new sterling silver, perfect for killing werewolves but very easy to scratch. Deep scratches could almost never be fixed. Frustrated, he punched his fist on the outside of the windowsill.

Wolf Adrian was thankful to hear the thumping sounds coming from upstairs. *Now maybe the stupid human will go aways,* he thought to himself. He continued to bite his paw hard to keep himself from howling out in pain over his tail. Finally, wolf Adrian couldn't take the pain any longer. He decided, *if that human still out there, he going to have all fucking sorrys! I hate stupid 'Oh, I paying my bills and commutings to work' weak baby humans.*

The werewolf chuckled at his roasting of humanity, then carefully opened the pantry door and tenderly picked up and inspected the tip of his tail. He licked it compassionately a few times as he walked out of the pantry and into the kitchen. Thankfully, the human was nowhere to be seen. Wolf Adrian walked out of the kitchen and down the hallway toward the front door. When he got to the entryway, he stopped suddenly when he saw the human about halfway up the stairs, looking scared and pathetic as he held a baseball bat.

Wolf Adrian began to limber up by stretching out his neck and bottom jaw. He quickly practiced a few appropriate *scary werewolf* attack faces. All the while, the human still did not notice a large werewolf behind him.

Back on the roof outside, one of the silver Bowie knives was reluctantly drawn out from the holster inside the lining of Curt's leather Bomber jacket. He jammed the tip of the shiny blade into the seam between the sill and window and attempted to pry it open. With one forceful push, the window latch broke off and fell to the floor inside the room. Curt tested the window, confirming it now opened easily, but at that moment, the bedroom door burst open and slammed shut again! Curt ducked behind the outside wall so as not to be seen.

Murdering this dude was imminent, but first thing was first—he examined his silver knife blade. In the full Moon's bright light, Curt saw the blade had deep scratches and was slightly bent. He was so angry that he felt like steam rose off his face, and he cursed silently. At that moment, a light popped on inside the room, snapping Curt's attention back into the present moment and refocusing him once more. Quietly, he slid open the window and stepped fully inside the room.

"P-P-please. You don't have to do this. You can take whatever you want," Ryan pleaded as he sensed Curt's presence and slowly turned around. Only then was the depth of his terror fully revealed as he saw a canine figure coming through the bedroom window.

"Hey Curt, the fucking '*oh, I cuts my lawn and do my serving jury duties*' human made the door hard with his *baby* strength. I could not break him down, so I went outside and climbed up the back wall," wolf Adrian justified, as he attempted to climb through the window in a less than graceful manner, but he stumbled and fell to the floor in a big werewolf heap.

"Scott, your human insults are fuckin terrible, man," Curt drawled while glancing down at his werewolf companion on the floor with a mixture of pity and annoyance, while still holding his knife with the bent tip out toward Ryan.

"Man?" wolf Adrian mulled the word over with disgust, as if he had just been called some sort of racial slur. "I am not a man! I am a Lycan-Hungarian."

"Dude, focus," Curt ordered, shutting down the conversation.

Ryan watched the squabbling intruders who were deliberately blocking the only exits in the room.

The werewolf began doing some stretches and asked, "Do you want I tear him apart now? I can do the fuck him up," wolf Adrian offered and did some karate chops in the air.

"Change of plans, Scott, my friend. Turns out I don't actually need you to kill this little bitch after all. I just needed you here so the girl would catch a glimpse of a werewolf. A little insurance policy I'll need later on down the line. You understand," Curt said in a sadistically cool manner.

"Werewolf?!" Ryan exclaimed in terror. Curt rolled an annoyed gaze over in his direction.

"Yeah, genius. What did you think this was? My roided out pet hamster?" Curt asked sarcastically.

Wolf Adrian went from looking excited to disappointed.

"Aw buddy, believe me, if this were any other human, I would let you kill him. *I would want you to kill him.* But trust me, when word gets out about this dumbass' death, you won't want the smell of his kill anywhere near your paws. Here," Curt reached into his pocket and fished out a large roll of cash, then handed it to the werewolf he thought was named Scott. "You can take off, Scott. Thanks for everything. I'll take it from here," Curt said as he turned back to face Ryan.

Then, something seemed to change in him. Instantly, Curt's entire demeanor transformed. A cold-blooded psychopath with a chillingly hollow stare replaced the cool, laid-back guy that was once there. All the humanity and soul drained from his face. He stepped up ominously close to Ryan's face.

"Ya know, I was asked to make this look like a normal 'human to human' scuffle, but just for funsies, I'm going to slash you up to make it look like a werewolf—just like that creature there..." Curt pointed to wolf Adrian with the bent tip of his silver blade, who still looked confused as he held the wad of money in his paws, "..is what killed you." Curt finished, stepped back, and rolled up his sleeves. He extracted a second brutal-looking silver Bowie knife from his jacket holster.

And then Ryan rushed Curt and endeavored to fight off his attacker, to defend the remnants of his final moments on earth as valiantly as he could—

Back on the 4th-floor rooftop courtyard, wolf Vittoria—with her hyper-keen senses—was the first to smell Curt's fear. She knew if this conversation continued the way it had been going, Curt would expose Cristian and tell everyone it was he, Erika's own cousin, who had ordered the hit on her boyfriend.

Wolf Vittoria began silently clocking everyone's positions with her senses on alert. First, she looked at the werewolves—Marius and Blake—who stood between herself and Curt and Erika near the crumbling pedestal railing. Next, she glanced down at werewolf Cristian, who was still on his knees on the ground. Then she watched as Curt desperately attempted to cling onto Erika, as he vehemently denied the she-wolf's accusations. Vittoria surmised that the only reason he had not yet played his card of revealing Cristian's involvement was simply because doing so meant admitting culpability. While Curt himself had been the one to kill her boyfriend several months prior, the fool was probably still holding out hope that there might be a chance he could salvage their relationship.

Now, having established everyone's positions and knowing that the time they had left was dwindling, wolf Vittoria shifted her gaze to wolf Cristian, who miraculously looked back at her at the same moment. With an almost imperceivable motion, wolf Vittoria nodded her head to her friend. He seemed to register her signal and returned a nod.

Then, the opportunity began to present itself the moment Erika started marching away from Curt. He reached out his hand to grab her arm to stop her. Wolf Marius and wolf Blake turned to face the escalating scene that was occurring with Curt and Erika behind them. Erika ripped her arm out of Curt's grasp. And then it happened. Curt pivoted around to try again to stop her from walking away. He turned and faced his back toward all the werewolves behind him. *Now* was the time. Wolf Vittoria darted off to the right in her decoy mission. And it worked. Both wolf Marius' and wolf Blake's attention snapped back toward wolf Vittoria. The two werewolves lurched after the she-wolf to thwart what they perceived was her resuming the attack. Instead, they inadvertently opened a pocket on the left for wolf Cristian, who seized his opportunity. Wolf Cristian sprang forward with such awful speed as he rushed Curt. But Curt did not notice until it was too late.

"No, No! It was him!" Curt frantically yelled out, but wolf Cristian was already upon him. Werewolf Cristian crouched down low, grabbed Curt around his knees and thighs, then, with a ferocious burst of strength and speed, he lifted Curt and heaved him up over the stone railing.

"CRISTIAN NO!" cried Marius.

Curt's form became smaller and smaller as he fell further and further toward the ground, all the time screaming. "It was Cris......!" But the sound of his body hitting the earth hard stopped his cries. A mortified Erika rushed toward the crumbling railing and stared down at Curt's lifeless body.

"Cristian, what did you do?" Marius asked in horror.

"I'm sorry, Uncle," wolf Cristian said while panting. "He told me downstairs he would kill her if that info came out about him murdering her boyfriend," wolf Cristian said, gesturing toward Erika. "We just found out what happened... Vittoria and I, from Adrian. Tonight. I thought," wolf Cristian tried to catch his breath and then pretended to get emotional. "I thought he was going to hurt Erika. I was only protecting my family."

The rain began to trickle down once again as Marius stared in shock and horror at his nephew. Then he glanced over at Erika, who was still looking down over the railing. She did not cry, nor seemed bothered by Curt's death at all. In fact, Marius thought she looked slightly glad. This was probably because Erika thought Curt was the lone murderer of her beloved fiancé, Ryan. However, Marius suspected that the late werewolf hunter was not the only perpetrator in this crime, as his gaze shifted back toward his werewolf nephew.

Cristian's large werewolf eyes met his uncle's. For a moment, the two stared at one another, unmoving. Wolf Cristian cocked his head to one side, as if wondering why his uncle was looking at him the way he was. Wolf Marius opened his mouth as if to say something but thought better of it. The moment was already too saturated with death, shocking revelations, and devastating disappointments. Marius closed his wolf jaws and said nothing more. Instead, the large silver werewolf lifted his head and gazed up at the magnificent blood Moon in the sky that night. It was a Hunter's Blood Moon in October, Marius realized. This revelation shot through his heart like a silver bullet as he turned and slowly walked back inside Dragos Manor to spend the rest of the evening alone in his room to ponder what should be done about this difficult situation. To ponder what should be done about his nephew... who Marius suspected might be *the real killer*.

Chapter Thirty-Five

Wolf Moon

My heart is on fire, Erika thought to herself as she stared at her reflection wearing an Andreea Constantin wedding dress. She leaned in close to the mirror and fixed a smudge in the eyeliner surrounding her misty, puffy eyes. It was an emotional day indeed. Not how she ever envisioned her wedding day before... before everything.

Erika Navarro turned away from the antique standing floor mirror and crossed the bedroom filled with early 20th-century Edwardian décor where she had lived for the past several months. Taking a seat at the antique vanity, she opened the top drawer and pulled out an old book—*The Adventures of Tom Sawyer*, by Mark Twain. Thumbing through the first couple of pages, Erika found what she was looking for. She pulled out a moderately worn photograph, edges dulled from being used as a secret bookmark. The photo was of her and Ryan holding each other on a bridge in front of the canals in Amsterdam. Big smiles were spread across the young lovers' faces.

She didn't get to reminisce in the memory for very long when the bedroom door abruptly burst open, and Ana Dragos walked in. The elderly Dragos Matriarch wore an elegant emerald satin dress that made *swooshing* sounds as she came striding into the room. Erika smoothly closed the book, concealing the photograph once more, and returned it to the vanity drawer. While doing so, her hand briefly passed over an antique pewter hand mirror. She paused as she considered its familiar paisley design on the back. With a sudden surge of rage, Erika slammed the vanity drawer shut with a loud *bang*.

"Are you almost ready?" Ana asked her grandniece in polished Romanian, ignoring the slammed drawer.

"Almost," Erika murmured in English without looking up.

"Well, come along soon," Ana said, switching to English with her thick Romanian accent. "Everybody is waiting, and there is no use prolonging the inevitable. This wedding was *your* decision after all," she said curtly, then reached over to latch the last couple of fastens on the back of Erika's bridal dress. Ana made one last rough adjustment on the dress, which Erika winced at, before turning and heading toward the exit again. Just before leaving, however, she paused and took a deep breath. "You should take solace in that this marriage was written in the stars. The rest of the family and I are proud of you for choosing *our* way of life. It's tradition, it's your destiny. This was always your fate. It happened just like this for me too once... long ago."

This last statement caught Erika's attention, and for a moment, she regarded her grandaunt in a new light. For a moment, Erika thought she saw the briefest flash of sympathy appear on her grandaunt's face—maybe even sadness. But the look disappeared as quickly as it had appeared, and then Ana turned and left without saying another word.

Erika sat in the stillness of her dimly lit bedroom. She gazed out from the room's 2nd story window over the sprawling woodlands adjacent to Dragos Manor. During this time of year, the woods contained a mixture of barren leafless trees and evergreens, and the landscape was blanketed in freshly fallen snow. Evening was approaching now as twilight crept in on the eastern horizon. The pale January sky was a blank canvas for the Full Wolf Moon that would be arriving later that night.

Despite Ana's urging, Erika found she couldn't move. She was frozen with the thoughts that were plaguing her mind. *Is this really my fate?* Whether or not this was true, she was unable to convince herself enough to quell the sinking feeling in her heart. Her mind was whirling with confusion. The truth was, she felt completely lost. Erika felt she no longer trusted herself, no longer trusted her instincts. It felt like every decision she had ever made only ever led her to heartache. Look where she was today—on the road to a wedding where she was merely a prop.

Maybe this really is my fate, she thought. *Or at least... maybe this is what I deserve.* She felt numb as she again stared down at the wedding dress she found herself wearing. *How did I get here?* No matter how many times she asked herself that question, she couldn't clearly see an answer.

On top of all the self-doubt, Erika was utterly disillusioned after the first lover she had taken since the gruesome murder of her fiancé had turned out to be the very same person who had brutally murdered him in cold blood. It had not even been a full year since Ryan's death.

After that revelation, Erika had agreed—out of despair and defeat—to marry Blake Farkas. If she was being honest with herself, she knew deep down that the decision had most likely come from a place of self-sabotage. Or perhaps she was actively *choosing* the opposite of what her instincts told her, just to see if it would yield a better result. Regardless, she didn't care where she ended up. It didn't matter if she wanted it or not; it was what she was doing. The helplessness tugged at her heartstrings.

Reaching her hand around the vanity mirror, Erika plucked out a bottle of whiskey she had hidden back there. She took a long pull from the bottle, then exhaled a high-octane sigh as something occurred to her. With abrupt force, she reached down, tore open the vanity drawer, and pushed aside the copy of *The Adventures of Tom Sawyer*. Erika firmly grasped the handle of the antique pewter hand mirror and lifted it to her face.

The last time she gazed into this mirror was inside the 3rd floor room she had once shared with her mother. At that time, Erika saw someone behind her in the room. She wasn't certain who this spirit was, but Erika longed for it now and wondered if the figure might reappear.

Again, Erika's image appeared haggard and unwell in the hand mirror's reflection despite it looking normal in the vanity mirror. Confused, she turned the mirror around to see if any apparent damage or flaws would cause the glass to show such a drastically different image of herself. Nothing jumped out, so Erika realized it must be a distortion of the glass itself that was causing the strange reflection.

She flipped the reflective surface back toward her face and became utterly unnerved when she did not see her reflection staring back as expected. In fact, she did not see any person in the mirror at all. This time, Erika saw an image of dark red bricks and graying mortar inside the mirror's glass. Perplexed, she again turned the antique over and examined the back. She felt her hand across the smooth paisley design before turning it over once more. The image of the dark red stacked bricks remained. Erika glanced up at the ceiling, then directly behind her, and then back down at the mirror. She tilted the hand mirror around, inspecting the image for another moment before deciding to pause and simply ponder the mysterious wall. Erika could feel the alluring power that existed behind this wall, even just through the image of it. It called to her...

Suddenly, it dawned on her what she was being beckoned to do. Erika arose from the vanity bench with purpose. She opened another drawer and withdrew the hammer and chisel she had been concealing. With thoughts of self-sabotage weaving webs inside her mind, she snatched up the bottle of whiskey and took another long swig. Erika spun sharply on her heel and was about to rush off toward her new mission when suddenly she came face-to-face with the feminine shadow entity. The figure's features were indiscernible. The only detail Erika could make out was the awful gaping mouth, revealing terrible darkness within. Unable to stop her forward momentum, Erika winced as she went head-on into the black hole of the open jaws. She had expected to feel the collision, yet she stumbled forward through the shadowy figure. Erika quickly regained her balance and spun around to where the figure had stood, but nobody was there.

"That's it!" Erika screamed with a renewed sense of anger. She would not call out for her mother this time! No. She was going to go directly to the source to find her.

Erika Navarro stepped out into the 2nd-floor hallway. She was on a mission and bristling with anger. For some inexplicable reason, her surroundings seemed to be buzzing with a strange scarlet hue. The walls, the floor, and even her white wedding dress had taken on an unnatural neon-red tint. Maybe this vermilion effect was caused by some new form of magic, or maybe it was caused by the rage that was burning behind Erika's eyes. Regardless, she had enough and no longer cared about any of it. Erika marched briskly down the stairs, clutching the hammer and chisel in her hands.

Jovial guests and ghosts chitchatted and laughed outside the grand ballroom downstairs in the lobby. Dragos Manor had been decorated for a wedding—Erika's wedding. Large flower arrangements, white satin ribbons, and drippy candles were heavily scattered throughout the entire 1st floor. The atmosphere was brimming with excitement and joy.

Many of their guests were awed at the bride-to-be as she descended the staircase. Their mouths spoke inaudible compliments of her beauty or congratulatory wishes on the upcoming union. However, Erika did not hear any of it as she moved past these individuals and said nothing. She tuned out her surroundings and walked with tunnel vision toward her intended target—the elevator in the back of the lobby. The doors parted open as if anticipating her arrival, but then Cristian Dragos stepped out of the lift looking very pleased with himself as he adjusted the collar of his fine groomsmen's tuxedo.

Cristian looked up just in time to see Erika beelining toward him. Something about her appearance and how she moved caused him to scream as he jumped out of her way. His cousin did not stop nor say a single word to him. She only stepped into the elevator cart and pressed a button. The doors closed soon after in response. Cristian stood with bewilderment. He exhaled heavily and then began to dramatically feel around his torso, almost as if inspecting himself for injuries. Once he was composed again, he cleared his throat, glancing around to ensure nobody had seen what had happened. As Cristian headed toward the crowd gathering in and around the ballroom, he stopped, hesitated for a moment, and glanced back toward the elevator. The lift's needle was still in motion. Unsure of what he had just witnessed, he shook it off and continued toward the ballroom.

Classical music from the string quartet inside the ballroom flowed softly throughout the lobby. As Cristian began encountering various guests, he started faking cheesy facial expressions in response to their equally—if not cheesier—remarks.

"Well, aren't you just a handsome devil!" Loki's mother, Mihaela Lupu said, to which Cristian batted his eyelashes and blew a kiss.

"Quite the she-wolf killer!" Kessler's mother, Elena Vulpe, agreed, to which Cristian made a flirtatious snarl as he clawed at the air.

"Such a gorgeous wedding!" River's father, John Landis, complimented, to which Cristian pressed his hands together in mock humility at the compliment and mouthed the words *thank you*.

"I'm glad that bitch cousin of yours finally decided to get this done," came the hostile comment from some old ghost who wore turn of the twentieth-century fashion.

"Tell me about it," Cristian agreed without batting an eyelash.

He passed through the ballroom entryway and marveled at the elegant welcome signage that read—*Welcome to the wedding of Blake and Erika on the 28th of January.* Cristian couldn't help but smile and feel proud of himself. There was no denying it; he had done well. Thank God his hard work had finally paid off, and he had gotten away with it. After everything, Blake and Erika were *finally* going to be married. Dragos Manor would finally be saved from political and financial burdens. Cristian had to commend himself for accomplishing everything in just under a year.

The elevator doors *dinged* open on the 4th floor. Erika stepped out into the long, dark hallway. It was quiet, save for the rustling of her wedding dress. She moved quickly, fearing losing her nerve, as she approached the brick wall and selected a random brick at eye level. Then, she raised the hammer and chisel, exhaled the breath she didn't realize she had been holding, and forcefully swung the hammer, bringing it down hard with a solid strike on the head of the chisel. The aged mortar did not put up much fight as a large chunk crumbled away from the wall and fell to the floor, leaving a long crack extending out from the origin of the strike.

Determination flowed through her veins as she worked until, finally, the brick appeared to loosen from the rest of the formation. She dropped the chisel and used the hammer to strike the brick directly before turning the tool around to use the handle as a ramming rod. Eventually, the crumbling brick fell backward into the dark cavity beyond the wall. Chalky dust from the mini-demolition project swirled in the air. Erika waved a hand to brush it away, then puffed out a breath to clear the newly exposed hole.

With a mixture of tantalizing trepidation, she leaned forward and peered into the dark void, waiting breathlessly for her eyes to adjust. Then she saw it. A small gasp escaped through her lips.

"Don't you look nice," came the silky, smooth voice of Beo Aristide.

"Beo!" Cristian exclaimed in hushed surprise as he nervously scanned the room for Ana. "I didn't expect to see you here today."

"Of course I'm here. All the Nocturne Lycan families are here. But don't worry, I'll stay *far* away from you, so I don't turn you *gay*. I just wanted to say hello and let you know I was here, so you can properly avoid me," Beo said distantly.

"You have no idea how much I've—" Cristian started to say but then spotted the former Heads of Household—his grandma, Ana, and ghostly grandaunt, Daniela. The pair chatted with each other as they nervously glanced around the ballroom. Most of the guests were in their seats now, anxiously awaiting the start of the ceremony. Ana's gaze drifted over in her grandson's direction. Cristian immediately pivoted away from Beo. "I'm sorry. I promise we'll talk about this soon," he whispered urgently, but despite Cristian's weak attempt to comfort his love, he still noticed the deep frown of heartache on Beo's lovely face as he walked away. Ana glared in their direction momentarily but became distracted when one of the guests approached her. She dropped her glower and refocused on the event that should be starting at any moment.

As Cristian approached both former Heads of Household—one living and one deceased—he silently fortified his confidence and reveled in his pride. After all, he had played a major role in making this day happen.

What a shame Bunica and Daniela will never know of the hard work I put in to make all of this happen, Cristian thought. He pondered all the tough decisions, sacrifices, and struggles he had orchestrated over the past year. He speculated that those were the actions that a *true* Head of Household would have taken, just like his great, great grandma Sophia Dragos would have done. Cristian felt good. Dare he chance an interaction with Bunica? His grandma had still largely been avoiding him since confirming he was gay. Feeling confident, he decided to go for it.

"Good evening, Grandaunt Daniela. Good evening, Grandmother. Well, this all turned out very well if I do say so—"

"Have you seen your cousin? She needs to get into position immediately,"

Ana urgently interrupted.

All guests were now in their seats. Blake stood handsomely, albeit nervously, in his tuxedo at the altar that had been erected on the stage by the large ballroom windows. The heavy curtains were drawn shut and would remain this way until the right moment in the ceremony when the Full Wolf Moon would be in its most magnificent position in the night sky. Then the signal would be given, the curtains would fall, and the werewolf groom would claim his bride.

Adrian's ghost floated beside him on the groom's side, and Cristian would join them both shortly. Vittoria stood alone on the bride's side. Arranging a wedding in only three months had been accomplished in such haste that Erika didn't have time to invite any other friends.

The abruptness of Ana's question momentarily caught Cristian off guard.

"Erika? Umm, yeah. I just saw her a moment ago. She went upstairs. She looked a little upset. Maybe a little..." Cristian made a motion of pouring an imaginary bottle into his mouth and made a small *glug glug* sound.

"Upstairs?" Daniela's ghost sharply asked. "You mean to her room on the 2nd floor?" *Crap,* Cristian thought to himself with a growing unease creeping over him.

"Umm... No... she ah... got into the elevator."

"Dear God! Did you see if she got off on the 3rd or the 4th?" Daniela asked with rapidly increasing alarm. At that moment, similar dark thoughts seemed to cross all three of their minds simultaneously, but none dared to voice those speculations aloud.

"Find her at once!" Ana urgently whispered.

"Yes, of course. I'll get her," Cristian said, rushing off to accomplish the task. *Ugh! Of course, she won't make this easy,* he thought as he began jogging through the ballroom toward the exit. *I will have to see this thing through to the bitter end. I can't wait for this all to be over already!*

Just as Cristian was about to exit the ballroom, preparing himself to talk Erika down off the preverbal—or possibly literal—ledge, the great old house let out a deep groan. Cristian abruptly stopped in his tracks. The musicians ceased playing. Guests and ghosts all looked around with confusion, searching for the origin of the sound. Then, they looked at one another in bewilderment. István and Irene Farkas peered around with alarmed expressions as they looked up toward their children on the stage. Blake and Vittoria only shook their heads with uncertainty.

"Oh no," the ghost of Daniela whispered solemnly. Her transparent eyes scanned the walls of Dragos Manor, wearing a look of ghostly terror in them as she whispered her realization aloud. "*She's* free..."

Cristian glanced back at Ana and the ghost of his late grandaunt.

"*What was that*?" he asked in a loud whisper from across the room, audible enough for everyone in the ballroom to hear. Ana and Daniela's ghost ignored the question and continued to look around as if searching for a physical manifestation that would confirm their greatest fear.

Chapter Thirty-Six

Amor Fati

Night of the Wolf Moon

Resuming his mission, Cristian took another step toward the ballroom exit to find his cousin, the bride-to-be. He did not get very far, however. Like the image of an empty shell, Erika appeared in the ballroom doorway.

"Oh, thank Gawd!" Cristian said, overflowing with relief as he walked up and hugged her. She stared up at him with a hollow expression in her eyes. As he released her, Cristian looked at his cousin for the first time in a long time. For a split second, he wondered if he should feel guilty about the hand he had forced in her life. Then, the stained-glass portrait above the staircase of his great-great-grandmother, Sophia Dragos, caught his eye. For a moment, Cristian thought he actually saw a smirk appear on the lips of the portrait. His conviction was restored once more. Every decision that Cristian had made, every single act, was done for the greater good of the Dragos family. He was only trying to act like a *true* Head of Household. No one would ever truly know how much he had done. While there was no one to thank him, he knew deep down that Sophia Dragos would have been proud.

"Mmkay, come on. Let's get this party started!" Cristian said lightheartedly, coaxing his despondent cousin forward. Then he spun around and called out loudly, "Okay! Places, everybody!" he said with a clap of his hands. He then turned to the classical musicians on the orchestral balcony and made a rapid rolling gesture with his arm, signaling them to start the music. The string quartet raised their instruments and softly began to play the lead-in song—*The Bridal Chorus.*

Marius hurriedly walked over, wearing a dark tuxedo. He adjusted his bowtie and extended his arm to escort Erika. The band skillfully played the melody and diligently watched Marius and Erika, waiting for the cue to begin the ceremony. Cristian trotted down the candlelit aisle and joined Adrian's ghost on the groom's side of the altar beside Blake.

Now that he was alone with Erika, Marius opened his mouth to check in with her.

"Don't," She warned in an icy tone without looking up at him. "I'm doing this," she reiterated sternly. Marius closed his mouth, not letting a single word escape, and solemnly nodded in acceptance.

Guilt plagued his mind. This was the first time in Marius Dragos' life that he felt utterly conflicted and spineless. He had always been a werewolf of strong morals and convictions. He had unintentionally allowed too much time to pass without confronting Cristian about his possible involvement in the scheme to murder Erika's fiancé, Ryan. This was partly because Marius had been completely shocked by the incident that had occurred on the rooftop that resulted in the death of a werewolf and a werewolf hunter. While Marius had not helped with the disposal of Curt's body, he was still participating in the coverup by omission of knowledge that any foul play had taken place.

Between Curt's murder and the clues Malcolm Aristide Sr. had sniffed out possibly implicating Cristian in Ryan's murder, Marius feared the consequences that could potentially befall his nephew. Whether right or wrong, Marius' instincts were to protect Cristian. If either bit of information were to come out, there would surely be consequences, and Marius dreaded what those consequences could be.

The hunters were straightforward in their agreement with the Lycan families. Should any harm be brought against a werewolf hunter by any Lycan participating in the Wolf/Hunter Agreement, that werewolf would be met with equitable punitive damages. Essentially, an eye for an eye.

However, it was the plotting and conspiring to kill Erika's late fiancé that Marius was more worried about—if Cristian did indeed do this. This crime was more nuanced. While the Lycan community had no laws against killing humans per se, this crime would also fall under werewolf hunter jurisdiction. With this, it was simply understood that werewolves should not kill humans in any reckless or frivolous manner. If it turned out Cristian was indeed involved in this crime, not only would he likely be punished at the family level, but the matter would almost certainly be escalated to the werewolf hunters as well. And if Erika, the new Head of Household at Dragos Manor, felt vengeful, the consequences could be very bad for Cristian.

After sitting up countless nights, speculating about worst-case scenarios, Marius had decided to ponder this matter for a while longer until he could figure out the best way forward. He knew this meant maintaining a level of deception between himself and Erika. This fact also tore his heart asunder.

The stage was now set. The ballroom was filled with all kinds of eclectic individuals in attendance. The werewolves—still in their human form—were composed of the Dragos family, the Farkas family, the local werewolf community, and visiting Lycans. The humans consisted of old Tom, Sabina, the hired catering staff, and the string musicians on the balcony. The ghostly attendees included individuals from various decades since the turn of the 20th century. Even some woodland creatures were in attendance—a few species of birds and a pack of Gray Wolves had been brought in as part of the wedding party. Ana stared at the wolves with a pained expression on her face.

The Aristide family sat next to the Farkas parents. Shanice Aristide—Beo and Malcolm Jr.'s mother—leaned over to congratulate István and Irene Farkas.

"You both must be so proud," Shanice whispered warmly. Irene Farkas looked startled by the comment, while István appeared as though he had not understood.

"Mit?" he asked his wife.

"Actually, no, not really. This whole thing is quite preposterous. *Feuds and quarrels.* It's all a bunch of nonsense! We simply cannot stand those insufferable Dragos," Irene whispered to Shanice with a distasteful look on her face. "We agreed to this for Blake so he can have a chance to create some magnificent offspring. That's it."

Shanice looked taken aback as she faced forward once more. An expression of quiet shock rested on her face.

The lights dimmed down low. The only illumination came from the soft glow of wall sconces and the long row of candles framing the aisle leading toward the altar. The coppery ambiance inadvertently gave the ballroom a reddish, almost blood-soaked atmosphere. Erika stepped forward, rousing Marius from his thoughts, as she pulled him along. He had to take command of his step to fall into pace with her. The band saw this action and softly rolled into playing the main melody of the classic wedding song.

About halfway down the aisle, two violinists jumped up from seats in the audience and began weaving in and out of the crowd and playing their instruments. They played melodically with the string quartet on the orchestral balcony as they danced in front of Marius and Erika. Wolf cubs pranced playfully ahead of them in place of flower girls. Song Sparrows, Blue Jays, and Robins flew in synchronized patterns through the air. Guests smiled and exchanged impressed looks with one another. No one in attendance noticed the small vines creeping throughout the floorboards, walls, and ceiling.

Blake waited at the altar and watched Erika as she approached. She looked so beautiful. He wanted to feel happy at that moment, yet for some reason he didn't. Instead, he closed his eyes and inhaled deeply through his nostrils, held his breath for a beat, and then softly exhaled through his mouth. When he opened his eyes next, Erika stood directly before him. She looked up at him with a joyless expression as Marius kissed her cheek and then went to take his seat in the crowd.

Silvery wisps of smoke-like material began to form in front of the couple to be married as a ghostly wedding officiant appeared. It had been decided beforehand—Blake had been the one who had made this request for Erika's sake—that the ceremony be conducted in traditional American form.

"Dearly beloved, we are gathered here tonight to join this Lycan and his mate in matrimony," the officiator started. The ceremony continued in a blur. Erika looked numb as Blake read aloud the heartfelt vows he had written in broken English. While they were simple, he promised her all the happiness and devotion he could offer.

When it came to Erika's turn to read her vows aloud, they were short, and she concluded by saying, "While I'm trying with every last ounce of my being not to be, I am still afraid." The words were honest, yet nobody in the crowd reacted to them. As soon as the ceremony was about to complete, old Tom climbed onto the stage and retracted the curtains. The bright light of the full Wolf Moon came flooding into the dimly lit ballroom, now containing more mysterious vine growth.

Blake immediately began to transform, as did many other werewolves in the audience. First, his large arms and legs with paws and claws burst out of his tuxedo sleeves and pant legs. His chest barreled broadly while his haunches grew large, furry, and muscular. Next, his thick black hair overtook his entire face, as his snout elongated. Soon, the majestic head of a black werewolf had replaced his human head. Finally, a thick, black tail came bursting out of the seat of his dress pants. The tattered remnants of his suit fell away from his large werewolf body as he stood next to a shocked-looking Erika. The crowd went wild, as this shredding of the tuxedo was a well-known ritual in the werewolf community.

The wedding officiant wore a pleased look on his ghostly face as he beheld the handsome couple before him. He took a deep breath and concluded the ceremony.

"By virtue of the authority vested in me under the laws of North American Lycans, I now pronounce you Werewolf and Wife." The ghostly officiant then turned to Blake, "You may kiss your bride." With that, Blake's lips curled back to reveal a pointed smile. Then, the werewolf lunged for his bride and effortlessly captured Erika in his arms.

"Whoa!" Erika yelped with alarm. "Will it always be this terrifying?"

Wolf Vittoria leaned forward and offered, "Always like this."

The wedding was about to conclude with the uniting kiss, but at that moment, a mysterious flash of lightning lit up the night sky outside. In an instant, the bizarre scene was lit up—*A werewolf wedding*. Attendees comprised of Lycans, ghosts, humans, as well as wolf cubs playing wrestling games in the aisles. There was also some overgrowth issue occurring in Dragos Manor, as vines now covered much of the floorboards, walls, and ceiling. Then suddenly, every single light blinked out. The entire room went dark. Even the light of the full Moon seemed to be gone.

Outside Dragos Manor, far off toward the border where the snow-covered east lawn met the edge of the dark woodlands, a dark figure stood, gaze fixated on the old house. He had been watching the lights from the ceremony going on inside. He saw the mysterious lightning strike despite no storm or rainfall anywhere. And now he watched on as the house was bathed in total darkness. He cursed the Dragos family silently, thinking he should have been there tonight. And this wedding should not be taking place.

Back inside the pitch-black ballroom, someone screamed in the back of the room. Then, a second brilliant lightning strike flashed, but this one was different somehow. The lightning seemed to be strobing for a prolonged period, again illuminating the wedding scene.

Erika screamed when she noticed that the ghostly face of the wedding officiant was suspended in an expression of horror. His translucent eyes and mouth were fixed wide open, with gaping, black emptiness replacing his eye sockets and mouth hole. The ghost of Adrian's face looked the same way.

Ana turned and looked at the ghost of her deceased sister-in-law. Daniela's eyes and mouth were the same—frozen in terror, with black holes replacing where her eyes and mouth ought to have been. Every ghost in the room had faces frozen in expressions of fright with sinking black holes in place of their eye sockets and open mouths. The small vines on the walls, floorboards, and ceiling, now lit up in the strobing light and gave the entire room the feeling as if the house had dark veins running through it.

A cellist on the orchestral balcony turned to her right and noticed a dark-haired woman dressed in old-timey fashion standing at the far edge of the balcony. The mysterious woman turned to the musician and revealed her twisted-up, demonic-looking face. Her eyes lit up unnaturally as her mouth opened in a silent scream, which made the violinist audibly scream.

And then it was over—the ballroom went completely dark again once more.

The lights slowly came back on again inside the ballroom. The light of the full Moon appeared in the sky once more. The mysterious lightning did not return. Everything seemed normal once more, with the exception that every ghost that had been in the room had now disappeared. The cellist on the balcony was relieved to see the mysterious woman with the twisted-up face had also disappeared. All the werewolves and the handful of humans looked around the ballroom, wearing shell-shocked expressions on their frightened faces, but not one of them truly had a sense of the horror that had just befallen Dragos Manor.

At that moment, a loud whistle sounded from the back of the ballroom near the entrance. Everyone turned to see three large men in long black jackets standing with arms folded menacingly.

"Excuse me!" the tall, burly guy with a pronounced brow and thick strawberry-blonde beard called out in a booming voice. "We're looking for Curt Siodmac. He is the hunter who is assigned to this region. He has not reported in for some months now, which is *not* alright with us!" he bellowed, his voice bouncing off the vine-covered walls and vaulted ceiling. "Now, the sooner we have positively located him, the sooner you all can get back to your little..." Then he paused and looked around the room. The ballroom looked like a tornado had come through it. He looked up at the altar to see Erika in the arms of a werewolf, standing beside two other werewolves in a room largely full of werewolves. "Um... sure," he scoffed. "Good luck with that!"

Epilogue

One Year Later

A small group of intoxicated women joyfully stumbled down the streets of North Hollywood. The young women were out for a night of dancing and fun to celebrate the bachelorette party for one of their friends in the group. They walked past an old couch abandoned on the curb, crossed a street crowded with parked cars, and then walked past a second couch abandoned similarly almost directly across from the first.

A soft bell announced the entrance of the boisterous crowd into a metaphysical shop called Stellar Remnants. The shop was flooded with a neon pink light, which burned from the large palm-shaped signage in the shop's window. Freshly burnt sage smoke hung thick in the air. Many candles were placed in small water dishes around the shop lobby, their wicks flickering and burning. An orange tabby cat hopped down from the sales counter and trotted over to greet the newcomers to the delight of two tipsy women, who bent down to pet the purring feline as she approached.

As the beads parted, Althea sensed that one of these people had carried some news about her fate, which she had been waiting for.

"Hello?" she asked, abandoning her normal greeting script, which had elements of tantalizing gypsy and carnival barker, depending on the customer.

The character she played for customers was in no way meant to beguile them into utilizing her services. Althea was simply a good businesswoman. She had intentionally developed this character as part of the product she sold. Doing so did not subtract from the earnestness of the service she provided to people, assuming they were open and would listen. Althea's readings always contained elements of the truth. Occasionally, individuals must go through moments, situations, or patterns without interference. In these circumstances, she would decidedly offer a small amount of guidance. After all, she knew that allowing people to own their karma was important. Her abilities were sharpened to such a fine point that Althea could discern when it was appropriate to intervene and when it was not.

But tonight, she would bypass her normal script, her business sense, and her customer because she needed to speak directly to one individual who was present there.

"Hey," one woman called out in a harmless yet inebriated manner. "My friend here is getting married! And she wants to find out if she is making a huge mistake," the woman said with a cynical laugh.

"You," Althea said, pointing to a mousy woman petting her cat, Gingersnaps, who was purring greedily at the attention.

"No, no, her!" the drunk woman who had been speaking corrected, pointing to a different woman in the crowd—the uncertain bride-to-be, questioning her decision in the upcoming nuptials.

"I need to speak with *her* first," Althea said, pointing to the mousy woman. "There is something I must ask you," Althea requested gently yet firmly. "I promise it won't take long, but this is important."

As she stood up, the woman looked alarmed at having been singled out. Althea recognized this person as the woman she had seen on the street just over a year ago. She knew it was only a matter of time before that woman would end up in her store.

The rest of her friend group began making spooky catcalls after the individual Althea had singled out. The woman smirked and followed the fortuneteller into the back room, where she gave tarot readings.

"Stop it you, guys... I could be dying," she called back humorously, to which the rest of the inebriated party laughed and called out more jokes after her.

Althea closed the door and composed herself, trying not to startle this person. The mousey woman wore a pleasant, albeit fake, smile on her face, seeming unsure of what was about to happen. So, Althea decided just to come right out and ask.

"Where is Erika?"

The End

A note for the reader –

Thank you to everyone who has read *Wolf Moon* thus far. Writing it has been a labor of love, and it was an absolute thrill for me to publish this first story. With that said, I humbly request your thoughts and feedback. Please leave an honest review if you are so inclined. I'm going to get working on the next three books. More to come!

All of my love and gratitude,

-Sea

Acknowledgments

I would like to express my gratitude to all the individuals that I did in the first edition and give recognition to a few more.

First, I want to thank my friend, Sylvia Rodemeyer, for your experience, creativity, and insight in helping me get the word out about my story. Thank you, Cara Oberfoell, for your sharp design eye and website expertise. Thank you to Lisa Birnbaum for giving Erika, Cristian, and all the other characters of Nocturne a voice. And last but certainly not least, thank you again to my family for being so supportive. Thank you, Dad, for being one of my biggest fans; thank you to my mother-in-law, Narelle, for your support and encouragement; and thank you to my wife, Raquel, and daughter, Frankie, for unconditional love and endless patience while I work on my passion project. You two are my whole world—Honey Bunny, you put the moon in the sky, and Frankie, you make the stars shine. I love you both so much.

About the Author

I have always loved a good story. And all I have ever wanted was to create at least one.

Woven into the fabric of my writing are the strands of my inspiration – colorful, strong, tactile writers, musicians and filmmakers who have left an indelible impression on me, wrapping me in their brilliance and warming my creative soul. They are the voices I hear in my head, my inspiration, and the flames that spark my creativity.

They are a varied lot, a tapestry that includes vibrant Pearl S. Buck, earnest Frank McCourt, compelling John Steinbeck, lyrical Tennessee Williams, satirical David Sedaris, irrepressible Quentin Tarantino, the incorrigible Coen Brothers, inventive John Cameron Mitchell, artful Akira Kurosawa, groundbreaking Thomas Vinterberg, spirited Michael Dante DiMartino and Bryan Konietzko, magnetic Nick Cave, and the powerfully poetic Leonard Cohen.

I invite you into my unusual and ethereal world. May each turn of the page incite your imagination, for while I write my stories for me, my wish is to share them with you. As Tennessee Williams said... "I'm only really alive when I'm writing."

Read more at https://www.seaellewolf.com.

www.ingramcontent.com/pod-product-compliance
Lightning Source LLC
Chambersburg PA
CBHW021002260626
47169CB00006B/1910